POLLYANNA

POLLYANNA GROWS UP

Pollyanna

❖

Pollyanna Grows Up

ELEANOR H. PORTER

WORDSWORTH CLASSICS

For my husband
ANTHONY JOHN RANSON
with love from your wife, the publisher.
Eternally grateful for your unconditional love.

Readers who are interested in other titles from
Wordsworth Editions are invited to visit our website at
www.wordsworth-editions.com

Pollyanna first published in 1994 by Wordsworth Editions Limited
8B East Street, Ware, Hertfordshire SG12 9HJ in 1994
This double volume containing
Pollyanna and *Pollyanna Grows Up* first published in 2011

ISBN 978 1 84022 675 1

Text © Wordsworth Editions Limited 2011

Wordsworth® is a registered trade mark of
Wordsworth Editions Limited

Wordsworth Editions
is the company founded in 1987 by
MICHAEL TRAYLER

Typeset in Great Britain by Antony Gray
Printed and bound by Clays Ltd, Elcograf S.p.A.

Contents

POLLYANNA

Pollyanna

ELEANOR H. PORTER

CONTENTS

CHAPTER I

Miss Polly

Miss Polly Harrington entered her kitchen a little hurriedly this June morning. Miss Polly did not usually make hurried movements; she specially prided herself on her repose of manner. But today she was hurrying – actually hurrying.

Nancy, washing dishes at the sink, looked up in surprise. Nancy had been working in Miss Polly's kitchen only two months, but already she knew that her mistress did not usually hurry.

'Nancy!'

'Yes, ma'am.' Nancy answered cheerfully, but she still continued wiping the pitcher in her hand.

'Nancy' – Miss Polly's voice was very stern now – 'when I'm talking to you, I wish you to stop your work and listen to what I have to say.'

Nancy flushed miserably. She set the pitcher down at once, with the cloth still about it, thereby nearly tipping it over – which did not add to her composure.

'Yes, ma'am; I will, ma'am,' she stammered, righting the pitcher, and turning hastily. 'I was only keepin' on with my work 'cause you specially told me this mornin' ter hurry with my dishes, ye know.'

Her mistress frowned.

'That will do, Nancy. I did not ask for explanations. I asked for your attention.'

'Yes, ma'am.' Nancy stifled a sigh. She was wondering if ever in any way she could please this woman. Nancy had never 'worked out' before; but a sick mother, suddenly widowed and left with three younger children besides Nancy herself, had forced the girl into doing something towards their support, and she had been so pleased when she found a place in the kitchen of the great house on the hill – Nancy had come from 'The Corners', six miles away, and she knew Miss Polly Harrington only as the mistress of the old Harrington homestead, and one of the wealthiest residents of the town. That was two months before. She knew Miss Polly now as a stern, severe-faced woman who frowned if a knife clattered to the floor, or if a door banged – but who never thought to smile even when knives and doors were still.

'When you've finished your morning work, Nancy,' Miss Polly was saying now, 'you may clear the little room at the head of the stairs in the attic, and make up the cot bed. Sweep the room and clean it, of course, after you clear out the trunks and boxes.'

'Yes, ma'am. And where shall I put the things, please, that I take out?'

'In the front attic.' Miss Polly hesitated, then went on: 'I suppose I may as well tell you now, Nancy. My niece, Miss Pollyanna Whittier, is coming to live with me. She is eleven years old, and will sleep in that room.'

'A little girl – coming here, Miss Harrington? Oh, won't that be nice!' cried Nancy, thinking of the sunshine her own little sisters made in the home at The Corners.

'Nice? Well, that isn't exactly the word I should use,' rejoined Miss Polly stiffly. 'However, I intend to make the best of it, of course. I am a good woman, I hope; and I know my duty.'

Nancy coloured hotly.

'Of course, ma'am; it was only that I thought a little girl here might – might brighten things up – for you,' she faltered.

'Thank you,' rejoined the lady drily. 'I can't say, however, that I see any immediate need for that.'

'But, of course, you – you'd want her, your sister's child,' ventured Nancy, vaguely feeling that somehow she must prepare a welcome for this lonely little stranger.

Miss Polly lifted her chin haughtily.

'Well, really, Nancy, just because I happened to have a sister who was silly enough to marry and bring unnecessary children into a world that was already quite full enough, I can't see how I should particularly *want* to have the care of them myself. However, as I said before, I hope I know my duty. See that you clean the corners, Nancy,' she finished sharply, as she left the room.

'Yes, ma'am,' sighed Nancy, picking up the half-dried pitcher – now so cold it must be rinsed again.

In her own room Miss Polly took out once more the letter which she had received two days before from the faraway Western town, and which had been so unpleasant a surprise to her. The letter was addressed to 'Miss Polly Harrington, Beldingsville, Vermont' and it read as follows:

DEAR MADAM – I regret to inform you that the Reverend John Whittier died two weeks ago, leaving one child, a girl eleven years old. He left practically nothing else save a few books; for, as you doubtless know, he was the pastor of this small mission church, and had a very meagre salary.

I believe he was your deceased sister's husband, but he gave me to understand the families were not on the best of terms. He thought, however, that for your sister's sake you might wish to take the child and bring her up among her own people in the East. Hence I am writing to you.

The little girl will be all ready to start by the time you get this letter; and if you can take her, we would appreciate it very much if you would write that she might come at once, as there is a man and his wife here who are going East very soon, and they would take her with them to Boston, and put her on the Beldingsville train. Of course you would be notified what day and train to expect Pollyanna on.

Hoping to hear favourably from you soon, I remain,

Respectfully yours,

JEREMIAH O. WHITE

With a frown Miss Polly folded the letter and tucked it into its envelope. She had answered it the day before, and she had said she would take the child, of course. She *hoped* she knew her duty well enough for that! – disagreeable as the task would be.

As she sat now, with the letter in her hands, her thoughts went back to her sister Jennie, who had been this child's mother, and to the time when Jennie, as a girl of twenty, had insisted upon marrying the young minister, in spite of her family's remonstrances. There had been a man of wealth who had wanted her – and the family had much preferred him to the minister; but Jennie had not. The man of wealth had more years, as well as more money, to his credit, while the minister had only a young head full of youth's ideals and enthusiasm, and a heart full of love. Jennie had preferred these – quite naturally, perhaps; so she had married the minister, and had gone South with him as a home missionary's wife.

The break had come then. Miss Polly remembered it well, though she had been but a girl of fifteen, the youngest, at the time. The family had had little more to do with the missionary's wife. To be sure, Jennie herself had written, for a time, and had named her last baby Pollyanna, for her two sisters, Polly and Anna – the other babies had all died. This had been the last time that Jennie had written; and in a few years there had come the news of her death, told in a short but heartbroken little note from the minister himself, dated at a little town in the West.

Meanwhile, time had not stood still for the occupants of the great house on the hill. Miss Polly, looking out at the far-reaching valley below, thought of the changes those twenty-five years had brought to her.

She was forty now, and quite alone in the world. Father, mother, sisters – all were dead. For years, now, she had been sole mistress of the house and of the thousands left her by her father. There were people who had openly pitied her lonely life, and who had urged her to have some friend or companion to live with her; but she had not welcomed either their sympathy or their advice. She was not lonely, she said. She liked being by herself. She preferred quiet. But now . . .

Miss Polly rose with frowning face and closely shut lips. She was glad, of course, that she was a good woman, and that she not only knew her duty, but had sufficient strength of character to perform it. But – *Pollyanna!* – what a ridiculous name!

CHAPTER 2

Old Tom and Nancy

In the little attic room Nancy swept and scrubbed vigorously, paying particular attention to the corners. There were times, indeed, when the vigour she put into her work was more of a relief to her feelings than it was an ardour to efface dirt – Nancy, in spite of her frightened submission to her mistress, was no saint.

'I – just – wish – I could – dig – out – the – corners – of – her – soul!' she muttered jerkily, punctuating her words with murderous jabs of her pointed cleaning-stick. 'There's plenty of 'em needs cleanin' all right, all right! The idea of stickin' that blessed child 'way off up here in this hot little room – with no fire in the winter, too; and all this big house ter pick and choose from! Unnecessary children, indeed! Humph!' snapped Nancy, wringing her rag so hard her fingers ached from the strain; 'I guess it ain't *children* what is *most* unnecessary just now, just now!'

For some time she worked in silence; then, her task finished, she looked about the bare little room in plain disgust.

'Well, it's done – my part, anyhow,' she sighed. 'There ain't no dirt here – and there's mighty little else. Poor little soul! – a pretty place this is ter put a homesick, lonesome child into!' she finished, going out and closing the door with a bang. 'Oh!' she ejaculated, biting her lip. Then, doggedly: 'Well, I don't care. I hope she did hear the bang – I do, I do!'

In the garden that afternoon Nancy found a few minutes in which to interview Old Tom, who had pulled the weeds and shovelled the paths about the place for uncounted years.

'Mr Tom,' began Nancy, throwing a quick glance over her shoulder to make sure she was unobserved; 'did you know a little girl was comin' here ter live with Miss Polly?'

'A – what?' demanded the old man, straightening his bent back with difficulty.

'A little girl – to live with Miss Polly.'

'Go on with yer jokin',' scoffed unbelieving Tom. 'Why don't ye tell me the sun is a-goin' ter set in the east termorrer?'

'But it's true. She told me so herself,' maintained Nancy. 'It's her niece; and she's eleven years old.'

The man's jaw fell.

'Sho! – I wonder, now,' he muttered; then a tender light came into his faded eyes. 'It ain't – but it must be – Miss Jennie's little gal! There wasn't none of the rest of 'em married. Why, Nancy, it must be Miss Jennie's little gal. Glory be ter praise! ter think of my old eyes a-seein' this!'

'Who was Miss Jennie?'

'She was an angel straight out of heaven,' breathed the man, fervently, 'but the old master and missus knew her as their oldest daughter. She was twenty when she married and went away from here long years ago. Her babies all died, I heard, except the last one; and that must be the one what's a-comin'.'

'She's eleven years old.'

'Yes, she might be,' nodded the old man.

'And she's goin' ter sleep in the attic – more shame ter *her*!' scolded Nancy, with another glance over her shoulder towards the house behind her.

Old Tom frowned. The next moment a curious smile curved his lips.

'I'm a-wonderin' what Miss Polly will do with a child in the house,' he said.

'Humph! Well, *I'm* a-wonderin' what a child will do with Miss Polly in the house!' snapped Nancy.

The old man laughed.

'I'm afraid you ain't fond of Miss Polly,' he grinned.

'As if ever anybody could be fond of her!' scorned Nancy.

Old Tom smiled oddly. He stooped and began to work again.

'I guess maybe you didn't know about Miss Polly's love affair,' he said slowly.

'Love affair – *her*! No! – and I guess nobody else didn't, neither.'

'Oh, yes, they did,' nodded the old man. 'And the feller's livin' terday – right in this town, too.'

'Who is he?'

'I ain't a-tellin' that. It ain't fit that I should.' The old man drew himself erect. In his dim blue eyes, as he faced the house, there was the loyal servant's honest pride in the family he has served and loved for long years.

'But it don't seem possible – her and a lover,' still maintained Nancy.

Old Tom shook his head.

'You didn't know Miss Polly as I did,' he argued. 'She used ter be real handsome – and she would be now, if she'd let herself be.'

'Handsome! Miss Polly!'

'Yes. If she'd just let that tight hair of hern all out loose and careless-like, as it used ter be, and wear the sort of bunnits with posies in 'em, and the kind o' dresses all lace and white things – you'd see she'd be handsome! Miss Polly ain't old, Nancy.'

'Ain't she, though? Well, then, she's got an awfully good imitation of it – she has, she has!' sniffed Nancy.

'Yes, I know. It begun then – at the time of the trouble with her lover,' nodded Old Tom; 'and it seems as if she'd been feedin' on wormwood an' thistles ever since – she's that bitter an' prickly ter deal with.'

'I should say she was,' declared Nancy, indignantly. 'There's no pleasin' her, nohow, no matter how you try! I wouldn't stay if 'twa'n't for the wages and the folks at home what's needin' 'em. But someday – someday I shall jest bile over; and when I do, of course, it'll be goodbye Nancy for me. It will, it will.'

Old Tom shook his head.

'I know. I've felt it. It's nart'ral – but 'tain't best, child; 'tain't best. Take my word for it, 'tain't best.' And again he bent his old head to the work before him.

'Nancy!' called a sharp voice.

'Y–yes, ma'am,' stammered Nancy; and hurried towards the house.

CHAPTER 3

The Coming of Pollyanna

In due time came the telegram announcing that Pollyanna would arrive in Beldingsville the next day, the 25th of June, at four o'clock. Miss Polly read the telegram, frowned, then climbed the stairs to the attic room. She still frowned as she looked about her.

The room contained a small bed, neatly made, two straight-backed chairs, a washstand, a bureau – without any mirror – and a small table. There were no drapery curtains at the dormer windows, no pictures on the wall. All day the sun had been pouring down upon the roof, and the little room was like an oven for heat. As there were no screens the windows had not been raised. A big fly was buzzing angrily at one of them now, up and down, up and down, trying to get out.

Miss Polly killed the fly, swept it through the window (raising the sash an inch for the purpose), straightened a chair, frowned again, and left the room.

'Nancy,' she said a few minutes later, at the kitchen door, 'I found a fly upstairs in Miss Pollyanna's room. The window must have been raised at some time. I have ordered screens, but until they come I shall expect you to see that the windows remain closed. My niece will arrive tomorrow at four o'clock. I desire you to meet her at the station. Timothy will take the open buggy and drive you over. The telegram says "light hair, red-checked gingham dress and straw hat". That is all I know, but I think it is sufficient for your purpose.'

'Yes, ma'am; but – you – '

Miss Polly evidently read the pause aright, for she frowned and said crisply: 'No, I shall not go. It is not necessary that I should, I think. That is all.' And she turned away – Miss Polly's arrangements for the comfort of her niece, Pollyanna, were complete.

In the kitchen, Nancy sent her flat-iron with a vicious dig across the dish-towel she was ironing.

' "Light hair, red-checked gingham dress and straw hat" – all she knows, indeed! Well, I'd be ashamed ter own it up, that I would, I would – and her my onliest niece what was a-comin' from 'way across the continent!'

Promptly at twenty minutes to four the next afternoon Timothy and Nancy drove off in the open buggy to meet the expected guest. Timothy was Old Tom's son. It was sometimes said in the town that if Old Tom was Miss Polly's right-hand man Timothy was her left.

Timothy was a good-natured youth, and a good-looking one as well. Short as had been Nancy's stay at the house, the two were already good friends. Today, however, Nancy was too full of her mission to be her usual talkative self; and almost in silence she took the drive to the station and alighted to wait for the train.

Over and over in her mind she was saying it – 'Light hair, red-checked dress, straw hat.' Over and over again she was wondering just what sort of child this Pollyanna was, anyway.

'I hope for her sake she's quiet and sensible, and don't drop knives nor bang doors,' she sighed to Timothy, who had sauntered up to her.

'Well, if she ain't, nobody knows what'll become of the rest of us,' grinned Timothy. 'Imagine Miss Polly and a *noisy* kid! Gorry! there goes the whistle now!'

'Oh, Timothy, I – I think it was mean ter send me,' chattered the suddenly frightened Nancy, as she turned and hurried to a point where she could best watch the passengers alight at the little station.

It was not long before Nancy saw her – the slender little girl in the red-checked gingham with two fat braids of flaxen hair hanging down her back. Beneath the straw hat an eager, freckled little face turned to the right and to the left, plainly searching for someone.

Nancy knew the child at once, but not for some time could she control her shaking knees sufficiently to go to her. The little girl was standing quite by herself when Nancy finally did approach her.

'Are you Miss – Pollyanna?' she faltered. The next moment she found herself half smothered in the clasp of two gingham-clad arms.

'Oh, I'm so glad, *glad, glad* to see you,' cried an eager voice in her ear. 'Of course I'm Pollyanna, and I'm so glad you came to meet me! I hoped you would.'

'You – you did?' stammered Nancy, vaguely wondering how Pollyanna could possibly have known her – and wanted her. 'You – you did?' she repeated, trying to straighten her hat.

'Oh, yes; and I've been wondering all the way here what you looked like,' cried the little girl, dancing on her toes, and sweeping the embarrassed Nancy from head to foot with her eyes. 'And now I know, and I'm glad you look just like you do look.'

Nancy was relieved just then to have Timothy come up. Pollyanna's words had been most confusing.

'This is Timothy. Maybe you have a trunk,' she stammered.

'Yes, I have,' nodded Pollyanna, importantly. 'I've got a brand-new one. The Ladies' Aid bought it for me – and wasn't it lovely of them, when they wanted the carpet so? Of course I don't know how much red carpet a trunk could buy, but it ought to buy some, anyhow – much as half an aisle, don't you think? I've got a little thing here in my bag that Mr Gray said was a check, and that I must give it to you before I could get my trunk. Mr Gray is Mrs Gray's husband. They're cousins of Deacon Carr's wife. I came East with them, and they're lovely! And – there, here 'tis,' she finished, producing the check after much fumbling in the bag she carried.

Nancy drew a long breath. Instinctively she felt that someone had to draw one – after that speech. Then she stole a glance at Timothy. Timothy's eyes were studiously turned away.

The three were off at last, with Pollyanna's trunk in behind, and Pollyanna herself snugly ensconced between Nancy and Timothy. During the whole process of getting started the little girl had kept up an uninterrupted stream of comments and questions, until the somewhat dazed Nancy found herself quite out of breath trying to keep up with her.

'There! Isn't this lovely? Is it far? I hope 'tis – I love to ride,' sighed Pollyanna, as the wheels began to turn. 'Of course, if 'tisn't far I shan't mind, though, 'cause I'll be glad to get there all the sooner, you know. What a pretty street! I knew 'twas going to be pretty; father told me.'

She stopped with a little choking breath. Nancy, looking at her apprehensively, saw that her small chin was quivering, and that her eyes were full of tears. In a moment, however, she hurried on, with a brave lifting of her head.

'Father told me all about it. He remembered. And – and I ought to have explained before. Mrs Gray told me to, at once – about this red gingham dress, you know, and why I'm not in black. She said you'd think 'twas queer. But there weren't any black things in the last missionary barrel, only a lady's velvet basque which Deacon Carr's wife said wasn't suitable for me at all; besides, it had white spots – worn, you know – on both elbows, and some other places. Part of the Ladies' Aid wanted to buy me a black dress and hat, but the other part thought the money ought to go towards the red carpet they're trying to get – for the church, you know. Mrs White said maybe it was just as well, anyway, for she didn't like children in black – that is, I mean, she liked the children, of course, but not the black part.'

Pollyanna paused for breath, and Nancy managed to stammer: 'Well, I'm sure it – it'll be all right.'

'I'm glad you feel that way. I do too,' nodded Pollyanna, again with that choking little breath. 'Of course, 'twould have been a good deal harder to be glad in black.'

'Glad!' gasped Nancy, surprised into an interruption.

'Yes – that father's gone to heaven to be with mother and the rest of us, you know. He said I must be glad. But it's been pretty hard to – to do it, even in red gingham, because I – I wanted him so; and I couldn't help feeling I *ought* to have him, specially as mother and the rest have God and all the angels, while I didn't have anybody but the Ladies' Aid. But now I'm sure it'll be easier because I've got you, Aunt Polly. I'm so glad I've got you!'

Nancy's aching sympathy for the poor little forlornness beside her turned suddenly into shocked terror.

'Oh, but – but you've made an awful mistake, d–dear,' she faltered. 'I'm only Nancy. I ain't your Aunt Polly, at all!'

'You – you *aren't*?' stammered the little girl, in plain dismay.

'No. I'm only Nancy. I never thought of your takin' me for her. We – we ain't a bit alike – we ain't, we ain't!'

Timothy chuckled softly; but Nancy was too disturbed to answer the merry flash from his eyes.

'But who *are* you?' questioned Pollyanna. 'You don't look a bit like a Ladies' Aider!'

Timothy laughed outright this time.

'I'm Nancy, the hired girl. I do all the work except the washin' an' hard ironin'. Mis' Durgin does that.'

'But there *is* an Aunt Polly?' demanded the child anxiously.

'You bet your life there is,' cut in Timothy.

Pollyanna relaxed visibly.

'Oh, that's all right, then.' There was a moment's silence, then she went on brightly: 'And do you know? I'm glad, after all, that she didn't come to meet me; because now I've got *her* still coming, and I've got you besides.'

Nancy flushed. Timothy turned to her with a quizzical smile.

'I call that a pretty slick compliment,' he said. 'Why don't you thank the little lady?'

'I – I was thinkin' about – Miss Polly,' faltered Nancy.

Pollyanna sighed contentedly.

'I was too. I'm so interested in her. You know she's all the aunt I've got, and I didn't know I had her for ever so long. Then father told me. He said she lived in a lovely great big house 'way on top of a hill.'

'She does. You can see it now,' said Nancy. 'It's that big white one with the green blinds, 'way ahead.'

'Oh, how pretty! – and what a lot of trees and grass all around it! I never saw such a lot of green grass, seems so, all at once. Is my Aunt Polly rich, Nancy?'

'Yes, miss.'

'I'm so glad. It must be perfectly lovely to have lots of money. I never knew anyone that did have, only the Whites – they're some rich. They have carpets in every room and ice-cream Sundays. Does Aunt Polly have ice-cream Sundays?'

Nancy shook her head. Her lips twitched. She threw a merry look into Timothy's eyes.

'No, miss. Your aunt don't like ice-cream, I guess; leastways, I never saw it on her table.'

Pollyanna's face fell.

'Oh, doesn't she? I'm so sorry! I don't see how she can help liking ice-cream. But – anyhow, I can be kinder glad about that, 'cause the ice-cream you don't eat can't make your stomach ache like Mrs White's did – that is, I ate hers, you know, lots of it. Maybe Aunt Polly has got the carpets, though.'

'Yes, she's got the carpets.'

'In every room?'

'Well, in almost every room,' answered Nancy, frowning suddenly at the thought of that bare little attic room where there was no carpet.

'Oh, I'm so glad,' exulted Pollyanna. 'I love carpets. We didn't have any, only two little rugs that came in a missionary barrel, and one of those had ink spots on it. Mrs White had pictures too, perfectly beautiful ones of roses and little girls kneeling and a kitty and some lambs and a lion – not together, you know – the lambs and the lion. Oh, of course the Bible says they will sometime, but they haven't yet – that is, I mean Mrs White's haven't. Don't you just love pictures?'

'I – I don't know,' answered Nancy, in a half-stifled voice.

'I do. We didn't have any pictures. They don't come in the barrels much, you know. There did two come once, though. But one was so good father sold it to get money to buy me some shoes with; and the other was so bad it fell to pieces just as soon as we hung it up. Glass – it broke, you know. And I cried. But I'm glad now we didn't have any of those nice things, 'cause I shall like Aunt Polly's all the better – not being used to 'em, you see. Just as it is when the *pretty* hair-ribbons come in the barrels after a lot of faded-out brown ones. My! but isn't this a perfectly beautiful house?' she broke off fervently, as they turned into the wide driveway.

It was when Timothy was unloading the trunk that Nancy found an opportunity to mutter low in his ear: 'Don't you never say nothin'

ter me again about leavin', Timothy Durgin. You couldn't *hire* me
ter leave!'

'Leave! I should say not,' grinned the youth. 'You couldn't drag
me away. It'll be more fun here now, with that kid around, than
movin'-picture shows, every day!'

'Fun! fun!' repeated Nancy, indignantly. 'I guess it'll be somethin'
more than fun for that blessed child – when them two tries ter live
tergether; and I guess she'll be a-needin' some rock ter fly to for
refuge. Well, I'm a-goin' ter be that rock, Timothy; I am, I am!' she
vowed, as she turned and led Pollyanna up the broad steps.

CHAPTER 4

The Little Attic Room

Miss Polly Harrington did not rise to meet her niece. She looked up
from her book, it is true, as Nancy and the little girl appeared in the
sitting-room doorway, and she held out a hand with 'duty' written
large on every coldly extended finger.

'How do you do, Pollyanna? I – ' She had no chance to say more.
Pollyanna had fairly flown across the room and flung herself into
her aunt's scandalised, unyielding lap.

'Oh, Aunt Polly, Aunt Polly, I don't know how to be glad enough
that you let me come to live with you,' she was sobbing. 'You don't
know how perfectly lovely it is to have you and Nancy and all this
after you've had just the Ladies' Aid!'

'Very likely – though I've not had the pleasure of the Ladies'
Aid's acquaintance,' rejoined Miss Polly, stiffly, trying to unclasp
the small, clinging fingers, and turning frowning eyes on Nancy in
the doorway. 'Nancy, that will do. You may go. Pollyanna, be good
enough, please, to stand erect in a proper manner. I don't know yet
what you look like.'

Pollyanna drew back at once, laughing a little hysterically.

'No, I suppose you don't; but you see I'm not very much to look at, anyway, on account of the freckles. Oh, and I ought to explain about the red gingham and the black velvet basque with white spots on the elbows. I told Nancy how father said – '

'Yes; well, never mind now what your father said,' interrupted Miss Polly crisply. 'You had a trunk, I presume?'

'Oh, yes, indeed, Aunt Polly. I've got a beautiful trunk that the Ladies' Aid gave me. I haven't got so very much in it – of my own, I mean. The barrels haven't had many clothes for little girls in them lately; but there were all father's books, and Mrs White said she thought I ought to have those. You see, father – '

'Pollyanna,' interrupted her aunt again sharply, 'there is one thing that might just as well be understood right away at once; and that is, I do not care to have you keep talking of your father to me.'

The little girl drew in her breath tremulously.

'Why, Aunt Polly, you – you mean – ' She hesitated, and her aunt filled the pause.

'We will go upstairs to your room. Your trunk is already there, I presume. I told Timothy to take it up – if you had one. You may follow me, Pollyanna.'

Without speaking Pollyanna turned and followed her aunt from the room. Her eyes were brimming with tears, but her chin was bravely high.

'After all, I – I reckon I'm glad she doesn't want me to talk about father,' Pollyanna was thinking. 'It'll be easier, maybe – if I don't talk about him. Probably, anyhow, that is why she told me not to talk about him.' And Pollyanna, convinced anew of her aunt's 'kindness', blinked off the tears and looked eagerly about her.

She was on the stairway now. Just ahead, her aunt's black silk skirt rustled luxuriously. Behind her an open door allowed a glimpse of soft-tinted rugs and satin-covered chairs. Beneath her feet a marvellous carpet was like green moss to the tread. On every side the gilt of picture frames or the glint of sunlight through the filmy mesh of lace curtains flashed in her eyes.

'Oh, Aunt Polly, Aunt Polly,' breathed the little girl rapturously; 'what a perfectly lovely, lovely house! How awfully glad you must be you're so rich!'

'Poll*anna*!' ejaculated her aunt, turning sharply about as she reached the head of the stairs. 'I'm surprised at you – making a speech like that to me!'

'Why, Aunt Polly, *aren't* you?' queried Pollyanna, in frank wonder.

'Certainly not, Pollyanna. I hope I could not so far forget myself as to be sinfully proud of any gift the Lord has seen fit to bestow upon me,' declared the lady; 'certainly not of *riches*!'

Miss Polly turned and walked down the hall towards the attic stairway door. She was glad, now, that she had put the child in the attic room. Her idea at first had been to get her niece as far away as possible from herself, and at the same time place her where her childish heedlessness would not destroy valuable furnishings. Now – with this evident strain of vanity showing thus early – it was all the more fortunate that the room planned for her was plain and sensible, thought Miss Polly.

Eagerly Pollyanna's small feet pattered behind her aunt. Still more eagerly her big blue eyes tried to look in all directions at once, that no thing of beauty or interest in this wonderful house might be passed unseen. Most eagerly of all her mind turned to the wondrously exciting problem about to be solved; behind which of all these fascinating doors was waiting now her room – the dear, beautiful room, full of curtains, rugs and pictures, that was to be her very own? Then, abruptly, her aunt opened a door and ascended another stairway.

There was little to be seen here. A bare wall rose on either side. At the top of the stairs wide reaches of shadowy space led to far corners where the roof came almost down to the floor, and where were stacked innumerable trunks and boxes. It was hot and stifling too. Unconsciously Pollyanna lifted her head higher – it seemed so hard to breathe. Then she saw that her aunt had thrown open a door at the right.

'There, Pollyanna, here is your room, and your trunk is here, I see. Have you your key?'

Pollyanna nodded dumbly. Her eyes were a little wide and frightened.

Her aunt frowned.

'When I ask a question, Pollyanna, I prefer that you should answer aloud – not merely with your head.'

'Yes, Aunt Polly.'

'Thank you; that is better. I believe you have everything that you need here,' she added, glancing at the well-filled towel-rack and water-pitcher. 'I will send Nancy up to help you unpack. Supper is at six o'clock,' she finished, as she left the room and swept downstairs.

For a moment after she had gone Pollyanna stood quite still, looking after her. Then she turned her wide eyes to the bare wall, the bare floor, the bare windows. She turned them last to the little trunk that had stood not so long before in her own little room in the faraway Western home. The next moment she stumbled blindly towards it and fell on her knees at its side, covering her face with her hands.

Nancy found her there when she came up a few minutes later.

'There, there, you poor lamb,' she crooned, dropping to the floor and drawing the little girl into her arms. 'I was just a-fearin' I'd find you like this, like this.'

Pollyanna shook her head.

'But I'm bad and wicked, Nancy – awful wicked,' she sobbed. 'I just can't make myself understand that God and the angels needed my father more than I did.'

'No more they did, neither,' declared Nancy stoutly.

'Oh–h! – *Nancy!*' The burning horror in Pollyanna's eyes dried the tears.

Nancy gave a shamefaced smile and rubbed her own eyes vigorously. 'There, there, child, I didn't mean it, of course,' she cried briskly. 'Come, let's have your key and we'll get inside this trunk and take out your dresses in no time, no time.'

Somewhat tearfully Pollyanna produced the key. 'There aren't very many there, anyway,' she faltered.

'Then they're all the sooner unpacked,' declared Nancy.

Pollyanna gave a sudden radiant smile. 'That's so! I can be glad of that, can't I?' she cried

Nancy stared. 'Why, of – course,' she answered a little uncertainly.

Nancy's capable hands made short work of unpacking the books, the patched undergarments, and the few pitifully unattractive dresses. Pollyanna, smiling bravely now, flew about, hanging the dresses in the closet, stacking the books on the table, and putting away the undergarments in the bureau drawers.

'I'm sure it – it's going to be a very nice room. Don't you think so?' she stammered, after a while.

There was no answer. Nancy was very busy, apparently, with her head in the trunk. Pollyanna, standing at the bureau, gazed a little wistfully at the bare wall above.

'And I can be glad there isn't any looking-glass here, too, 'cause where there *isn't* any glass I can't see my freckles.'

Nancy made a sudden queer little sound with her mouth – but when Pollyanna turned, her head was in the trunk again. At one of the windows, a few minutes later, Pollyanna gave a glad cry and clapped her hands joyously.

'Oh, Nancy, I hadn't seen this before,' she breathed. 'Look – 'way off there, with those trees and the houses and that lovely church spire, and the river shining just like silver. Why, Nancy, there doesn't anybody need any pictures with that to look at. Oh, I'm so glad now she let me have this room!'

To Pollyanna's surprise and dismay, Nancy burst into tears. Pollyanna hurriedly crossed to her side.

'Why, Nancy, Nancy – what is it?' she cried; then, fearfully: 'This wasn't – *your* room, was it?'

'My room!' stormed Nancy, hotly, choking back the tears. 'If you ain't a little angel straight from heaven, and if some folks don't eat dirt before – Oh, land! there's her bell!' After which amazing speech, Nancy sprang to her feet, dashed out of the room, and went clattering down the stairs.

Left alone, Pollyanna went back to her 'picture', as she mentally designated the beautiful view from the window. After a time she touched the sash tentatively. It seemed as if no longer could she endure the stifling heat. To her joy the sash moved under her fingers. The next moment the window was wide open, and Pollyanna was leaning far out, drinking in the fresh, sweet air.

She ran then to the other window. That, too, soon flew up under her eager hands. A big fly swept past her nose, and buzzed noisily about the room. Then another came, and another; but Pollyanna paid no heed. Pollyanna had made a wonderful discovery – against this window a huge tree flung great branches. To Pollyanna they looked like arms outstretched, inviting her.

Suddenly she laughed aloud.

'I believe I can do it,' she chuckled. The next moment she had climbed nimbly to the window ledge. From there it was an easy matter to step to the nearest tree-branch. Then, clinging like a monkey, she swung herself from limb to limb until the lowest branch was reached. The drop to the ground was – even for Pollyanna, who was used to climbing trees – a little fearsome. She took it, however, with bated breath, swinging from her strong little arms, and landing on all fours in the soft grass. Then she picked herself up and looked eagerly about her.

She was at the back of the house. Before her lay a garden in which a bent old man was working. Beyond the garden a little path through an open field led up a steep hill, at the top of which a lone pine tree stood on guard beside the huge rock. To Pollyanna, at the moment, there seemed to be just one place in the world worth being – on the top of that big rock.

With a run and a skilful turn, Pollyanna skipped by the bent old man, threaded her way between the orderly rows of green growing things, and – a little out of breath – reached the path that ran through the open field. Then, determinedly, she began to climb. Already, however, she was thinking what a long long way off that rock must be, when back at the window it had looked so near!

Fifteen minutes later the great clock in the hallway of the Harrington homestead struck six. At precisely the last stroke Nancy sounded the bell for supper.

One, two, three minutes passed. Miss Polly frowned and tapped the floor with her slipper. A little jerkily she rose to her feet, went into the hall, and looked upstairs, plainly impatient. For a minute she listened intently; then she turned and swept into the dining-room.

'Nancy,' she said with decision, as soon as the little serving-maid appeared; 'my niece is late. No, you need not call her,' she added severely, as Nancy made a move towards the hall door. 'I told her what time supper was, and now she will have to suffer the consequences. She may as well begin at once to learn to be punctual. When she comes down she may have bread and milk in the kitchen.'

'Yes, ma'am.' It was well, perhaps, that Miss Polly did not happen to be looking at Nancy's face just then.

At the earliest possible moment after supper, Nancy crept up the back stairs and thence to the attic room.

'Bread and milk, indeed! – and when the poor lamb hain't only just cried herself to sleep,' she was muttering fiercely, as she softly pushed open the door. The next moment she gave a frightened cry. 'Where are you? Where've you gone? Where *have* you gone?' she panted, looking in the closet, under the bed, and even in the trunk and down the water-pitcher. Then she flew downstairs and out to Old Tom in the garden.

'Mr Tom, Mr Tom, that blessed child's gone,' she wailed. 'She's vanished right up into heaven where she come from, poor lamb – and me told ter give her bread and milk in the kitchen – her what's eatin' angel food this minute, I'll warrant, I'll warrant!'

The old man straightened up.

'Gone? Heaven?' he repeated stupidly, unconsciously sweeping the brilliant sunset sky with his gaze. He stopped, stared a moment intently, then turned, with a slow grin. 'Well, Nancy, it do look like as if she'd tried ter get as nigh heaven as she could, and that's a fact,' he agreed, pointing with a crooked finger to where, sharply outlined against the reddening sky, a slender, wind-blown figure was poised on top of a huge rock.

'Well, she ain't goin' ter heaven that way ternight – not if I has my say,' declared Nancy, doggedly. 'If the mistress asks, tell her I ain't furgettin' the dishes, but I gone on a stroll,' she flung back over her shoulder, as she sped towards the path that led through the open field.

CHAPTER 5

The Game

'For the land's sake, Miss Pollyanna, what a scare you did give me,' panted Nancy, hurrying up to the big rock, down which Pollyanna had just regretfully slid.

'Scare? Oh, I'm so sorry; but you mustn't, really, ever get scared about me, Nancy. Father and the Ladies' Aid used to do it, too, till they found I always came back all right.'

'But I didn't even know you'd went,' cried Nancy, tucking the little girl's hand under her arm and hurrying her down the hill. 'I didn't see you go, and nobody didn't. I guess you flew right up through the roof; I do, I do.'

Pollyanna skipped gleefully.

'I did, 'most – only I flew down instead of up. I came down the tree.'

Nancy stopped short. 'You did – what?'

'Came down the tree, outside my window.'

'My stars and stockings!' gasped Nancy, hurrying on again. 'I'd like ter know what yer aunt would say ter that!'

'Would you? Well, I'll tell her, then, so you can find out,' promised the little girl cheerfully.

'Mercy!' gasped Nancy. 'No – no!'

'Why, you don't mean she'd *care*!' cried Pollyanna, plainly disturbed.

'No – er – yes – well, never mind. I – I ain't so very particular about knowin' what she'd say, truly,' stammered Nancy, determined to keep one scolding from Pollyanna, if nothing more. 'But, say, we better hurry. I've got ter get them dishes done, ye know.'

'I'll help,' promised Pollyanna promptly.

'Oh, Miss Pollyanna!' demurred Nancy.

For a moment there was silence. The sky was darkening fast. Pollyanna took a firmer hold of her friend's arm.

'I reckon I'm glad, after all, that you *did* get scared – a little, 'cause then you came after me,' she shivered.

'Poor little lamb! And you must be hungry, too. I – I'm afraid you'll have ter have bread and milk in the kitchen with me. Yer aunt didn't like it – because you didn't come down ter supper, ye know.'

'But I couldn't. I was up here.'

'Yes; but – she didn't know that, you see,' observed Nancy, drily, stifling a chuckle. 'I'm sorry about the bread and milk; I am, I am.'

'Oh, I'm not. I'm glad.'

'Glad! Why?'

'Why, I like bread and milk, and I'd like to eat with you. I don't see any trouble about being glad about that.'

'You don't seem ter see any trouble bein' glad about everythin',' retorted Nancy, choking a little over her remembrance of Pollyanna's brave attempts to like the bare little attic room.

Pollyanna laughed softly.

'Well, that's the game, you know, anyway.'

'The – *game*?'

'Yes; the "just being glad" game.'

'Whatever in the world are you talkin' about?'

'Why, it's a game. Father told it to me, and it's lovely,' rejoined Pollyanna. 'We've played it always, ever since I was a little, little girl. I told the Ladies' Aid, and they played it – some of them.'

'What is it? I ain't much on games, though.'

Pollyanna laughed again, but she sighed, too; and in the gathering twilight her face looked thin and wistful.

'Why, we began it on some crutches that came in a missionary barrel.'

'*Crutches!*'

'Yes. You see I'd wanted a doll, and father had written them so; but when the barrel came the lady wrote that there hadn't any dolls come in, but the little crutches had. So she sent 'em along as they might come in handy for some child, sometime. And that's when we began it.'

'Well, I must say I can't see any game about that, about that,' declared Nancy, almost irritably.

'Oh, yes; the game was to just find something about everything to be glad about – no matter what 'twas,' rejoined Pollyanna earnestly. 'And we began right then – on the crutches.'

'Well, goodness me! I can't see anythin' ter be glad about – gettin' a pair of crutches when you wanted a doll!'

Pollyanna clapped her hands.

'There is – there is,' she crowed. 'But I couldn't see it, either, Nancy, at first,' she added, with quick honesty. 'Father had to tell it to me.'

'Well, then, suppose *you* tell *me*,' almost snapped Nancy.

'Goosey! Why, just be glad because you *don't – need – 'em*!' exulted Pollyanna triumphantly. 'You see it's just as easy – when you know how!'

'Well, of all the queer doin's!' breathed Nancy, regarding Pollyanna with almost fearful eyes.

'Oh, but it isn't queer – it's lovely,' maintained Pollyanna enthusiastically. 'And we've played it ever since. And the harder 'tis, the more fun 'tis to get 'em out; only – only – sometimes it's almost too hard – like when your father goes to heaven, and there isn't anybody but the Ladies' Aid left.'

'Yes, or when you're put in a snippy little room 'way at the top of the house with nothin' in it,' growled Nancy.

Pollyanna sighed.

'That *was* a hard one, at first,' she admitted, 'specially when I was so kind of lonesome. I just didn't feel like playing the game, anyway, and I *had* been wanting pretty things, so! Then I happened to think how I hated to see my freckles in the looking-glass, and I saw that lovely picture out the window too; so then I knew I'd found the things to be glad about. You see, when you're hunting for the glad things, you sort of forget the other kind – like the doll you wanted, you know.'

'Humph!' choked Nancy, trying to swallow the lump in her throat.

'Most generally it doesn't take so long,' sighed Pollyanna; 'and lots of times now I just think of them *without* thinking, you know.

I've got so used to playing it. It's a lovely game. F–father and I used to like it so much,' she faltered. 'I suppose, though, it – it'll be a little harder now, as long as I haven't anybody to play it with. Maybe Aunt Polly will play it, though,' she added, as an afterthought.

'My stars and stockings! – *her*!' breathed Nancy, behind her teeth. Then, aloud, she said doggedly: 'See here, Miss Pollyanna, I ain't sayin' that I'll play it very well, and I ain't sayin' that I know how, anyway; but I'll play it with ye, after a fashion – I just will, I will!'

'Oh, Nancy!' exulted Pollyanna, giving her a rapturous hug. 'That'll be splendid! Won't we have fun?'

'Er – maybe,' conceded Nancy, in open doubt. 'But you mustn't count too much on me, ye know. I never was no case fur games, but I'm a-goin' ter make a most awful old try on this one. You're goin' ter have someone ter play it with, anyhow,' she finished, as they entered the kitchen together.

Pollyanna ate her bread and milk with good appetite; then, at Nancy's suggestion, she went into the sitting-room, where her aunt sat reading.

Miss Polly looked up coldly.

'Have you had your supper, Pollyanna?'

'Yes, Aunt Polly.'

'I'm very sorry, Pollyanna, to have been obliged so soon to send you into the kitchen to eat bread and milk.'

'But I was real glad you did it, Aunt Polly. I like bread and milk, and Nancy too. You mustn't feel bad about that one bit.'

Aunt Polly sat suddenly a little more erect in her chair.

'Pollyanna, it's quite time you were in bed. You have had a hard day, and tomorrow we must plan your hours and go over your clothing to see what it is necessary to get for you. Nancy will give you a candle. Be careful how you handle it. Breakfast will be at half-past seven. See that you are down to that. Good-night.'

Quite as a matter of course, Pollyanna came straight to her aunt's side and gave her an affectionate hug.

'I've had such a beautiful time, so far,' she sighed happily. 'I know I'm going to just love living with you – but then, I knew I should before I came. Good-night,' she called cheerfully, as she ran from the room.

'Well, upon my soul!' ejaculated Miss Polly, half aloud. 'What a most extraordinary child!' Then she frowned. 'She's "glad" I punished her, and I "mustn't feel bad one bit", and she's going to "love to live" with me! Well, upon my soul!' ejaculated Miss Polly again, as she took up her book.

Fifteen minutes later, in the attic room, a lonely little girl sobbed into the tightly clutched sheet: 'I know, father-among-the-angels, I'm not playing the game one bit now – not one bit; but I don't believe even you could find anything to be glad about sleeping all alone 'way off up here in the dark – like this. If only I was near Nancy or Aunt Polly, or even a Ladies' Aider, it would be easier!'

Downstairs in the kitchen, Nancy, hurrying with her belated work, jabbed her dish-mop into the milk pitcher, and muttered jerkily: 'If playin' a silly-fool game – about bein' glad you've got crutches when you want dolls – is got ter be – my way – o' bein' that rock o' refuge – why, I'm a-goin' ter play it – I am, I am!'

CHAPTER 6

A Question of Duty

It was nearly seven o'clock when Pollyanna awoke that first day after her arrival. Her windows faced the south and the west, so she could not see the sun yet; but she could see the hazy blue of the morning sky, and she knew that the day promised to be a fair one.

The little room was cooler now, and the air blew in fresh and sweet. Outside, the birds were twittering joyously, and Pollyanna flew to the window to talk to them. She saw then that down in the garden her aunt was already out among the rose-bushes. With rapid fingers, therefore, she made herself ready to join her.

Down the attic stairs sped Pollyanna, leaving both doors wide open. Through the hall, down the next flight, then bang through the front screened door and around to the garden she ran.

Aunt Polly, with the bent old man, was leaning over a rose-bush when Pollyanna, gurgling with delight, flung herself upon her.

'Oh, Aunt Polly, Aunt Polly, I reckon I am glad this morning just to be alive!'

'Polly*anna*!' remonstrated the lady sternly, pulling herself as erect as she could with a dragging weight of ninety pounds hanging about her neck. 'Is this the usual way you say good-morning?'

The little girl dropped to her toes, and danced lightly up and down.

'No, only when I love folks so I just can't help it! I saw you from my window, Aunt Polly, and I got to thinking how you *weren't* a Ladies' Aider, and you were my really truly aunt; and you looked so good I just had to come down and hug you!'

The bent old man turned his back suddenly. Miss Polly attempted a frown – not with her usual success.

'Pollyanna, you – I – Thomas, that will do for this morning. I think you understand – about those rose-bushes,' she said stiffly. Then she turned and walked rapidly away.

'Do you always work in the garden, Mr – Man?' asked Pollyanna interestedly.

The man turned. His lips were twitching, but his eyes looked blurred as if with tears.

'Yes, miss. I'm Old Tom, the gardener,' he answered. Timidly, but as if impelled by an irresistible force, he reached out a shaking hand and let it rest for a moment on her bright hair. 'You are so like your mother, little miss! I used ter know her when she was even littler than you be. You see, I used ter work in the garden – then.'

Pollyanna caught her breath audibly.

'You did? And you knew my mother, really – when she was just a little earth angel, and not a heaven one? Oh, please tell me about her!' And down plumped Pollyanna in the middle of the dirt path by the old man's side.

A bell sounded from the house. The next moment Nancy was seen flying out the back door.

'Miss Pollyanna, that bell means breakfast – mornin's,' she panted, pulling the little girl to her feet and hurrying her back to the house; 'and other times it means other meals. But it always means that you're ter run like time when ye hear it, no matter where ye be. If ye don't – well, it'll take somethin' smarter'n we be ter find *anythin'* ter be glad about in that!' she finished, shooing Pollyanna into the house as she would shoo an unruly chicken into a coop.

Breakfast, for the first five minutes, was a silent meal; then Miss Polly, her disapproving eyes following the airy wings of two flies darting here and there over the table, said sternly: 'Nancy, where did those flies come from?'

'I don't know, ma'am. There wasn't one in the kitchen.' Nancy had been too excited to notice Pollyanna's up-flung windows the afternoon before.

'I reckon maybe they're my flies, Aunt Polly,' observed Pollyanna amiably. 'There were lots of them this morning having a beautiful time upstairs.'

Nancy left the room precipitately, though to do so she had to carry out the hot muffins she had just brought in.

'Yours!' gasped Miss Polly. 'What do you mean? Where did they come from?'

'Why, Aunt Polly, they came from out of doors, of course, through the windows. I *saw* some of them come in.'

'You saw them! You mean you raised those windows without any screens?'

'Why, yes. There weren't any screens there, Aunt Polly.'

Nancy, at this moment, came in again with the muffins. Her face was grave, but very red.

'Nancy,' directed her mistress sharply, 'you may set the muffins down and go at once to Miss Pollyanna's room and shut the windows. Shut the doors, also. Later, when your morning work is done, go through every room with the spatter. See that you make a thorough search.'

To her niece she said: 'Pollyanna, I have ordered screens for those windows. I knew, of course, that it was my duty to do that. But it seems to me that you have quite forgotten *your* duty.'

'My – duty?' Pollyanna's eyes were wide with wonder.

'Certainly. I know it is warm, but I consider it your duty to keep your windows closed till those screens come. Flies, Pollyanna, are not only unclean and annoying, but very dangerous to health. After breakfast, I will give you a little pamphlet on this matter to read.'

'To read? Oh, thank you, Aunt Polly. I love to read!'

Miss Polly drew in her breath audibly, then she shut her lips together hard. Pollyanna, seeing her stern face, frowned a little thoughtfully.

'Of course I'm sorry about the duty I forgot, Aunt Polly,' she apologised timidly. 'I won't raise the windows again.'

Her aunt made no reply. She did not speak, indeed, until the meal was over. Then she rose, went to the bookcase in the sitting-room, took out a small paper booklet, and crossed the room to her niece's side.

'This is the article I spoke of, Pollyanna. I desire you to go to your room at once and read it. I will be up in half an hour to look over your things.'

Pollyanna, her eyes on the illustration of a fly's head, many times magnified, cried joyously: 'Oh, thank you, Aunt Polly!' The next moment she skipped merrily from the room, banging the door behind her.

Miss Polly frowned, hesitated, then crossed the room majestically and opened the door; but Pollyanna was already out of sight, clattering up the attic stairs.

Half an hour later when Miss Polly, her face expressing stern duty in every line, climbed those stairs and entered Pollyanna's room, she was greeted with a burst of eager enthusiasm.

'Oh, Aunt Polly, I never saw anything so perfectly lovely and interesting in my life. I'm so glad you gave me that book to read. Why, I didn't suppose flies could carry such a lot of things on their feet and – '

'That will do,' observed Aunt Polly, with dignity. 'Pollyanna, you may bring out your clothes now, and I will look them over. What are not suitable for you I shall give to the Sullivans, of course.'

With visible reluctance Pollyanna laid down the pamphlet and turned towards the closet.

'I'm afraid you'll think they're worse than the Ladies' Aid did – and *they* said they were shameful,' she sighed. 'But there were mostly things for boys and older folks in the last two or three barrels; and – did you ever have a missionary barrel, Aunt Polly?'

At her aunt's look of shocked anger, Pollyanna corrected herself at once.

'Why, no, of course you didn't, Aunt Polly!' she hurried on, with a hot blush. 'I forgot; rich folks never have to have them. But you see sometimes I kind of forget that you *are* rich – up here in this room, you know.'

Miss Polly's lips parted indignantly, but no words came. Pollyanna, plainly unaware that she had said anything in the least unpleasant, was hurrying on.

'Well, as I was going to say, you can't tell a thing about missionary barrels – except that you won't find in 'em what you think you're going to – even when you think you won't. It was the barrels every time, too, that were hardest to play the game on, for father and – '

Just in time Pollyanna remembered that she was not to talk of her father to her aunt. She dived into her closet then, hurriedly, and brought out all the poor little dresses in both her arms.

'They aren't nice, at all,' she choked, 'and they'd have been black if it hadn't been for the red carpet for the church; but they're all I've got.'

With the tips of her fingers Miss Polly turned over the conglomerate garments, so obviously made for anybody but Pollyanna. Next she bestowed frowning attention on the patched undergarments in the bureau drawers.

'I've got the best ones on,' confessed Pollyanna anxiously. 'The Ladies' Aid bought me one set straight through all whole. Mrs Jones – she's the president – told 'em I should have that if they had to clatter down bare aisles themselves the rest of their days. But they won't. Mr White doesn't like the noise. He's got nerves, his wife says; but he's got money, too, and they expect he'll give a lot towards the carpet – on account of the nerves, you know. I should think he'd be glad that if he did have the nerves he'd got money, too; shouldn't you?'

Miss Polly did not seem to hear. Her scrutiny of the under-garments finished, she turned to Pollyanna somewhat abruptly.

'You have been to school, of course, Pollyanna?'

'Oh, yes, Aunt Polly. Besides, fath – I mean, I was taught at home some, too.'

Miss Polly frowned.

'Very good. In the fall you will enter school here, of course. Mr Hall, the principal, will doubtless settle in which grade you belong. Meanwhile, I suppose I ought to hear you read aloud half an hour each day.'

'I love to read; but if you don't want to hear me I'd be just glad to read to myself – truly, Aunt Polly. And I wouldn't have to half try to be glad, either, for I like best to read to myself – on account of the big words, you know.'

'I don't doubt it,' rejoined Miss Polly grimly. 'Have you studied music?'

'Not much. I don't like my music – I like other people's though. I learned to play on the piano a little. Miss Gray – she plays for church – she taught me. But I'd just as soon let that go as not, Aunt Polly. I'd rather, truly.'

'Very likely,' observed Aunt Polly, with slightly uplifted eyebrows. 'Nevertheless I think it is my duty to see that you are properly instructed in at least the rudiments of music. You sew, of course.'

'Yes, ma'am.' Pollyanna sighed. 'The Ladies' Aid taught me that. But I had an awful time. Mrs Jones didn't believe in holding your needle like the rest of 'em did on buttonholing, and Mrs White thought backstitching ought to be taught you before hemming (or else the other way), and Mrs Harriman didn't believe in putting you on patchwork, ever, at all.'

'Well, there will be no difficulty of that kind any longer, Pollyanna. I shall teach you sewing myself, of course. You do not know how to cook, I presume.'

Pollyanna laughed suddenly.

'They were just beginning to teach me that this summer, but I hadn't got far. They were more divided up on that than they were on the sewing. They were *going* to begin on bread; but there wasn't two of 'em that made it alike, so after arguing it all one sewing-meeting, they decided to take turns at me one forenoon a week – in their own kitchens, you know. I'd only learned chocolate fudge and fig cake, though, when – when I had to stop.' Her voice broke.

'Chocolate fudge and fig cake, indeed!' scorned Miss Polly. 'I think we can remedy that very soon.' She paused in thought for a minute, then went on slowly: 'At nine o'clock every morning you will read aloud one half-hour to me. Before that you will use the time to put this room in order. Wednesday and Saturday forenoons, after half-past nine, you will spend with Nancy in the kitchen, learning to cook. Other mornings you will sew with me. That will leave the afternoons for your music. I shall, of course, procure a teacher at once for you,' she finished decisively, as she arose from her chair.

Pollyanna cried out in dismay.

'Oh, but Aunt Polly, Aunt Polly, you haven't left me any time at all just to – to live.'

'To live, child! What do you mean? As if you weren't living all the time!'

'Oh, of course I'd be *breathing* all the time I was doing those things, Aunt Polly, but I wouldn't be living. You breathe all the time you're asleep, but you aren't living. I mean *living* – doing the things you want to do: playing outdoors, reading (to myself, of course), climbing hills, talking to Mr Tom in the garden, and Nancy, and finding out all about the houses and the people and everything everywhere all through the perfectly lovely streets I came through yesterday. That's what I call living, Aunt Polly. Just breathing isn't living!'

Miss Polly lifted her head irritably.

'Pollyanna, you *are* the most extraordinary child! You will be allowed a proper amount of playtime, of course. But, surely, it seems to me if I am willing to do my duty in seeing that you have proper care and instruction, you ought to be willing to do yours by seeing that that care and instruction are not ungratefully wasted.'

Pollyanna looked shocked.

'Oh, Aunt Polly, as if I ever could be ungrateful – to *you*! Why, I *love* you – and you aren't even a Ladies' Aider; you're an aunt!'

'Very well; then see that you don't act ungratefully,' vouchsafed Miss Polly, as she turned towards the door.

She had gone halfway down the stairs when a small, unsteady voice called after her: 'Please, Aunt Polly, you didn't tell me which of my things you wanted to – to give away.'

Aunt Polly emitted a tired sigh – a sigh that ascended straight to Pollyanna's ears.

'Oh, I forgot to tell you, Pollyanna. Timothy will drive us into town at half-past one this afternoon. Not one of your garments is fit for my niece to wear. Certainly I should be very far from doing my duty by you if I should let you appear out in any one of them.'

Pollyanna sighed now – she believed she was going to hate that word – duty.

'Aunt Polly, please,' she called wistfully, 'isn't there *any* way you can be glad about all that – duty business?'

'What?' Miss Polly looked up in dazed surprise; then, suddenly, with very red cheeks, she turned and swept angrily down the stairs. 'Don't be impertinent, Pollyanna!'

In the hot little attic room Pollyanna dropped herself on to one of the straight-backed chairs. To her, existence loomed ahead one endless round of duty.

'I don't see, really, what there was impertinent about that,' she sighed. 'I was only asking her if she couldn't tell me something to be glad about in all that duty business.'

For several minutes Pollyanna sat in silence, her rueful eyes fixed on the forlorn heap of garments on the bed. Then, slowly, she rose and began to put away the dresses.

'There just isn't anything to be glad about, that I can see,' she said aloud; 'unless – it's to be glad when the duty's done!' Whereupon she laughed suddenly.

CHAPTER 7

Pollyanna and Punishments

At half-past one o'clock Timothy drove Miss Polly and her niece to the four or five principal dry goods stores, which were about half a mile from the homestead.

Fitting Pollyanna with a new wardrobe proved to be more or less of an exciting experience for all concerned. Miss Polly came out of it with the feeling of limp relaxation that one might have at finding oneself at last on solid earth after a perilous walk across the very thin crust of a volcano. The various clerks who had waited upon the pair came out of it with very red faces, and enough amusing stories of Pollyanna to keep their friends in gales of laughter the rest of the week. Pollyanna herself came out of it with radiant smiles and a heart content; for, as she expressed it to one of the clerks: 'When you haven't had anybody but missionary barrels and Ladies' Aiders to dress you, it is perfectly lovely to just walk right in and buy clothes that are brand-new, and that don't have to be tucked up or let down because they don't fit!'

The shopping expedition consumed the entire afternoon; then came supper and a delightful talk with Old Tom in the garden, and another with Nancy on the back porch, after the dishes were done and while Aunt Polly paid a visit to a neighbour.

Old Tom told Pollyanna wonderful things of her mother, that made her very happy indeed; and Nancy told her all about the little farm six miles away at The Corners, where lived her own dear mother, and her equally dear brother and sisters. She promised, too, that sometimes, if Miss Polly were willing, Pollyanna should be taken to see them.

'And *they've* got lovely names, too. You'll like *their* names,' sighed Nancy. 'They're Algernon and Florabelle and Estelle. I – I just hate "Nancy"!'

'Oh, Nancy, what a dreadful thing to say! Why?'

'Because it isn't pretty like the others. You see I was the first baby, and mother hadn't begun ter read so many stories with the pretty names in 'em then.'

'But I love "Nancy", just because it's you,' declared Pollyanna.

'Humph! Well, I guess you could love "Clarissa Mabelle" just as well,' retorted Nancy, 'and it would be a heap happier for me. I think *that* name's just grand!'

Pollyanna laughed. 'Well, anyhow,' she chuckled, 'you can be glad it isn't "Hephzibah". '

'Hephzibah!'

'Yes. Mrs White's name is that. Her husband calls her "Hep", and she doesn't like it. She says when he calls out, "Hep! Hep!" she feels just as if the next minute he was going to yell, "Hurrah!" And she doesn't like to be hurrahed at.'

Nancy's gloomy face relaxed into a broad smile.

'Well, if you don't beat the Dutch! Say, do you know? – I shan't never hear "Nancy" now that I don't think o' that "Hep! Hep!" and giggle. My, I guess I *am* glad – ' She stopped short and turned amazed eyes on the little girl. 'Say, Miss Pollyanna, do you mean – was you playin' that 'ere game *then* – about my bein' glad I wasn't named Hephzibah?'

Pollyanna frowned; then she laughed.

'Why, Nancy, that's so! I *was* playing the game – but that's one of the times I just did it without thinking, I reckon. You see, you *do*, lots of times; you get so used to it – looking for something to be glad about, you know. And most generally there is something about everything that you can be glad about, if you keep hunting long enough to find it.'

'Well, m–maybe,' granted Nancy, with open doubt.

At half-past eight Pollyanna went up to bed. The screens had not yet come, and the close little room was like an oven. With longing eyes Pollyanna looked at the two fast-closed windows – but she did not raise them. She undressed, folded her clothes neatly, said her prayers, blew out her candle and climbed into bed.

Just how long she lay in sleepless misery, tossing from side to side of the hot little cot, she did not know; but it seemed to her that it must have been hours before she finally slipped out of bed, felt her way across the room and opened her door.

Out in the main attic all was velvet blackness save where the moon flung a path of silver halfway across the floor from the east dormer window. With a resolute ignoring of that fearsome darkness to the right and to the left, Pollyanna drew a quick breath and pattered straight into that silvery path, and on to the window.

She had hoped, vaguely, that this window might have a screen, but it did not. Outside, however, there was a wide world of fairylike beauty, and there was, too, she knew, fresh, sweet air that would feel so good to hot cheeks and hands!

As she stepped nearer and peered longingly out, she saw something else: she saw, only a little way below the window, the wide, flat tin roof of Miss Polly's sun-parlour built over the *porte-cochère*. The sight filled her with longing. If only, now, she were out there!

Fearfully she looked behind her. Back there, somewhere, were her hot little room and her still hotter bed; but between her and them lay a horrid desert of blackness across which one must feel one's way with outstretched, shrinking arms; while before her, out on the sun-parlour roof, were the moonlight and the cool, sweet night air.

If only her bed were out there! And folks did sleep out of doors. Joel Hartley at home, who was so sick with the consumption, *had* to sleep out of doors.

Suddenly Pollyanna remembered that she had seen near this attic window a row of long white bags hanging from nails. Nancy had said that they contained the winter clothing, put away for the summer. A little fearfully now, Pollyanna felt her way to these bags, selected a nice fat soft one (it contained Miss Polly's sealskin coat) for a bed; and a thinner one to be doubled up for a pillow, and still another (which was so thin it seemed almost empty) for a covering. Thus equipped, Pollyanna in high glee pattered to the moonlit window again, raised the sash, stuffed her burden through to the roof below, then let herself down after it, closing the window carefully behind her – Pollyanna had not forgotten those flies with the marvellous feet that carried things.

How deliciously cool it was! Pollyanna quite danced up and down with delight, drawing in long, full breaths of the refreshing air. The tin roof under her feet crackled with little resounding snaps that Pollyanna rather liked. She walked, indeed, two or three times back and forth from end to end – it gave her such a pleasant sensation of airy space after her hot little room; and the roof was so broad and flat that she had no fear of falling off. Finally, with a sigh of content, she curled herself up on the sealskin-coat mattress, arranged one bag for a pillow and the other for a covering, and settled herself to sleep.

'I'm so glad now that the screens didn't come,' she murmured, blinking up at the stars; 'else I couldn't have had this!'

Downstairs in Miss Polly's room next to the sun-parlour, Miss Polly herself was hurrying into dressing-gown and slippers, her face white and frightened. A minute before she had been telephoning in a shaking voice to Timothy: 'Come up quick! – you and your father. Bring lanterns. Somebody is on the roof of the sun-parlour. He must have climbed up the rose-trellis or somewhere and of course he can get right into the house through the east window in the attic. I have locked the attic door down here – but hurry, quick!'

Some time later, Pollyanna, just dropping off to sleep, was startled by a lantern flash, and a trio of amazed ejaculations. She opened her eyes to find Timothy at the top of a ladder near her, Old Tom just getting through the window, and her aunt peering out at her from behind him.

'Pollyanna, what does this mean?' cried Aunt Polly.

Pollyanna blinked sleepy eyes and sat up.

'Why, Mr Tom – Aunt Polly!' she stammered. 'Don't look so scared! It isn't that I've got the consumption, you know, like Joel Hartley. It's only that I was so hot – in there. But I shut the window Aunt Polly, so the flies couldn't carry those germ-things in.'

Timothy disappeared suddenly down the ladder. Old Tom, with almost equal precipitation, handed his lantern to Miss Polly, and followed his son. Miss Polly bit her lip hard – until the men were gone – then she said sternly: 'Pollyanna, hand those things to me at once and come in here. Of all the extraordinary children!' she ejaculated a little later, as, with Pollyanna by her side and the lantern in her hand, she turned back into the attic.

To Pollyanna the air was all the more stifling after that cool breath of the out-of-doors; but she did not complain. She only drew a long, quivering sigh.

At the top of the stairs, Miss Polly jerked out crisply: 'For the rest of the night, Pollyanna, you are to sleep in my bed with me. The screens will be here tomorrow, but until then I consider it my duty to keep you where I know where you are.'

Pollyanna drew in her breath.

'With you? – in your bed?' she cried rapturously. 'Oh, Aunt Polly, Aunt Polly, how perfectly lovely of you! And when I've so wanted to sleep with someone sometime – someone that belonged to me, you know; not a Ladies' Aider. I've *had* them. My! I reckon I am glad now those screens didn't come! Wouldn't you be?'

There was no reply. Miss Polly was stalking on ahead. Miss Polly, to tell the truth, was feeling curiously helpless. For the third time since Pollyanna's arrival, Miss Polly was punishing Pollyanna – and for the third time she was being confronted with the amazing fact that her punishment was being taken as a special reward of merit. No wonder Miss Polly was feeling curiously helpless.

CHAPTER 8

Pollyanna Pays a Visit

It was not long before life at the Harrington homestead settled into something like order – though not exactly the order that Miss Polly had at first prescribed. Pollyanna sewed, practised, read aloud, and studied cooking in the kitchen, it is true; but she did not give to any of these things quite so much time as had first been planned. She had more time, also, to 'just live', as she expressed it, for almost all of every afternoon from two until six o'clock was hers to do with as she liked – provided she did not 'like' to do certain things already prohibited by Aunt Polly.

It is a question, perhaps, whether all this leisure time was given to the child as a relief to Pollyanna from work – or as a relief to Aunt Polly from Pollyanna. Certainly, as those first July days passed, Miss Polly found occasion many times to ejaculate, 'What an extraordinary child!' and certainly the reading and sewing-lessons found her at their conclusion each day somewhat dazed and wholly exhausted.

Nancy, in the kitchen, fared better. She was not dazed nor exhausted. Wednesdays and Saturdays came to be, indeed, red-letter days to her.

There were no children in the immediate neighbourhood of the Harrington homestead for Pollyanna to play with. The house itself was on the outskirts of the village, and though there were other houses not far away, they did not chance to contain any boys or girls near Pollyanna's age. This, however, did not seem to disturb Polly-anna in the least.

'Oh, no, I don't mind it at all,' she explained to Nancy. 'I'm happy just to walk around and see the streets and the houses and watch the people. I just love people. Don't you, Nancy?'

'Well, I can't say I do – all of 'em,' retorted Nancy tersely.

Almost every pleasant afternoon found Pollyanna begging for 'an errand to run', so that she might be off for a walk in one direction or another; and it was on these walks that frequently she met the man. To herself Pollyanna always called him 'the man', no matter if she met a dozen other men the same day.

The man often wore a long black coat and a high silk hat – two things that the 'just men' never wore. His face was clean-shaven and rather pale, and his hair, showing below his hat, was somewhat grey. He walked erect, and rather rapidly, and he was always alone, which made Pollyanna vaguely sorry for him. Perhaps it was because of this that she one day spoke to him.

'How do you do, sir? Isn't this a nice day?' she called cheerily, as she approached him.

The man threw a hurried glance about him, then stopped uncertainly.

'Did you speak – to me?' he asked in a sharp voice.

'Yes, sir,' beamed Pollyanna. 'I say, it's a nice day, isn't it?'

'Eh? Oh! Humph!' he grunted; and strode on again.

Pollyanna laughed. He was such a funny man, she thought.

The next day she saw him again. ' 'Tisn't quite so nice as yesterday, but it's pretty nice,' she called out cheerfully.

'Eh? Oh! Humph!' grunted the man as before; and once again Pollyanna laughed happily.

When for the third time Pollyanna accosted him in much the same manner the man stopped abruptly.

'See here, child, who are you, and why are you speaking to me every day?'

'I'm Pollyanna Whittier, and I thought you looked lonesome. I'm so glad you stopped. Now we're introduced – only I don't know your name yet.'

'Well, of all the – ' The man did not finish his sentence, but strode on faster than ever.

Pollyanna looked after him with a disappointed droop to her usually smiling lips.

'Maybe he didn't understand – but that was only half an introduction. I don't know *his* name, yet,' she murmured, as she proceeded on her way.

Pollyanna was carrying calf's-foot jelly to Mrs Snow today. Miss Polly Harrington always sent something to Mrs Snow once a week. She said she thought that it was her duty, inasmuch as Mrs Snow was poor, sick, and a member of her church – it was the duty of all the church members to look out for her, of course. Miss Polly did her duty by Mrs Snow usually on Thursday afternoons – not personally, but through Nancy. Today Pollyanna had begged the privilege, and Nancy had promptly given it to her in accordance with Miss Polly's orders.

'And it's glad that I am ter get rid of it,' Nancy had declared in private afterwards to Pollyanna; 'though it's a shame ter be tuckin' the job off on ter you, poor lamb, so it is, it is!'

'But I'd love to do it, Nancy.'

'Well, you won't – after you've done it once,' predicted Nancy sourly.

'Why not?'

'Because nobody does. If folks wa'n't sorry for her there wouldn't a soul go near her from mornin' till night, she's that cantankerous. All is, I pity her daughter what *has* ter take care of her.'

'But why, Nancy?'

Nancy shrugged her shoulders. 'Well, in plain words, it's just that nothin' whatever has happened, has happened right in Mis' Snow's eyes. Even the days of the week ain't run ter her mind. If it's Monday she's bound ter say she wished 'twas Sunday; and if you take her jelly you're pretty sure ter hear she wanted chicken – but if you *did* bring her chicken, she'd be jest hankerin' for lamb broth!'

'Why, what a funny woman,' laughed Pollyanna. 'I think I shall like to go to see her. She must be so surprising and – and different. I love *different* folks.'

'Humph! Well, Mis' Snow's "different", all right – I hope, for the sake of the rest of us!' Nancy had finished grimly.

Pollyanna was thinking of these remarks today as she turned in at the gate of the shabby little cottage. Her eyes were quite sparkling, indeed, at the prospect of meeting this 'different' Mrs Snow.

A pale-faced, tired-looking young girl answered her knock at the door.

'How do you do?' began Pollyanna politely. 'I'm from Miss Polly Harrington, and I'd like to see Mrs Snow, please.'

'Well, if you would, you're the first one that ever "liked" to see her,' muttered the girl under her breath; but Pollyanna did not hear this. The girl had turned and was leading the way through the hall to a door at the end of it.

In the sick-room, after the girl had ushered her in and closed the door, Pollyanna blinked a little before she could accustom her eyes to the gloom. Then she saw, dimly outlined, a woman half-sitting up in the bed across the room. Pollyanna advanced at once.

'How do you do, Mrs Snow? Aunt Polly says she hopes you are comfortable today, and she's sent you some calf's-foot jelly.'

'Dear me! Jelly?' murmured a fretful voice. 'Of course I'm very much obliged, but I was hoping 'twould be lamb broth today.'

Pollyanna frowned a little.

'Why, I thought it was *chicken* you wanted when folks brought you jelly,' she said.

'What?' The sick woman turned sharply.

'Why, nothing much,' apologised Pollyanna hurriedly; 'and of course it doesn't really make any difference. It's only that Nancy said it was chicken you wanted when we brought jelly, and lamb broth when we brought chicken – but maybe 'twas the other way, and Nancy forgot.'

The sick woman pulled herself up till she sat erect in the bed – a most unusual thing for her to do, though Pollyanna did not know this. 'Well, Miss Impertinence, who are you?' she demanded.

Pollyanna laughed gleefully.

'Oh, *that* isn't my name, Mrs Snow – and I'm so glad 'tisn't, too! That would be worse than Hephzibah, wouldn't it? I'm Pollyanna Whittier, Miss Polly Harrington's niece, and I've come to live with her. That's why I'm here with the jelly this morning.'

All through the first part of this sentence the sick woman had sat interestedly erect; but at the reference to the jelly she fell back on her pillow listlessly.

'Very well; thank you. Your aunt is very kind, of course, but my appetite isn't very good this morning, and I was wanting lamb – ' She stopped suddenly, then went on with an abrupt change of subject. 'I never slept a wink last night – not a wink!'

'Oh, dear, I wish I didn't,' sighed Pollyanna, placing the jelly on the little stand and seating herself comfortably in the nearest chair. 'You lose such a lot of time just sleeping! Don't you think so?'

'Lose time – sleeping!' exclaimed the sick woman.

'Yes, when you might be just living, you know. It seems such a pity we can't live at night, too.'

Once again the woman pulled herself erect in her bed.

'Well, if you ain't the amazing young one!' she cried. 'Here! do you go to that window and pull up the curtain,' she directed. 'I should like to know what you look like!'

Pollyanna rose to her feet, but she laughed a little ruefully. 'Oh, dear! then you'll see my freckles, won't you?' she sighed, as she went to the window; 'and just when I was being so glad it was dark and you couldn't see 'em. There! Now you can – oh!' she broke off excitedly, as she turned back to the bed; 'I'm so glad you wanted to see me, because now I can see you! They didn't tell me you were so pretty!'

'Me! – pretty!' scoffed the woman bitterly.

'Why, yes. Didn't you know it?' cried Pollyanna.

'Well, no, I didn't,' retorted Mrs Snow drily. Mrs Snow had lived forty years, and for fifteen of those years she had been too busy wishing things were different to find much time to enjoy things as they were.

'Oh, but your eyes are so big and dark, and your hair's all dark, too, and curly,' cooed Pollyanna. 'I love black curls. (That's one of the things I'm going to have when I get to heaven.) And you've got two little red spots in your cheeks. Why, Mrs Snow, you *are* pretty! I should think you'd know it when you looked at yourself in the glass.'

'The glass!' snapped the sick woman, falling back on her pillow. 'Yes, well, I hain't done much prinkin' before the mirror these days – and you wouldn't, if you was flat on your back as I am!'

'Why, no, of course not,' agreed Pollyanna sympathetically. 'But wait – just let me show you,' she exclaimed, skipping over to the bureau and picking up a small hand-glass.

On the way back to the bed she stopped, eyeing the sick woman with a critical gaze.

'I reckon maybe, if you don't mind, I'd like to fix your hair just a little before I let you see it,' she proposed. 'May I fix your hair, please?'

'Why, I – suppose so, if you want to,' permitted Mrs Snow grudgingly; 'but 'twon't stay, you know.'

'Oh, thank you. I love to fix people's hair,' exulted Pollyanna, carefully laying down the hand-glass and reaching for a comb. 'I shan't do much today, of course – I'm in such a hurry for you to see how pretty you are; but someday I'm going to take it all down and have a perfectly lovely time with it,' she cried, touching with soft fingers the waving hair above the sick woman's forehead.

For five minutes Pollyanna worked swiftly, deftly, combing a refractory curl into fluffiness, perking up a drooping ruffle at the neck, or shaking a pillow into plumpness so that the head might have a better pose. Meanwhile the sick woman, frowning prodigiously, and openly scoffing at the whole procedure, was, in spite of herself, beginning to tingle with a feeling perilously near to excitement.

'There!' panted Pollyanna, hastily plucking a pink from a vase near by and tucking it into the dark hair where it would give the best effect. 'Now I reckon we're ready to be looked at!' And she held out the mirror in triumph.

'Humph!' grunted the sick woman, eyeing her reflection severely. 'I like red pinks better than pink ones; but then, it'll fade, anyhow, before night, so what's the difference!'

'But I should think you'd be glad they did fade,' laughed Pollyanna, ' 'cause then you can have the fun of getting some more. I just love your hair fluffed out like that,' she finished with a satisfied gaze. 'Don't you?'

'Hm–m; maybe. Still – 'twon't last, with me tossing back and forth on the pillow as I do.'

'Of course not – and I'm glad, too,' nodded Pollyanna cheerfully, 'because then I can fix it again. Anyhow, I should think *you'd* be glad it's black – black shows up so much nicer on a pillow than yellow hair like mine does.'

'Maybe; but I never did set much store by black hair – shows grey too soon,' retorted Mrs Snow. She spoke fretfully, but she still held the mirror before her face.

'Oh, I love black hair! I should be so glad if I only had it,' sighed Pollyanna.

Mrs Snow dropped the mirror and turned irritably.

'Well, you wouldn't! – not if you were me. You wouldn't be glad for black hair nor anything else – if you had to lie here all day as I do!'

Pollyanna bent her brows in a thoughtful frown.

'Why, 'twould be kind of hard – to do it then, wouldn't it?' she mused aloud.

'Do what?'

'Be glad about things.'

'Be glad about things – when you're sick in bed all your days? Well, I should say it would,' retorted Mrs Snow. 'If you don't think so, just tell me something to be glad about; that's all!'

To Mrs Snow's unbounded amazement, Pollyanna sprang to her feet and clapped her hands.

'Oh, goody! That'll be a hard one – won't it? I've got to go, now, but I'll think and think all the way home; and maybe the next time I come I can tell it to you. Goodbye. I've had a lovely time! Goodbye,' she called again, as she tripped through the doorway.

'Well, I never! Now, what does she mean by that?' ejaculated Mrs Snow, staring after her visitor. By and by she turned her head and picked up the mirror, eyeing her reflection critically.

'That little thing *has* got a knack with hair – and no mistake,' she muttered under her breath. 'I declare, I didn't know it could look so pretty. But then, what's the use?' she sighed, dropping the little glass into the bedclothes, and rolling her head on the pillow fretfully.

A little later, when Milly, Mrs Snow's daughter, came in, the mirror still lay among the bedclothes – though it had been carefully hidden from sight.

'Why, mother – the curtain is up!' cried Milly, dividing her amazed stare between the window and the pink in her mother's hair.

'Well, what if it is?' snapped the sick woman. 'I needn't stay in the dark all my life, if I am sick, need I?'

'Why, n–no, of course not,' rejoined Milly, in hasty conciliation, as she reached for the medicine bottle. 'It's only – well, you know very well that I've tried to get you to have a lighter room for ages – and you wouldn't.'

There was no reply to this. Mrs Snow was picking at the lace on her nightgown. At last she spoke fretfully.

'I should think *somebody* might give me a new nightdress – instead of lamb broth, for a change!'

'Why – mother!'

No wonder Milly quite gasped aloud with bewilderment. In the drawer behind her at that moment lay two new nightdresses that Milly for months had been vainly urging her mother to wear.

CHAPTER 9

Which Tells of the Man

It rained the next time Pollyanna saw the man. She greeted him, however, with a bright smile.

'It isn't so nice today, is it?' she called blithesomely. 'I'm glad it doesn't rain always, anyhow!'

The man did not even grunt this time, nor turn his head. Pollyanna decided that of course he did not hear her. The next time, therefore (which happened to be the following day), she spoke up louder. She thought it particularly necessary to do this, anyway, for the man was striding along, his hands behind his back, and his eyes on the ground – which seemed, to Pollyanna, preposterous in the face of the glorious sunshine and the freshly washed morning air; Pollyanna, as a special treat, was on a morning errand today.

'How do you do?' she chirped. 'I'm so glad it isn't yesterday, aren't you?'

The man stopped abruptly. There was an angry scowl on his face.

'See here, little girl, we might just as well settle this thing right now, once for all,' he began testily. 'I've got something besides the weather to think of. I don't know whether the sun shines or not.'

Pollyanna beamed joyously.

'No, sir; I thought you didn't. That's why I told you.'

'Yes; well – Eh? What?' he broke off sharply, in sudden understanding of her words.

'I say, that's why I told you – so you would notice it, you know – that the sun shines, and all that. I knew you'd be glad it did if you only stopped to think of it – and you didn't look a bit as if you *were* thinking of it!'

'Well, of all the – ' ejaculated the man, with an oddly impotent gesture. He started forward again, but after the second step he turned back, still frowning. 'See here, why don't you find someone your own age to talk to?'

'I'd like to, sir, but there aren't any around here, Nancy says. Still, I don't mind so very much. I like old folks just as well, maybe better, sometimes – being used to the Ladies' Aid, so.'

'Humph! The Ladies' Aid, indeed! Is that what you took me for?' The man's lips were threatening to smile, but the scowl above them was still trying to hold them grimly stern.

Pollyanna laughed gleefully.

'Oh, no, sir. You don't look a mite like a Ladies' Aider – not but that you're just as good, of course – maybe better,' she added in hurried politeness. 'You see, I'm sure you're much nicer than you look!'

The man made a queer noise in his throat.

'Well, of all the – ' he ejaculated again, as he turned and strode on as before.

The next time Pollyanna met the man, his eyes were gazing straight into hers, with a quizzical directness that made his face look really pleasant, Pollyanna thought.

'Good-afternoon,' he greeted her a little stiffly. 'Perhaps I'd better say right away that I *know* the sun is shining today.'

'But you don't have to tell me,' nodded Pollyanna brightly. 'I *knew* you knew it just as soon as I saw you.'

'Oh, you did, did you?'

'Yes, sir; I saw it in your eyes, you know, and in your smile.'

'Humph!' grunted the man, as he passed on.

The man always spoke to Pollyanna after this, and frequently he spoke first, though usually he said little but, 'Good-afternoon.' Even that, however, was a great surprise to Nancy, who chanced to be with Pollyanna one day when the greeting was given.

'Sakes alive, Miss Pollyanna,' she gasped, 'did that man *speak* to *you*?'

'Why, yes, he always does – now,' smiled Pollyanna.

'He always does! Goodness! Do you know who – he – is?' demanded Nancy.

Pollyanna frowned and shook her head.

'I reckon he forgot to tell me. You see, I did my part of the introducing, but he didn't.'

Nancy's eyes widened.

'But he never speaks ter anybody, child – he hain't for years, I guess, except when he just has to, for business, and all that. He's John Pendleton. He lives all by himself in the big house on Pendleton Hill. He won't even have anyone round ter cook for him – comes down ter the hotel for his meals three times a day. I know Sally Miner, who waits on him, and she says he hardly opens his head enough ter tell what he wants ter eat. She has ter guess it more'n half the time – only it'll be somethin' *cheap*! She knows that without no tellin'.'

Pollyanna nodded sympathetically.

'I know. You have to look for cheap things when you're poor. Father and I took meals out a lot. We had beans and fish-balls most generally. We used to say how glad we were we liked beans – that is, we said it specially when we were looking at the roast turkey place, you know, that was sixty cents. Does Mr Pendleton like beans?'

'Like 'em! What if he does – or don't? Why, Miss Pollyanna, he ain't poor. He's got loads of money, John Pendleton has – from his father. There ain't nobody in town as rich as he is. He could eat dollar bills, if he wanted to – and not know it.'

Pollyanna giggled.

'As if anybody *could* eat dollar bills and not know it, Nancy, when they come to try to chew 'em!'

'Ho! I mean he's rich enough ter do it,' shrugged Nancy. 'He ain't spendin' his money, that's all. He's a-savin' of it.'

'Oh, for the heathen,' surmised Pollyanna. 'How perfectly splendid! That's denying yourself and taking up your cross. I know; father told me.'

Nancy's lips parted abruptly, as if there were angry words all ready to come; but her eyes, resting on Pollyanna's jubilantly trustful face, saw something that prevented the words being spoken.

'Humph!' she vouchsafed. Then, showing her old-time interest, she went on: 'But, say, it *is* queer, his speakin' to you, honestly, Miss Pollyanna. He don't speak ter no one; and he lives all alone in a great big lovely house all full of jest grand things, they say. Some says he's crazy, and some jest cross; and some says he's got a skeleton in his closet.'

'Oh, Nancy!' shuddered Pollyanna. 'How can he keep such a dreadful thing? I should think he'd throw it away!'

Nancy chuckled. That Pollyanna had taken the skeleton literally instead of figuratively, she knew very well; but, perversely, she refrained from correcting the mistake.

'And *everybody* says he's mysterious,' she went on. 'Some years he jest travels, week in and week out, and it's always in heathen countries – Egypt and Asia and the desert of Sarah, you know.'

'Oh, a missionary,' nodded Pollyanna.

Nancy laughed oddly.

'Well, I didn't say that, Miss Pollyanna. When he comes back he writes books – queer, odd books, they say, about some gimcrack he's found in them heathen countries. But he don't never seem ter want ter spend no money here – leastways, not for jest livin'.'

'Of course not – if he's saving it for the heathen,' declared Pollyanna. 'But he is a funny man, and he's different, too, just like Mrs Snow, only he's a different different.'

'Well, I guess he is – rather,' chuckled Nancy.

'I'm gladder'n ever now, anyhow, that he speaks to me,' sighed Pollyanna contentedly.

CHAPTER 10

A Surprise for Mrs Snow

The next time Pollyanna went to see Mrs Snow, she found that lady, as at first, in a darkened room.

'It's the little girl from Miss Polly's, mother,' announced Milly, in a tired manner; then Pollyanna found herself alone with the invalid.

'Oh, it's you, is it?' asked a fretful voice from the bed. 'I remember you. *Anybody*'d remember you, I guess, if they saw you once. I wish you had come yesterday. I *wanted* you yesterday.'

'Did you? Well, I'm glad 'tisn't any farther away from yesterday than today is, then,' laughed Pollyanna, advancing cheerily into the room, and setting her basket carefully down on a chair. 'My! but aren't you dark here, though? I can't see you a bit,' she cried, unhesitatingly crossing to the window and pulling up the shade. 'I want to see if you've fixed your hair like I did – oh, you haven't! But, never mind; I'm glad you haven't, after all, 'cause maybe you'll let me do it – later. But *now* I want you to see what I've brought you.'

The woman stirred restlessly.

'Just as if how it looks would make any difference to how it tastes,' she scoffed – but she turned her eyes towards the basket. 'Well, what is it?'

'Guess! What do you want?' Pollyanna had skipped back to the basket. Her face was alight.

The sick woman frowned.

'Why, I don't *want* anything, as I know of,' she sighed. 'After all, they all taste alike!'

Pollyanna chuckled.

'This won't. Guess! If you *did* want something, what would it be?'

The woman hesitated. She did not realise it herself, but she had so long been accustomed to wanting what she did not have, that to state offhand what she *did* want seemed impossible – until she knew what she had. Obviously, however, she must say something. This extraordinary child was waiting.

'Well, of course, there's lamb broth.'

'I've got it!' crowed Pollyanna.

'But that's what I *didn't* want,' sighed the sick woman, sure now of what her stomach craved. 'It was chicken I wanted.'

'Oh, I've got that too,' chuckled Pollyanna.

The woman turned in amazement.

'Both of them?' she demanded.

'Yes – and calf's-foot jelly,' triumphed Pollyanna. 'I was just bound you should have what you wanted for once; so Nancy and I fixed it.

Oh, of course, there's only a little of each – but there's *some* of all of 'em! I'm so glad you did want chicken,' she went on contentedly, as she lifted the three little bowls from her basket. 'You see, I got to thinking on the way here – what if you should say tripe, or onions, or something like that, that I didn't have! Wouldn't it have been a shame – when I tried so hard?' she laughed merrily.

There was no reply. The sick woman seemed to be trying – mentally – to find something she had lost.

'There! I'm to leave them all,' announced Pollyanna, as she arranged the three bowls in a row on the table. 'Like enough it'll be lamb broth you want tomorrow. How do you do today?' she finished in polite enquiry.

'Very poorly, thank you,' murmured Mrs Snow, falling back into her usual listless attitude. 'I lost my nap this morning. Nellie Higgins next door has begun music lessons, and her practising drives me nearly wild. She was at it all the morning – every minute! I'm sure, I don't know what I shall do!'

Pollyanna nodded sympathetically.

'I know. It *is* awful! Mrs White had it once – one of my Ladies' Aiders, you know. She had rheumatic fever, too, at the same time, so she couldn't thrash around. She said 'twould have been easier if she could have. Can you?'

'Can I – what?'

'Thrash around – move, you know, so as to change your position when the music gets too hard to stand.'

Mrs Snow stared a little.

'Why, of course I can move – anywhere – in bed,' she rejoined a little irritably.

'Well, you can be glad of that, then, anyhow, can't you?' nodded Pollyanna. 'Mrs White couldn't. You can't thrash when you have rheumatic fever – though you want to something awful, Mrs White says. She told me afterwards she reckoned she'd have gone raving crazy if it hadn't been for Mr White's sister's ears – being deaf, so.'

'Sister's – *ears*! What do you mean?'

Pollyanna laughed.

'Well, I reckon I didn't tell it all, and I forgot you didn't know Mrs

White. You see, Miss White was deaf – awfully deaf; and she came to visit 'em and to help take care of Mrs White and the house. Well, they had such an awful time making her understand *anything*, that after that, every time the piano commenced to play across the street, Mrs White felt so glad she *could* hear it, that she didn't mind so much that she *did* hear it, 'cause she couldn't help thinking how awful 'twould be if she was deaf and couldn't hear anything, like her husband's sister. You see, she was playing the game too. I'd told her about it.'

'The – game?'

Pollyanna clapped her hands.

'There! I 'most forgot; but I've thought it up, Mrs Snow – what you can be glad about.'

'*Glad* about! What do you mean?'

'Why, I told you I would. Don't you remember? You asked me to tell you something to be glad about – glad, you know, even though you did have to lie here abed all day.'

'Oh!' scoffed the woman. '*That?* Yes, I remember that; but I didn't suppose you were in earnest any more than I was.'

'Oh, yes, I was,' nodded Pollyanna triumphantly; 'and I found it, too. But 'twas hard. It's all the more fun, though, always, when 'tis hard. And I will own up, honest to true, that I couldn't think of anything for a while. Then I got it.'

'Did you, really? Well, what is it?' Mrs Snow's voice was sarcastically polite.

Pollyanna drew a long breath.

'I thought – how glad you could be – that other folks weren't like you – all sick in bed like this, you know,' she announced impressively.

Mrs Snow stared. Her eyes were angry.

'Well, really!' she ejaculated, in a not quite agreeable tone of voice.

'And now I'll tell you the game,' proposed Pollyanna, blithely confident. 'It'll be just lovely for you to play – it'll be so hard. And there's so much more fun when it is hard! You see, it's like this.' And she began to tell of the missionary barrel, the crutches and the doll that did not come.

The story was just finished when Milly appeared at the door.

'Your aunt is wanting you, Miss Pollyanna,' she said with dreary listlessness. 'She telephoned down to the Harlows across the way. She says you're to hurry – that you've got some practising to make up before dark.'

Pollyanna rose reluctantly.

'All right,' she sighed. 'I'll hurry.' Suddenly she laughed. 'I suppose I ought to be glad I've got legs to hurry with, hadn't I, Mrs Snow?'

There was no answer. Mrs Snow's eyes were closed. But Milly, whose eyes were wide open with surprise, saw that there were tears on the wasted cheeks.

'Goodbye,' flung Pollyanna over her shoulder, as she reached the door. 'I'm awfully sorry about the hair – I wanted to do it. But maybe I can next time!'

One by one the July days passed. To Pollyanna, they were happy days, indeed. She often told her aunt, joyously, how very happy they were. Whereupon her aunt would usually reply, wearily: 'Very well, Pollyanna. I am gratified, of course, that they are happy; but I trust that they are profitable, as well – otherwise I should have failed signally in my duty.'

Generally Pollyanna would answer this with a hug and a kiss – a proceeding that was still always most disconcerting to Miss Polly; but one day she spoke. It was during the sewing hour.

'Do you mean that it wouldn't be enough then, Aunt Polly, that they should be just happy days?' she asked wistfully.

'That is what I mean, Pollyanna.'

'They must be pro–fi–ta–ble as well?'

'Certainly.'

'What is being pro–fi–ta–ble?'

'Why, it – it's just being profitable – having profit, something to show for it, Pollyanna. What an extraordinary child you are!'

'Then just being glad isn't pro–fi–ta–ble?' questioned Pollyanna, a little anxiously.

'Certainly not.'

'Oh, dear! Then you wouldn't like it, of course. I'm afraid, now, you won't ever play the game, Aunt Polly.'

'Game? What game?'

'Why, that father – ' Pollyanna clapped her hand to her lips. 'N–nothing,' she stammered.

Miss Polly frowned.

'That will do for this morning, Pollyanna,' she said tersely. And the sewing-lesson was over.

It was that afternoon that Pollyanna, coming down from her attic room, met her aunt on the stairway.

'Why, Aunt Polly, how perfectly lovely!' she cried. 'You were coming up to see me! Come right in. I love company,' she finished, scampering up the stairs and throwing her door wide open.

Now Miss Polly had not been intending to call on her niece. She had been planning to look for a certain white wool shawl in the cedar chest near the east window. But to her unbounded surprise, now, she found herself, not in the main attic before the cedar chest, but in Pollyanna's little room sitting in one of the straight-backed chairs – so many, many times since Pollyanna came, Miss Polly had found herself like this, doing some utterly unexpected, surprising thing, quite unlike the thing she had set out to do!

'I love company,' said Pollyanna, again, flitting about as if she were dispensing the hospitality of a palace; 'specially since I've had this room, all mine, you know. Oh, of course, I had a room, always, but 'twas a hired room, and hired rooms aren't half as nice as owned ones, are they? And of course I do own this one, don't I?'

'Why, y–yes, Pollyanna,' murmured Miss Polly, vaguely wondering why she did not get up at once and go to look for that shawl.

'And of course *now* I just love this room, even if it hasn't got the carpets and curtains and pictures that I'd been want – ' With a painful blush Pollyanna stopped short. She was plunging into an entirely different sentence when her aunt interrupted her sharply.

'What's that, Pollyanna?'

'N–nothing, Aunt Polly, truly. I didn't mean to say it.'

'Probably not,' returned Miss Polly coldly; 'but you did say it, so suppose we have the rest of it.'

'But it wasn't anything – only that I'd been kind of planning on pretty carpets and lace curtains and things, you know. But, of course – '

'*Planning* on them!' interrupted Miss Polly sharply.

Pollyanna blushed still more painfully.

'I ought not to have, of course, Aunt Polly,' she apologised. 'It was only because I'd always wanted them and hadn't had them, I suppose. Oh, we'd had two rugs in the barrels, but they were little, you know, and one had ink spots, and the other holes; and there never were only those two pictures; the one fath – I mean the good one we sold, and the bad one that broke. Of course if it hadn't been for all that I shouldn't have wanted them so – pretty things, I mean; and I shouldn't have got to planning all through the hall that first day how pretty mine would be here, and – and – But, truly, Aunt Polly, it wasn't but just a minute – I mean, a few minutes – before I was being glad that the bureau *didn't* have a looking-glass, because it didn't show my freckles; and there couldn't be a nicer picture than the one out of my window there; and you've been so good to me, that – '

Miss Polly rose suddenly to her feet. Her face was very red.

'That will do, Pollyanna,' she said stiffly. 'You have said quite enough, I'm sure.' The next minute she had swept down the stairs – and not until she reached the first floor did it suddenly occur to her that she had gone up into the attic to find a white wool shawl in the cedar chest near the east window.

Less than twenty-four hours later, Miss Polly said to Nancy crisply: 'Nancy, you may move Miss Pollyanna's things downstairs this morning to the room directly beneath. I have decided to have my niece sleep there for the present.'

'Yes, ma'am,' said Nancy aloud. 'Oh, glory!' said Nancy to herself.

To Pollyanna, a minute later, she cried joyously: 'And won't ye jest be listenin' ter this, Miss Pollyanna. You're ter sleep downstairs in the room straight under this. You are – you are!'

Pollyanna actually grew white.

'You mean – why, Nancy, not really – really and truly?'

'I guess you'll think it's really and truly,' prophesied Nancy, exultingly, nodding her head to Pollyanna over the armful of dresses she had taken from the closet. 'I'm told ter take down yer things, and I'm goin' ter take 'em, too, 'fore she gets a chance ter change her mind.'

Pollyanna did not stop to hear the end of this sentence. At the imminent risk of being dashed headlong, she was flying downstairs, two steps at a time.

Bang went two doors and a chair before Pollyanna at last reached her goal – Aunt Polly.

'Oh, Aunt Polly, Aunt Polly, did you mean it, really? Why, that room's got *everything* – the carpet and curtains and three pictures, besides the one outdoors, too, 'cause the windows look the same way. Oh, Aunt Polly!'

'Very well, Pollyanna. I am gratified that you like the change, of course; but if you think so much of all those things, I trust you will take proper care of them; that's all. Pollyanna, please pick up that chair, and you have banged two doors in the last half-minute.' Miss Polly spoke sternly, all the more sternly because for some inexplicable reason, she felt inclined to cry – and Miss Polly was not used to feeling inclined to cry.

Pollyanna picked up the chair.

'Yes'm; I know I banged 'em – those doors,' she admitted cheerfully. 'You see I'd just found out about the room, and I reckon you'd have banged doors if – ' Pollyanna stopped short and eyed her aunt with new interest. 'Aunt Polly, *did* you ever bang doors?'

'I hope – not, Pollyanna!' Miss Polly's voice was properly shocked.

'Why, Aunt Polly, what a shame!' Pollyanna's face expressed only concerned sympathy.

'A shame!' repeated Aunt Polly, too dazed to say more.

'Why, yes. You see, if you'd felt like banging doors you'd have banged 'em, of course; and if you didn't, that must have meant that you weren't ever glad over anything – or you would have banged 'em. You couldn't have helped it. And I'm so sorry you weren't ever glad over anything!'

'Poll*ya*nna!' gasped the lady; but Pollyanna was gone, and only the distant bang of the attic-stairway door answered for her. Pollyanna had gone to help Nancy bring down 'her things'.

Miss Polly, in the sitting-room, felt vaguely disturbed; – but then, of course she *had* been glad – over some things!

CHAPTER II

Introducing Jimmy

August came. August brought several surprises and also some changes – none of which, however, were really a surprise to Nancy. Nancy, since Pollyanna's arrival, had come to look for surprises and changes.

First there was the kitten.

Pollyanna found the kitten mewing pitifully some distance down the road. When systematic questioning of the neighbours failed to find anyone who claimed it, Pollyanna brought it home at once, as a matter of course.

'And I was glad I didn't find anyone who owned it, too,' she told her aunt in happy confidence; ' 'cause I wanted to bring it home all the time. I love kitties. I knew you'd be glad to let it live here.'

Miss Polly looked at the forlorn little grey bunch of neglected misery in Pollyanna's arms, and shivered. Miss Polly did not care for cats – not even pretty, healthy, clean ones.

'Ugh! Pollyanna! What a dirty little beast! And it's sick, I'm sure, and all mangy and fleay.'

'I know it, poor little thing,' crooned Pollyanna, tenderly looking into the little creature's frightened eyes. 'And it's all trembly too, it's so scared. You see it doesn't know, yet, that we're going to keep it, of course.'

'No – nor anybody else,' retorted Miss Polly, with meaning emphasis.

'Oh, yes, they do,' nodded Pollyanna, entirely misunderstanding her aunt's words. 'I told everybody we should keep it, if I didn't find where it belonged. I knew you'd be glad to have it – poor little lonesome thing!'

Miss Polly opened her lips and tried to speak; but in vain. The curious helpless feeling, that had been hers so often since Pollyanna's arrival, had her now fast in its grip.

'Of course I knew,' hurried on Pollyanna gratefully, 'that you wouldn't let a dear little lonesome kitty go hunting for a home when you'd just taken me in; and I said so to Mrs Ford when she asked if you'd let me keep it. Why, *I* had the Ladies' Aid, you know, and kitty didn't have anybody. I knew you'd feel that way,' she nodded happily, as she ran from the room.

'But, Pollyanna, Pollyanna,' remonstrated Miss Polly. 'I don't – '

'But Pollyanna was already halfway to the kitchen, calling: 'Nancy, Nancy, just see this dear little kitty that Aunt Polly is going to bring up along with me!' And Aunt Polly, in the sitting-room – who abhorred cats – fell back in her chair with a gasp of dismay, powerless to remonstrate.

The next day it was a dog, even dirtier and more forlorn, perhaps, than was the kitten; and again Miss Polly, to her dumbfounded amazement, found herself figuring as a kind protector and an angel of mercy – a role that Pollyanna so unhesitatingly thrust upon her as a matter of course that the woman – who abhorred dogs even more than she did cats, if possible – found herself, as before, powerless to remonstrate.

When, in less than a week, however, Pollyanna brought home a small, ragged boy, and confidently claimed the same protection for him, Miss Polly did have something to say. It happened after this wise.

On a pleasant Thursday morning Pollyanna had been taking calf's-foot jelly again to Mrs Snow. Mrs Snow and Pollyanna were the best of friends now. Their friendship had started from the third visit Pollyanna had made, the one after she had told Mrs Snow of the game. Mrs Snow herself was playing the game now, with Pollyanna. To be sure, she was not playing it very well – she had been sorry for everything for so long, that it was not easy to be glad for anything now. But under Pollyanna's cheery instructions and merry laughter at her mistakes, she was learning fast. Today, even, to Pollyanna's huge delight, she had said that she was glad Pollyanna had brought calf's-foot jelly, because that was just what she had been wanting – she did not know that Milly, at the front door, had told Pollyanna that the minister's wife had already that day sent over a great bowlful of that same kind of jelly.

Pollyanna was thinking of this now when suddenly she saw the boy.

The boy was sitting in a disconsolate little heap by the roadside, whittling half-heartedly at a small stick.

'Hallo,' smiled Pollyanna engagingly.

The boy glanced up, but he looked away again, at once.

'Hallo yourself,' he mumbled.

Pollyanna laughed.

'Now you don't look as if you'd be glad even for calf's-foot jelly,' she chuckled, stopping before him.

The boy stirred restlessly, gave her a surprised look, and began to whittle again at his stick with the dull, broken-bladed knife in his hand.

Pollyanna hesitated, then dropped herself comfortably down on the grass near him. In spite of Pollyanna's brave assertion that she was 'used to Ladies' Aiders', and 'didn't mind', she had sighed at times for some companion of her own age. Hence her determination to make the most of this one.

'My name's Pollyanna Whittier,' she began pleasantly. 'What's yours?'

Again the boy stirred restlessly. He even almost got to his feet. But he settled back.

'Jimmy Bean,' he grunted with ungracious indifference.

'Good! Now we're introduced. I'm glad you did your part – some folks don't, you know. I live at Miss Polly Harrington's house. Where do you live?'

'Nowhere.'

'Nowhere! Why, you can't do that – everybody lives somewhere,' asserted Pollyanna.

'Well, I don't – just now. I'm huntin' up a new place.'

'Oh! Where is it?'

The boy regarded her with scornful eyes.

'Silly! As if I'd be a-huntin' for it – if I knew!'

Pollyanna tossed her head a little. This was not a nice boy, and she did not like to be called 'silly'. Still, he was somebody besides – old folks.

'Where did you live – before?' she queried.

'Well, if you ain't the beat 'em for askin' questions!' sighed the boy impatiently.

'I have to be,' retorted Pollyanna calmly, 'else I couldn't find out a thing about you. If you'd talk more I wouldn't talk so much.'

The boy gave a short laugh. It was a sheepish laugh, and not quite a willing one; but his face looked a little pleasanter when he spoke this time.

'All right then – here goes! I'm Jimmy Bean, and I'm ten years old goin' on eleven. I come last year ter live at the Orphans' Home; but they've got so many kids there ain't much room for me, an' I wa'n't never wanted, anyhow, I don't believe. So I've quit. I'm goin' ter live somewheres else – but I hain't found the place, yet. I'd *like* a home – jest a common one, ye know, with a mother in it, instead of a matron. If ye has a home, ye has folks; an' I hain't had folks since – dad died. So I'm a-huntin' now. I've tried four houses, but – they didn't want me – though I said I expected ter work, 'course. There! Is that all you want ter know?' The boy's voice had broken a little over the last two sentences.

'Why, what a shame!' sympathised Pollyanna. 'And didn't there anybody want you? Oh, dear! I know just how you feel, because after – after my father died, too, there wasn't anybody but the Ladies' Aid for me, until Aunt Polly said she'd take – ' Pollyanna stopped abruptly. The dawning of a wonderful idea began to show in her face.

'Oh, I know just the place for you,' she cried. 'Aunt Polly'll take you – I know she will! Didn't she take me? And didn't she take Fluffy and Buffy, when they didn't have anyone to love them, or any place to go? – and they're only cats and dogs. Oh, come, I know Aunt Polly'll take you! You don't know how good and kind she is!'

Jimmy Bean's thin little face brightened.

'Honest Injun? Would she, now? I'd work, ye know, an' I'm real strong!' He bared a small, bony arm.

'Of course she would! Why, my Aunt Polly is the nicest lady in the world – now that my mama has gone to be a heaven angel. And there's rooms – heaps of 'em,' she continued, springing to her feet, and tugging at his arm. 'It's an awful big house. Maybe, though,' she added a little anxiously, as they hurried on, 'maybe you'll have to sleep in the attic room. I did, at first. But there's screens there now, so 'twon't be so hot, and the flies can't get in, either, to bring in the germ-things on their feet. Did you know about that? It's perfectly lovely! Maybe she'll let you read the book if you're good – I mean, if you're bad. And you've got freckles, too' – with a critical glance – 'so you'll be glad there isn't any looking-glass; and the outdoor picture is nicer than any wall-one could be, so you won't mind sleeping in that room at all, I'm sure,' panted Pollyanna, finding suddenly that she needed the rest of her breath for purposes other than talking.

'Gorry!' exclaimed Jimmy Bean tersely and uncomprehendingly, but admiringly. Then he added: 'I shouldn't think anybody who could talk like that, runnin', would need ter ask no questions ter fill up time with!'

Pollyanna laughed.

'Well, anyhow, you can be glad of that,' she retorted; 'for when I'm talking, *you* don't have to!'

When the house was reached Pollyanna unhesitatingly piloted her companion straight into the presence of her amazed aunt.

'Oh, Aunt Polly,' she triumphed. 'Just look a-here! I've got something ever so much nicer, even, than Fluffy and Buffy for you to bring up. It's a real live boy. He won't mind a bit sleeping in the attic, at first, you know, and he says he'll work; but I shall need him the most of the time to play with, I reckon.'

Miss Polly grew white, then very red. She did not quite understand; but she thought she understood enough.

'Pollyanna, what does this mean? Who is this dirty little boy? Where did you find him?' she demanded sharply.

The 'dirty little boy' fell back a step and looked towards the door. Pollyanna laughed merrily.

'There, if I didn't forget to tell you his name! I'm as bad as the man.

And he is dirty, too, isn't he? – I mean, the boy is – just like Fluffy and Buffy were when you took them in. But I reckon he'll improve all right by washing, just as they did, and – Oh, I 'most forgot again,' she broke off with a laugh. 'This is Jimmy Bean, Aunt Polly.'

'Well, what is he doing here?'

'Why, Aunt Polly, I just told you!' Pollyanna's eyes were wide with surprise. 'He's for you. I brought him home – so he could live here, you know. He wants a home and folks. I told him how good you were to me, and to Fluffy and Buffy, and that I knew you would be to him, because of course he's even nicer than cats and dogs.'

Miss Polly dropped back in her chair and raised a shaking hand to her throat. The old helplessness was threatening once more to overcome her. With a visible struggle, however, Miss Polly pulled herself suddenly erect.

'That will do, Pollyanna. This is a little the most absurd thing you've done yet. As if tramp cats and mangy dogs weren't bad enough but you must needs bring home ragged little beggars from the street, who – '

There was a sudden stir from the boy. His eyes flashed and his chin came up. With two strides of his sturdy little legs he confronted Miss Polly fearlessly.

'I ain't a beggar, marm, an' I don't want nothin' o' you. I was calc'latin' ter work, of course, fur my board an' keep. I wouldn't have come ter your old house, anyhow, if there 'ere girl hadn't 'a' made me, a-tellin' me how you was so good an' kind that you'd be jest dyin' ter take me in. So, there!' And he wheeled about and stalked from the room with a dignity that would have been absurd had it not been so pitiful.

'Oh, Aunt Polly,' choked Pollyanna. 'Why, I thought you'd be *glad* to have him here! I'm sure, I should think you'd be glad.'

Miss Polly raised her hand with a peremptory gesture of silence. Miss Polly's nerves had snapped at last. The 'good and kind' of the boy's words were still ringing in her ears, and the old helplessness was almost upon her, she knew. Yet she rallied her forces with the last atom of her willpower.

'Pollyanna,' she cried sharply, '*will* you stop using that everlasting word "glad"! It's "glad" – "glad" – "glad" from morning till night until I think I shall grow wild!'

From sheer amazement Pollyanna's jaw dropped.

'Why, Aunt Polly,' she breathed, 'I should think you'd be glad to have me gl – Oh!' she broke off, clapping her hand to her lips and hurrying blindly from the room.

Before the boy had reached the end of the driveway, Pollyanna overtook him.

'Boy! Boy! Jimmy Bean, I want you to know how – how sorry I am,' she panted, catching him with a detaining hand.

'Sorry nothin'! I ain't blamin' you,' retorted the boy sullenly. 'But I ain't no beggar!' he added with sudden spirit.

'Of course you aren't! But you mustn't blame Auntie,' appealed Pollyanna. 'Probably I didn't do the introducing right, anyhow; and I reckon I didn't tell her much who you were. She *is* good and kind, really – she's always been; but I probably didn't explain it right. I do wish I could find some place for you, though!'

The boy shrugged his shoulders and half turned away. 'Never mind. I guess I can find one myself. I ain't no beggar, you know.'

Pollyanna was frowning thoughtfully. Of a sudden she turned, her face illumined.

'Say, I'll tell you what I *will* do! The Ladies' Aid meets this afternoon. I heard Aunt Polly say so. I'll lay your case before them. That's what father always did, when he wanted anything – educating the heathen and new carpets, you know.'

The boy turned fiercely.

'Well, I ain't a heathen or a new carpet. Besides – what is a Ladies' Aid?'

Pollyanna stared in shocked disapproval.

'Why, Jimmy Bean, wherever have you been brought up? – not to know what a Ladies' Aid is!'

'Oh, all right – if you ain't tellin',' grunted the boy, turning and beginning to walk away indifferently.

Pollyanna sprang to his side at once.

'It's – it's – why, it's just a lot of ladies that meet and sew and give suppers and raise money and – and talk; that's what a Ladies' Aid is.

They're awfully kind – that is, most of mine was, back home. I haven't seen this one here, but they're always good, I reckon. I'm going to tell them about you this afternoon.'

Again the boy turned fiercely.

'Not much you will! Maybe you think I'm goin' ter stand round an' hear a whole *lot* o' women call me a beggar, instead of jest *one*! Not much!'

'Oh, but you wouldn't be there,' argued Pollyanna quickly. 'I'd go alone, of course, and tell them.'

'You would?'

'Yes; and I'd tell it better this time,' hurried on Pollyanna, quick to see the signs of relenting in the boy's face. 'And there'd be some of 'em, I know, that would be glad to give you a home.'

'I'd work – don't forget ter say that,' cautioned the boy.

'Of course not,' promised Pollyanna happily, sure now that her point was gained. 'Then I'll let you know tomorrow.'

'Where?'

'By the road – where I found you today; near Mrs Snow's house.'

'All right. I'll be there.' The boy paused before he went on slowly: 'Maybe I'd better go back, then, for ternight, ter the Home. You see I hain't no other place ter stay; and – and I didn't leave till this mornin'. I slipped out. I didn't tell 'em I wasn't comin' back, else they'd pretend I couldn't come – though I'm thinkin' they won't do no worryin' when I don't show up sometime. They ain't like *folks*, ye know. They don't *care*!'

'I know,' nodded Pollyanna, with understanding eyes. 'But I'm sure, when I see you tomorrow, I'll have just a common home and folks that do care all ready for you. Goodbye!' she called brightly, as she turned back towards the house.

In the sitting-room window at that moment, Miss Polly, who had been watching the two children, followed with sombre eyes the boy until a bend of the road hid him from sight. Then she sighed, turned, and walked listlessly upstairs – and Miss Polly did not usually move listlessly. In her ears still was the boy's scornful 'you was so good and kind'. In her heart was a curious sense of desolation – as of something lost.

CHAPTER 12

Before the Ladies' Aid

Dinner, which came at noon in the Harrington homestead, was a silent meal on the day of the Ladies' Aid meeting. Pollyanna, it is true, tried to talk; but she did not make a success of it, chiefly because four times she was obliged to break off a "glad" in the middle of it, much to her blushing discomfort. The fifth time it happened Miss Polly moved her head wearily.

'There, there, child, say it, if you want to,' she sighed. 'I'm sure I'd rather you did than not – if it's going to make all this fuss.'

Pollyanna's puckered little face cleared.

'Oh, thank you. I'm afraid it would be pretty hard – not to say it. You see I've played it so long.'

'You've – what?' demanded Aunt Polly.

'Played it – the game, you know, that father –' Pollyanna stopped with a painful blush at finding herself so soon again on forbidden ground.

Aunt Polly frowned and said nothing. The rest of the meal was a silent one.

Pollyanna was not sorry to hear Aunt Polly tell the minister's wife over the telephone, a little later, that she would not be at the Ladies' Aid meeting that afternoon, owing to a headache. When Aunt Polly went upstairs to her room and closed the door, Pollyanna tried to be sorry for the headache; but she could not help feeling glad that her aunt was not to be present that afternoon when she laid the case of Jimmy Bean before the Ladies' Aid. She could not forget that Aunt Polly had called Jimmy Bean a little beggar; and she did not want Aunt Polly to call him that – before the Ladies' Aid.

Pollyanna knew that the Ladies' Aid met at two o'clock in the chapel next the church, not quite half a mile from home. She planned her going, therefore, so that she should get there a little before three.

'I want them all to be there,' she said to herself; 'else the very one that wasn't there might be the one who would be wanting to give Jimmy Bean a home; and, of course, two o'clock always means three, really – to Ladies' Aiders.'

Quietly, but with confident courage, Pollyanna ascended the chapel steps, pushed open the door and entered the vestibule. A soft babel of feminine chatter and laughter came from the main room. Hesitating only a brief moment Pollyanna pushed open one of the inner doors.

The chatter dropped to a surprised hush. Pollyanna advanced a little timidly. Now that the time had come, she felt unwontedly shy. After all, these half-strange, half-familiar faces about her were not her own dear Ladies' Aid.

'How do you do, Ladies' Aiders?' she faltered politely. 'I'm Polly-anna Whittier. I – I reckon some of you know me, maybe; anyway, I do *you* – only I don't know you all together this way.'

The silence could almost be felt now. Some of the ladies did know this rather extraordinary niece of their fellow-member, and nearly all had heard of her; but not one of them could think of anything to say, just then.

'I – I've come to – to lay a case before you,' stammered Pollyanna, after a moment, unconsciously falling into her father's familiar phraseology.

There was a slight rustle.

'Did – did your aunt send you, my dear?' asked Mrs Ford, the minister's wife.

Pollyanna coloured a little.

'Oh, no. I came all by myself. You see, I'm used to Ladies' Aiders. It was Ladies' Aiders that brought me up – with father.'

Somebody tittered hysterically, and the minister's wife frowned.

'Yes, dear. What is it?'

'Well, it – it's Jimmy Bean,' sighed Pollyanna. 'He hasn't any home except the orphans' one, and they're full, and don't want him, anyhow, so he thinks; so he wants another. He wants one of the common kind, that has a mother instead of a matron in it – folks, you know, that'll care. He's ten years old going on eleven. I thought some of you might like him – to live with you, you know.'

'Well, did you ever!' murmured a voice, breaking the dazed pause that followed Pollyanna's words.

With anxious eyes Pollyanna swept the circle of faces about her.

'Oh, I forgot to say; he will work,' she supplemented eagerly.

Still there was silence; then, coldly, one or two women began to question her. After a time they all had the story and began to talk among themselves, animatedly, not quite pleasantly.

Pollyanna listened with growing anxiety. Some of what was said she could not understand. She did gather, after a time, however, that there was no woman there who had a home to give him, though every woman seemed to think that some of the others might take him, as there were several who had no little boys of their own already in their homes. But there was no one who agreed herself to take him. Then she heard the minister's wife suggest timidly that they, as a society, might perhaps assume his support and education instead of sending quite so much money this year to the little boys in faraway India.

A great many ladies talked then, and several of them talked all at once, and even more loudly and more unpleasantly than before. It seemed that their society was famous for its offering to Hindu missions, and several said they should die of mortification if it should be less this year. Some of what was said at this time Pollyanna again thought she could not have understood, too, for it sounded almost as if they did not care at all what the money *did*, so long as the sum opposite the name of their society in a certain 'report' 'headed the list' – and of course that could not be what they meant at all! But it was all very confusing, and not quite pleasant, so that Pollyanna was glad, indeed, when at last she found herself outside in the hushed, sweet air – only she was very sorry, too; for she knew it was not going to be easy, or anything but sad, to tell Jimmy Bean tomorrow that the Ladies' Aid had decided that they would rather send all their money to bring up the little India boys than to save out enough to bring up one little boy in their own town, for which they would not get 'a bit of credit in the report', according to the tall lady who wore spectacles.

'Not but that it's good, of course, to send money to the heathen, and I shouldn't want 'em not to send some there,' sighed Pollyanna to herself, as she trudged sorrowfully along. 'But they acted as if little boys *here* weren't any account – only little boys 'way off. I should *think*, though, they'd rather see Jimmy Bean grow – than just a report!'

CHAPTER 13

In Pendleton Woods

Pollyanna had not turned her steps towards home when she left the chapel. She had turned them, instead, towards Pendleton Hill. It had been a hard day, for all it had been a 'vacation one' (as she termed the infrequent days when there was no sewing- or cooking-lesson), and Pollyanna was sure that nothing would do her quite so much good as a walk through the green quiet of Pendleton Woods. Up Pendleton Hill, therefore, she climbed steadily, in spite of the warm sun on her back.

'I don't have to get home till half-past five, anyway,' she was telling herself; 'and it'll be so much nicer to go around by the way of the woods, even if I do have to climb to get there.'

It was very beautiful in the Pendleton Woods, as Pollyanna knew by experience. But today it seemed even more delightful than ever, notwithstanding her disappointment over what she must tell Jimmy Bean tomorrow.

'I wish they were up here – all those ladies who talked so loud,' sighed Pollyanna to herself, raising her eyes to the patches of vivid blue between the sunlit green of the treetops. 'Anyhow, if they were up here, I just reckon they'd change and take Jimmy Bean for their little boy, all right,' she finished, secure in her conviction, but unable to give a reason for it, even to herself.

Suddenly Pollyanna lifted her head and listened. A dog had barked some distance ahead. A moment later he came dashing towards her, still barking.

'Hallo, doggie – hallo!' Pollyanna snapped her fingers at the dog and looked expectantly down the path. She had seen the dog once before, she was sure. He had been then with the man, Mr John Pendleton. She was looking now, hoping to see him. For some minutes she watched eagerly, but he did not appear. Then she turned her attention towards the dog.

The dog, as even Pollyanna could see, was acting strangely. He was still barking – giving little short, sharp yelps, as if of alarm. He was running back and forth, too, in the path ahead. Soon they reached a side-path, and down this the little dog fairly flew, only to come back at once, whining and barking.

'Ho! That isn't the way home,' laughed Pollyanna, still keeping to the main path.

The little dog seemed frantic now. Back and forth, back and forth, between Pollyanna and the side-path he vibrated, barking and whining pitifully. Every quiver of his little brown body, and every glance from his beseeching brown eyes were eloquent with appeal – so eloquent that at last Pollyanna understood, turned, and followed him.

Straight ahead, now, the little dog dashed madly, and it was not long before Pollyanna came upon the reason for it all: a man lying motionless at the foot of a steep, overhanging mass of rock a few yards from the side-path.

A twig cracked sharply under Pollyanna's foot, and the man turned his head. With a cry of dismay Pollyanna ran to his side.

'Mr Pendleton! Oh, are you hurt?'

'Hurt? Oh, no! I'm just taking a siesta in the sunshine,' snapped the man irritably. 'See here, how much do you know? What can you do? Have you got any sense?'

Pollyanna caught her breath with a little gasp, but – as was her habit – she answered the questions literally, one by one.

'Why, Mr Pendleton, I – I don't know so very much, and I can't do a great many things; but most of the Ladies' Aiders, except Mrs Rawson, said I had real good sense. I heard 'em say so one day – they didn't know I heard, though.'

The man smiled grimly. 'There, there, child, I beg your pardon, I'm sure; it's only this confounded leg of mine. Now listen.' He paused, and with some difficulty reached his hand into his trousers-pocket and brought out a bunch of keys, singling out one between his thumb and forefinger. 'Straight through the path there, about five minutes' walk, is my house. This key will admit you to the side-door under the *porte-cochère*. Do you know what a *porte-cochère* is?'

'Oh, yes, sir. Auntie has one with a sun-parlour over it. That's the roof I slept on – only I didn't sleep, you know. They found me.'

'Eh? Oh! Well, when you get into the house, go straight through the vestibule and hall to the door at the end. On the big, flat-topped desk in the middle of the room you'll find a telephone. Do you know how to use a telephone?'

'Oh, yes, sir! Why, once when Aunt Polly – '

'Never mind Aunt Polly now,' cut in the man scowlingly, as he tried to move himself a little. 'Hunt up Dr Thomas Chilton's number on the card you'll find somewhere around there – it ought to be on the hook down at the side, but it probably won't be. You know a telephone card, I suppose, when you see one!'

'Oh, yes, sir! I just love Aunt Polly's. There's such a lot of queer names, and – '

'Tell Dr Chilton that John Pendleton is at the foot of Little Eagle Ledge in Pendleton Woods with a broken leg, and to come at once with a stretcher and two men. He'll know what to do besides that. Tell him to come by the path from the house.'

'A broken leg? Oh, Mr Pendleton, how perfectly awful!' shuddered Pollyanna. 'But I'm so glad I came! Can't *I* do – '

'Yes, you can – but evidently you won't! *Will* you go and do what I ask and stop talking?' moaned the man faintly.

And, with a little sobbing cry, Pollyanna went. She did not stop now to look up at the patches of blue between the sunlit tops of the trees. She kept her eyes on the ground to make sure that neither twig nor stone tripped her hurrying feet.

It was not long before she came in sight of the house. She had seen it before, though never so near as this. She was almost frightened now at the massiveness of the great pile of grey stone with its pillared verandas and its imposing entrance. Pausing only a moment, however, she sped across the big neglected lawn and around the house to the side door under the *porte-cochère*. Her fingers, stiff from their tight clutch upon the keys, were anything but skilful in their efforts to turn the bolt in the lock; but at last the heavy, carved door swung slowly back on its hinges.

Pollyanna caught her breath. In spite of her feeling of haste, she paused a moment and looked fearfully through the vestibule to the wide, sombre hall beyond, her thoughts in a whirl. This was John Pendleton's house; the house of mystery; the house into which no one but its master entered; the house which sheltered, somewhere – a skeleton. Yet she, Pollyanna, was expected to enter alone these fearsome rooms, and telephone the doctor that the master of the house lay now . . .

With a little cry Pollyanna, looking neither to the right nor the left, fairly ran through the hall to the door at the end and opened it.

The room was large and sombre, with dark woods and hangings like the hall; but through the west window the sun threw a long shaft of gold across the floor, gleamed dully on the tarnished brass andirons in the fireplace and touched the nickel of the telephone on the great desk in the middle of the room. It was towards this desk that Pollyanna hurriedly tiptoed.

The telephone card was not on its hook; it was on the floor. But Pollyanna found it, and ran her shaking forefinger down through the Cs to 'Chilton'. In due time she had Dr Chilton himself at the other end of the wires, and was tremblingly delivering her message and answering the doctor's terse, pertinent questions. This done, she hung up the receiver and drew a long breath of relief.

Only a brief glance did Pollyanna give about her; then, with a confused vision in her eyes of crimson draperies, book-lined walls, a littered floor, an untidy desk, innumerable closed doors (any one of which might conceal a skeleton), and everywhere dust, dust, dust, she fled back through the hall to the great carved door, still half open as she had left it.

In what seemed, even to the injured man, an incredibly short time, Pollyanna was back in the woods at the man's side.

'Well, what is the trouble? Couldn't you get in?' he demanded.

Pollyanna opened wide her eyes.

'Why, of course I could! I'm *here*,' she answered. 'As if I'd be here if I hadn't got in! And the doctor will be right up just as soon as possible with the men and things. He said he knew just where you were, so I didn't stay to show him. I wanted to be with you.'

'Did you?' smiled the man grimly. 'Well, I can't say I admire your taste. I should think you might find pleasanter companions.'

'Do you mean – because you're so – cross?'

'Thanks for your frankness. Yes.'

Pollyanna laughed softly.

'But you're only cross *outside* – you aren't cross inside a bit!'

'Indeed! How do you know that?' asked the man, trying to change the position of his head without moving the rest of his body.

'Oh, lots of ways; there – like that – the way you act with the dog,' she added, pointing to the long, slender hand that rested on the dog's sleek head near him. 'It's funny how dogs and cats know the insides of folks better than other folks do, isn't it? Say, I'm going to hold your head,' she finished abruptly.

The man winced several times and groaned once softly while the change was being made; but in the end he found Pollyanna's lap a very welcome substitute for the rocky hollow in which his head had lain before.

'Well, that is – better,' he murmured faintly.

He did not speak again for some time. Pollyanna, watching his face, wondered if he were asleep. She did not think he was. He looked as if his lips were tight shut to keep back moans of pain. Pollyanna herself almost cried aloud as she looked at his great, strong body lying there so helpless. One hand, with fingers tightly clenched, lay out-flung, motionless. The other, limply open, lay on the dog's head. The dog, his wistful, eager eyes on his master's face, was motionless, too.

Minute by minute the time passed. The sun dropped lower in the west and the shadows grew deeper under the trees. Pollyanna sat so still she hardly seemed to breathe. A bird alighted fearlessly within reach of her hand, and a squirrel whisked his bushy tail on a tree-branch almost under her nose – yet with his bright little eyes all the while on the motionless dog.

At last the dog pricked up his ears and whined softly; then he gave a short, sharp bark. The next moment Pollyanna heard voices, and very soon their owners appeared – three men carrying a stretcher and various other articles.

The tallest of the party – a smooth-shaven, kind-eyed man whom Pollyanna knew by sight as Dr Chilton – advanced cheerily.

'Well, my little lady, playing nurse?'

'Oh, no, sir,' smiled Pollyanna. 'I've only held his head – I haven't given him a mite of medicine. But I'm glad I was here.'

'So am I,' nodded the doctor, as he turned his absorbed attention to the injured man.

CHAPTER 14

Just a Matter of Jelly

Pollyanna was a little late for supper on the night of the accident to John Pendleton; but, as it happened, she escaped without reproof.

Nancy met her at the door.

'Well, if I ain't glad ter be settin' my two eyes on you,' she sighed in obvious relief. 'It's half-past six!'

'I know it,' admitted Pollyanna anxiously; 'but I'm not to blame – truly I'm not. And I don't think even Aunt Polly will say I am, either.'

'She won't have the chance,' retorted Nancy, with huge satisfaction. 'She's gone.'

'Gone!' gasped Pollyanna. 'You don't mean that I've driven her away?' Through Pollyanna's mind at that moment trooped remorseful memories of the morning with its unwanted boy, cat and dog, and its unwelcome 'glad' and forbidden 'father' that would spring to her forgetful little tongue. 'Oh, I *didn't* drive her away?'

'Not much you did,' scoffed Nancy. 'Her cousin died suddenly down in Boston, and she had ter go. She had one o' them yeller telegram letters after you went away this afternoon, and she won't be back for three days. Now I guess we're glad all right. We'll be keepin' house tergether, jest you and me, all that time. We will, we will!'

Pollyanna looked shocked.

'Glad! Oh, Nancy, when it's a funeral?'

'Oh, but 'twa'n't the funeral I was glad for, Miss Pollyanna. It was – ' Nancy stopped abruptly. A shrewd twinkle came into her eyes. 'Why, Miss Pollyanna, as if it wa'n't yerself that was teachin' me ter play the game,' she reproached her gravely.

Pollyanna puckered her forehead into a troubled frown.

'I can't help it, Nancy,' she argued, with a shake of her head. 'It must be that there are some things that 'tisn't right to play the game on – and I'm sure funerals is one of them. There's nothing in a funeral to be glad about.'

Nancy chuckled.

'We can be glad 'tain't our'n,' she observed demurely. But Pollyanna did not hear. She had begun to tell of the accident; and in a moment Nancy, open-mouthed, was listening.

At the appointed place the next afternoon Pollyanna met Jimmy Bean according to agreement. As was to be expected, of course, Jimmy showed keen disappointment that the Ladies' Aid preferred a little India boy to himself.

'Well, maybe 'tis natural,' he sighed. 'Of course things you don't know about are always nicer'n things you do, same as the pertater on t'other side of the plate is always the biggest. But I wish I looked that way ter somebody 'way off. Wouldn't it be jest great, now, if only somebody over in India wanted *me*?'

Pollyanna clapped her hands.

'Why, of course! That's the very thing, Jimmy! I'll write to *my* Ladies' Aiders about you. They aren't over in India; they're only out West – but that's awful far away, just the same. I reckon you'd think so if you'd come all the way here, as I did!'

Jimmy's face brightened.

'Do you think they would – truly – take me?' he asked.

'Of course they would! Don't they take little boys in India to bring up? Well, they can just play you are the little India boy this time. I reckon you're far enough away to make a report, all right. You wait. I'll write 'em. I'll write Mrs White. No, I'll write Mrs Jones. Mrs White has got the most money, but Mrs Jones gives the most – which is kind of funny, isn't it? – when you think of it. But I reckon some of the Aiders will take you.'

'All right – but don't furgit ter say I'll work fur my board an' keep,' put in Jimmy. 'I ain't no beggar, an' bis'ness is bis'ness, even with Ladies' Aiders, I'm thinkin'.' He hesitated, then added: 'An' I s'pose I better stay where I be fur a spell yet – till you hear.'

'Of course,' nodded Pollyanna emphatically. 'Then I'll know just where to find you. And they'll take you – I'm sure you're far enough away for that. Didn't Aunt Polly take – Say!' she broke off suddenly, '*do* you suppose I was Aunt Polly's little girl from India?'

'Well, if you ain't the queerest kid,' grinned Jimmy as he turned away.

It was about a week after the accident in Pendleton Woods that Pollyanna said to her aunt one morning: 'Aunt Polly, please would you mind very much if I took Mrs Snow's calf's-foot jelly this week to someone else? I'm sure Mrs Snow wouldn't mind – this once.'

'Dear me, Pollyanna, what *are* you up to now?' sighed her aunt. 'You *are* the most extraordinary child!'

Pollyanna frowned a little anxiously.

'Aunt Polly, please, what is extraordinary? If you're *ex*traordinary you can't be *or*dinary, can you?'

'You certainly cannot.'

'Oh, that's all right, then. I'm glad I'm *ex*traordinary,' sighed Pollyanna, her face clearing. 'You see, Mrs White used to say Mrs Rawson was a very ordinary woman – and she disliked Mrs Rawson something awful. They were always fight – I mean, father had – that is, I mean, *we* had more trouble keeping peace between them than we did between any of the rest of the Aiders,' corrected Pollyanna, a little breathless from her efforts to steer between the Scylla of her father's past commands in regard to speaking of church quarrels, and the Charybdis of her aunt's present commands in regard to speaking of her father.

'Yes, yes; well, never mind,' interposed Aunt Polly, a trifle impatiently. 'You do run on so, Pollyanna, and no matter what we're talking about you always bring up at those Ladies' Aiders!'

'Yes'm,' smiled Pollyanna cheerfully. 'I reckon I do, maybe. But you see they used to bring me up, and –'

'That will do, Pollyanna,' interrupted a cold voice. 'Now what is it about this jelly?'

'Nothing, Aunt Polly, truly, that you would mind, I'm sure. You let me take jelly to *her*, so I thought you would to *him* – this once. You see, broken legs aren't like – like lifelong invalids, so his won't last for ever as Mrs Snow's does, and *she* can have all the rest of the things after just once or twice.'

'Him? He? Broken leg? What are you talking about, Pollyanna?'

Pollyanna stared; then her face relaxed.

'Oh, I forgot. I reckon you didn't know. You see, it happened while you were gone. It was the very day you went that I found him in the woods, you know; and I had to unlock his house and telephone for the men and the doctor, and hold his head, and everything. And of course then I came away and haven't seen him since. But when Nancy made the jelly for Mrs Snow this week I thought how nice it would be if I could take it to him instead of her, just this once. Aunt Polly, may I?'

'Yes, yes, I suppose so,' acquiesced Miss Polly, a little wearily. 'Who did you say he was?'

'The man. I mean, Mr John Pendleton.'

Miss Polly almost sprang from her chair. '*John Pendleton!*'

'Yes. Nancy told me his name. Maybe you know him?'

Miss Polly did not answer this. Instead she asked: 'Do *you* know him?'

Pollyanna nodded. 'Oh, yes. He always speaks and smiles – now. He's only cross *outside*, you know. I'll go and get the jelly. Nancy had it 'most fixed when I came in,' finished Pollyanna, already halfway across the room.

'Pollyanna, wait!' Miss Polly's voice was suddenly very stern. 'I've changed my mind. I would prefer that Mrs Snow had that jelly today – as usual. That is all. You may go now.'

Pollyanna's face fell.

'Oh, but Aunt Polly, *hers* will last. She can always be sick and have things, you know; but *his* is just a broken leg, and legs don't last – I mean, broken ones. He's had it a whole week now.'

'Yes, I remember. I heard Mr John Pendleton had met with an accident,' said Miss Polly, a little stiffly; 'but – I do not care to be sending jelly to John Pendleton, Pollyanna.'

'I know, he is cross – outside,' admitted Pollyanna, sadly, 'so I suppose you don't like him. But I wouldn't say 'twas you sent it. I'd say 'twas me. I like him. I'd be glad to send him jelly.'

Miss Polly began to shake her head again. Then, suddenly, she stopped, and asked in a curiously quiet voice: 'Does he know who you – are, Pollyanna?'

The little girl sighed. 'I reckon not. I told him my name, once, but he never calls me it – never.'

'Does he know where you – live?'

'Oh, no. I never told him that.'

'Then he doesn't know you're my – niece?'

'I don't think so.'

For a moment there was silence. Miss Polly was looking at Pollyanna with eyes that did not seem to see her at all. The little girl, shifting impatiently from one small foot to the other, sighed audibly. Then Miss Polly roused herself with a start.

'Very well, Pollyanna,' she said at last, still in that queer voice, so unlike her own: 'you may – you may take the jelly to Mr Pendleton as your own gift. But understand, I do not send it. Be very sure that he does not think I do!'

'Yes'm – no'm – thank you, Aunt Polly,' exulted Pollyanna, as she flew through the door.

CHAPTER 15

Dr Chilton

The great grey pile of masonry looked very different to Pollyanna when she made her second visit to the house of Mr John Pendleton. Windows were open, an elderly woman was hanging out clothes in the back yard, and the doctor's gig stood under the *porte-cochère*.

As before Pollyanna went to the side door. This time she rang the bell – her fingers were not stiff today from a tight clutch on a bunch of keys.

A familiar-looking small dog bounded up the steps to greet her, but there was a slight delay before the woman who had been hanging out the clothes opened the door.

'If you please, I've brought some calf's-foot jelly for Mr Pendleton,' smiled Pollyanna.

'Thank you,' said the woman, reaching for the bowl in the little girl's hand. 'Who shall I say sent it? And it's calf's-foot jelly?'

The doctor, coming into the hall at that moment, heard the woman's words and saw the disappointed look on Pollyanna's face. He stepped quickly forward.

'Ah! Some calf's-foot jelly?' he asked genially. 'That will be fine! Maybe you'd like to see our patient, eh?'

'Oh, yes, sir,' beamed Pollyanna; and the woman, in obedience to a nod from the doctor, led the way down the hall at once, though plainly with vast surprise on her face.

Behind the doctor, a young man (a trained nurse from the nearest city) gave a disturbed exclamation.

'But, doctor, didn't Mr Pendleton give orders not to admit anyone?'

'Oh, yes,' nodded the doctor, imperturbably. 'But I'm giving orders now. I'll take the risk.' Then he added whimsically: 'You don't know, of course; but that little girl is better than a six-quart bottle of tonic any day. If anything or anybody can take the grouch out of Pendleton this afternoon, she can. That's why I sent her in.'

'Who is she?'

For one brief moment the doctor hesitated.

'She's the niece of one of our best-known residents. Her name is Pollyanna Whittier. I – I don't happen to enjoy a very extensive personal acquaintance with the little lady as yet; but lots of my patients do – I'm thankful to say!'

The nurse smiled.

'Indeed! And what are the special ingredients of this wonder-working – tonic of hers?'

The doctor shook his head.

'I don't know. As near as I can find out it is an overwhelming, unquenchable gladness for everything that has happened or is going to happen. At any rate, her quaint speeches are constantly being repeated to me, and, as near as I can make out, "just being glad" is the tenor of most of them. All is,' he added, with another whimsical smile, as he stepped out on to the porch, 'I wish I could prescribe her – and buy her – as I would a box of pills; though if there gets to be many of her in the world, you and I might as well go to ribbon-selling and ditch-digging for all the money we'd get out of nursing and doctoring,' he laughed, picking up the reins and stepping into the gig.

Pollyanna, meanwhile, in accordance with the doctor's orders, was being escorted to John Pendleton's rooms.

Her way led through the great library at the end of the hall, and, rapid as was her progress through it, Pollyanna saw at once that great changes had taken place. The book-lined walls and the crimson curtains were the same; but there was no litter on the floor, no untidiness on the desk, and not so much as a grain of dust in sight. The telephone card hung in its proper place, and the brass andirons had been polished. One of the mysterious doors was open, and it was towards this that the maid led the way. A moment later Polly-anna found herself in a sumptuously furnished bedroom while the maid was saying in a frightened voice: 'If you please, sir, here – here's a little girl with some jelly. The doctor said I was to – to bring her in.'

The next moment Pollyanna found herself alone with a very cross-looking man lying flat on his back in bed.

'See here, didn't I say – ' began an angry voice. 'Oh, it's you!' it broke off not very graciously, as Pollyanna advanced towards the bed.

'Yes, sir,' smiled Pollyanna. 'Oh, I'm so glad they let me in! You see, at first the lady 'most took my jelly, and I was so afraid I wasn't going to see you at all. Then the doctor came, and he said I might. Wasn't he lovely to let me see you?'

In spite of himself the man's lips twitched into a smile; but all he said was, 'Humph!'

'And I've brought you some jelly,' resumed Pollyanna; 'calf's-foot. I hope you like it?' There was a rising inflection in her voice.

'Never ate it.' The fleeting smile had gone, and the scowl had come back to the man's face.

For a brief instant Pollyanna's countenance showed disappointment; but it cleared as she set the bowl of jelly down.

'Didn't you? Well, if you didn't, then you can't know you *don't* like it, anyhow, can you? So I reckon I'm glad you haven't, after all. Now, if you knew – '

'Yes, yes; well, there's one thing I know all right, and that is that I'm flat on my back right here this minute, and that I'm liable to stay here – till doomsday, I guess.'

Pollyanna looked shocked.

'Oh, no! It couldn't be till doomsday, you know, when the Angel Gabriel blows his trumpet, unless it should come quicker than we think it will – oh, of course, I know the Bible says it may come quicker than we think, but I don't think it will – that is, of course I believe the Bible; but I mean I don't think it will come as much quicker as it would if it should come now, and – '

John Pendleton laughed suddenly – and aloud. The nurse, coming in at that moment, heard the laugh, and beat a hurried – but a very silent – retreat. He had the air of a frightened cook who, seeing the danger of a breath of cold air striking a half-done cake, hastily shuts the oven door.

'Aren't you getting a little mixed?' asked John Pendleton of Pollyanna.

The little girl laughed.

'Maybe. But what I mean is that legs don't last – broken ones, you know – like lifelong invalids, same as Mrs Snow has got. So yours won't last till doomsday at all. I should think you could be glad of that.'

'Oh, I am,' retorted the man grimly.

'And you didn't break but one. You can be glad 'twasn't two.' Pollyanna was warming to her task.

'Of course! So fortunate,' sniffed the man, with uplifted eyebrows; 'looking at it from that standpoint, I suppose I might be glad I wasn't a centipede and didn't break fifty!'

Pollyanna chuckled.

'Oh, that's the best yet,' she crowed. 'I know what a centipede is; they've got lots of legs. And you can be glad – '

'Oh, of course,' interrupted the man sharply, all the old bitterness coming back to his voice; 'I can be glad, too, for all the rest, I suppose – the nurse, and the doctor, and that confounded woman in the kitchen!'

'Why, yes, sir – only think how bad 'twould be if you *didn't* have them!'

'Well, I – eh?' he demanded sharply.

'Why, I say, only think how bad it would be if you didn't have 'em – and you lying here like this!'

'As if that wasn't the very thing that was at the bottom of the whole matter,' retorted the man testily, 'because I *am* lying here like this! And yet you expect me to say I'm glad because of a fool woman who disarranges the whole house and calls it "regulating", and a man who aids and abets her in it, and calls it "nursing", to say nothing of a doctor who eggs 'em both on – and the whole bunch of them, meanwhile, expecting me to pay them for it, and pay them well, too!'

Pollyanna frowned sympathetically.

'Yes, I know. *That* part is too bad – about the money – when you've been saving it, too, all this time.'

'When – eh?'

'Saving it – buying beans and fish-balls, you know. Say, *do* you like beans? – or do you like turkey better, and it's only on account of the sixty cents?'

'Look a-here, child, what are you talking about?'

Pollyanna smiled radiantly.

'About your money, you know – denying yourself, and saving it for the heathen. You see, I found out about it. Why, Mr Pendleton, that's one of the ways I knew you weren't cross inside. Nancy told me.'

The man's jaw dropped.

'Nancy told you I was saving money for the – Well, may I enquire who Nancy is?'

'Our Nancy. She works for Aunt Polly.'

'Aunt Polly! Well, who is Aunt Polly?'

'She's Miss Polly Harrington. I live with her.'

The man made a sudden movement.

'Miss – Polly – Harrington!' he breathed. 'You live with – *her!*'

'Yes; I'm her niece. She's taken me to bring up – on account of my mother, you know,' faltered Pollyanna, in a low voice. 'She was her sister. And after father – went to be with her and the rest of us in heaven, there wasn't anyone left for me down here but the Ladies' Aid; so she took me.'

The man did not answer. His face, as he lay back on the pillow now, was very white – so white that Pollyanna was frightened. She rose uncertainly to her feet.

'I reckon maybe I'd better go now,' she proposed. 'I – I hope you'll like – the jelly.'

The man turned his head suddenly, and opened his eyes. There was a curious longing in their dark depths which even Pollyanna saw, and at which she marvelled.

'And so you are – Miss Polly Harrington's niece,' he said gently.

'Yes, sir.' Still the man's dark eyes lingered on her face, until Pollyanna, feeling vaguely restless, murmured: 'I – I suppose you know – her.'

John Pendleton's lips curved in an odd smile.

'Oh, yes; I know her.' He hesitated, then went on, still with that curious smile. 'But – you don't mean – you can't mean that it was Miss Polly Harrington who sent that jelly – to me?' he said slowly.

Pollyanna looked distressed.

'N–no, sir; she didn't. She said I must be very sure not to let you think she did send it. But I – '

'I thought as much,' vouchsafed the man, shortly, turning away his head. And Pollyanna, still more distressed, tiptoed from the room.

Under the *porte-cochère* she found the doctor waiting in his gig. The nurse stood on the steps.

'Well, Miss Pollyanna, may I have the pleasure of seeing you home?' asked the doctor smilingly. 'I started to drive on a few minutes ago, then it occurred to me that I'd wait for you.'

'Thank you, sir. I'm glad you did. I just love to ride,' beamed Pollyanna, as he reached out his hand to help her in.

'Do you?' smiled the doctor, nodding his head in farewell to the young man on the steps. 'Well, as near as I can judge, there are a good many things you "love" to do – eh?' he added, as they drove briskly away.

Pollyanna laughed.

'Why, I don't know. I reckon perhaps there are,' she admitted. 'I like to do 'most everything that's *living*. Of course I don't like the other things very well – sewing, and reading out loud, and all that. But *they* aren't *living*.'

'No? What are they, then?'

'Aunt Polly says they're "learning to live",' sighed Pollyanna, with a rueful smile.

The doctor smiled now – a little queerly.

'Does she? Well, I should think she might say – just that.'

'Yes,' responded Pollyanna. 'But I don't see it that way at all. I don't think you have to *learn* how to live. I didn't, anyhow.'

The doctor drew a long sigh.

'After all, I'm afraid some of us – do have to, little girl,' he said. Then, for a time he was silent. Pollyanna, stealing a glance at his face, felt vaguely sorry for him. He looked so sad. She wished, uneasily, that she could 'do something'.

It was this, perhaps, that caused her to say in a timid voice: 'Dr Chilton, I should think being a doctor would be the very gladdest kind of a business there was.'

The doctor turned in surprise. 'Gladdest! – when I see so much suffering always, everywhere I go?' he cried.

She nodded. 'I know; but you're *helping* it – don't you see? – and of course you're glad to help it! And so that makes you the gladdest of any of us, all the time.'

The doctor's eyes filled with sudden hot tears. The doctor's life was a singularly lonely one. He had no wife and no home save his two-room office in a boarding house. His profession was very dear to him. Looking now into Pollyanna's shining eyes, he felt as if a loving hand had been suddenly laid on his head in blessing. He knew, too, that never again would a long day's work or a long night's weariness be quite without that new-found exaltation that had come to him through Pollyanna's eyes.

'God bless you, little girl,' he said unsteadily. Then, with the bright smile his patients knew and loved so well, he added: 'And I'm thinking, after all, that it was the doctor, quite as much as his patients, that needed a draft of that tonic!' All of which puzzled Pollyanna very much – until a chipmunk, running across the road, drove the whole matter from her mind.

The doctor left Pollyanna at her own door, smiled at Nancy, who was sweeping off the front porch, then drove rapidly away.

'I've had a perfectly beautiful ride with the doctor,' announced Pollyanna, bounding up the steps. 'He's lovely, Nancy!'

'Is he?'

'Yes. And I told him I should think his business should be the very gladdest one there was.'

'What! – goin' ter see sick folks – an' folks what ain't sick but thinks they is, which is worse?' Nancy's face showed open scepticism.

Pollyanna laughed gleefully. 'Yes. That's 'most what he said, too; but there is a way to be glad, even then. Guess!'

Nancy frowned in meditation. Nancy was getting so she could play this game of 'being glad' quite successfully, she thought. She rather enjoyed studying out Pollyanna's 'posers', too, as she called some of the little girl's questions.

'Oh, I know,' she chuckled. 'It's just the opposite from what you told Mis' Snow.'

'Opposite?' repeated Pollyanna, obviously puzzled.

'Yes. You told her she could be glad because other folks wasn't like her – all sick, you know.'

'Yes,' nodded Pollyanna.

'Well, the doctor can be glad because *he* isn't like other folks – the sick ones, I mean, what he doctors,' finished Nancy in triumph.

It was Pollyanna's turn to frown.

'Why, y–yes,' she admitted. 'Of course that *is* one way, but it isn't the way I said; and – someway, I don't seem to quite like the sound of it. It isn't exactly as if he said he was glad they *were* sick, but – You do play the game so funny, sometimes, Nancy,' she sighed, as she went into the house.

Pollyanna found her aunt in the sitting-room.

'Who was that man – the one who drove into the yard, Pollyanna?' questioned the lady a little sharply.

'Why, Aunt Polly, that was Dr Chilton! Don't you know him?'

'Dr Chilton! What was he doing – here?'

'He drove me home. Oh, and I gave the jelly to Mr Pendleton, and –'

Miss Polly lifted her head quickly.

'Pollyanna, he did not think I sent it?'

'Oh, no, Aunt Polly. I told him you didn't.'

Miss Polly grew a sudden vivid pink.

'You *told* him I didn't!'

Pollyanna opened wide her eyes at the remonstrative dismay in her aunt's voice.

'Why, Aunt Polly, you *said* to!'

Aunt Polly sighed.

'I *said*, Pollyanna, that I did not send it, and for you to be very sure that he did not think I *did*! – which is a very different matter from *telling* him outright that I did not send it.' And she turned vexedly away.

'Dear me! Well, I don't see where the difference is,' sighed Polly-anna, as she went to hang her hat on the one particular hook in the house upon which Aunt Polly had said that it must be hung.

CHAPTER 16

A Red Rose and a Lace Shawl

It was on a rainy day about a week after Pollyanna's visit to Mr John Pendleton, that Miss Polly was driven by Timothy to an early afternoon committee meeting of the Ladies' Aid Society. When she returned at three o'clock her cheeks were a bright, pretty pink, and her hair, blown by the damp wind, had fluffed into kinks and curls wherever the loosened pins had given leave.

Pollyanna had never before seen her aunt look like this.

'Oh – oh – oh! Why, Aunt Polly, you've got 'em, too,' she cried rapturously, dancing round and round her aunt, as that lady entered the sitting-room.

'Got what, you impossible child?'

Pollyanna was still revolving round and round her aunt.

'And I never knew you had 'em! *Can* folks have 'em when you don't know they've got 'em? Do you suppose I could? – 'fore I get to heaven, I mean,' she cried, pulling out with eager fingers the straight locks above her ears. 'But then, they wouldn't be black, if they did come. You can't hide the black part.'

'Pollyanna, what does all this mean?' demanded Aunt Polly, hurriedly removing her hat, and trying to smooth back her disordered hair.

'No, no – please, Aunt Polly!' Pollyanna's jubilant voice turned to one of distressed appeal. 'Don't smooth 'em out! It's those that I'm talking about – those darling little black curls. Oh, Aunt Polly, they're so pretty!'

'Nonsense! What do you mean, Pollyanna, by going to the Ladies' Aid the other day in that absurd fashion about that beggar boy?'

'But it isn't nonsense,' urged Pollyanna, answering only the first of her aunt's remarks. 'You don't know how pretty you look with your hair like that! Oh, Aunt Polly, please, mayn't I do your hair like

I did Mrs Snow's, and put in a flower? I'd so love to see you that way! Why, you'd be ever so much prettier than she was!'

'Pollyanna!' (Miss Polly spoke very sharply – all the more sharply because Pollyanna's words had given her an odd throb of joy: when before had anybody cared how she, or her hair, looked? When before had anybody 'loved' to see her 'pretty'?) 'Pollyanna, you did not answer my question. Why did you go to the Ladies' Aid in that absurd fashion?'

'Yes'm, I know; but, please, I didn't know it *was* absurd until I went and found out they'd rather see their report grow than Jimmy. So then I wrote to *my* Ladies' Aiders – 'cause Jimmy *is* far away from them, you know; and I thought maybe he could be their little India boy same as – Aunt Polly, *was* I your little India girl? And, Aunt Polly, you *will* let me do your hair, won't you?'

Aunt Polly put her hand to her throat – the old, helpless feeling was upon her, she knew.

'But, Pollyanna, when the ladies told me this afternoon how you came to them, I was so ashamed! I –

Pollyanna began to dance up and down lightly on her toes.

'You didn't! – you didn't say I *couldn't* do your hair,' she crowed triumphantly; 'and so I'm sure it means just the other way round, sort of – like it did the other day about Mr Pendleton's jelly that you didn't send, but didn't want me to say you didn't send, you know. Now wait just where you are. I'll get a comb.'

'But Pollyanna, Pollyanna,' remonstrated Aunt Polly, following the little girl from the room and panting upstairs after her.

'Oh, did you come up here?' Pollyanna greeted her at the door of Miss Polly's own room. 'That'll be nicer yet! I've got the comb. Now sit down, please, right here. Oh, I'm so glad you let me do it!'

'But, Pollyanna, I –!'

Miss Polly did not finish her sentence. To her helpless amazement she found herself in the low chair before the dressing-table, with her hair already tumbling about her ears under ten eager, but very gentle fingers.

'Oh, my! what pretty hair you've got,' prattled Pollyanna; 'and there's so much more of it than Mrs Snow has, too! But, of course, you need more, anyhow, because you're well and can go to places where folks can see it. My! I reckon folk'll be glad when they do see it – and surprised, too, 'cause you've hid it so long. Why, Aunt Polly, I'll make you so pretty everybody'll just love to look at you!'

'Pollyanna!' gasped a stifled but shocked voice from a veil of hair. 'I – I'm sure I don't know why I'm letting you do this silly thing.'

'Why, Aunt Polly, I should think you'd be glad to have folks like to look at you! Don't you like to look at pretty things? I'm ever so much happier when I look at pretty folks, 'cause when I look at the other kind I'm so sorry for them.'

'But – but – '

'And I just love to do folks' hair,' purred Pollyanna contentedly. 'I did quite a lot of the Ladies' Aiders' – but there wasn't any of them so nice as yours. Mrs White's was pretty nice, though, and she looked just lovely one day when I dressed her up in – Oh, Aunt Polly, I've just happened to think of something! But it's a secret, and I shan't tell. Now your hair is almost done, and pretty quick I'm going to leave you just a minute; and you must promise – promise – *promise* not to stir, nor peek, even, till I come back. Now remember!' she finished, as she ran from the room.

Aloud Miss Polly said nothing. To herself she said that of course she should at once undo the absurd work of her niece's fingers, and put her hair up properly again. As for 'peeking' – just as if she cared how –

At that moment – unaccountably – Miss Polly caught a glimpse of herself in the mirror of the dressing-table. And what she saw sent such a flush of rosy colour to her cheeks that – she only flushed the more at the sight.

She saw a face – not young, it is true – but just now alight with excitement and surprise. The cheeks were a pretty pink. The eyes sparkled. The hair, dark, and still damp from the outdoor air, lay in loose waves about the forehead and curved back over the ears in wonderfully becoming lines, with softening little curls here and there.

So amazed and so absorbed was Miss Polly with what she saw in the glass that she quite forgot her determination to do over her hair, until she heard Pollyanna enter the room again. Before she could move, then, she felt a folded something slipped across her eyes and tied at the back.

'Pollyanna, Pollyanna! What are you doing?' she cried.

Pollyanna chuckled.

'That's just what I don't want you to know, Aunt Polly, and I was afraid you *would* peek, so I tied on the handkerchief. Now sit still. It won't take but just a minute, then I'll let you see.'

'But, Pollyanna,' began Miss Polly, struggling blindly to her feet, 'you must take this off! You – child, child! what *are* you doing?' she gasped, as she felt a soft something slipped about her shoulders.

Pollyanna only chuckled the more gleefully. With trembling fingers she was draping about her aunt's shoulders the fleecy folds of a beautiful lace shawl, yellowed from long years of packing away, and fragrant with lavender. Pollyanna had found the shawl the week before when Nancy had been regulating the attic; and it had occurred to her today that there was no reason why her aunt, as well as Mrs White of her Western home, should not be 'dressed up'.

Her task completed, Pollyanna surveyed her work with eyes that approved, but that saw yet one touch wanting. Promptly, therefore, she pulled her aunt towards the sun-parlour where she could see a belated red rose blooming on the trellis within reach of her hand.

'Pollyanna, what are you doing? Where are you taking me to?' recoiled Aunt Polly, vainly trying to hold herself back. 'Pollyanna, I shall not.'

'It's just to the sun-parlour – only a minute! I'll have you ready now quicker'n no time,' panted Pollyanna, reaching for the rose and thrusting it into the soft hair above Miss Polly's left ear. 'There!' she exulted, untying the knot of the handkerchief and flinging the bit of linen far from her. 'Oh, Aunt Polly, now I reckon you'll be glad I dressed you up!'

For one dazed moment Miss Polly looked at her bedecked self, and at her surroundings; then she gave a low cry and fled to her room. Pollyanna, following the direction of her aunt's last dismayed gaze, saw, through the open windows of the sun-parlour, the horse and gig turning into the driveway. She recognised at once the man who held the reins.

Delightedly she leaned forward.

'Dr Chilton, Dr Chilton! Did you want to see me? I'm up here.'

'Yes,' smiled the doctor, a little gravely. 'Will you come down, please?'

In the bedroom Pollyanna found a flushed-faced, angry-eyed woman plucking at the pins that held a lace shawl in place.

'Pollyanna, how could you?' moaned the woman. 'To think of your rigging me up like this, and then letting me – *be seen*!'

Pollyanna stopped in dismay.

'But you looked lovely – perfectly lovely, Aunt Polly; and – '

'Lovely!' scorned the woman, flinging the shawl to one side and attacking her hair with shaking fingers.

'Oh, Aunt Polly, please, please let the hair – stay!'

'Stay? Like this? As if I would!' And Miss Polly pulled the locks so tightly back that the last curl lay stretched dead at the ends of her fingers.

'Oh, dear! And you did look so pretty,' almost sobbed Pollyanna, as she stumbled through the door.

Downstairs Pollyanna found the doctor waiting in his gig.

'I've prescribed you for a patient, and he's sent me to get the prescription filled,' announced the doctor. 'Will you go?'

'You mean – an errand – to the drug-store?' asked Pollyanna, a little uncertainly. 'I used to go some – for the Ladies' Aiders.'

The doctor shook his head with a smile.

'Not exactly. It's Mr John Pendleton. He would like to see you today, if you'll be so good as to come. It's stopped raining, so I drove down after you. Will you come? I'll call for you and bring you back before six o'clock.'

'I'd love to!' exclaimed Pollyanna. 'Let me ask Aunt Polly.'

In a few moments she returned, hat in hand, but with rather a sober face.

'Didn't your aunt want you to go?' asked the doctor, a little diffidently, as they drove away.

'Y–yes,' sighed Pollyanna. 'She – she wanted me to go *too* much, I'm afraid.'

'Wanted you to go *too much*!'

Pollyanna sighed again.

'Yes. I reckon she meant she didn't want me there. You see, she said: "Yes, yes, run along, run along – do! I wish you'd gone before."'

The doctor smiled – but with his lips only. His eyes were very grave. For some time he said nothing; then, a little hesitatingly, he asked: 'Wasn't it – your aunt I saw with you a few minutes ago – in the window of the sun-parlour?'

Pollyanna drew a long breath.

'Yes; that's what's the whole trouble, I suppose. You see I'd dressed her up in a perfectly lovely lace shawl I found upstairs, and I'd fixed her hair and put in a rose, and she looked so pretty. Didn't *you* think she looked just lovely?'

For a moment the doctor did not answer. When he did speak his voice was so low Pollyanna could but just hear the words.

'Yes, Pollyanna, I – I thought she did look – just lovely.'

'Did you? I'm so glad! I'll tell her,' nodded the little girl contentedly.

To her surprise the doctor gave a sudden exclamation.

'Never! Pollyanna, I – I'm afraid I shall have to ask you not to tell her – that.'

'Why, Dr Chilton! Why not? I should think you'd be glad –'

'But she might not be,' cut in the doctor.

Pollyanna considered this for a moment.

'That's so – maybe she wouldn't,' she sighed. 'I remember now; 'twas 'cause she saw you that she ran. And she – she spoke afterwards about her being seen in that rig.'

'I thought as much,' declared the doctor, under his breath.

'Still, I don't see why,' maintained Pollyanna, '– when she looked so pretty!'

The doctor said nothing. He did not speak again, indeed, until they were almost at the great stone house in which John Pendleton lay with a broken leg.

CHAPTER 17

'Just Like a Book'

John Pendleton greeted Pollyanna today with a smile.

'Well, Miss Pollyanna, I'm thinking you must be a very forgiving little person, else you wouldn't have come to see me again today.'

'Why, Mr Pendleton, I was real glad to come, and I'm sure I don't see why I shouldn't be, either.'

'Oh, well, you know, I was pretty cross with you, I'm afraid, both the other day when you so kindly brought me the jelly, and that time when you found me with the broken leg at first. By the way, too, I don't think I've ever thanked you for that. Now I'm sure that even you would admit that you were very forgiving to come and see me, after such ungrateful treatment as that!'

Pollyanna stirred uneasily.

'But I was glad to find you – that is, I don't mean I was glad your leg was broken, of course,' she corrected hurriedly.

John Pendleton smiled.

'I understand. Your tongue does get away with you once in a while, doesn't it, Miss Pollyanna? I do thank you, however; and I consider you a very brave little girl to do what you did that day. I thank you for the jelly, too,' he added in a lighter voice.

'Did you like it?' asked Pollyanna with interest.

'Very much. I suppose – there isn't any more today that – that Aunt Polly *didn't* send, is there?' he asked, with an odd smile.

His visitor looked distressed.

'N–no, sir.' She hesitated, then went on with heightened colour. 'Please, Mr Pendleton, I didn't mean to be rude the other day when I said Aunt Polly did *not* send the jelly.'

There was no answer. John Pendleton was not smiling now. He was looking straight ahead of him with eyes that seemed to be gazing through and beyond the objects before them. After a time he drew a long sigh and turned to Pollyanna. When he spoke his voice carried the old nervous fretfulness.

'Well, well, this will never do at all! I didn't send for you to see me moping this time. Listen! Out in the library – the big room where the telephone is, you know – you will find a carved box on the lower shelf of the big case with glass doors in the corner not far from the fireplace. That is, it'll be there if that confounded woman hasn't "regulated" it to somewhere else! You may bring it to me. It is heavy, but not too heavy for you to carry, I think.'

'Oh, I'm awfully strong,' declared Pollyanna, cheerfully, as she sprang to her feet. In a minute she had returned with the box.

It was a wonderful half-hour that Pollyanna spent then. The box was full of treasures – curios that John Pendleton had picked up in years of travel – and concerning each there was some entertaining story, whether it were a set of exquisitely carved chessmen from China, or a little jade idol from India.

It was after she had heard the story about the idol that Pollyanna murmured wistfully: 'Well, I suppose it *would* be better to take a little boy in India to bring up – one that didn't know any more than to think that God was in that doll-thing – than it would be to take Jimmy Bean, a little boy who knows God is up in the sky. Still, I can't help wishing they had wanted Jimmy Bean, too, besides the India boys.'

John Pendleton did not seem to hear. Again his eyes were staring straight before him, looking at nothing. But soon he had roused himself, and had picked up another curio to talk about.

The visit, certainly, was a delightful one, but before it was over Pollyanna was realising that they were talking about something besides the wonderful things in the beautiful carved box. They were talking of herself, of Nancy, of Aunt Polly, and of her daily life. They were talking, too, even of the life and home long ago in the far Western town.

Not until it was nearly time for her to go, did the man say, in a voice Pollyanna had never before heard from stern John Pendleton: 'Little girl, I want you to come to see me often. Will you? I'm lonesome, and I need you. There's another reason – and I'm going to tell you that, too. I thought, at first, after I found out who you were, the other day, that I didn't want you to come any more. You reminded me of – of something I have tried for long years to forget. So I said to myself that I never wanted to see you again; and every day, when the doctor asked if I wouldn't let him bring you to me, I said no.

'But after a time I found I was wanting to see you so much that – that the fact that I *wasn't* seeing you was making me remember all the more vividly the thing I was so wanting to forget. So now I want you to come. Will you – little girl?'

'Why, yes, Mr Pendleton,' breathed Pollyanna, her eyes luminous with sympathy for the sad-faced man lying back on the pillow before her. 'I'd love to come!'

'Thank you,' said John Pendleton gently.

After supper that evening Pollyanna, sitting on the back porch, told Nancy all about Mr John Pendleton's wonderful carved box, and the still more wonderful things it contained.

'And ter think,' sighed Nancy, 'that he *showed* ye all them things, and told ye about 'em like that – him that's so cross he never talks ter no one – no one!'

'Oh, but he isn't cross, Nancy, only outside,' demurred Pollyanna, with quick loyalty. 'I don't see why everybody thinks he's so bad, either. They wouldn't, if they knew him. But even Aunt Polly doesn't like him very well. She wouldn't send the jelly to him, you know, and she was so afraid he'd think she did send it!'

'Probably she didn't call him no duty,' shrugged Nancy. 'But what beats me is how he happened ter take ter you so, Miss Pollyanna – meanin' no offence ter you, of course – but he ain't the sort o' man that gen'rally takes ter kids; he ain't, he ain't.'

Pollyanna smiled happily.

'But he did, Nancy,' she nodded, 'only I reckon even he didn't want to – *all* the time. Why, only today he owned up that one time he just felt he never wanted to see me again, because I reminded him of something he wanted to forget. But afterwards – '

'What's that?' interrupted Nancy excitedly. 'He said you reminded him of something he wanted to forget?'

'Yes. But afterwards – '

'What was it?' Nancy was eagerly insistent.

'He didn't tell me. He just said it was something.'

'*The mystery!*' breathed Nancy, in an awestruck voice. 'That's why he took to you in the first place. Oh, Miss Pollyanna! Why, that's just like a book – I've read lots of 'em: *Lady Maud's Secret* and *The Lost Heir* and *Hidden for Years* – all of 'em had mysteries and things just like this. My stars and stockings! Just think of havin' a book lived right under yer nose like this – an' me not knowin' it all this time! Now tell me everythin' – everythin' he said, Miss Pollyanna, there's a dear! No wonder he took ter you; no wonder – no wonder!'

'But he didn't,' cried Pollyanna, 'not till *I* talked to *him*, first. And he didn't even know who I was till I took the calf's-foot jelly, and had to make him understand that Aunt Polly didn't send it, and – '

Nancy sprang to her feet and clasped her hands together suddenly. 'Oh, Miss Pollyanna, I know, I know – I *know* I know!' she exulted rapturously. The next minute she was down at Pollyanna's side again. 'Tell me – now think, and answer straight and true,' she urged excitedly. 'It was after he found out you was Miss Polly's niece that he said he didn't ever want ter see ye again, wa'n't it?'

'Oh, yes. I told him that the last time I saw him, and he told me this today.'

'I thought as much,' triumphed Nancy. 'And Miss Polly wouldn't send the jelly herself, would she?'

'No.'

'And you told him she didn't send it?'

'Why, yes; I – '

'And he began ter act queer and cry out sudden after he found out you was her niece. He did that, didn't he?'

'Why, y–yes; he did act a little queer – over that jelly,' admitted Pollyanna, with a thoughtful frown.

Nancy drew a long sigh.

'Then I've got it, sure! Now listen. *Mr John Pendleton was Miss Polly Harrington's lover!*' she announced impressively, but with a furtive glance over her shoulder.

'Why, Nancy, he couldn't be! She doesn't like him,' objected Pollyanna.

Nancy gave her a scornful glance.

'Of course she don't! *That's* the quarrel!'

Pollyanna still looked incredulous as, with another long breath, Nancy happily settled herself to tell the story.

'It's like this. Just before you come Mr Tom told me Miss Polly had had a lover once. I didn't believe it. I couldn't – her and a lover! But Mr Tom said she had, and that he was livin' now right in this town. And *now* I know, of course. It's John Pendleton. Hain't he got a mystery in his life? Don't he shut himself up in that grand house alone, and never speak ter no one? Didn't he act queer when he found out you was Miss Polly's niece? And now hain't he owned up that you remind him of somethin' he wants ter forget? Just as if *anybody* couldn't see 'twas Miss Polly! – an' her sayin' she wouldn't send him no jelly, too. Why, Miss Pollyanna, it's as plain as the nose on yer face; it is, it is!'

'Oh–h!' breathed Pollyanna, in wide-eyed amazement. 'But, Nancy, I should think if they loved each other they'd make up sometime. Both of 'em all alone so, all these years. I should think they'd be glad to make up!'

Nancy sniffed disdainfully.

'I guess maybe you don't know much about lovers, Miss Pollyanna. You ain't big enough yet, anyhow. But if there is a set o' folks in the world that wouldn't have no use for that 'ere "glad game" o' your'n, it'd be a pair o' quarrellin' lovers; and that's what they be. Ain't he cross as sticks, most gen'rally? – and ain't she – '

Nancy stopped abruptly, remembering just in time to whom, and about whom, she was speaking. Suddenly, however, she chuckled.

'I ain't sayin', though, Miss Pollyanna, but what it would be a pretty slick piece of business if you could *get* 'em ter playin' it – so they *would* be glad ter make up. But, my land! wouldn't folks stare some – Miss Polly and him! I guess, though, there ain't much chance, much chance!'

Pollyanna said nothing; but when she went into the house a little later her face was very thoughtful.

CHAPTER 18

Prisms

As the warm August days passed Pollyanna went very frequently to the great house on Pendleton Hill. She did not feel, however, that her visits were really a success. Not but that the man seemed to want her there – he sent for her, indeed, frequently; but that when she was there he seemed scarcely any the happier for her presence – at least, so Pollyanna thought.

He talked to her, it was true, and he showed her many strange and beautiful things – books, pictures and curios. But he still fretted audibly over his own helplessness, and he chafed visibly under the rules and "regulatings" of the unwelcome members of his household. He did, indeed, seem to like to hear Pollyanna talk, however, and Pollyanna talked. Pollyanna liked to talk – but she was never sure that she would not look up and find him lying back on his pillow with that white, hurt look that always pained her; and she was never sure which – if any – of her words had brought it there. As for telling him the 'glad game', and trying to get him to play it – Pollyanna had never seen the time yet when she thought he would care to hear about it. She had twice tried to tell him; but neither time had she got beyond the beginning of what her father had said – John Pendleton had on each occasion turned the conversation abruptly to another subject.

Pollyanna never doubted now that John Pendleton was her Aunt Polly's one-time lover; and with all the strength of her loving, loyal heart, she wished she could in some way bring happiness into their – to her mind – miserably lonely lives.

Just how she was to do this, however, she could not see. She talked to Mr Pendleton about her aunt; and he listened, sometimes politely, sometimes irritably, frequently with a quizzical smile on his usually stern lips. She talked to her aunt about Mr Pendleton – or rather, she tried to talk to her about him. As a general thing, however, Miss Polly would not listen long. She always found something else to talk about. She frequently did that, however, when Pollyanna was talking of others – of Dr Chilton, for instance. Pollyanna laid this, though, to the fact that it had been Dr Chilton who had seen her in the sun-parlour with the rose in her hair and the lace shawl draped about her shoulders. Aunt Polly, indeed, seemed particularly bitter against Dr Chilton, as Pollyanna found out one day when a hard cold shut her up in the house.

'If you are not better by night I shall send for the doctor,' Aunt Polly said.

'Shall you? Then I'm going to be worse,' gurgled Pollyanna. 'I'd love to have Dr Chilton come to see me!'

She wondered, then, at the look that came to her aunt's face.

'It will not be Dr Chilton, Pollyanna,' Miss Polly said sternly. 'Dr Chilton is not our family physician. I shall send for Dr Warren – if you are worse.'

Pollyanna did not grow worse, however, and Dr Warren was not summoned.

'And I'm so glad, too,' Pollyanna said to her aunt that evening. 'Of course I like Dr Warren, and all that; but I like Dr Chilton better, and I'm afraid he'd feel hurt if I didn't have him. You see, he wasn't really to blame, after all, that he happened to see you when I'd dressed you up so pretty that day, Aunt Polly,' she finished wistfully.

'That will do, Pollyanna. I really do not wish to discuss Dr Chilton – or his feelings,' reproved Miss Polly decisively.

Pollyanna looked at her for a moment with mournfully interested eyes; then she sighed: 'I just love to see you when your cheeks are pink like that, Aunt Polly; but I would so like to fix your hair. If – Why, Aunt Polly!' But her aunt was already out of sight down the hall.

It was towards the end of August that Pollyanna, making an early morning call on John Pendleton, found the flaming band of blue and gold and green edged with red and violet lying across his pillow. She stopped short in awed delight.

'Why, Mr Pendleton, it's a baby rainbow – a real rainbow come in to pay you a visit!' she exclaimed, clapping her hands together softly. 'Oh – oh – oh, how pretty it is! But how *did* it get in?' she cried.

The man laughed a little grimly; John Pendleton was particularly out of sorts with the world this morning.

'Well, I suppose it "got in" through the bevelled edge of that glass thermometer in the window,' he said wearily. 'The sun shouldn't strike it at all – but it does in the morning.'

'Oh, but it's so pretty, Mr Pendleton! And does just the sun do that? My! if it was mine I'd have it hang in the sun all day long!'

'Lots of good you'd get out of the thermometer, then,' laughed the man. 'How do you suppose you could tell how hot it was, or how cold it was, if the thermometer hung in the sun all day?'

'I shouldn't care,' breathed Pollyanna, her fascinated eyes on the brilliant band of colours across the pillow. 'Just as if anybody'd care – when they were living all the time in a rainbow!'

The man laughed. He was watching Pollyanna's rapt face a little curiously. Suddenly a new thought came to him. He touched the bell at his side.

'Nora,' he said, when the elderly maid appeared at the door, 'bring me one of the big brass candlesticks from the mantel in the front drawing-room.'

'Yes, sir,' murmured the woman, looking slightly dazed. In a minute she had returned. A musical tinkling entered the room with her as she advanced wonderingly towards the bed. It came from the prism pendants encircling the old-fashioned candelabrum in her hand.

'Thank you. You may set it here on the stand,' directed the man. 'Now get a string and fasten it to the sash-curtain fixtures of that window there. Take down the sash-curtain, and let the string reach straight across the window from side to side. That will be all. Thank you,' he said, when she had carried out his directions.

As she left the room he turned smiling eyes towards the wondering Pollyanna.

'Bring me the candlestick now, please, Pollyanna.'

With both hands she brought it; and in a moment he was slipping off the pendants, one by one, until they lay, a round dozen of them, side by side, on the bed.

'Now, my dear, suppose you take them and hook them to that little string Nora fixed across the window. If you really want to *live* in a rainbow – I don't see but we'll have to have a rainbow for you to live in!'

Pollyanna had not hung up three of the pendants in the sunlit window before she saw a little of what was going to happen. She was so excited that she could scarcely control her shaking fingers enough to hang up the rest. But at last her task was finished, and she stepped back with a low cry of delight.

It had become a fairyland – that sumptuous, but dreary bedroom. Everywhere were bits of dancing red and green, violet and orange, gold and blue. The wall, the floor, and the furniture, even the bed itself, were aflame with shimmering bits of colour.

'Oh, oh, oh, how lovely!' breathed Pollyanna; then she laughed suddenly. 'I just reckon the sun himself is trying to play the game now, don't you?' she cried, forgetting for the moment that Mr Pendleton could not know what she was talking about. 'Oh, how I wish I had a lot of those things! How I would like to give them to Aunt Polly and Mrs Snow and – lots of folks. I reckon *then* they'd be glad all right! Why, I think even Aunt Polly'd get so glad she couldn't help banging doors – if she lived in a rainbow like that. Don't you?'

Mr Pendleton laughed.

'Well, from my remembrance of your aunt, Miss Pollyanna, I must say I think it would take something more than a few prisms in the sunlight to – to make her bang many doors – for gladness. But come, now really, what do you mean?'

Pollyanna stared slightly; then she drew a long breath.

'Oh, I forgot. You don't know about the game. I remember now.'

'Suppose you tell me, then.'

And this time Pollyanna told him. She told him the whole thing from the very first – from the crutches that should have been a doll. As she talked, she did not look at his face. Her rapt eyes were still on the dancing flecks of colour from the prism pendants swaying in the sunlit window.

'And that's all,' she sighed, when she had finished. 'And now you know why I said the sun was trying to play it – that game.'

For a moment there was silence. Then a low voice from the bed said unsteadily: 'Perhaps; but I'm thinking that the very finest prism of them all is yourself, Pollyanna.'

'Oh, but I don't show beautiful red and green and purple when the sun shines through me, Mr Pendleton!'

'Don't you?' smiled the man. And Pollyanna, looking into his face, wondered why there were tears in his eyes.

'No,' she said. Then, after a minute she added mournfully: 'I'm afraid, Mr Pendleton, the sun doesn't make anything but freckles – out of me. Aunt Polly says it *does* make them!'

The man laughed a little; and again Pollyanna looked at him; the laugh had sounded almost like a sob.

CHAPTER 19

Which is Somewhat Surprising

Pollyanna entered school in September. Preliminary examinations showed that she was well advanced for a girl of her years, and she was soon a happy member of a class of girls and boys her own age.

School, in some ways, was a surprise to Pollyanna; and Pollyanna, certainly, in many ways, was very much of a surprise to school. They were soon on the best of terms, however, and to her aunt Pollyanna confessed that going to school *was* living, after all – though she had had her doubts before.

In spite of her delight in her new work, Pollyanna did not forget her old friends. True, she could not give them quite so much time now, of course; but she gave them what time she could. Perhaps John Pendleton, of them all, however, was the most dissatisfied.

One Saturday afternoon he spoke to her about it.

'See here, Pollyanna, how would you like to come and live with me?' he asked, a little impatiently. 'I don't see anything of you, nowadays.'

Pollyanna laughed – Mr Pendleton was such a funny man!

'I thought you didn't like to have folks around,' she said.

He made a wry face.

'Oh, but that was before you taught me to play that wonderful game of yours. *Now* I'm glad to be waited on, hand and foot! Never mind, I'll be on my own two feet yet, one of these days; then I'll see who steps around,' he finished, picking up one of the crutches at his side and shaking it playfully at the little girl. They were sitting in the great library today.

'Oh, but you aren't really glad at all for things; you just say you are,' pouted Pollyanna, her eyes on the dog, dozing before the fire. 'You know you don't play the game right *ever*, Mr Pendleton – you know you don't!'

The man's face grew suddenly very grave. 'That's why I want you, little girl – to help me play it. Will you come?'

Pollyanna turned in surprise.

'Mr Pendleton, you don't really mean – that?'

'But I do. I want you. Will you come?'

Pollyanna looked distressed.

'Why, Mr Pendleton, I can't – you know I can't. Why, I'm – Aunt Polly's!'

A quick something crossed the man's face that Pollyanna could not quite understand. His head came up almost fiercely.

'You're no more hers than – Perhaps she would let you come to me,' he finished more gently. 'Would you come – if she did?'

Pollyanna frowned in deep thought.

'But Aunt Polly has been so – good to me,' she began slowly; 'and she took me when I didn't have anybody left but the Ladies' Aid, and – '

Again that spasm of something crossed the man's face; but this time, when he spoke, his voice was low and very sad.

'Pollyanna, long years ago I loved somebody very much. I hoped to bring her, someday, to this house. I pictured how happy we'd be together in our home all the long years to come.'

'Yes,' pitied Pollyanna, her eyes shining with sympathy.

'But – well, I didn't bring her here. Never mind why. I just didn't – that's all. And ever since then this great grey pile of stone has been a house – never a home. It takes a woman's hand and heart, or a child's presence, to make a home, Pollyanna; and I have not had either. Now will you come, my dear?'

Pollyanna sprang to her feet. Her face was fairly illumined.

'Mr Pendleton, you – you mean that you wish you – you had had that woman's hand and heart all this time?'

'Why, y–yes, Pollyanna.'

'Oh, I'm so glad! Then it's all right,' sighed the little girl. 'Now you can take us both, and everything will be lovely.'

'Take – you – both?' repeated the man dazedly.

A faint doubt crossed Pollyanna's countenance.

'Well, of course, Aunt Polly isn't won over, yet; but I'm sure she will be if you tell it to her just as you did to me, and then we'd both come, of course.'

A look of actual terror leaped to the man's eyes.

'Aunt Polly come – *here*!'

Pollyanna's eyes widened a little.

'Would you rather go *there*?' she asked. 'Of course the house isn't quite so pretty, but it's nearer – '

'Pollyanna, what *are* you talking about?' asked the man, very gently now.

'Why, about where we're going to live, of course,' rejoined Pollyanna, in obvious surprise. 'I *thought* you meant here, at first. You said it was here that you had wanted Aunt Polly's hand and heart all these years to make a home, and – '

An inarticulate cry came from the man's throat. He raised his hand and began to speak; but the next moment he dropped his hand nervelessly at his side.

'The doctor, sir,' said the maid in the doorway.

Pollyanna rose at once.

John Pendleton turned to her feverishly. 'Pollyanna, for heaven's sake, say nothing of what I asked you – yet,' he begged, in a low voice.

Pollyanna dimpled into a sunny smile.

'Of course not! Just as if I didn't know you'd rather tell her yourself!' she called back merrily over her shoulder.

John Pendleton fell limply back in his chair.

'Why, what's up?' demanded the doctor, a minute later, his fingers on his patient's galloping pulse.

A whimsical smile trembled on John Pendleton's lips.

'Overdose of your – tonic, I guess,' he laughed, as he noted the doctor's eyes following Pollyanna's little figure down the driveway.

CHAPTER 20

Which is More Surprising

Sunday mornings Pollyanna usually attended church and Sunday school. Sunday afternoons she frequently went for a walk with Nancy. She had planned one for the day after her Saturday-afternoon visit to Mr John Pendleton; but on the way home from Sunday school Dr Chilton overtook her in his gig, and brought his horse to a stop.

'Suppose you let me drive you home, Pollyanna,' he suggested. 'I want to speak to you a minute. I was just driving out to your place to tell you,' he went on, as Pollyanna settled herself at his side. 'Mr Pendleton sent a special request for you to go to see him this afternoon, *sure*. He says it's very important.'

Pollyanna nodded happily.

'Yes, it is, I know. I'll go.'

The doctor eyed her with some surprise.

'I'm not sure I shall let you, after all,' he declared, his eyes twinkling. 'You seemed more upsetting than soothing yesterday, young lady.'

Pollyanna laughed.

'Oh, it wasn't me, truly – not really, you know; not so much as it was Aunt Polly.'

The doctor turned with a quick start.

'Your – aunt!' he ejaculated.

Pollyanna gave a happy little bounce in her seat.

'Yes. And it's so exciting and lovely, just like a story, you know. I – I'm going to tell you,' she burst out, with sudden decision. 'He said not to mention it; but he wouldn't mind your knowing, of course. He meant not to mention it to *her*.'

'*Her?*'

'Yes; Aunt Polly. And, of course he *would* want to tell her himself instead of having me do it – with lovers it should be so! '

'Lovers!' As the doctor said the word, the horse started violently, as if the hand that held the reins had given them a sharp jerk.

'Yes,' nodded Pollyanna happily. 'That's the story part, you see. I didn't know it till Nancy told me. She said Aunt Polly had a lover years ago, and they quarrelled. She didn't know who it was at first. But we've found out now. It's Mr Pendleton, you know.'

The doctor relaxed suddenly. The hand holding the reins fell limply to his lap.

'Oh! No; I – didn't know,' he said quietly.

Pollyanna hurried on – they were nearing the Harrington homestead.

'Yes; and I'm so glad now. It's come out lovely. Mr Pendleton asked me to come and live with him, but of course I wouldn't leave Aunt Polly like that after she'd been so good to me. Then he told me all about the woman's hand and heart that he used to want, and I found out that he wanted it now; and I was so glad! For of course if he *wants* to make up the quarrel, everything will be all right now, and Aunt Polly and I will both go to live there, or else he'll come to live with us. Of course Aunt Polly doesn't know yet, and we haven't got everything settled; so I suppose that is why he wanted to see me this afternoon, sure.'

The doctor sat suddenly erect. There was an odd smile on his lips.

'Yes; I can well imagine that Mr John Pendleton does – want to see you, Pollyanna,' he nodded, as he pulled his horse to a stop before the door.

'There's Aunt Polly now in the window,' cried Pollyanna; then, a second later: 'Why, no, she isn't – but I thought I saw her!'

'No; she isn't there – now,' said the doctor. His lips had suddenly lost their smile.

Pollyanna found a very nervous John Pendleton waiting for her that afternoon.

'Pollyanna,' he began at once. 'I've been trying all night to puzzle out what you meant by all that, yesterday – about my wanting your Aunt Polly's hand and heart here all those years. What did you mean?'

'Why, because you were lovers, you know – once; and I was so glad you still felt that way now.'

'Lovers! – your Aunt Polly and I?'

At the obvious surprise in the man's voice, Pollyanna opened wide her eyes.

'Why, Mr Pendleton, Nancy said you were!'

The man gave a short little laugh.

'Indeed! Well, I'm afraid I shall have to say that Nancy – didn't know.'

'Then you – weren't lovers?' Pollyanna's voice was tragic with dismay.

'Never!'

'And it *isn't* all coming out like a book?'

There was no answer. The man's eyes were moodily fixed out the window.

'Oh, dear! And it was all going so splendidly,' almost sobbed Pollyanna. 'I'd have been so glad to come – with Aunt Polly.'

'And you won't – now?' The man asked the question without turning his head.

'Of course not! I'm Aunt Polly's.'

The man turned now, almost fiercely.

'Before you were hers, Pollyanna, you were – your mother's. And – it was your mother's hand and heart that I wanted long years ago.'

'My mother's!'

'Yes. I had not meant to tell you, but perhaps it's better, after all, that I do – now.' John Pendleton's face had grown very white. He was speaking with evident difficulty. Pollyanna, her eyes wide and frightened, and her lips parted, was gazing at him fixedly. 'I loved your mother; but she – didn't love me. And after a time she went away with – your father. I did not know until then how much I did – care. The whole world suddenly seemed to turn black under my fingers, and – But never mind. For long years I have been a cross, crabbed, unlovable, unloved old man – though I'm not nearly sixty, yet, Pollyanna. Then, one day, like one of the prisms that you love so well, little girl, you danced into my life, and flecked my dreary old world with dashes of the purple and gold and scarlet of your own bright cheeriness. I found out, after a time, who you were, and – and I thought then I never wanted to see you again. I didn't want to be reminded of – your mother. But – you know how that came out. I just had to have you come. And now I want you always. Pollyanna, won't you come – *now?*'

'But, Mr Pendleton! There's Aunt Polly!' Pollyanna's eyes were blurred with tears.

The man made an impatient gesture.

'What about me? How do you suppose I'm going to be "glad" about anything – without you? Why, Pollyanna, it's only since you came that I've been even half glad to live! But if I had you for my own little girl, I'd be glad for – anything; and I'd try to make you glad too, my dear. You shouldn't have a wish ungratified. All my money, to the last cent, should go to make you happy.'

Pollyanna looked shocked.

'Why, Mr Pendleton, as if I'd let you spend it on me – all that money you've saved for the heathen!'

A dull red came to the man's face. He started to speak, but Pollyanna was still talking.

'Besides, anybody with such a lot of money as you have doesn't need me to make you glad about things. You're making other folks so glad giving them things that you just can't help being glad yourself! Why, look at those prisms you gave Mrs Snow and me, and the gold piece you gave Nancy on her birthday, and – '

'Yes, yes – never mind about all that,' interrupted the man. His face was very, very red now – and no wonder, perhaps; it was not for 'giving things' that John Pendleton had been best known in the past. 'That's all nonsense. 'Twasn't much, anyhow – but what there was,

was because of you. You gave those things; not I! Yes, you did,' he repeated, in answer to the shocked denial in her face. 'And that only goes to prove all the more how I need you, little girl,' he added, his voice softening into tender pleading once more. 'If ever, ever I am to play the "glad game", Pollyanna, you'll have to come and play it with me.'

The little girl's forehead puckered into a wistful frown.

'Aunt Polly has been so good to me,' she began; but the man interrupted her sharply. The old irritability had come back to his face. Impatience which would brook no opposition had been a part of John Pendleton's nature too long to yield very easily now to restraint.

'Of course she's been good to you! But she doesn't want you, I'll warrant, half so much as I do,' he contested.

'Why, Mr Pendleton, she's glad, I know, to have – '

'Glad!' interrupted the man, thoroughly losing his patience now. 'I'll wager Miss Polly doesn't know how to be glad – for anything! Oh, she does her duty, I know. She's a very *dutiful* woman. I've had experience of her "duty", before. I'll acknowledge we haven't been the best of friends for the last fifteen or twenty years. But I know her. Everyone knows her – and she isn't the "glad" kind, Pollyanna. She doesn't know how to be. As for your coming to me – you just ask her and see if she won't let you come. And, oh, little girl, little girl, I want you so!' he finished brokenly.

Pollyanna rose to her feet with a long sigh.

'All right. I'll ask her,' she said wistfully. 'Of course I don't mean that I wouldn't like to live here with you, Mr Pendleton, but – ' She did not complete her sentence. There was a moment's silence, then she added: 'Well, anyhow, I'm glad I didn't tell her yesterday – 'cause then I supposed *she* was wanted too.'

John Pendleton smiled grimly.

'Well, yes, Pollyanna; I guess it is just as well you didn't mention it – yesterday.'

'I didn't – only to the doctor; and of course he doesn't count.'

'The doctor!' cried John Pendleton, turning quickly. 'Not – Dr Chilton?'

'Yes; when he came to tell me you wanted to see me today, you know.'

'Well, of all the – ' muttered the man, falling back in his chair. Then he sat up with sudden interest. 'And what did Dr Chilton say?' he asked.

Pollyanna frowned thoughtfully.

'Why, I don't remember. Not much, I reckon. Oh, he did say he could well imagine you did want to see me.'

'Oh, did he, indeed!' answered John Pendleton. And Pollyanna wondered why he gave that sudden queer little laugh.

CHAPTER 21

A Question Answered

The sky was darkening fast with what appeared to be an approaching thunder shower when Pollyanna hurried down the hill from John Pendleton's house. Halfway home she met Nancy with an umbrella. By that time, however, the clouds had shifted their position and the shower was not so imminent.

'Guess it's goin' round ter the north,' announced Nancy, eyeing the sky critically. 'I thought 'twas, all the time, but Miss Polly wanted me ter come with this. She was *worried* about ye!'

'Was she?' murmured Pollyanna abstractedly, eyeing the clouds in her turn.

Nancy sniffed a little.

'You don't seem ter notice what I said,' she observed aggrievedly. 'I said yer aunt was *worried* about ye!'

'Oh,' sighed Pollyanna, remembering suddenly the question she was so soon to ask her aunt. 'I'm sorry. I didn't mean to scare her.'

'Well, I'm glad,' retorted Nancy unexpectedly. 'I am, I am.'

Pollyanna stared.

'*Glad* that Aunt Polly was scared about me! Why, Nancy, *that* isn't the way to play the game – to be glad for things like that!' she objected.

'There wa'n't no game in it,' retorted Nancy. 'Never thought of it. You don't seem ter sense what it means ter have Miss Polly *worried* about ye, child!'

'Why, it means worried – and worried is horrid – to feel,' maintained Pollyanna. 'What else can it mean?'

Nancy tossed her head.

'Well, I'll tell ye what it means. It means she's at last gettin' down somewheres near human – like folks; an' that she ain't jest doin' her duty by ye all the time.'

'Why, Nancy,' demurred the scandalised Pollyanna, 'Aunt Polly always does her duty. She – she's a very dutiful woman!' Unconsciously Pollyanna repeated John Pendleton's words of half an hour before.

Nancy chuckled. 'You're right she is – and she always was, I guess. But she's somethin' more, now, since you came.'

Pollyanna's face changed. Her brows drew into a troubled frown.

'There, that's what I was going to ask you, Nancy,' she sighed. 'Do you think Aunt Polly likes to have me here? Would she mind – if – if I wasn't here any more?'

Nancy threw a quick look into the little girl's absorbed face. She had expected to be asked this question long before, and she had dreaded it. She had wondered how she should answer it – how she could answer it honestly without cruelly hurting the questioner. But now, *now*, in the face of the new suspicions that had become convictions with the afternoon's umbrella-sending – Nancy only welcomed the question with open arms. She was sure that today, with a clean conscience, she could set the love-hungry little girl's heart at rest.

'Likes ter have ye here? Would she miss ye if ye wa'n't here?' cried Nancy indignantly. 'As if that wa'n't jest what I was tellin' ye of! Didn't she send me post-haste with an umbrella 'cause she see a little cloud in the sky? Didn't she make me tote yer things all downstairs, so you could have the pretty room you wanted? Why, Miss Polly-anna, when ye remember how at first she hated ter have – '

With a choking cough Nancy pulled herself up just in time.

'And it ain't jest things I can put my fingers on, neither,' rushed on Nancy breathlessly. 'It's little ways she has that shows how you've been softenin' her up an' mellerin' her down – the cat, and the dog, and the way she speaks ter me, and – oh, lots o' things. Why, Miss Pollyanna, there ain't no tellin' how she'd miss ye – if ye wa'n't here,' finished Nancy, speaking with an enthusiastic certainty that was meant to hide the perilous admission she had almost made before. Even then she was not quite prepared for the sudden joy that illumined Pollyanna's face.

'Oh, Nancy, I'm so glad – glad – glad! You don't know how glad I am that Aunt Polly – wants me!'

'As if I'd leave her now!' thought Pollyanna, as she climbed the stairs to her room a little later. 'I always knew I wanted to live with Aunt Polly – but I reckon maybe I didn't know quite how much I wanted Aunt Polly to want to live with *me*!'

The task of telling John Pendleton of her decision would not be an easy one, Pollyanna knew, and she dreaded it. She was very fond of John Pendleton, and she was very sorry for him – because he seemed to be so sorry for himself. She was sorry, too, for the long, lonely life that had made him so unhappy; and she was grieved that it had been because of her mother that he had spent those dreary years. She pictured the great grey house as it would be after its master was well again, with its silent rooms, its littered floors, its disordered desk; and her heart ached for his loneliness. She wished that somewhere, someone might be found who – And it was at this point that she sprang to her feet with a little cry of joy at the thought that had come to her.

As soon as she could, after that, she hurried up the hill to John Pendleton's house; and in due time she found herself in the great dim library, with John Pendleton himself sitting near her, his long, thin hands lying idle on the arms of his chair, and his faithful little dog at his feet.

'Well, Pollyanna, is it to be the "glad game" with me, all the rest of my life?' asked the man gently.

'Oh, yes,' cried Pollyanna. 'I've thought of the very gladdest kind of a thing for you to do, and – '

'With – *you*?' asked John Pendleton, his mouth growing a little stern at the corners.

'N–no; but – '

'Pollyanna, you aren't going to say no!' interrupted a voice deep with emotion.

'I – I've got to, Mr Pendleton; truly I have. Aunt Polly – '

'Did she *refuse* – to let you – come?'

'I – I didn't ask her,' stammered the little girl miserably.

'Pollyanna!'

Pollyanna turned away her eyes. She could not meet the hurt, grieved gaze of her friend.

'So you didn't even ask her!'

'I couldn't, sir – truly,' faltered Pollyanna. 'You see, I found out – without asking. Aunt Polly *wants* me with her, and – and I want to stay, too,' she confessed bravely. 'You don't know how good she's been to me; and – and I think, really, sometimes she's beginning to be glad about things – lots of things. And you know she never used to be. You said it yourself. Oh, Mr Pendleton, I *couldn't* leave Aunt Polly – now!'

There was a long pause. Only the snapping of the wood fire in the grate broke the silence. At last, however, the man spoke. 'No, Pollyanna; I see. You couldn't leave her – now,' he said. 'I won't ask you – again.' The last word was so low it was almost inaudible; but Pollyanna heard.

'Oh, but you don't know about the rest of it,' she reminded him eagerly. 'There's the very gladdest thing you *can* do – truly there is!'

'Not for me, Pollyanna.'

'Yes, sir, for you. You *said* it. You said only a – a woman's hand and heart or a child's presence could make a home. And I can get it for you – a child's presence – not me, you know, but another one.'

'As if I would have any but you!' resented an indignant voice.

'But you will – when you know; you're so kind and good! Why, think of the prisms and the gold pieces, and all that money you save for the heathen, and – '

'Pollyanna!' interrupted the man savagely. 'Once for all let us end that nonsense! I've tried to tell you half a dozen times before. There *is* no money for the heathen. I never sent a penny to them in my life. There!'

He lifted his chin and braced himself to meet what he expected – the grieved disappointment of Pollyanna's eyes. To his amazement, however, there was neither grief nor disappointment in Pollyanna's eyes. There was only surprised joy.

'Oh, oh!' she cried, clapping her hands. 'I'm so glad! That is,' she corrected, colouring distressfully, 'I don't mean that I'm not sorry for the heathen, only just now I can't help being glad that you don't want the little India boys, because all the rest have wanted them. And so I'm glad you'd rather have Jimmy Bean. Now I know you'll take him!'

'Take – *who*?'

'Jimmy Bean. He's the "child's presence", you know; and he'll be so glad to be it. I had to tell him last week that even my Ladies' Aid out West wouldn't take him, and he was so disappointed. But now – when he hears of this – he'll be so glad!'

'Will he? Well, I won't,' ejaculated the man decisively. 'Pollyanna, this is sheer nonsense!'

'You don't mean – you won't take him?'

'I certainly do mean just that.'

'But he'd be a lovely child's presence,' faltered Pollyanna. She was almost crying now. 'And you *couldn't* be lonesome – with Jimmy around.'

'I don't doubt it,' rejoined the man; 'but – I think I prefer the lonesomeness.'

It was then that Pollyanna, for the first time in weeks, suddenly remembered something Nancy had once told her. She raised her chin aggrievedly.

'Maybe you think a nice live little boy wouldn't be better than that old dead skeleton you keep somewhere; but I think it would!'

'*Skeleton?*'

'Yes. Nancy said you had one in your closet, somewhere.'

'Why, what – ' Suddenly the man threw back his head and laughed. He laughed very heartily indeed – so heartily that Pollyanna began to cry from pure nervousness. When he saw that, John Pendleton sat erect very promptly. His face grew grave at once.

'Pollyanna, I suspect you are right – more right than you know,' he said gently. 'In fact, I *know* that a "nice live little boy" would be far better than – my skeleton in the closet; only – we aren't always willing to make the exchange. We are apt still to cling to – our skeletons, Pollyanna. However, suppose you tell me a little more about this nice little boy.' And Pollyanna told him.

Perhaps the laugh cleared the air; or perhaps the pathos of Jimmy Bean's story as told by Pollyanna's eager little lips touched a heart already strangely softened. At all events, when Pollyanna went home that night she carried with her an invitation for Jimmy Bean himself to call at the great house with Pollyanna the next Saturday afternoon.

'And I'm so glad, and I'm sure you'll like him,' sighed Pollyanna, as she said goodbye. 'I do so want Jimmy Bean to have a home – and folks that care, you know.'

CHAPTER 22

Sermons and Woodboxes

On the afternoon that Pollyanna told John Pendleton of Jimmy Bean, the Reverend Paul Ford climbed the hill and entered the Pendleton Woods, hoping that the hushed beauty of God's out-of-doors would still the tumult that His children of men had wrought.

The Reverend Paul Ford was sick at heart. Month by month, for a year past, conditions in the parish under him had been growing worse and worse; until it seemed that now, turn which way he would, he encountered only wrangling, backbiting, scandal and jealousy. He had argued, pleaded, rebuked and ignored by turns; and always and through all he had prayed – earnestly, hopefully. But today, miserably, he was forced to own that matters were no better, but rather worse.

Two of his deacons were at swords' points over a silly something that only endless brooding had made of any account. Three of his most energetic women workers had withdrawn from the Ladies' Aid Society because a tiny spark of gossip had been fanned by wagging tongues into a devouring flame of scandal. The choir had split over the amount of solo work given to a fanciedly preferred singer. Even the Christian Endeavour Society was in a ferment of unrest owing to open criticism of two of its officers. As to the Sunday school – it had been the resignation of its superintendent and two of its teachers that had been the last straw, and that had sent the harassed minister to the quiet woods for prayer and meditation.

Under the green arch of the trees, the Reverend Paul Ford faced the thing squarely. To his mind, the crisis had come. Something must be done – and done at once. The entire work of the church was at a standstill. The Sunday services, the weekday prayer meetings, the missionary teas, even the suppers and socials were becoming less and less well attended. True, a few conscientious workers were still left. But they pulled at cross purposes, usually, and always they showed themselves to be acutely aware of the critical eyes all about them, and of the tongues that had nothing to do but to talk about what the eyes saw.

And because of all this the Reverend Paul Ford understood very well that he (God's minister), the church, the town and even Christianity itself was suffering; and must suffer still more unless . . .

Clearly something must be done, and done at once. But what?

Slowly the minister took from his pocket the notes he had made for his next Sunday's sermon. Frowningly he looked at them. His mouth settled into stern lines, as aloud, very impressively, he read the verses on which he had determined to speak:

'But woe unto you, scribes and Pharisees, hypocrites! for ye shut up the kingdom of heaven against men; for ye neither go in yourselves, neither suffer ye them that are entering to go in.

Woe unto you, scribes and Pharisees, hypocrites! for ye devour widows' houses, and for a pretence make long prayer; therefore ye shall receive the greater damnation.

Woe unto you, scribes and Pharisees, hypocrites! for ye pay tithe of mint and anise and cummin, and have omitted the weightier matters of the law, judgment, mercy and faith; these ought ye to have done, and not to leave the other undone.'

It was a bitter denunciation. In the green aisles of the woods the minister's deep voice rang out with scathing effect. Even the birds and squirrels seemed hushed into awed silence. It brought to the minister a vivid realisation of how those words would sound the next Sunday when he should utter them before his people in the sacred hush of the church.

His people! – they *were* his people. Could he do it? Dare he do it? Dare he *not* do it? It was a fearful denunciation, even without the words that would follow – his own words. He had prayed and prayed. He had pleaded earnestly for help, for guidance. He longed – oh, how earnestly he longed! – to take now, in this crisis, the right step. But was this the right step?

Slowly the minister folded the papers and thrust them back into his pocket. Then, with a sigh that was almost a moan, he flung himself down at the foot of a tree, and covered his face with his hands.

It was there that Pollyanna, on her way home from the Pendleton house, found him. With a little cry she ran forward. 'Oh, oh, Mr Ford! You – *you* haven't broken *your* leg or – anything, have you?' she gasped.

The minister dropped his hands, and looked up quickly. He tried to smile.

'No, dear – no, indeed! I'm just – resting.'

'Oh,' sighed Pollyanna, falling back a little 'That's all right, then. You see, Mr Pendleton *had* broken his leg when I found him – but he was lying down, though. And you are sitting up.'

'Yes, I am sitting up; and I haven't broken anything – that doctors can mend.'

The last words were very low, but Pollyanna heard them. A swift change crossed her face. Her eyes glowed with tender sympathy.

'I know what you mean – something plagues you. Father used to feel like that, lots of times. I reckon ministers do – most generally. You see there's such a lot depends on 'em, somehow.'

The Reverend Paul Ford turned a little wonderingly.

'Was *your* father a minister, Pollyanna?'

'Yes, sir. Didn't you know? I supposed everybody knew that. He married Aunt Polly's sister, and she was my mother.'

'Oh, I understand But, you see, I haven't been here many years, so I don't know all the family histories.'

'Yes, sir – I mean, no, sir,' smiled Pollyanna.

There was a long pause. The minister, still sitting at the foot of the tree, appeared to have forgotten Pollyanna's presence. He had pulled some papers from his pocket and unfolded them; but he was not looking at them. He was gazing, instead, at a leaf on the ground a little distance away – and it was not even a pretty leaf. It was brown and dead. Pollyanna, looking at him, felt vaguely sorry for him.

'It – it's a nice day,' she began hopefully.

For a moment there was no answer; then the minister looked up with a start.

'What? Oh! – yes, it is a very nice day.'

'And 'tisn't cold at all, either, even if 'tis October,' observed Pollyanna, still more hopefully. 'Mr Pendleton had a fire, but he said he didn't need it. It was just to look at. I like to look at fires, don't you?'

There was no reply this time, though Pollyanna waited patiently, before she tried again – by a new route.

'Do you like being a minister?'

The Reverend Paul Ford looked up now, very quickly.

'Do I like – Why, what an odd question! Why do you ask that, my dear?'

'Nothing – only the way you looked. It made me think of my father. He used to look like that – sometimes.'

'Did he?' The minister's voice was polite, but his eyes had gone back to the dried leaf on the ground.

'Yes, and I used to ask him just as I did you if he was glad he was a minister.'

The man under the tree smiled a little sadly.

'Well – what did he say?'

'Oh, he always said he was, of course, but 'most always he said, too, that he wouldn't *stay* a minister a minute if 'twasn't for the rejoicing texts.'

'The – *what*?' The Reverend Paul Ford's eyes left the leaf and gazed wonderingly into Pollyanna's merry little face.

'Well, that's what father used to call 'em,' she laughed. 'Of course the Bible didn't name 'em that. But it's all those that begin "Be glad in the Lord", or "Rejoice greatly", or "Shout for joy", and all that, you know – such a lot of 'em. Once, when father felt specially bad, he counted 'em. There were eight hundred of 'em.'

'Eight hundred!'

'Yes – that told you to rejoice and be glad, you know; that's why father named 'em the "rejoicing texts". '

'Oh!' There was an odd look on the minister's face. His eyes had fallen to the words on the top paper in his hands – 'But woe unto you, scribes and Pharisees, hypocrites!' 'And so your father – liked those "rejoicing texts",' he murmured.

'Oh, yes,' nodded Pollyanna emphatically. 'He said he felt better right away, that first day he thought to count 'em. He said if God took the trouble to tell us eight hundred times to be glad and rejoice, He must want us to do it – *some*. And father felt ashamed that he hadn't done it more. After that, they got to be such a comfort to him, you know, when things went wrong; when the Ladies' Aiders got to fight – I mean, when they *didn't agree* about something,' corrected Pollyanna hastily. 'Why it was those texts, too, father said, that made *him* think of the game – he began with *me* on the crutches – but he said 'twas the rejoicing texts that started him on it.'

'And what game might that be?' asked the minister.

'About finding something in everything to be glad about, you know. As I said, he began with me on the crutches.' And once more Pollyanna told her story – this time to a man who listened with tender eyes and understanding ears.

A little later Pollyanna and the minister descended the hill, hand in hand. Pollyanna's face was radiant. Pollyanna loved to talk, and she had been talking now for some time; there seemed to be so many, many things about the game, her father and the old home-life that the minister wanted to know.

At the foot of the hill their ways parted and Pollyanna, down one road, and the minister, down another, walked on alone

In the Reverend Paul Ford's study that evening the minister sat thinking. Near him on the desk lay a few loose sheets of paper – his sermon notes. Under the suspended pencil in his fingers lay other sheets of paper, blank – his sermon to be. But the minister was not thinking of what he had written, or of what he intended to write. In his imagination he was far away in a little Western town with a missionary minister who was poor, sick, worried and almost alone in the world – but who was poring over the Bible to find how many times his Lord and Master had told him to 'rejoice and be glad'.

After a time, with a long sigh, the Reverend Paul Ford aroused himself, came back from the far Western town, and adjusted the sheets of paper under his hand.

'Matthew 23: 13–14 and 23,' he wrote; then, with a gesture of impatience, he dropped his pencil and pulled towards him a magazine left on the desk by his wife a few minutes before. Listlessly his tired eyes turned from paragraph to paragraph until these words arrested them:

A father one day said to his son Tom, who he knew had refused to fill his mother's woodbox that morning: 'Tom, I'm sure you'll be glad to go and bring in some wood for your mother.' And without a word Tom went. Why? Just because his father showed so plainly that he expected him to do the right thing. Suppose he had said: 'Tom, I overheard what you said to your mother this morning, and I'm ashamed of you. Go at once and fill that woodbox!' I'll warrant that woodbox would be empty yet, so far as Tom was concerned!

On and on read the minister – a word here, a line there, a paragraph somewhere else:

What men and women need is encouragement. Their natural resisting powers should be strengthened, not weakened . . . Instead of always harping on a man's faults, tell him of his virtues. Try to pull him out of his rut of bad habits. Hold up to him his better self, his *real* self that can dare and do and win out! . . . The influence of a beautiful, helpful, hopeful character is contagious, and may revolutionise a whole town . . . People radiate what is in their minds and in their hearts. If a man feels kindly and obliging, his neighbours will feel that way, too, before long. But if he scolds and scowls and criticises – his neighbours will return scowl for scowl, and add interest! . . . When you look for the bad, expecting it, you will get it. When you *know* you will find the good – you will get that . . . Tell your son Tom you *know* he'll be glad to fill that woodbox – then watch him start, alert and interested!

The minister dropped the paper and lifted his chin. In a moment he was on his feet, tramping the narrow room back and forth, back and forth. Later, some time later, he drew a long breath, and dropped himself in the chair at his desk.

'God helping me, I'll do it!' he cried softly. 'I'll tell all my Toms I *know* they'll be glad to fill that woodbox! I'll give them work to do, and I'll make them so full of the very joy of doing it that they won't have *time* to look at their neighbours' woodboxes!' And he picked up his sermon notes, tore straight through the sheets, and cast them from him, so that on one side of his chair lay 'But woe unto you', and on the other, 'scribes and Pharisees, hypocrites!' while across the smooth white paper before him his pencil fairly flew – after first drawing one black line through 'Matthew 23; 13–14 and 23'.

Thus it happened that the Reverend Paul Ford's sermon the next Sunday was a veritable bugle-call to the best that was in every man and woman and child that heard it; and its text was one of Pollyanna's shining eight hundred: 'Be glad in the Lord and rejoice, ye righteous, and shout for joy all ye that are upright in heart.'

CHAPTER 23

An Accident

At Mrs Snow's request Pollyanna went one day to Dr Chilton's office to get the name of a medicine which Mrs Snow had forgotten. As it chanced, Pollyanna had never before seen the inside of Dr Chilton's office.

'I've never been to your home before! This is your home, isn't it?' she said, looking interestedly about her.

The doctor smiled a little sadly.

'Yes – such as 'tis,' he answered, as he wrote something on the pad of paper in his hand; 'but it's a pretty poor apology for a home, Pollyanna. They're just rooms that's all – not a home.'

Pollyanna nodded her head wisely. Her eyes glowed with sympathetic understanding.

'I know. It takes a woman's hand and heart, or a child's presence to make a home,' she said.

'Eh?' The doctor wheeled about abruptly.

'Mr Pendleton told me,' nodded Pollyanna again; 'about the woman's hand and heart, or the child's presence, you know. Why don't you get a woman's hand and heart, Dr Chilton? Or maybe you'd take Jimmy Bean – if Mr Pendleton doesn't want him.'

Dr Chilton laughed a little constrainedly.

'So Mr Pendleton says it takes a woman's hand and heart to make a home, does he?' he asked evasively.

'Yes. He says his is just a house, too. Why don't you, Dr Chilton?'

'Why don't I – what?' The doctor had turned back to his desk.

'Get a woman's hand and heart. Oh – and I forgot.' Pollyanna's face showed suddenly a painful colour. 'I suppose I ought to tell you. It wasn't Aunt Polly that Mr Pendleton loved long ago; and so we – we aren't going there to live. You see, I told you it was – but I made a mistake. I hope you didn't tell anyone,' she finished anxiously.

'No – I didn't tell anyone, Pollyanna,' replied the doctor, a little queerly.

'Oh, that's all right, then,' sighed Pollyanna in relief. 'You see you're the only one I told, and I thought Mr Pendleton looked sort of funny when I said I'd told *you*.'

'Did he?' The doctor's lips twitched.

'Yes. And of course he wouldn't want many people to know it – when 'twasn't true. But why don't you get a woman's hand and heart, Dr Chilton?'

There was a moment's silence; then very gravely the doctor said: 'They're not always to be had – for the asking, little girl.'

Pollyanna frowned thoughtfully.

'But I should think *you* could get 'em,' she argued. The flattering emphasis was unmistakable.

'Thank you,' laughed the doctor, with uplifted eyebrows. Then, gravely again: 'I'm afraid some of your older sisters would not be quite so – confident. At least, they – they haven't shown themselves to be so – obliging,' he observed.

Pollyanna frowned again. Then her eyes widened in surprise.

'Why, Dr Chilton, you don't mean – you didn't try to get somebody's hand and heart once, like Mr Pendleton, and – and couldn't, did you?'

The doctor got to his feet a little abruptly.

'There, there, Pollyanna, never mind about that now. Don't let other people's troubles worry your little head. Suppose you run back now to Mrs Snow. I've written down the name of the medicine, and the directions how she is to take it. Was there anything else?'

Pollyanna shook her head. 'No, sir; thank you, sir,' she murmured soberly, as she turned towards the door. From the little hallway she called back, her face suddenly alight: 'Anyhow, I'm glad 'twasn't my mother's hand and heart that you wanted and couldn't get, Dr Chilton. Goodbye!'

It was on the last day of October that the accident occurred. Pollyanna, hurrying home from school, crossed the road at an apparently safe distance in front of a swiftly approaching motor car.

Just what happened, no one could seem to tell afterwards. Neither was there anyone found who could tell why it happened or who was to blame that it did happen. Pollyanna, however, at five o'clock, was borne, limp and unconscious, into the little room that was so dear to her. There, by a white-faced Aunt Polly and a weeping Nancy she was undressed tenderly and put to bed, while from the village, hastily summoned by telephone, Dr Warren was hurrying as fast as another motor car could bring him.

'And ye didn't need ter more'n look at her aunt's face,' Nancy was sobbing to Old Tom in the garden, after the doctor had arrived and was closeted in the hushed room; 'ye didn't need ter more'n look at her aunt's face ter see that 'twa'n't no duty that was eatin' her. Yer hands don't shake, and yer eyes don't look as if ye was tryin' ter hold back the Angel o' Death himself, when you're jest doin' yer *duty*, Mr Tom – they don't, they don't!'

'Is she hurt – bad?' The old man's voice shook.

'There ain't no tellin',' sobbed Nancy. 'She lay back that white an' still she might easy be dead; but Miss Polly said she wa'n't dead – an' Miss Polly had oughter know, if anyone would – she kept up such a listenin' an' feelin' for her heartbeats an' her breath!'

'Couldn't ye tell anythin' what it done to her? – that – that – ' Old Tom's face worked convulsively.

Nancy's lips relaxed a little.

'I wish ye *would* call it somethin', Mr Tom – an' somethin' good an' strong, too. Drat it! Ter think of its runnin' down our little girl! I always hated the evil-smellin' things, anyhow – I did, I did!'

'But where is she hurt?'

'I don't know, I don't know,' moaned Nancy. 'There's a little cut on her blessed head, but 'tain't bad – that ain't – Miss Polly says. She says she's afraid it's infernally she's hurt.'

A faint flicker came into Old Tom's eyes.

'I guess you mean in*ter*nally, Nancy,' he said drily. 'She's hurt infernally, all right – plague take that autymobile! – but I don't guess Miss Polly'd be usin' that word, all the same.'

'Eh? Well, I don't know, I don't know,' moaned Nancy, with a shake of her head as she turned away. 'Seems as if I jest couldn't stand it till that doctor gits out o' there. I wish I had a washin' ter do – the biggest washin' I ever see, I do, I do!' she wailed, wringing her hands helplessly.

Even after the doctor was gone, however, there seemed to be little that Nancy could tell Mr Tom. There appeared to be no bones broken, and the cut was of slight consequence; but the doctor had looked very grave, had shaken his head slowly, and had said that time alone could tell. After he had gone Miss Polly had shown a face even whiter and more drawn-looking than before. The patient had not fully recovered consciousness, but at present she seemed to be resting as comfortably as could be expected. A trained nurse had been sent for, and would come that night.

That was all. And Nancy turned sobbingly, and went back to her kitchen.

It was sometime during the next forenoon that Pollyanna opened conscious eyes and realised where she was.

'Why, Aunt Polly, what's the matter? Isn't it daytime? Why don't I get up?' she cried. 'Why, Aunt Polly, I can't get up,' she moaned, falling back on the pillow, after an ineffectual attempt to lift herself.

'No, dear, I wouldn't try – just yet,' soothed her aunt quickly, but very quietly.

'But what is the matter? Why can't I get up?'

Miss Polly's eyes asked an agonised question of the white-capped young woman standing in the window, out of range of Pollyanna's eyes.

The young woman nodded.

'Tell her,' the lips said.

Miss Polly cleared her throat, and tried to swallow the lump that would scarcely let her speak.

'You were hurt, dear, by the automobile last night. But never mind that now. Auntie wants you to rest and go to sleep again.'

'Hurt? Oh, yes; I – I ran.' Pollyanna's eyes were dazed. She lifted her hand to her forehead. 'Why, it's – done up, and it – hurts!'

'Yes, dear; but never mind. Just – just rest.'

'But Aunt Polly, I feel so funny, and so bad! My legs feel so – so queer – only they don't *feel* – at all!'

With an imploring look into the nurse's face, Miss Polly struggled to her feet, and turned away. The nurse came forward quickly.

'Suppose you let me talk to you now,' she began cheerily. 'I'm sure I think it's high time we were getting acquainted, and I'm going to introduce myself. I am Miss Hunt, and I've come to help your aunt take care of you. And the very first thing I'm going to do is to ask you to swallow these little white pills for me.'

Pollyanna's eyes grew a bit wild.

'But I don't want to be taken care of – that is, not for long! I want to get up. You know I go to school. Can't I go to school tomorrow?'

From the window where Aunt Polly stood now there came a half-stifled cry.

'Tomorrow?' smiled the nurse brightly. 'Well, I may not let you out quite as soon as that, Miss Pollyanna. But just swallow these little pills for me, and we'll see what *they'll* do.'

'All right,' agreed Pollyanna, somewhat doubtfully; 'but I *must* go to school the day after tomorrow – there are examinations then, you know.'

She spoke again, a minute later. She spoke of school, and of the automobile, and of how her head ached; but very soon her voice trailed into silence under the blessed influence of the little white pills she had swallowed.

CHAPTER 24

John Pendleton

Pollyanna did not go to school 'tomorrow', nor the 'day after tomorrow'. Pollyanna, however, did not realise this, except momentarily when a brief period of full consciousness sent insistent questions to her lips. Pollyanna did not realise anything, in fact, very clearly until a week had passed; then the fever subsided, the pain lessened somewhat, and her mind awoke to full consciousness. She had then to be told all over again what had occurred.

'And so it's hurt that I am, and not sick,' she sighed at last. 'Well, I'm glad of that.'

'G–glad, Pollyanna?' asked her aunt, who was sitting by the bed.

'Yes. I'd so much rather have broken legs like Mr Pendleton's than lifelong invalids like Mrs Snow you know. Broken legs get well, and lifelong invalids don't.'

Miss Polly – who had said nothing whatever about broken legs – got suddenly to her feet and walked to the little dressing-table across the room. She was picking up one object after another now, and putting each down, in an aimless fashion quite unlike her usual decisiveness. Her face was not aimless-looking at all, however; it was white and drawn.

On the bed Pollyanna lay blinking at the dancing band of colours on the ceiling, which came from one of the prisms in the window.

'I'm glad it isn't smallpox that ails me, too,' she murmured contentedly. 'That would be worse than freckles. And I'm glad 'tisn't whooping cough – I've had that, and it's horrid – and I'm glad 'tisn't appendicitis nor measles, 'cause they're catching – measles are, I mean – and they wouldn't let you stay here.'

'You seem to – to be glad of a good many things, my dear,' faltered Aunt Polly, putting her hand to her throat as if her collar bound.

Pollyanna laughed softly.

'I am. I've been thinking of 'em – lots of 'em – all the time I've been looking up at that rainbow. I love rainbows. I'm so glad Mr Pendleton gave me those prisms! I'm glad of some things I haven't said yet. I don't know but I'm most glad I was hurt.'

'Pollyanna!'

Pollyanna laughed softly again. She turned luminous eyes on her aunt. 'Well, you see, since I have been hurt, you've called me "dear" lots of times – and you didn't before. I love to be called "dear" – by folks that belong to you, I mean. Some of the Ladies' Aiders did call me that; and of course that was pretty nice, but not so nice as if they had belonged to me, like you do. Oh, Aunt Polly, I'm so glad you belong to me!'

Aunt Polly did not answer. Her hand was at her throat again. Her eyes were full of tears. She had turned away and was hurrying from the room through the door by which the nurse had just entered.

It was that afternoon that Nancy ran out to Old Tom, who was cleaning harnesses in the barn. Her eyes were wild.

'Mr Tom, Mr Tom, guess what's happened,' she panted. 'You couldn't guess in a thousand years – you couldn't, you couldn't!'

'Then I calc'late I won't try,' retorted the man grimly, 'specially as I hain't got more'n *ten* ter live, anyhow, probably. You'd better tell me first off, Nancy.'

'Well, listen, then. Who do you s'pose is in the parlour now with the mistress? Who, I say?'

Old Tom shook his head.

'There's no tellin',' he declared.

'Yes, there is. I'm tellin'. It's John Pendleton!'

'Sho, now! You're jokin', girl.'

'Not much I am – an' me a-lettin' him in myself – crutches an' all! An' the team he come in a-waitin' this minute at the door for him, jest as if he wa'n't the cranky old crosspatch he is, what never talks ter no one! Jest think, Mr Tom – *him* a-callin' on *her*!'

'Well, why not?' demanded the old man, a little aggressively.

Nancy gave him a scornful glance.

'As if you didn't know better'n me!' she derided,

'Eh?'

'Oh, you needn't be so innercent,' she retorted with mock indignation; 'you what led me wild-goose chasin' in the first place!'

'What do ye mean?'

Nancy glanced through the open barn door towards the house, and came a step nearer to the old man.

'Listen! 'Twas you that was tellin' me Miss Polly had a lover in the first place, wa'n't it? Well, one day I thinks I finds two and two, and I puts 'em tergether an' makes four. But it turns out ter be five – an' no four at all, at all!'

With a gesture of indifference, Old Tom turned and fell to work. 'If you're goin' ter talk ter me, you've got ter talk plain horse sense,' he declared testily. 'I never was no hand for figgers.'

Nancy laughed.

'Well, it's this,' she explained. 'I heard somethin' that made me think him an' Miss Polly was lovers.'

'*Mr Pendleton?*' Old Tom straightened up.

'Yes. Oh, I know now; he wasn't. It was that blessed child's mother he was in love with, and that's why he wanted – but never mind that part,' she added hastily, remembering just in time her promise to Pollyanna not to tell that Mr Pendleton had wished her to come and live with him. 'Well, I've been askin' folks about him some, since, and I've found out that him an' Miss Polly hain't been friends for years, an' that she's been hatin' him like pisen owin' ter the silly gossip that coupled their names tergether when she was eighteen or twenty.'

'Yes, I remember,' nodded Old Tom. 'It was three or four years after Miss Jennie give him the mitten and went off with the other chap. Miss Polly knew about it, of course, and was sorry for him. So she tried ter be nice to him. Maybe she overdid it a little – she hated that minister chap so who had took off her sister. At any rate, somebody begun ter make trouble. They said she was runnin' after him.'

'Runnin' after any man – her!' interjected Nancy.

'I know it; but they did,' declared Old Tom, 'and of course no gal of any spunk'll stand that. Then about that time come her own lover an' the trouble with *him*. After that she shut up like an oyster an' wouldn't have nothin' ter do with nobody fur a spell. Her heart jest seemed to turn bitter at the core.'

'Yes, I know. I've heard about that now,' rejoined Nancy; 'an' that's why you could 'a' knocked me down with a feather when I see *him* at the door – him, what she hain't spoke to for years! But I let him in an' went an' told her.'

'What did she say?' Old Tom held his breath.

'Nothin' – at first. She was so still I thought she hadn't heard; and I was jest goin' ter say it over when she speaks up quiet like: "Tell Mr Pendleton I will be down at once." An' I come an' told him. Then I come out here an' told you,' finished Nancy, casting another backward glance towards the house.

'Humph!' grunted Old Tom; and fell to work again.

In the ceremonious 'parlour' of the Harrington homestead, Mr John Pendleton did not have to wait long before a swift step warned him of Miss Polly's coming. As he attempted to rise, she made a gesture of remonstrance. She did not offer her hand, however, and her face was coldy reserved.

'I called to ask for – Pollyanna,' he began at once, a little brusquely.

'Thank you. She is about the same,' said Miss Polly.

'And that is – won't you tell me *how* she is?' His voice was not quite steady this time.

A quick spasm of pain crossed the woman's face.

'I can't. I wish I could!'

'You mean – you don't know?'

'Yes.'

'But – the doctor?'

'Dr Warren himself seems – at sea. He is in correspondence now with a New York specialist. They have arranged for a consultation – at once.'

'But – but what *were* her injuries that you do know?'

'A slight cut on the head, one or two bruises, and – and an injury to the spine which has seemed to cause – paralysis from the hips down.'

A low cry came from the man. There was a brief silence; then, huskily, he asked: 'And Pollyanna – how does she – take it?'

'She doesn't understand – at all – how things really are. And I can't tell her.'

'But she must know – something!'

Miss Polly lifted her hand to the collar at her throat in the gesture that had become so common to her of late.

'Oh, yes. She knows she can't – move; but she thinks her legs are – broken. She says she's glad it's broken legs like yours rather than "lifelong invalids" like Mrs Snow's; because broken legs get well, and the other – doesn't. She talks like that all the time until it – it seems as if I should – die!'

Through the blur of tears in his own eyes, the man saw the drawn face opposite, twisted with emotion. Involuntarily his thoughts went back to what Pollyanna had said when he had made his final plea for her presence: 'Oh, I couldn't leave Aunt Polly – now!'

It was this thought that made him ask very gently, as soon as he could control his voice: 'I wonder if you know, Miss Harrington, how hard I tried to get Pollyanna to come and live with me.'

'With *you*! – Pollyanna!'

The man winced a little at the tone of her voice; but his own voice was still impersonally cool when he spoke again. 'Yes. I wanted to adopt her – legally, you understand; making her my heir, of course.'

The woman in the opposite chair relaxed a little. It came to her, suddenly, what a brilliant future it would have meant to Pollyanna – this adoption; and she wondered if Pollyanna were old enough – and mercenary enough – to be tempted by this man's money and position.

'I am very fond of Pollyanna,' the man was continuing. 'I am fond of her both for her own sake, and for – her mother's. I stood ready to give Pollyanna the love that had been twenty-five years in storage.'

'*Love*.' Miss Polly remembered suddenly why *she* had taken this child in the first place – and with the recollection came the remembrance of Pollyanna's own words uttered that very morning: 'I love to be called "dear" by folks that belong to you!' And it was this love-hungry little girl that had been offered the stored-up affection of twenty-five years; and she *was* old enough to be tempted by love! With a sinking heart Miss Polly realised that. With a sinking heart, too, she realised something else; the dreariness of her own future now – without Pollyanna.

'Well?' she said. And the man, recognising the self-control that vibrated through the harshness of the tone, smiled sadly.

'She would not come,' he answered.

'Why?'

'She would not leave you. She said you had been so good to her. She wanted to stay with you – and she said she *thought* you wanted her to stay,' he finished, as he pulled himself to his feet.

He did not look towards Miss Polly. He turned his face resolutely towards the door. But instantly he heard a swift step at his side, and found a shaking hand thrust towards him.

'When the specialist comes, and I know anything – definite about Pollyanna, I will let you hear from me,' said a trembling voice. 'Goodbye – and thank you for coming. Pollyanna will be – pleased.'

CHAPTER 25

A Waiting Game

On the day after John Pendleton's call at the Harrington homestead Miss Polly set herself to the task of preparing Pollyanna for the visit of the specialist.

'Pollyanna, my dear,' she began gently, 'we have decided that we want another doctor besides Dr Warren to see you. Another one might tell us something new to do – to help you get well faster, you know.'

A joyous light came to Pollyanna's face.

'Dr Chilton! Oh, Aunt Polly, I'd so love to have Dr Chilton! I've wanted him all the time, but I was afraid you didn't, on account of his seeing you in the sun-parlour that day, you know; so I didn't like to say anything. But I'm so glad you do want him!'

Aunt Polly's face had turned white, then red, then back to white again. But when she answered, she showed very plainly that she was trying to speak lightly and cheerfully.

'Oh, no, dear! It wasn't Dr Chilton at all that I meant. It is a new doctor – a very famous doctor from New York, who – who knows a great deal about – hurts like yours.'

Pollyanna's face fell.

'I don't believe he knows half so much as Dr Chilton.'

'Oh, yes, he does, I'm sure, dear.'

'But it was Dr Chilton who doctored Mr Pendleton's broken leg, Aunt Polly. If – if you don't mind *very* much, I *would like* to have Dr Chilton – truly! I would!'

A distressed colour suffused Miss Polly's face. For a moment she did not speak at all; then she said gently – though yet with a touch of her old stern decisiveness: 'But I do mind, Pollyanna. I mind very much. I would do anything – almost anything for you, my dear; but

I – for reasons which I do not care to speak of now, I don't wish Dr Chilton called in on – on this case. And believe me, he can*not* know so much about – about your trouble, as this great doctor does, who will come from New York tomorrow.'

Pollyanna still looked unconvinced.

'But, Aunt Polly, if you *loved* Dr Chilton – '

'*What*, Pollyanna?' Aunt Polly's voice was very sharp now. Her cheeks were very red, too.

'I say, if you loved Dr Chilton, and didn't love the other one,' sighed Pollyanna, 'seems to me that would make some difference in the good he would do; and I love Dr Chilton.'

The nurse entered the room at that moment, and Aunt Polly rose to her feet abruptly, a look of relief on her face.

'I am very sorry, Pollyanna,' she said, a little stiffly; 'but I'm afraid you'll have to let me be the judge, this time. Besides, it's already arranged. The New York doctor is coming tomorrow.'

As it happened, however, the New York doctor did not come 'tomorrow'. At the last moment a telegram told of an unavoidable delay owing to the sudden illness of the specialist himself. This led Pollyanna into a renewed pleading for the substitution of Dr Chilton – 'which would be so easy, now, you know'.

But as before, Aunt Polly shook her head and said, 'No, dear,' very decisively, yet with a still more anxious assurance that she would do anything – anything but that – to please her dear Pollyanna.

As the days of waiting passed, one by one, it did indeed seem that Aunt Polly was doing everything (but that) that she could do to please her niece.

'I wouldn't 'a' believed it – you couldn't 'a' made me believe it,' Nancy said to Old Tom one morning. 'There don't seem ter be a minute in the day that Miss Polly ain't jest hangin' round waitin' ter do somethin' for that blessed lamb, if 'tain't more than ter let in the cat – an' her what wouldn't let Fluff nor Buff upstairs for love nor money a week ago; an' now she lets 'em tumble all over the bed jest 'cause it pleases Miss Pollyanna!

'An' when she ain't doin' nothin' else, she's movin' them little glass danglers round ter diff'rent winders in the room so the sun'll make the "rainbows dance", as that blessed child calls it. She's sent Timothy down ter Cobb's greenhouse three times for fresh flowers – an' that besides all the posies fetched in ter her, too. An' the other day, if I didn't find her sittin' 'fore the bed with the nurse actually doin' her hair, an' Miss Pollyanna lookin' on an' bossin' from the bed, her eyes all shinin' an' happy. An' I declare ter goodness, if Miss Polly hain't wore her hair like that every day now – jest ter please that blessed child!'

Old Tom chuckled.

'Well, it strikes me Miss Polly herself ain't lookin' none the worse – for wearin' them 'ere curls round her forehead,' he observed drily

' 'Course she ain't,' retorted Nancy indignantly. 'She looks like *folks*, now. She's actually almost – '

'Keerful, now, Nancy!' interrupted the old man, with a slow grin. 'You know what you said when I told ye she was handsome once.'

Nancy shrugged her shoulders.

'Oh, she ain't handsome, of course; but I will own up she don't look like the same woman, what with the ribbons an' lace jiggers Miss Pollyanna makes her wear round her neck.'

'I told ye so,' nodded the man. 'I told ye she wa'n't – old.'

Nancy laughed.

'Well, I'll own up she *hain't* got quite so good an imitation of it – as she did have, 'fore Miss Pollyanna come. Say, Mr Tom, who *was* her lover? I hain't found that out, yet; I hain't, I hain't!'

'Hain't ye?' asked the old man, with an odd look on his face. 'Well, I guess ye won't then – from me.'

'Oh, Mr Tom, come on, now,' wheedled the girl. 'Ye see, there ain't many folks here that I *can* ask.'

'Maybe not. But there's one, anyhow, that ain't answerin',' grinned Old Tom. Then, abruptly, the light died from his eyes. 'How is she, terday – the little gal?'

Nancy shook her head. Her face, too, had sobered.

'Just the same, Mr Tom. There ain't no special diff'rence, as I can see – or anybody, I guess. She jest lays there an' sleeps an' talks some, an' tries ter smile an' be "glad" 'cause the sun sets or the moon rises, or some other such thing, till it's enough ter make yer heart break with achin'.'

'I know; it's the "game" – bless her sweet heart!' nodded Old Tom, blinking a little.

'She told *you* then, about that 'ere – game?'

'Oh, yes. She told me long ago.' The old man hesitated, then went on, his lips twitching a little. 'I was growlin' one day 'cause I was so bent up and crooked; an' what do ye s'pose the little thing said?'

'I couldn't guess. I wouldn't think she could find *anythin'* about *that* ter be glad about!'

'She did. She said I could be glad, anyhow, that I didn't have ter *stoop so far ter do my weedin'* – 'cause I was already bent part way over.'

Nancy gave a wistful laugh

'Well, I ain't surprised, after all. You might know she'd find somethin'. We've been playin' it – that game – since almost the first, 'cause there wa'n't no one else she could play it with – though she did speak of – her aunt.'

'*Miss Polly!*'

Nancy chuckled.

'I guess you hain't got such an awful diff'rent opinion o' the mistress than I have,' she bridled.

Old Tom stiffened.

'I was only thinkin' 'twould be – some of a surprise – to her,' he explained, with dignity.

'Well, yes, I guess 'twould be – *then*,' retorted Nancy. 'I ain't sayin' what 'twould be *now*. I'd believe anythin' o' the mistress now – even that she'd take ter playin' it herself!'

'But hain't the little gal told her – ever? She's told ev'ryone else, I guess. I'm hearin' of it ev'rywhere, now, since she was hurted,' said Tom.

'Well, she didn't tell Miss Polly,' rejoined Nancy. 'Miss Pollyanna told me long ago that she couldn't tell her, 'cause her aunt didn't like ter have her talk about her father; an' 'twas her father's game, an' she'd have to talk about him if she did tell her. So she never told her.'

'Oh, I see, I see.' The old man nodded his head slowly. 'They was always bitter against the minister chap – all of 'em, 'cause he took Miss Jennie away from 'em. An' Miss Polly – young as she was – couldn't never forgive him; she was that fond of Miss Jennie – in them days. I see, I see. 'Twas a bad mess,' he sighed, as he turned away.

'Yes, 'twas – all round, all round,' sighed Nancy in her turn, as she went back to her kitchen.

For no one were those days of waiting easy. The nurse tried to look cheerful, but her eyes were troubled. The doctor was openly nervous and impatient. Miss Polly said little; but even the softening waves of hair about her face, and the becoming laces at her throat, could not hide the fact that she was growing thin and pale. As to Pollyanna – Pollyanna petted the dog, smoothed the cat's sleek head, admired the flowers and ate the fruits and jellies that were sent in to her; and returned innumerable cheery answers to the many messages of love and enquiry that were brought to her bedside. But she too grew pale and thin; and the nervous activity of the poor little hands and arms only emphasised the pitiful motionlessness of the once active little feet and legs now lying so woefully quiet under the blankets.

As to the game – Pollyanna told Nancy these days how glad she was going to be when she could go to school again, go to see Mrs Snow, go to call on Mr Pendleton and go to ride with Dr Chilton; nor did she seem to realise that all this 'gladness' was in the future, not the present. Nancy, however, did realise it – and cry about it, when she was alone.

CHAPTER 26

A Door Ajar

Just a week from the time Dr Mead, the specialist, was first expected, he came. He was a tall, broad-shouldered man, with kind grey eyes and a cheerful smile. Pollyanna liked him at once, and told him so.

'You look quite a lot like *my* doctor, you see,' she added engagingly.

'*Your* doctor?' Dr Mead glanced in evident surprise at Dr Warren, talking with the nurse a few feet away. Dr Warren was a small, brown-eyed man with a pointed brown beard.

'Oh, *that* isn't my doctor,' smiled Pollyanna, divining his thought. 'Dr Warren is Aunt Polly's doctor. My doctor is Dr Chilton.'

'Oh–h!' said Dr Mead, a little oddly, his eyes resting on Miss Polly, who, with a vivid blush, had turned hastily away.

'Yes.' Pollyanna hesitated, then continued with her usual truthfulness. 'You see, *I* wanted Dr Chilton all the time, but Aunt Polly wanted you. She said you knew more than Dr Chilton, anyway, about – about broken legs like mine. And of course if you do, I can be glad for that. Do you?'

A swift something crossed the doctor's face that Pollyanna could not quite translate.

'Only time can tell that, little girl,' he said gently; then he turned a grave face towards Dr Warren, who had just come to the bedside.

Everyone said afterwards that it was the cat that did it. Certainly, if Fluffy had not poked an insistent paw and nose against Pollyanna's unlatched door, the door would not have swung noiselessly open on its hinges until it stood perhaps a foot ajar; and if the door had not been open, Pollyanna would not have heard her aunt's words.

In the hall the two doctors, the nurse, and Miss Polly stood talking. In Pollyanna's room Fluffy had just jumped on to the bed with a little purring *meow* of joy when through the open door sounded clearly and sharply Aunt Polly's agonised exclamation.

'Not that! Doctor, not that! You don't mean – the child – will *never walk* again!'

It was all confusion then. First, from the bedroom came Pollyanna's terrified, 'Aunt Polly – Aunt Polly!' Then Miss Polly, seeing the open door and realising that her words had been heard, gave a low little moan and – for the first time in her life – fainted dead away.

The nurse, with a choking, 'She heard!' stumbled towards the open door. The two doctors stayed with Miss Polly. Dr Mead had to stay – he had caught Miss Polly as she fell. Dr Warren stood by helplessly. It was not until Pollyanna cried out again sharply and the nurse closed the door, that the two men, with a despairing glance into each other's eyes, awoke to the immediate duty of bringing the woman in Dr Mead's arms back to unhappy consciousness.

In Pollyanna's room, the nurse had found a purring grey cat on the bed vainly trying to attract the attention of a white-faced, wild-eyed little girl.

'Miss Hunt, please, I want Aunt Polly. I want her right away, quick, please!'

The nurse closed the door and came forward hurriedly. Her face was very pale.

'She – she can't come just this minute, dear. She will – a little later. What is it? Can't I – get it?'

Pollyanna shook her head.

'But I want to know what she said – just now. Did you hear her? I want Aunt Polly – she said something. I want her to tell me 'tisn't true – 'tisn't true!'

The nurse tried to speak, but no words came. Something in her face sent an added terror to Pollyanna's eyes.

'Miss Hunt, you *did* hear her! It *is* true! Oh, it *isn't* true! You don't mean I can't ever – walk again?'

'There, there, dear – don't, don't!' choked the nurse. 'Perhaps he didn't know. Perhaps he was mistaken. There's lots of things that could happen, you know.'

'But Aunt Polly said he did know! She said he knew more than anybody else about – about broken legs like mine!'

'Yes, yes, I know, dear; but all doctors make mistakes sometimes. Just – just don't think any more about it now – please don't, dear.'

Pollyanna flung out her arms wildly.

'But I can't help thinking about it,' she sobbed. 'It's all there is now to think about. Why, Miss Hunt, how am I to go to school, or to see Mr Pendleton, or Mrs Snow, or – or anybody?' She caught her breath and sobbed wildly for a moment. Suddenly she stopped and looked up, a new terror in her eyes. 'Why, Miss Hunt, if I can't walk, how am I ever going to be glad for – *anything*?'

Miss Hunt did not know 'the game'; but she did know that her patient must be quieted, and that at once. In spite of her own perturbation and heartache, her hands had not been idle, and she stood now at the bedside with the quieting powder ready.

'There, there, dear, just take this,' she soothed; 'and by and by we'll be more rested, and we'll see what can be done then. Things aren't half as bad as they seem, dear, lots of times, you know.'

Obediently Pollyanna took the medicine, and sipped the water from the glass in Miss Hunt's hand.

'I know; that sounds like things father used to say,' faltered Pollyanna, blinking off the tears. 'He said there was always something about everything that might be worse; but I reckon he'd never just heard he couldn't ever walk again. I don't see how there *can* be anything about that that could be worse – do you?'

Miss Hunt did not reply. She could not trust herself to speak just then.

CHAPTER 27

Two Visits

It was Nancy who was sent to tell Mr John Pendleton of Dr Mead's verdict. Miss Polly had remembered her promise to let him have direct information from the house. To go herself or to write a letter she felt to be almost equally out of the question. It occurred to her then to send Nancy.

There had been a time when Nancy would have rejoiced greatly at this extraordinary opportunity to see something of the House of Mystery and its master. But today her heart was too heavy to rejoice at anything. She scarcely even looked about her at all, indeed, during the few minutes she waited for Mr John Pendleton to appear.

'I'm Nancy, sir,' she said respectfully, in response to the surprised questioning of his eyes, when he came into the room. 'Miss Harrington sent me to tell you about – Miss Pollyanna.'

'Well?'

In spite of the curt terseness of the word, Nancy quite understood the anxiety that lay behind that short, 'Well?'

'It ain't well, Mr Pendleton,' she choked.

'You don't mean –' He paused, and she bowed her head miserably.

'Yes, sir. He says – she can't walk again – never.' For a moment there was absolute silence in the room; then the man spoke, in a voice shaken with emotion.

'Poor – little – girl! Poor – little – girl!'

Nancy glanced at him, but dropped her eyes at once. She had not supposed that sour, cross, stern John Pendleton could look like that. In a moment he spoke again, still in the low, unsteady voice.

'It seems cruel – never to dance in the sunshine again! My little prism girl!'

There was another silence; then, abruptly, the man asked: 'She herself doesn't know yet – of course – does she?'

'But she does, sir,' sobbed Nancy; 'an' that's what makes it all the harder. She found out – drat that cat! I begs yer pardon,' apologised the girl hurriedly. 'It's only that the cat pushed open the door an' Miss Pollyanna overheard 'em talkin'. She found out – that way.'

'Poor – little – girl!' sighed the man again.

'Yes, sir. You'd say so, sir, if you could see her,' choked Nancy. 'I hain't seen her but twice since she knew about it, an' it done me up both times. Ye see it's all so fresh an' new to her, an' she keeps thinkin' all the time of new things she can't do – *now*. It worries her, too, 'cause she can't seem ter be glad – maybe you don't know about her game, though – ' broke off Nancy apologetically.

'The "glad game"?' asked the man. 'Oh yes; she told me of that.'

'Oh, she did! Well, I guess she has told it generally ter most folks. But ye see, now she – she can't play it herself, an' it worries her. She says she can't think of a thing – not a thing about this not walkin' again ter be glad about.'

'Well, why should she?' retorted the man, almost savagely.

Nancy shifted her feet uneasily. 'That's the way I felt too – till I happened ter think – it *would* be easier if she *could* find somethin', ye know. So I tried to – to remind her.'

'To remind her! Of what?' John Pendleton's voice was still angrily impatient.

'Of – of how she told others ter play it – Mis' Snow and the rest, ye know – and what she said for them ter do. But the poor little lamb just cries, an' says it don't seem the same, somehow. She says it's easy ter *tell* lifelong invalids how ter be glad, but 'tain't the same thing when you're the lifelong invalid yerself an' have ter try ter do it. She says she's told herself over an' over again how glad she is that other folks ain't like her; but that all the time she's sayin' it, she ain't really *thinkin'* of anythin' only how she can't ever walk again.'

Nancy paused, but the man did not speak. He sat with his hand over his eyes.

'Then I tried ter remind her how she used ter say the game was all the nicer ter play when – when it was hard,' resumed Nancy, in a dull voice. 'But she says that too is diff'rent – when it really *is* hard. An' I must be goin', now, sir,' she broke off abruptly.

At the door she hesitated, turned, and asked timidly: 'I couldn't be tellin' Miss Pollyanna that – that you'd seen Jimmy Bean again, I s'pose, sir, could I?'

'I don't see how you could – as I haven't seen him,' observed the man a little shortly. 'Why?'

'Nothin', sir, only – well, ye see, that's one of the things that she was feelin' bad about, that she couldn't take him ter see you, now. She said she'd taken him once, but she didn't think he showed off very well that day, and that she was afraid you didn't think he would make a very nice child's presence, after all. Maybe you know what she means by that; but I didn't, sir.'

'Yes, I know – what she means.'

'All right, sir. It was only that she was wantin' ter take him again, she said, so's ter show ye he really was a lovely child's presence. And now she – can't! – drat that autymobile! I begs yer pardon, sir. Goodbye!' And Nancy fled precipitately.

It did not take long for the entire town of Beldingsville to learn that the great New York doctor had said Pollyanna Whittier would never walk again; and certainly never before had the town been so stirred. Everybody knew by sight now the piquant little freckled face that had always a smile of greeting; and almost everybody knew of the 'game' that Pollyanna was in the habit of playing. To think that now never again would that smiling face be seen on their streets – never again would that cheery little voice proclaim the gladness of some everyday experience! It seemed unbelievable, impossible, cruel.

In kitchens and sitting-rooms and over backyard fences women talked of it, and wept openly. On street corners and in store lounging-places the men talked too, and wept – though not so openly. And neither the talking nor the weeping grew less when fast on the heels of the news itself, came Nancy's pitiful story that Pollyanna, face to face with what had come to her, was bemoaning most of all the fact that she could not play the game; that she could not now be glad over – anything.

It was then that the same thought must have, in some way, come to Pollyanna's friends. At all events, almost at once, the mistress of the Harrington homestead, greatly to her surprise, began to receive calls: calls from people she knew, and people she did not know; calls from men, women and children – many of whom Miss Polly had not supposed that her niece knew at all.

Some came in and sat down for a stiff five or ten minutes. Some stood awkwardly on the porch steps, fumbling with hats or handbags, according to their sex. Some brought a book, a bunch of flowers, or a dainty to tempt the palate. Some cried frankly. Some turned their backs and blew their noses furiously. But all enquired very anxiously for the little injured girl; and all sent to her some message – and it was these messages which, after a time, stirred Miss Polly to action.

First came Mr John Pendleton. He came without his crutches today.

'I don't need to tell you how shocked I am,' he began almost harshly. 'But can – nothing be done?'

Miss Polly gave a gesture of despair.

'Oh, we're "doing", of course, all the time. Dr Mead prescribed certain treatments and medicines that might help, and Dr Warren is carrying them out to the letter, of course. But – Dr Mead held out almost no hope.'

John Pendleton rose abruptly – though he had but just come. His face was white, and his mouth was set into stern lines. Miss Polly, looking at him, knew very well why he felt that he could not stay longer in her presence.

At the door he turned. 'I have a message for Pollyanna,' he said. 'Will you tell her, please, that I have seen Jimmy Bean and – that he's going to be my boy hereafter. Tell her I thought she would be – *glad* to know I shall adopt him, probably.'

For a brief moment Miss Polly lost her usual well-bred self-control. 'You will adopt Jimmy Bean!' she gasped.

The man lifted his chin a little.

'Yes. I think Pollyanna will understand. You will tell her I thought she would be – *glad*?'

'Why, of – of course,' faltered Miss Polly.

'Thank you,' bowed John Pendleton, as he turned to go.

In the middle of the floor Miss Polly stood, silent and amazed, still looking after the man who had just left her. Even yet she could scarcely believe what her ears had heard. John Pendleton *adopt* Jimmy Bean? John Pendleton, wealthy, independent, morose, reputed to be miserly and supremely selfish, to adopt a little boy – and such a little boy?

With a somewhat dazed face Miss Polly went upstairs to Polly-anna's room.

'Pollyanna, I have a message for you from Mr John Pendleton. He has just been here. He says to tell you he has taken Jimmy Bean for his little boy. He said he thought you'd be glad to know it.'

Pollyanna's wistful little face flamed into sudden joy. 'Glad? *Glad?* Well, I reckon I am glad! Oh, Aunt Polly, I've so wanted to find a place for Jimmy – and that's such a lovely place! Besides, I'm so glad for Mr Pendleton, too. You see, now he'll have the child's presence.'

'The – what?'

Pollyanna coloured painfully. She had forgotten that she had never told her aunt of Mr Pendleton's desire to adopt her – and certainly she would not wish to tell her now that she had ever thought for a minute of leaving her – this dear Aunt Polly!

'The child's presence,' stammered Pollyanna, hastily. 'Mr Pendle-ton told me once, you see, that only a woman's hand and heart or a child's presence could make a – a home. And now he's got it – the child's presence.'

'Oh, I – see,' said Miss Polly very gently; and she did see – more than Pollyanna realised. She saw something of the pressure that was probably brought to bear on Pollyanna herself at the time John Pendleton was asking *her* to be the 'child's presence', which was to transform his great pile of grey stone into a home. 'I see,' she finished, her eyes stinging with sudden tears.

Pollyanna, fearful that her aunt might ask further embarrassing questions, hastened to lead the conversation away from the Pendleton house and its master.

'Dr Chilton says so, too – that it takes a woman's hand and heart, or a child's presence, to make a home, you know,' she remarked.

Miss Polly turned with a start.

'*Dr Chilton!* How do you know – that?'

'He told me so. 'Twas when he said he lived in just rooms, you know – not a home.'

Miss Polly did not answer. Her eyes were out the window.

'So I asked him why he didn't get 'em – a woman's hand and heart, and have a home.'

'Pollyanna!' Miss Polly had turned sharply. Her cheeks showed a sudden colour.

'Well, I did. He looked so – so sorrowful.'

'What did he – say?' Miss Polly asked the question as if in spite of some force within her that was urging her not to ask it.

'He didn't say anything for a minute; then he said very low that you couldn't always get 'em for the asking.'

There was a brief silence. Miss Polly's eyes had turned again to the window. Her cheeks were still unnaturally pink.

Pollyanna sighed.

'He wants one, anyhow, I know, and I wish he could have one.'

'Why, Pollyanna, *how* do you know?'

'Because, afterwards, on another day, he said something else. He said that low, too, but I heard him. He said that he'd give all the world if he did have one woman's hand and heart. Why, Aunt Polly, what's the matter?' Aunt Polly had risen hurriedly and gone to the window.

'Nothing, dear. I was changing the position of this prism,' said Aunt Polly, whose whole face now was aflame.

CHAPTER 28

The Game and its Player

It was not long after John Pendleton's second visit that Milly Snow called one afternoon. Milly Snow had never before been to the Harrington homestead. She blushed and looked very embarrassed when Miss Polly entered the room.

'I – I came to enquire for the little girl,' she stammered.

'You are very kind. She is about the same. How is your mother?' rejoined Miss Polly wearily.

'That is what I came to tell you – that is, to ask you to tell Miss Pollyanna,' hurried on the girl breathlessly and incoherently. 'We think it's – so awful – so perfectly awful that the little thing can't ever walk again; and after all she's done for us, too – for mother, you know, teaching her to play the game, and all that. And when we heard how now she couldn't play it herself – poor little dear! I'm sure I don't see how she *can*, either, in her condition! – but when we remembered all the things she'd said to us, we thought if she could only know what she *had* done for us, that it would *help*, you know, in her own case, about the game, because she could be glad – that is, a little glad –' Milly stopped helplessly, and seemed to be waiting for Miss Polly to speak.

Miss Polly had sat politely listening, but with a puzzled questioning in her eyes. Only about half of what had been said, had she understood. She was thinking now that she always had known that Milly Snow was "queer", but she had not supposed she was crazy. In no other way, however, could she account for this incoherent, illogical, unmeaning rush of words.

When the pause came she filled it with a quiet: 'I don't think I quite understand, Milly. Just what is it that you want me to tell my niece?'

'Yes, that's it; I want you to tell her,' answered the girl feverishly. 'Make her see what she's done for us. Of course she's *seen* some things, because she's been there, and she's known mother is different; but I want her to know *how* different she is – and me, too. I'm different. I've been trying to play it – the game – a little.'

Miss Polly frowned. She would have asked what Milly meant by this 'game', but there was no opportunity. Milly was rushing on again with nervous volubility.

'You know nothing was ever right before – for mother. She was always wanting 'em different. And, really, I don't know as one could blame her much – under the circumstances. But now she lets me keep the shades up, and she takes an interest in things – how she looks, and her nightdress, and all that. And she's actually begun to knit little things – reins and baby blankets for fairs and hospitals. And she's so interested and so *glad* to think she can do it! – and that was all Miss Pollyanna's doing, you know, 'cause she told mother she could be glad she'd got her hands and arms, anyway; and that made mother wonder right away why she didn't *do* something with her hands and arms. And so she began to do something – to knit, you know. And you can't think what a different room it is now, what with the red and blue and yellow worsteds, and the prisms in the window that *she* gave her – why, it actually makes you feel *better* just to go in there now; and before I used to dread it awfully, it was so dark and gloomy, and mother was so – so unhappy, you know.

'And so we want you to please tell Miss Pollyanna that we understand it's all because of her. And please say we're so glad we know her that we thought, maybe if she knew it, it would make her a little glad that she knew us. And – and that's all,' sighed Milly, rising hurriedly to her feet. 'You'll tell her?'

'Why, of course,' murmured Miss Polly, wondering just how much of this remarkable discourse she could remember to tell.

These visits of John Pendleton and Milly Snow were only the first of many; and always there were the messages – the messages which were in some ways so curious that they caused Miss Polly more and more to puzzle over them.

One day there was the little Widow Benton. Miss Polly knew her well, though they had never called upon each other. By reputation she knew her as the saddest little woman in town – one who was always in black. Today, however, Mrs Benton wore a knot of pale blue at the throat, though there were tears in her eyes. She spoke of her grief and horror at the accident; then she asked diffidently if she might see Pollyanna.

Miss Polly shook her head.

'I am sorry, but she sees no one yet. A little later – perhaps.'

Mrs Benton wiped her eyes, rose, and turned to go. But after she had almost reached the hall door she came back hurriedly.

'Miss Harrington, perhaps you'd give her – a message,' she stammered.

'Certainly, Mrs Benton; I shall be very glad to.'

Still the little woman hesitated; then she spoke. 'Will you tell her, please, that – that I've put on *this*,' she said, just touching the blue bow at her throat. Then, at Miss Polly's ill-concealed look of surprise, she added: 'The little girl has been trying for so long to make me wear – some colour, that I thought she'd be – glad to know I'd begun. She said that Freddy would be so glad to see it, if I would. You know Freddy's *all* I have now. The others have all –' Mrs Benton shook her head and turned away. 'If you'll just tell Pollyanna – *she'll* understand.' And the door closed after her.

A little later, that same day, there was the other widow – at least, she wore widow's garments. Miss Polly did not know her at all. She wondered vaguely how Pollyanna could have known her. The lady gave her name as 'Mrs Tarbell'.

'I'm a stranger to you, of course,' she began at once. 'But I'm not a stranger to your little niece, Pollyanna. I've been at the hotel all summer, and every day I've had to take long walks for my health. It was on these walks that I've met your niece – she's such a dear little girl! I wish I could make you understand what she's been to me. I was very sad when I came up here; and her bright face and cheery ways reminded me of – my own little girl that I lost years ago. I was so shocked to hear of the accident; and then when I learned that the poor child would never walk again, and that she was so unhappy because she couldn't be glad any longer – the dear child! – I just had to come to you.'

'You are very kind,' murmured Miss Polly.

'But it is you who are to be kind,' demurred the other. 'I – I want you to give her a message from me. Will you?'

'Certainly.'

'Will you just tell her, then, that Mrs Tarbell is glad now. Yes, I know it sounds odd, and you don't understand. But – if you'll pardon me, I'd rather not explain.' Sad lines came to the lady's mouth, and the smile left her eyes. 'Your niece will know just what I mean; and I felt that I must tell – her. Thank you; and pardon me, please, for any seeming rudeness in my call,' she begged, as she took her leave.

Thoroughly mystified now, Miss Polly hurried upstairs to Pollyanna's room.

'Pollyanna, do you know a Mrs Tarbell?'

'Oh, yes. I love Mrs Tarbell. She's sick, and awfully sad; and she's at the hotel, and takes long walks. We go together. I mean – we used to.' Pollyanna's voice broke, and two big tears rolled down her cheeks.

Miss Polly cleared her throat hurriedly.

'Well, she's just been here, dear. She left a message for you – but she wouldn't tell me what it meant. She said to tell you that Mrs Tarbell is glad now.'

Pollyanna clapped her hands softly.

'Did she say that – really? Oh, I'm so glad!'

'But, Pollyanna, what did she mean?'

'Why, it's the game, and – ' Pollyanna stopped short, her fingers to her lips.

'What game?'

'N–nothing much, Aunt Polly; that is – I can't tell it unless I tell other things that – that I'm not to speak of.'

It was on Miss Polly's tongue to question her niece further; but the obvious distress on the little girl's face stayed the words before they were uttered.

Not long after Mrs Tarbell's visit the climax came. It came in the shape of a call from a certain young woman with unnaturally pink cheeks and abnormally yellow hair; a young woman who wore high heels and cheap jewellery; a young woman whom Miss Polly knew very well by reputation – but whom she was angrily amazed to meet beneath the roof of the Harrington homestead.

Miss Polly did not offer her hand. She drew back, indeed, as she entered the room.

The woman rose at once. Her eyes were very red, as if she had been crying. Half defiantly she asked if she might, for a moment, see the little girl, Pollyanna.

Miss Polly said no. She began to say it very sternly; but something in the woman's pleading eyes made her add the civil explanation that no one was allowed yet to see Pollyanna.

The woman hesitated; then a little brusquely she spoke. Her chin was still at a slightly defiant tilt.

'My name is Mrs Payson – Mrs Tom Payson. I presume you've heard of me – most of the good people in the town have – and maybe some of the things you've heard ain't true. But never mind that. It's about the little girl I came. I heard about the accident, and – and it broke me all up. Last week I heard how she couldn't ever walk again, and – and I wished I could give up my two uselessly well legs for hers. She'd do more good trotting around on 'em one hour than I could in a hundred years. But never mind that. Legs ain't always given to the one who can make the best use of 'em, I notice.'

She paused, and cleared her throat; but when she resumed her voice was still husky.

'Maybe you don't know it, but I've seen a good deal of that little girl of yours. We live on the Pendleton Hill Road, and she used to go by often – only she didn't always *go by*. She came in and played with the kids and talked to me – and my man, when he was home. She seemed to like it, and to like us. She didn't know, I suspect, that her kind of folks don't generally call on my kind. Maybe if they *did* call more, Miss Harrington, there wouldn't be so many – of my kind,' she added, with sudden bitterness.

'Be that as it may, she came; and she didn't do herself no harm, and she did do us good – a lot o' good. How much she won't know – nor can't know, I hope; 'cause if she did, she'd know other things – that I don't want her to know.

'But it's just this. It's been hard times with us this year, in more ways than one. We've been blue and discouraged – my man and me, and ready for – 'most anything. We was reckoning on getting a divorce about now, and letting the kids – well, we didn't know what we would do with the kids. Then came the accident, and what we heard about the little girl's never walking again. And we got to thinking how she used to come and sit on our doorstep and train with the kids, and laugh, and – and just be glad. She was always being glad about something; and then, one day, she told us why, and about the game, you know; and tried to coax us to play it.

'Well, we've heard now that she's fretting her poor little life out of her, because she can't play it no more – that there's nothing to be glad about. And that's what I came to tell her today – that maybe she can be a little glad for us, 'cause we've decided to stick to each other, and play the game ourselves. I knew she would be glad, because she used to feel kind of bad – at things we said, sometimes. Just how the game is going to help us, I can't say that I exactly see, yet; but maybe 'twill. Anyhow, we're going to try – 'cause she wanted us to. Will you tell her?'

'Yes, I will tell her,' promised Miss Polly, a little faintly. Then, with sudden impulse, she stepped forward and held out her hand. 'And thank you for coming, Mrs Payson,' she said simply.

The defiant chin fell. The lips above it trembled visibly. With an incoherently mumbled something, Mrs Payson blindly clutched at the outstretched hand, turned, and fled.

The door had scarcely closed behind her before Miss Polly was confronting Nancy in the kitchen.

'Nancy!'

Miss Polly spoke sharply. The series of puzzling, disconcerting visits of the last few days, culminating as they had in the extraordinary experience of the afternoon, had strained her nerves to the snapping point. Not since Miss Pollyanna's accident had Nancy heard her mistress speak so sternly.

'Nancy, *will* you tell me what this absurd "game" is that the whole town seems to be babbling about? And what, please, has my niece to do with it? *Why* does everybody, from Milly Snow to Mrs Tom Payson, send word to her that they're "playing it"? As near as I can judge, half the town are putting on blue ribbons, or stopping family quarrels, or learning to like something they never liked before, and all because of Pollyanna. I tried to ask the child herself about it, but I can't seem to make much headway, and of course I don't like to worry her – now. But from something I heard her say to you last night, I should judge you were one of them, too. Now *will* you tell me what it all means?'

To Miss Polly's surprise and dismay Nancy burst into tears.

'It means that ever since last June that blessed child has jest been makin' the whole town glad, an' now they're turnin' round an' tryin' ter make her a little glad, too.'

'Glad of what?'

'Just glad! That's the game.'

Miss Polly actually stamped her foot.

'There you go like all the rest, Nancy. *What* game?'

Nancy lifted her chin. She faced her mistress and looked her squarely in the eye.

'I'll tell ye, ma'am. It's a game Miss Pollyanna's father learned her ter play. She got a pair of crutches once in a missionary barrel when she was wantin' a doll; an' she cried, of course, like any child would. It seems 'twas then her father told her that there wasn't ever anythin' but what there was somethin' about it that you could be glad about; an' that she could be glad about them crutches.'

'Glad for – *crutches*!' Miss Polly choked back a sob – she was thinking of the helpless little legs on the bed upstairs.

'Yes'm. That's what I said, an' Miss Pollyanna said that's what *she* said too. But he told her she *could* be glad – 'cause she *didn't need 'em.*'

'Oh–h!' cried Miss Polly.

'And after that she said he made a regular game of it – findin' somethin' in everythin' ter be glad about. An' she said she could do it too, and that she didn't seem ter mind not havin' the doll so much, 'cause she was so glad she *didn't* need the crutches. An' they called it the "jest bein' glad game". That's the game, ma'am. She's played it ever since.'

'But, how – how – ' Miss Polly came to a helpless pause.

'An' you'd be surprised ter find how cute it works, ma'am, too,' maintained Nancy, with almost the eagerness of Pollyanna herself. 'I wish I could tell ye what a lot she's done for mother an' the folks out at home. She's been ter see 'em, ye know, twice, with me. She's made me glad, too, on such a lot o' things – little things, an' big things; an' it's made 'em so much easier. For instance, I don't mind "Nancy" for a name half as much since she told me I could be glad 'twa'n't "Hephzibah". An' there's Monday mornin's, too, that I used ter hate so. She's actually made me glad for Monday mornin's.'

'Glad – for Monday mornings!'

Nancy laughed.

'I know it does sound nutty, ma'am. But let me tell ye. That blessed lamb found out I hated Monday mornin's somethin' awful; an' what does she up an' tell me one day but this: "Well, anyhow, Nancy, I should think you could be gladder on Monday mornin' than on any other day in the week, because 'twould be a whole *week* before you'd have another one!" An' I'm blest if I hain't thought of it ev'ry Monday mornin' since – an' it *has* helped, ma'am. It made me laugh, anyhow, ev'ry time I thought of it; an' laughin' helps, ye know – it does, it does!'

'But why hasn't – she told me – the game?' faltered Miss Polly. 'Why has she made such a mystery of it, when I asked her?'

Nancy hesitated.

'Beggin' yer pardon, ma'am, you told her not ter speak of – her father; so she couldn't tell ye. 'Twas her father's game, ye see.'

Miss Polly bit her lip.

'She wanted ter tell ye, first off,' continued Nancy, a little unsteadily. 'She wanted somebody ter play it with, ye know. That's why I begun it – so she could have someone.'

'And – and – these others?' Miss Polly's voice shook now.

'Oh, ev'rybody, 'most, knows it now, I guess. Anyhow, I should think they did from the way I'm hearin' of it ev'rywhere I go. Of course she told a lot, and they told the rest. Them things go, ye know, when they gets started. An' she was always so smilin' an' pleasant ter ev'ryone, an' so – so jest glad herself all the time, that they couldn't help knowin' it, anyhow. Now, since she's hurt, ev'rybody feels so bad – specially when they heard how bad *she* feels 'cause she can't find anythin' ter be glad about. An' so they've been comin' ev'ry day ter tell her how glad she's made *them*, hopin' that'll help some. Ye see, she's always wanted ev'rybody ter play the game with her.'

'Well, I know somebody who'll play it – now,' choked Miss Polly, as she turned and sped through the kitchen doorway.

Behind her, Nancy stood staring amazedly.

'Well, I'll believe anythin' – anythin' now,' she muttered to herself. 'Ye can't stump me with anythin' I wouldn't believe now – o' Miss Polly!'

A little later, in Pollyanna's room, the nurse left Miss Polly and Pollyanna alone together.

'And you've had still another caller today, my dear,' announced Miss Polly, in a voice she vainly tried to steady. 'Do you remember Mrs Payson?'

'Mrs Payson? Why, I reckon I do! She lives on the way to Mr Pendleton's, and she's got the prettiest little girl baby three years old, and a boy 'most five. She's awfully nice, and so's her husband – only they don't seem to know how nice each other is. Sometimes they fight – I mean, they don't quite agree. They're poor, too, they say, and of course they don't ever have barrels, 'cause he isn't a missionary minister, you know, like – well, he isn't.'

A faint colour stole into Pollyanna's cheeks which was duplicated suddenly in those of her aunt.

'But she wears real pretty clothes, sometimes, in spite of their being so poor,' resumed Pollyanna, in some haste. 'And she's got perfectly beautiful rings with diamonds and rubies and emeralds in them; but she says she's got one ring too many, and that she's going to throw it away and get a divorce instead. What is a divorce, Aunt Polly? I'm afraid it isn't very nice, because she didn't look happy when she talked about it. And she said if she did get it, they wouldn't live there any more, and that Mr Payson would go 'way off, and maybe the children, too. But I should think they'd rather keep the ring, even if they did have so many more. Shouldn't you? Aunt Polly, what is a divorce?'

'But they aren't going 'way off, dear,' evaded Aunt Polly hurriedly. 'They're going to stay right there together.'

'Oh, I'm so glad! Then they'll be there when I go up to see – Oh, dear!' broke off the little girl, miserably. 'Aunt Polly, why *can't* I remember that my legs don't go any more, and that I won't ever, ever go up to see Mr Pendleton again?'

'There, there, don't,' choked her aunt. 'Perhaps you'll drive up sometime. But listen! I haven't told you, yet, all that Mrs Payson said. She wanted me to tell you that they – they were going to stay together and to play the game, just as you wanted them to.'

Pollyanna smiled through tear-wet eyes. 'Are they? Are they, really? Oh, I am glad of that!'

'Yes, she said she hoped you'd be. That's why she told you, to make you – *glad*, Pollyanna.'

Pollyanna looked up quickly.

'Why, Aunt Polly, you – you spoke just as if you knew – *Do* you know about the game, Aunt Polly?'

'Yes, dear.' Miss Polly sternly forced her voice to be cheerfully matter-of-fact. 'Nancy told me. I think it's a beautiful game. I'm going to play it now – with you.'

'Oh, Aunt Polly – *you*? I'm so glad! You see, I've really wanted you most of anybody, all the time.'

Aunt Polly caught her breath a little sharply. It was even harder this time to keep her voice steady, but she did it.

'Yes, dear; and there are all those others, too. Why, Pollyanna, I think all the town is playing that game now with you – even to the minister! I haven't had a chance to tell you yet, but this morning I met Mr Ford when I was down to the village, and he told me to say to you that just as soon as you could see him, he was coming to tell you that he hadn't stopped being glad over those eight hundred rejoicing texts that you told him about. So you see, dear, it's just you that have done it. The whole town is playing the game, and the whole town is wonderfully happier – and all because of one little girl who taught the people a new game, and how to play it.'

Pollyanna clapped her hands.

'Oh, I'm so glad,' she cried. Then, suddenly, a wonderful light illumined her face. 'Why, Aunt Polly, there *is* something I can be glad about, after all. I can be glad I've *had* my legs, anyway – else I couldn't have done – that!'

CHAPTER 29

Through an Open Window

One by one the short winter days came and went – but they were not short to Pollyanna. They were long, and sometimes full of pain. Very resolutely, these days, however, Pollyanna was turning a cheerful face towards whatever came. Was she not specially bound to play the game, now that Aunt Polly was playing it too? And Aunt Polly found so many things to be glad about! It was Aunt Polly, too, who discovered the story one day about the two poor little waifs in a snowstorm who found a blown-down door to crawl under, and who wondered what poor folks did that didn't have any door! And it was Aunt Polly who brought home the other story that she had heard about the poor old lady who had only two teeth, but who was so glad that those two teeth 'hit'!

Pollyanna now, like Mrs Snow, was knitting wonderful things out of bright-coloured worsteds that trailed their cheery lengths across the white spread, and made Pollyanna – again like Mrs Snow – so glad she had her hands and arms, anyway.

Pollyanna saw people now, occasionally, and always there were the loving messages from those she could not see; and always they brought her something new to think about – and Pollyanna needed new things to think about.

Once she had seen John Pendleton, and twice she had seen Jimmy Bean. John Pendleton had told her what a fine boy Jimmy was getting to be, and how well he was doing. Jimmy had told her what a first-rate home he had, and what bang-up 'folks' Mr Pendleton made; and both had said that it was all owing to her.

'Which makes me all the gladder, you know, that I *have* had my legs,' Pollyanna confided to her aunt afterwards.

The winter passed, and spring came. The anxious watchers over Pollyanna's condition could see little change wrought by the prescribed treatment. There seemed every reason to believe, indeed, that Dr Mead's worst fears would be realised – that Pollyanna would never walk again.

Beldingsville, of course, kept itself informed concerning Pollyanna; and of Beldingsville, one man in particular fumed and fretted himself into a fever of anxiety over the daily bulletins which he managed in some way to procure from the bed of suffering. As the days passed, however, and the news came to be no better, but rather worse, something besides anxiety began to show in the man's face: despair and a very dogged determination, each fighting for the mastery. In the end the dogged determination won; and it was then that Mr John Pendleton, somewhat to his surprise, received one Saturday morning a call from Dr Thomas Chilton.

'Pendleton,' began the doctor abruptly, 'I've come to you because you, better than anyone else in town, know something of my relations with Miss Polly Harrington.'

John Pendleton was conscious that he must have started visibly – he did know something of the affair between Polly Harrington and Thomas Chilton, but the matter had not been mentioned between them for fifteen years, or more.

'Yes,' he said, trying to make his voice sound concerned enough for sympathy, and not eager enough for curiosity. In a moment he saw that he need not have worried, however; the doctor was quite too intent on his errand to notice how that errand was received.

'Pendleton, I want to see that child. I want to make an examination. I *must* make an examination.'

'Well – can't you?'

'*Can't* I! Pendleton, you know very well I haven't been inside that door for more than fifteen years. You don't know – but I will tell you – that the mistress of that house told me that the *next* time she *asked* me to enter it, I might take it that she was begging my pardon, and that all would be as before – which meant that she'd marry me. Perhaps you see her summoning me now – but I don't!'

'But couldn't you go – without a summons?'

The doctor frowned. 'Well, hardly. *I* have some pride, you know.'

'But if you're so anxious – couldn't you swallow your pride and forget the quarrel.'

'Forget the quarrel!' interrupted the doctor savagely. 'I'm not talking of that kind of pride. So far as *that* is concerned, I'd go from here to there on my knees – or on my head – if that would do any good. It's *professional* pride I'm talking about. It's a case of sickness, and I'm a doctor. I can't butt in and say, "Here, take me!" – can I?'

'Chilton, what *was* the quarrel?' demanded Pendleton.

The doctor made an impatient gesture, and got to his feet. 'What was it? What's any lovers' quarrel – after it's over?' he snarled, pacing the room angrily. 'A silly wrangle over the size of the moon or the depth of a river, maybe – it might as well be, so far as its having any real significance compared to the years of misery that follow it! Never mind the quarrel! So far as I am concerned, I am willing to say there was no quarrel. Pendleton, I must see that child. It may mean life or death. It will mean – I honestly believe – nine chances out of ten that Pollyanna Whittier will walk again!'

The words were spoken clearly, impressively; and they were spoken just as the one who uttered them had almost reached the open window near John Pendleton's chair. Thus it happened that very distinctly they reached the ears of a small boy kneeling beneath the window on the ground outside.

Jimmy Bean, at his Saturday-morning task of pulling up the first little green weeds from the flower-beds, sat up with ears and eyes wide open.

'Walk! Pollyanna!' John Pendleton was saying. 'What do you mean?'

'I mean that from what I can hear and learn – a mile from her bedside – her case is very much like one that a college friend of mine has just helped. For years he's been making this sort of thing a special study. I've kept in touch with him, and studied, too, in a way. And from what I hear – but I want to *see* the girl!'

John Pendleton came erect in his chair.

'You must see her, man! Couldn't you – say, through Dr Warren?'

The other shook his head.

'I'm afraid not. Warren has been very decent, though. He told me himself that he suggested consultation with me at the first, but – Miss Harrington said no so decisively that he didn't dare venture it again, even though he knew of my desire to see the child. Lately, some of his best patients have come over to me – so of course that ties my hands still more effectually. But, Pendleton, I've got to see that child! Think of what it may mean to her – if I do!'

'Yes, and think of what it will mean – if you don't!' retorted Pendleton.

'But how can I – without a direct request from her aunt? – which I'll never get!'

'She must be made to ask you!'

'How?'

'I don't know.'

'No, I guess you don't – nor anybody else. She's too proud and too angry to ask me – after what she said years ago it would mean if she did ask me. But when I think of that child, doomed to lifelong misery, and when I think that maybe in my hands lies a chance of escape, but for that confounded nonsense we call pride and professional etiquette, I – ' He did not finish his sentence, but with his hands thrust deep into his pockets he turned and began to tramp up and down the room again, angrily.

'But if she could be made to see – to understand,' urged John Pendleton.

'Yes; and who's going to do it?' demanded the doctor, with a savage turn.

'I don't know, I don't know,' groaned the other miserably.

Outside the window Jimmy Bean stirred suddenly. Up to now he had scarcely breathed, so intently had he listened to every word.

'Well, by Jinks, I know!' he whispered exultingly. '*I'm* a-goin' ter do it!' And forthwith he rose to his feet, crept stealthily round the corner of the house, and ran with all his might down Pendleton Hill.

CHAPTER 30

Jimmy Takes the Helm

'It's Jimmy Bean. He wants ter see ye, ma'am,' announced Nancy in the doorway.

'Me?' rejoined Miss Polly, plainly surprised. 'Are you sure he did not mean Miss Pollyanna? He may see her a few minutes today, if he likes.'

'Yes'm. I told him. But he said it was you he wanted.'

'Very well, I'll come down.' And Miss Polly arose from her chair a little wearily.

In the sitting-room she found waiting for her a round-eyed, flushed-faced boy, who began to speak at once.

'Ma'am, I s'pose it's dreadful – what I'm doin', an' what I'm sayin'; but I can't help it. It's for Pollyanna, and I'd walk over hot coals for her, or face you, or – or anythin' like that, any time. An' I think you would, too, if you thought there *was* a chance for her ter walk again. An' so that's why I come ter tell ye that as long as it's only pride an' et – et – somethin' that's keepin' Pollyanna from walkin', why I knew you *would* ask Dr Chilton here if you understood.'

'Wh–at?' interrupted Miss Polly, the look of stupefaction on her face changing to one of angry indignation.

Jimmy sighed despairingly. 'There, I didn't mean ter make ye mad. That's why I begun by tellin' ye about her walkin' again. I thought you'd listen ter that.'

'Jimmy, what are you talking about?'

Jimmy sighed again. 'That's what I'm tryin' ter tell ye.'

'Well, then tell me. But begin at the beginning, and be sure I understand each thing as you go. Don't plunge into the middle of it as you did before – and mix everything all up!'

Jimmy wet his lips determinedly.

'Well, ter begin with, Dr Chilton come ter see Mr Pendleton, an' they talked in the library. Do you understand that?'

'Yes, Jimmy.' Miss Polly's voice was rather faint.

'Well, the window was open, and I was weedin' the flower-bed under it; an' I heard 'em talk.'

'Oh, Jimmy! *Listening?*'

' 'Twa'n't about me, an' 'twa'n't sneak listenin',' bridled Jimmy. 'And I'm glad I listened. You will be when I tell ye. Why, it may make Pollyanna – walk!'

'Jimmy, what do you mean?' Miss Polly was leaning forward eagerly.

'There, I told ye so,' nodded Jimmy contentedly. 'Well, Dr Chilton knows some doctor somewhere that can cure Pollyanna, he thinks – make her walk, ye know; but he can't tell sure till he *sees* her. And he wants ter see her somethin' awful, but he told Mr Pendleton that you wouldn't let him.'

Miss Polly's face turned very red.

'But, Jimmy, I – I can't – I couldn't! That is, I didn't know!' Miss Polly was twisting her fingers together helplessly.

'Yes, an' that's why I come ter tell ye, so you *would* know,' asserted Jimmy eagerly. 'They said that for some reason – I didn't rightly catch what – you wouldn't let Dr Chilton come, an' you told Dr Warren so; an' Dr Chilton couldn't come himself, without you asked him, on account of pride an' professional et – et – well, et– somethin', anyway. An' they was wishin' somebody could make you understand, only they didn't know who could; an' I was outside the winder, an' I says ter myself right away, "By Jinks, I'll do it!" An' I come – an' have I made ye understand?'

'Yes; but, Jimmy, about that doctor,' implored Miss Polly feverishly. 'Who was he? What does he do? Are they *sure* he could make Pollyanna – walk?'

'I don't know who he was. They didn't say. Dr Chilton knows him, an' he's just cured somebody just like her, Dr Chilton thinks. Anyhow, they didn't seem ter be doin' no worryin' about *him*. 'Twas *you* they was worryin' about, 'cause you wouldn't let Dr Chilton see her. An' say – you will let him come, won't you? – now you understand?'

Miss Polly turned her head from side to side. Her breath was coming in little uneven, rapid gasps.

Jimmy, watching her with anxious eyes, thought she was going to cry. But she did not cry. After a minute she said brokenly: 'Yes – I'll let – Dr Chilton – see her. Now run home, Jimmy – quick! I've got to speak to Dr Warren. He's upstairs now. I saw him drive in a few minutes ago.'

A little later Dr Warren was surprised to meet an agitated, flushed-faced Miss Polly in the hall. He was still more surprised to hear the lady say, a little breathlessly: 'Dr Warren, you asked me once to allow Dr Chilton to be called in in consultation, and – I refused. Since then I have reconsidered. I very much desire that you *should* call in Dr Chilton. Will you not ask him at once – please? Thank you.'

CHAPTER 31

A New Uncle

The next time Dr Warren entered the chamber where Pollyanna lay watching the dancing shimmer of colour on the ceiling, a tall, broad-shouldered man followed close behind him.

'Dr Chilton! – oh, Dr Chilton, how glad I am to see *you*!' cried Pollyanna. And at the joyous rapture of the voice, more than one pair of eyes in the room brimmed hot with sudden tears. 'But, of course, if Aunt Polly doesn't want – '

'It is all right, my dear; don't worry,' soothed Miss Polly agitatedly, hurrying forward. 'I have told Dr Chilton that – that I want him to look you over – with Dr Warren, this morning.'

'Oh, then you asked him to come,' murmured Pollyanna contentedly.

'Yes, dear, I asked him. That is – ' But it was too late. The adoring happiness that had leaped to Dr Chilton's eyes was unmistakable, and Miss Polly had seen it. With very pink cheeks she turned and left the room hurriedly.

Over in the window the nurse and Dr Warren were talking earnestly. Dr Chilton held out both his hands to Pollyanna.

'Little girl, I'm thinking that one of the very gladdest jobs you ever did has been done today,' he said in a voice shaken with emotion.

At twilight a wonderfully tremulous, wonderfully different Aunt Polly crept to Pollyanna's bedside. The nurse was at supper. They had the room to themselves.

'Pollyanna, dear, I'm going to tell you – the very first one of all. Someday I'm going to give Dr Chilton to you for your – uncle. And it's you that have done it all. Oh, Pollyanna, I'm so – happy! And so – glad! – darling!'

Pollyanna began to clap her hands; but even as she brought her small palms together the first time, she stopped, and held them suspended.

'Aunt Polly, Aunt Polly, were *you* the woman's hand and heart he wanted so long ago? You were – I know you were! And that's what he meant by saying I'd done the gladdest job of all – today. I'm so glad! Why, Aunt Polly, I don't know but I'm so glad that I don't mind even my legs, now!'

Aunt Polly swallowed a sob.

'Perhaps, someday, dear – '

But Aunt Polly did not finish. Aunt Polly did not dare to tell, yet, the great hope that Dr Chilton had put into her heart. But she did say this – and surely this was quite wonderful enough – to Pollyanna's mind: 'Pollyanna, next week you're going to take a journey. On a nice comfortable little bed you're going to be carried in cars and carriages to a great doctor who has a big house many miles from here made on purpose for just such people as you are. He's a dear friend of Dr Chilton's, and we're going to see what he can do for you!'

CHAPTER 32

Which is a Letter from Pollyanna

DEAR AUNT POLLY AND UNCLE TOM – Oh, I can – I can – I *can* walk! I did today all the way from my bed to the window! It was six steps. My, how good it was to be on legs again!

All the doctors stood around and smiled, and all the nurses stood beside of them and cried. A lady in the next ward who walked last week first, peeked into the door, and another one who hopes she can walk next month, was invited in to the party, and she lay on my nurse's bed and clapped her hands. Even Black Tilly, who washes the floor, looked through the piazza window and called me 'Honey, child' when she wasn't crying too much to call me anything.

I don't see why they cried. I wanted to sing and shout and yell! Oh – oh – oh! Just think, I can walk – walk – *walk*! Now I don't mind being here almost ten months, and I didn't miss the wedding, anyhow. Wasn't that just like you, Aunt Polly, to come on here and get married right beside my bed, so I could see you. You always do think of the gladdest things!

Pretty soon, they say, I shall go home. I wish I could walk all the way there. I do. I don't think I shall ever want to ride anywhere any more. It will be so good just to walk. Oh, I'm so glad! I'm glad for everything. Why, I'm glad now I lost my legs for a while, for you never, never know how perfectly lovely legs are till you haven't got them – that go, I mean. I'm going to walk eight steps tomorrow.

With heaps of love to everybody,

POLLYANNA

POLLYANNA GROWS UP

Pollyanna Grows Up

ELEANOR H. PORTER

CONTENTS

CHAPTER I

Della Speaks Her Mind

Della Wetherby tripped up the somewhat imposing steps of her sister's Commonwealth Avenue home and pressed an energetic finger against the electric-bell button. From the tip of her wing-trimmed hat to the toe of her low-heeled shoe she radiated health, capability and alert decision. Even her voice, as she greeted the maid who opened the door, vibrated with the joy of living.

'Good-morning, Mary. Is my sister in?'

'Y–yes, ma'am, Mrs Carew is in,' hesitated the girl; 'but – she gave orders she'd see no one.'

'Did she? Well, I'm no one,' smiled Miss Wetherby, 'so she'll see me. Don't worry – I'll take the blame,' she nodded, in answer to the frighten(ed remonstrance in the girl's eyes. 'Where is she – in her sitting-room?'

'Y–yes, ma'am; but – that is, she said – ' Miss Wetherby, however, was already halfway up the broad stairway; and, with a despairing backward glance, the maid turned away.

In the hall above Della Wetherby unhesitatingly walked towards a half-open door and knocked.

'Well, Mary,' answered a 'dear-me-what-now' voice. 'Haven't I – Oh, Della!' The voice grew suddenly warm with love and surprise. 'You dear girl, where did you come from?'

'Yes, it's Della,' smiled that young woman, blithely, already half-way across the room. 'I've come from an over-Sunday at the beach with two of the other nurses, and I'm on my way back to the Sanatorium now. That is, I'm here now, but I shan't be long. I stepped in for – this,' she finished, giving the owner of the 'dear-me-what-now' voice a hearty kiss.

Mrs Carew frowned and drew back a little coldly. The slight

touch of joy and animation that had come into her face fled, leaving only a dispirited fretfulness that was plainly very much at home there.

'Oh, of course! I might have known,' she said. 'You never stay – here.'

'Here!' Della Wetherby laughed merrily, and threw up her hands; then, abruptly, her voice and manner changed. She regarded her sister with grave, tender eyes. 'Ruth, dear, I couldn't – I just couldn't live in this house. You know I couldn't,' she finished gently.

Mrs Carew stirred irritably.

'I'm sure I don't see why not,' she fenced.

Della Wetherby shook her head.

'Yes, you do, dear. You know I'm entirely out of sympathy with it all: the gloom, the lack of aim, the insistence on misery and bitterness.'

'But I *am* miserable and bitter.'

'You ought not to be.'

'Why not? What have I to make me otherwise?'

Della Wetherby gave an impatient gesture.

'Ruth, look here,' she challenged. 'You're thirty-three years old. You have good health – or would have, if you treated yourself properly – and you certainly have an abundance of time and a superabundance of money. Surely anybody would say you ought to find *something* to do this glorious morning besides sitting moped up in this tomb-like house with instructions to the maid that you'll see no one.'

'But I don't *want* to see anybody.'

'Then I'd *make* myself want to.'

Mrs Carew sighed wearily and turned away her head.

'Oh, Della, why won't you ever understand? I'm not like you. I can't – forget.'

A swift pain crossed the younger woman's face.

'You mean Jamie, I suppose. I don't forget that, dear. I couldn't, of course. But moping won't help us find him.'

'As if I hadn't *tried* to find him, for eight long years – and by something besides moping,' flashed Mrs Carew, indignantly, with a sob in her voice.

'Of course you have, dear,' soothed the other, quickly; 'and we shall keep on hunting, both of us, till we do find him – or die. But *this* sort of thing doesn't help.'

'But I don't want to do – anything else,' murmured Ruth Carew, drearily.

For a moment there was silence. The younger woman sat regarding her sister with troubled, disapproving eyes.

'Ruth,' she said, at last, with a touch of exasperation, 'forgive me, but – are you always going to be like this? You're widowed, I'll admit; but your married life lasted only a year, and your husband was much older than yourself. You were little more than a child at the time, and that one short year can't seem much more than a dream now. Surely that ought not to embitter your whole life!'

'No, oh, no,' murmured Mrs Carew, still drearily.

'Then *are* you going to be always like this?'

'Well, of course, if I could find Jamie – '

'Yes, yes, I know; but, Ruth, dear, isn't there anything in the world but Jamie – to make you *any* happy?'

'There doesn't seem to be, that I can think of,' sighed Mrs Carew, indifferently.

'Ruth!' ejaculated her sister, stung into something very like anger. Then suddenly she laughed. 'Oh, Ruth, Ruth, I'd like to give you a dose of Pollyanna. I don't know anyone who needs it more!'

Mrs Carew stiffened a little.

'Well, what pollyanna may be I don't know, but whatever it is, I don't want it,' she retorted sharply, nettled in her turn. 'This isn't your beloved Sanatorium, and I'm not your patient to be dosed and bossed, please remember.'

Della Wetherby's eyes danced, but her lips remained unsmiling.

'Pollyanna isn't a medicine, my dear,' she said demurely, ' – though I have heard some people call her a tonic. Pollyanna is a little girl.'

'A child? Well, how should I know,' retorted the other, still aggrievedly. 'You have your "belladonna", so I'm sure I don't see why not "pollyanna". Besides, you're always recommending something for me to take, and you distinctly said "dose" – and dose usually means medicine, of a sort.'

'Well, Pollyanna *is* a medicine – of a sort,' smiled Della. 'Anyway, the Sanatorium doctors all declare that she's better than any medicine they can give. She's a little girl, Ruth, twelve or thirteen years old, who was at the Sanatorium all last summer and most of the winter. I didn't see her but a month or two, for she left soon after I arrived. But that was long enough for me to come fully under her spell. Besides, the whole Sanatorium is still talking Pollyanna, and playing her game.'

'*Game!*'

'Yes,' nodded Della, with a curious smile. 'Her "glad game". I'll never forget my first introduction to it. One feature of her treatment was particularly disagreeable and even painful. It came every Tuesday morning, and very soon after my arrival it fell to my lot to give it to her. I was dreading it, for I knew from past experience with other children what to expect: fretfulness and tears, if nothing worse. To my unbounded amazement she greeted me with a smile and said she was glad to see me; and, if you'll believe it, there was never so much as a whimper from her lips through the whole ordeal, though I knew I was hurting her cruelly.

'I fancy I must have said something that showed my surprise, for she explained earnestly: "Oh, yes, I used to feel that way, too, and I did dread it so, till I happened to think 'twas just like Nancy's washdays, and I could be gladdest of all on *Tuesdays*, 'cause there wouldn't be another one for a whole week." '

'Why, how extraordinary!' frowned Mrs Carew, not quite comprehending. 'But, I'm sure I don't see any *game* to that.'

'No, I didn't, till later. Then she told me. It seems she was the motherless daughter of a poor minister in the West, and was brought up by the Ladies' Aid Society and missionary barrels. When she was a tiny girl she wanted a doll, and confidently expected it in the next barrel; but there turned out to be nothing but a pair of little crutches.

'The child cried, of course, and it was then that her father taught her the game of hunting for something to be glad about, in everything that happened; and he said she could begin right then by being glad she didn't *need* the crutches. That was the beginning. Pollyanna said it was a lovely game, and she'd been playing it ever since; and that the harder it was to find the glad part, the more fun it was, except when it was too *awful* hard, like she had found it sometimes.'

'Why, how extraordinary!' murmured Mrs Carew, still not entirely comprehending.

'You'd think so – if you could see the results of that game in the Sanatorium,' nodded Della; 'and Dr Ames says he hears she's revolutionised the whole town she comes from, just the same way. He knows Dr Chilton very well – the man that married Pollyanna's aunt. And, by the way, I believe that marriage was one of her ministrations. She patched up an old lovers' quarrel between them.

'You see, two years ago, or more, Pollyanna's father died, and the little girl was sent East to this aunt. In October she was hurt by an automobile, and was told she could never walk again. In April Dr Chilton sent her to the Sanatorium, and she was there till last March – almost a year. She went home practically cured. You should have seen the child! There was just one cloud to mar her happiness: that she couldn't *walk* all the way there. As near as I can gather, the whole town turned out to meet her with brass bands and banners.

'But you can't *tell* about Pollyanna. One has to *see* her. And that's why I say I wish you could have a dose of Pollyanna. It would do you a world of good.'

Mrs Carew lifted her chin a little.

'Really, indeed, I must say I beg to differ with you,' she returned coldly. 'I don't care to be "revolutionised", and I have no lovers' quarrel to be patched up; and if there is *anything* that would be insufferable to me, it would be a little Miss Prim with a long face preaching to me how much I had to be thankful for. I never could bear – '

But a ringing laugh interrupted her. 'Oh, Ruth, Ruth,' choked her sister, gleefully. 'Miss Prim, indeed – *Pollyanna*! Oh, oh, if only you could see that child now! But there, I might have known. I *said* one couldn't *tell* about Pollyanna. And of course there's no way you can see her. But – Miss Prim, indeed!' And off she went into another gale of laughter. Almost at once, however, she sobered and gazed at her sister with the old troubled look in her eyes.

'Seriously, dear, can't anything be done?' she pleaded. 'You ought not to waste your life like this. Won't you try to get out a little more, and – meet people?'

'Why should I, when I don't want to? I'm tired of – people. You know society always bored me.'

'Then why not try some sort of work – charity?'

Mrs Carew gave an impatient gesture.

'Della, dear, we've been all over this before. I do give money – lots of it, and that's enough. In fact, I'm not sure but it's too much. I don't believe in pauperising people.'

'But if you'd give a little of yourself, dear,' ventured Della, gently. 'If you could only get interested in something outside of your own life, it would help so much; and – '

'Now, Della, dear,' interrupted the elder sister, restively, 'I love you, and I love to have you come here; but I simply cannot endure being preached to. It's all very well for you to turn yourself into an angel of mercy and give cups of cold water, and bandage up broken heads, and all that. Perhaps *you* can forget Jamie that way; but I couldn't. It would only make me think of him all the more, wondering if *he* had anyone to give him water and bandage up his head. Besides, the whole thing would be very distasteful to me – mixing with all sorts and kinds of people like that.'

'Did you ever try it?'

'Why, no, of course not!' Mrs Carew's voice was scornfully indignant.

'Then how can you know – till you do try?' asked the young nurse, rising to her feet a little wearily. 'But I must go, dear. I'm to meet the girls at the South Station. Our train goes at twelve-thirty. I'm sorry if I've made you cross with me,' she finished, as she kissed her sister goodbye.

'I'm not cross with you, Della,' sighed Mrs Carew; 'but if you only would understand!'

One minute later Della Wetherby made her way through the silent, gloomy halls, and out to the street. Face, step and manner were very different from what they had been when she tripped up the steps less than half an hour before. All the alertness, the springiness, the joy of living were gone. For half a block she listlessly dragged one foot after the other. Then, suddenly, she threw back her head and drew a long breath.

'One week in that house would kill me,' she shuddered. 'I don't believe even Pollyanna herself could so much as make a dent in the gloom! And the only thing she could be glad for there would be that she didn't have to stay.'

That this avowed disbelief in Pollyanna's ability to bring about a change for the better in Mrs Carew's home was not Della Wetherby's real opinion, however, was quickly proved; for no sooner had the nurse reached the Sanatorium than she learned something that sent her flying back over the fifty-mile journey to Boston the very next day.

So exactly as before did she find circumstances at her sister's home that it seemed almost as if Mrs Carew had not moved since she left her.

'Ruth,' she burst out eagerly, after answering her sister's surprised greeting, 'I just *had* to come, and you must, this once, yield to me and let me have my way. Listen! You can have that little Pollyanna here, I think, if you will.'

'But I won't,' returned Mrs Carew, with chilly promptness.

Della Wetherby did not seem to have heard. She plunged on excitedly. 'When I got back yesterday I found that Dr Ames had had a letter from Dr Chilton, the one who married Pollyanna's aunt, you know. Well, it seems in it he said he was going to Germany for the winter for a special course, and was going to take his wife with him, if he could persuade her that Pollyanna would be all right in some boarding school here meantime. But Mrs Chilton didn't want to leave Pollyanna in just a school, and so he was afraid she wouldn't go. And now, Ruth, there's our chance. I want *you* to take Pollyanna this winter, and let her go to some school around here.'

'What an absurd idea, Della! As if I wanted a child here to bother with!'

'She won't bother a bit. She must be nearly or quite thirteen by this time, and she's the most capable little thing you ever saw.'

'I don't like "capable" children,' retorted Mrs Carew perversely –

but she laughed; and because she did laugh, her sister took sudden courage and redoubled her efforts.

Perhaps it was the suddenness of the appeal, or the novelty of it. Perhaps it was because the story of Pollyanna had somehow touched Ruth Carew's heart. Perhaps it was only her unwillingness to refuse her sister's impassioned plea. Whatever it was that finally turned the scale, when Della Wetherby took her hurried leave half an hour later, she carried with her Ruth Carew's promise to receive Pollyanna into her home.

'But just remember,' Mrs Carew warned her at parting, 'just remember that the minute that child begins to preach to me and to tell me to count my mercies, back she goes to you, and you may do what you please with her. *I* shan't keep her!'

'I'll remember – but I'm not worrying any,' nodded the younger woman, in farewell. To herself she whispered, as she hurried away from the house: 'Half my job is done. Now for the other half – to get Pollyanna to come. But she's just got to come. I'll write that letter so they can't help letting her come!'

CHAPTER 2

Some Old Friends

In Beldingsville that August day, Mrs Chilton waited until Pollyanna had gone to bed before she spoke to her husband about the letter that had come in the morning mail. For that matter, she would have had to wait, anyway, for crowded office hours and the doctor's two long drives over the hills had left no time for domestic conferences.

It was about half-past nine, indeed, when the doctor entered his wife's sitting-room. His tired face lighted at sight of her, but at once a perplexed questioning came to his eyes.

'Why, Polly, dear, what is it?' he asked concernedly.

His wife gave a rueful laugh.

'Well, it's a letter – though I didn't mean you should find out by just looking at me.'

'Then you mustn't look so I can,' he smiled. 'But what is it?'

Mrs Chilton hesitated, pursed her lips, then picked up a letter near her.

'I'll read it to you,' she said. 'It's from a Miss Della Wetherby at Dr Ames's Sanatorium.'

'All right. Fire away,' directed the man, throwing himself at full length on to the couch near his wife's chair.

But his wife did not at once 'fire away'. She got up first and covered her husband's recumbent figure with a grey worsted afghan. Mrs Chilton's wedding day was but a year behind her. She was forty-two now. It seemed sometimes as if into that one short year of wifehood she had tried to crowd all the loving service and 'babying' that had been accumulating through twenty years of lovelessness and loneliness. Nor did the doctor – who had been forty-five on his wedding day, and who could remember nothing but loneliness and lovelessness – on his part object in the least to this concentrated 'tending'. He acted, indeed, as if he quite enjoyed it – though he was careful not to show it too ardently: he had discovered that Mrs Polly had for so long been Miss Polly that she was inclined to retreat in a panic and dub her ministrations 'silly', if they were received with too much notice and eagerness. So he contented himself now with a mere pat of her hand as she gave the afghan a final smooth, and settled herself to read the letter aloud.

'My dear Mrs Chilton – Just six times I have commenced a letter to you, and torn it up; so now I have decided not to "commence" at all, but just to tell you what I want at once. I want Pollyanna. May I have her?

I met you and your husband last March when you came on to take Pollyanna home, but I presume you don't remember me. I am asking Dr Ames (who does know me very well) to write your husband, so that you may (I hope) not fear to trust your dear little niece to us.

I understand that you would go to Germany with your husband

but for leaving Pollyanna; and so I am making so bold as to ask you to let us take her. Indeed, I am begging you to let us have her, dear Mrs Chilton. And now let me tell you why.

My sister, Mrs Carew, is a lonely, broken-hearted, discontented, unhappy woman. She lives in a world of gloom, into which no sunshine penetrates. Now I believe that if anything on earth can bring the sunshine into her life, it is your niece, Pollyanna. Won't you let her try? I wish I could tell you what she has done for the Sanatorium here, but nobody could *tell*. You would have to see it. I long ago discovered that you can't *tell* about Pollyanna. The minute you try to, she sounds priggish and preachy, and – impossible. Yet you and I know she is anything but that. You just have to bring Pollyanna on to the scene and let her speak for herself. And so I want to take her to my sister – and let her speak for herself. She would attend school, of course, but meanwhile I truly believe she would be healing the wound in my sister's heart.

I don't know how to end this letter. I believe it's harder than it was to begin it. I'm afraid I don't want to end it at all. I just want to keep talking and talking, for fear, if I stop, it'll give you a chance to say no. And so, if you *are* tempted to say that dreadful word, won't you please consider that – that I'm still talking, and telling you how much we want and need Pollyanna.

Hopefully yours,

DELLA WETHERBY.'

'There!' ejaculated Mrs Chilton, as she laid the letter down. 'Did you ever read such a remarkable letter, or hear of a more preposterous, absurd request?'

'Well, I'm not so sure,' smiled the doctor. 'I don't think it's absurd to want Pollyanna.'

'But – but the way she puts it – healing the wound in her sister's heart, and all that. One would think the child was some sort of – of medicine!'

The doctor laughed outright, and raised his eyebrows.

'Well, I'm not so sure but she is, Polly. I *always* said I wished I could prescribe her and buy her as I would a box of pills; and Charlie

Ames says they always made it a point at the Sanatorium to give their patients a dose of Pollyanna as soon as possible after their arrival, during the whole year she was there.'

' "Dose", indeed!' scorned Mrs Chilton.

'Then – you don't think you'll let her go?'

'Go? Why, of course not! Do you think I'd let that child go to perfect strangers like that? – and such strangers! Why, Thomas, I should expect that that nurse would have her all bottled and labelled, with full directions on the outside how to take her, by the time I'd got back from Germany.'

Again the doctor threw back his head and laughed heartily, but only for a moment. His face changed perceptibly as he reached into his pocket for a letter.

'I heard from Dr Ames myself, this morning,' he said, with an odd something in his voice that brought a puzzled frown to his wife's brow. 'Suppose I read you my letter now.

'DEAR TOM – Miss Della Wetherby has asked me to give her and her sister a "character", which I am very glad to do. I have known the Wetherby girls from babyhood. They come from a fine old family, and are thoroughbred gentlewomen. You need not fear on that score.

There were three sisters, Doris, Ruth and Della. Doris married a man named John Kent, much against the family's wishes. Kent came from good stock, but was not much himself, I guess, and was certainly a very eccentric, disagreeable man to deal with. He was bitterly angry at the Wetherbys' attitude towards him, and there was little communication between the families until the baby came. The Wetherbys worshipped the little boy, James – 'Jamie', as they called him. Doris, the mother, died when the boy was four years old, and the Wetherbys were making every effort to get the father to give the child entirely up to them, when suddenly Kent disappeared, taking the boy with him. He has never been heard from since, though a worldwide search has been made.

The loss practically killed old Mr and Mrs Wetherby. They both died soon after. Ruth was already married and widowed. Her husband was a man named Carew, very wealthy and much older than herself. He lived but a year or so after marriage, and left her with a young son who also died within a year.

From the time little Jamie disappeared, Ruth and Della seemed to have but one object in life, and that was to find him. They have spent money like water, and have all but moved heaven and earth; but without avail. In time Della took up nursing. She is doing splendid work, and has become the cheerful, efficient, sane woman that she was meant to be – though still never forgetting her lost nephew, and never leaving unfollowed any possible clue that might lead to his discovery.

But with Mrs Carew it is quite different. After losing her own boy, she seemed to concentrate all her thwarted mother-love on her sister's son. As you can imagine, she was frantic when he disappeared. That was eight years ago – for her, eight long years of misery, gloom and bitterness. Everything that money can buy, of course, is at her command; but nothing pleases her, nothing interests her. Della feels that the time has come when she must be gotten out of herself, at all hazards; and Della believes that your wife's sunny little niece, Pollyanna, possesses the magic key that will unlock the door to a new existence for her. Such being the case, I hope you will see your way clear to granting her request. And may I add that I, too, personally, would appreciate the favour; for Ruth Carew and her sister are very old, dear friends of my wife and myself; and what touches them touches us.

As ever yours,

CHARLIE.'

The letter finished, there was a long silence, so long a silence that the doctor uttered a quiet, 'Well, Polly?'

Still there was silence. The doctor, watching his wife's face closely, saw that the usually firm lips and chin were trembling. He waited then quietly until his wife spoke.

'How soon – do you think – they'll expect her?' she asked at last. In spite of himself Dr Chilton gave a slight start.

'You – mean – that you *will* let her go?' he cried.

His wife turned indignantly. 'Why, Thomas Chilton, what a question! Do you suppose, after a letter like that, I could do anything *but* let her go? Besides, didn't Dr Ames *himself* ask us to? Do you think, after what that man has done for Pollyanna, that I'd refuse him *anything* – no matter what it was?'

'Dear, dear! I hope, now, that the doctor won't take it into his head to ask for – for *you*, my love,' murmured the husband-of-a-year, with a whimsical smile.

But his wife only gave him a deservedly scornful glance, and said: 'You may write Dr Ames that we'll send Pollyanna; and ask him to tell Miss Wetherby to give us full instructions. It must be sometime before the tenth of next month, of course, for you sail then; and I want to see the child properly established myself before I leave, naturally.'

'When will you tell Pollyanna?'

'Tomorrow, probably.'

'What will you tell her?'

'I don't know – exactly; but not any more than I can't help, certainly. Whatever happens, Thomas, we don't want to spoil Pollyanna; and no child could help being spoiled if she once got it into her head that she was a sort of – of – '

'Of medicine bottle with a label of full instructions for taking?' interpolated the doctor, with a smile.

'Yes,' sighed Mrs Chilton. 'It's her unconsciousness that saves the whole thing. *You* know that, dear.'

'Yes, I know,' nodded the man.

'She knows, of course, that you and I, and half the town are playing the game with her, and that we – we are wonderfully happier because we *are* playing it.' Mrs Chilton's voice shook a little, then went on more steadily.' But if, consciously, she should begin to be anything but her own natural, sunny, happy little self, playing the game that her father taught her, she would be – just what that nurse said she sounded like – "impossible". So, whatever I tell her, I shan't tell her that she's going down to Mrs Carew's to cheer her up,' concluded Mrs Chilton, rising to her feet with decision, and putting away her work.

'Which is where I think you're wise,' approved the doctor.

Pollyanna was told the next day; and this was the manner of it.

'My dear,' began her aunt, when the two were alone together that morning, 'how would you like to spend next winter in Boston?'

'With you?'

'No; I have decided to go with your uncle to Germany. But Mrs Carew, a dear friend of Dr Ames, has asked you to come and stay with her for the winter, and I think I shall let you go.'

Pollyanna's face fell.

'But in Boston I won't have Jimmy, or Mr Pendleton, or Mrs Snow, or anybody that I know, Aunt Polly.'

'No, dear; but you didn't have them when you came here – till you found them.'

Pollyanna gave a sudden smile.

'Why, Aunt Polly, so I didn't! And that means that down to Boston there are some Jimmys and Mr Pendletons and Mrs Snows waiting for me that I don't know, doesn't it?'

'Yes, dear.'

'Then I can be glad of that. I believe now, Aunt Polly, you know how to play the game better than I do. I never thought of the folks down there waiting for me to know them. And there's such a lot of 'em, too! I saw some of them when I was there two years ago with Mrs Gray. We were there two whole hours, you know, on my way here from out West.

'There was a man in the station – a perfectly lovely man who told me where to get a drink of water. Do you suppose he's there now? I'd like to know him. And there was a nice lady with a little girl. They live in Boston. They said they did. The little girl's name was Susie Smith. Perhaps I could get to know them. Do you suppose I could? And there was a boy, and another lady with a baby – only they lived in Honolulu, so probably I couldn't find them there now. But there'd be Mrs Carew, anyway. Who is Mrs Carew, Aunt Polly? Is she a relation?'

'Dear me, Pollyanna!' exclaimed Mrs Chilton, half-laughingly, half-despairingly. 'How do you expect anybody to keep up with your tongue, much less your thoughts, when they skip to Honolulu and back again in two seconds! No, Mrs Carew isn't any relation to us. She's Miss Della Wetherby's sister. Do you remember Miss Wetherby at the Sanatorium?'

Pollyanna clapped her hands.

'*Her* sister? Miss Wetherby's sister? Oh, then she'll be lovely, I know. Miss Wetherby was. I loved Miss Wetherby. She had little smile-wrinkles all around her eyes and mouth, and she knew the *nicest* stories. I only had her two months, though, because she only got there a little while before I came away. At first I was sorry that I hadn't had her *all* the time, but afterwards I was glad; for you see if I *had* had her all the time, it would have been harder to say goodbye than 'twas when I'd only had her a little while. And now it'll seem as if I had her again, 'cause I'm going to have her sister.'

Mrs Chilton drew in her breath and bit her lip.

'But, Pollyanna, dear, you must not expect that they'll be quite alike,' she ventured.

'Why, they're *sisters*, Aunt Polly,' argued the little girl, her eyes widening; 'and I thought sisters were always alike. We had two sets of 'em in the Ladies' Aiders. One set was twins, and *they* were so alike you couldn't tell which was Mrs Peck and which was Mrs Jones, until a wart grew on Mrs Jones's nose, then of course we could, because we looked for the wart the first thing. And that's what I told her one day when she was complaining that people called her Mrs Peck, and I said if they'd only look for the wart as I did, they'd know right off. But she acted real cross – I mean displeased, and I'm afraid she didn't like it – though I don't see why; for I should have thought she'd been glad there was something they could be told apart by, specially as she was the president, and didn't like it when folks didn't *act* as if she was the president – best seats and introductions and special attentions at church suppers, you know. But she didn't, and afterwards I heard Mrs White tell Mrs Rawson that Mrs Jones had done everything she could think of to get rid of that wart, even to trying to put salt on a bird's tail. But I don't see how *that* could do any good. Aunt Polly, *does* putting salt on a bird's tail help the warts on people's noses?'

'Of course not, child! How you do run on, Pollyanna, especially if you get started on those Ladies' Aiders!'

'Do I, Aunt Polly?' asked the little girl, ruefully. 'And does it plague you? I don't mean to plague you, honestly, Aunt Polly. And, anyway, if I do plague you about those Ladies' Aiders, you can be kind o' glad, for if I'm thinking of the Aiders, I'm sure to be thinking how glad I am that I don't belong to them any longer, but have got an aunt all my own. You can be glad of that, can't you, Aunt Polly?'

'Yes, yes, dear, of course I can, of course I can,' laughed Mrs Chilton, rising to leave the room, and feeling suddenly very guilty that she was conscious sometimes of a little of her old irritation against Pollyanna's perpetual gladness.

During the next few days, while letters concerning Pollyanna's winter stay in Boston were flying back and forth, Pollyanna herself was preparing for that stay by a series of farewell visits to her Beldingsville friends.

Everybody in the little Vermont village knew Pollyanna now, and almost everybody was playing the game with her. The few who were not, were not refraining because of ignorance of what the glad game was. So to one house after another Pollyanna carried the news now that she was going down to Boston to spend the winter; and loudly rose the clamour of regret and remonstrance, all the way from Nancy in Aunt Polly's own kitchen to the great house on the hill where lived John Pendleton.

Nancy did not hesitate to say – to everyone except her mistress – that *she* considered this Boston trip all foolishness, and that for her part she would have been glad to take Miss Pollyanna home with her to The Corners, she would, she would; and then Mrs Polly could have gone to Germany all she wanted to.

On the hill John Pendleton said practically the same thing, only he did not hesitate to say it to Mrs Chilton herself. As for Jimmy, the twelve-year-old boy whom John Pendleton had taken into his home because Pollyanna wanted him to, and whom he had now adopted – because he wanted to himself – as for Jimmy, Jimmy was indignant, and he was not slow to show it.

'But you've just come,' he reproached Pollyanna, in the tone of voice a small boy is apt to use when he wants to hide the fact that he has a heart.

'Why, I've been here ever since the last of March. Besides, it isn't as if I was going to stay. It's only for this winter.'

'I don't care. You've just been away for a whole year, 'most, and if I'd s'posed you was going away again right off, the first thing, I wouldn't have helped one mite to meet you with flags and bands and things that day you come from the Sanatorium.'

'Why, Jimmy Bean!' ejaculated Pollyanna, in amazed disapproval. Then, with a touch of superiority born of hurt pride, she observed: 'I'm sure I didn't *ask* you to meet me with bands and things – and you made two mistakes in that sentence. You shouldn't say "you was"; and I think "you come" is wrong. It doesn't sound right, anyway.'

'Well, who cares if I did?'

Pollyanna's eyes grew still more disapproving.

'You *said* you did – when you asked me this summer to tell you when you said things wrong, because Mr Pendleton was trying to make you talk right.'

'Well, if you'd been brought up in a 'sylum without any folks that cared, instead of by a whole lot of old women who didn't have anything to do but tell you how to talk right, maybe you'd say "you was", and a whole lot more worse things, Pollyanna Whittier!'

'Why, Jimmy Bean!' flared Pollyanna. 'My Ladies' Aiders weren't old women – that is, not many of them, so very old,' she corrected hastily, her usual proclivity for truth and literalness superseding her anger; 'and – '

'Well, I'm not Jimmy Bean, either,' interrupted the boy, uptilting his chin.

'You're – not – Why, Jimmy Be – what do you mean?' demanded the little girl.

'I've been adopted, *legally*. He's been intending to do it, all along, he says, only he didn't get to it. Now he's done it. I'm to be called "Jimmy Pendleton" and I'm to call him Uncle John, only I ain't – are not – I mean, I *am* not used to it yet, so I hain't – haven't begun to call him that, much.'

The boy still spoke crossly, aggrievedly, but every trace of displeasure had fled from the little girl's face at his words. She clapped her hands joyfully.

'Oh, how splendid! Now you've really got *folks* – folks that care, you know. And you won't ever have to explain that he wasn't *born* your folks, 'cause your name's the same now. I'm so glad, *glad*, *GLAD*!'

The boy got up suddenly from the stone wall where they had been sitting, and walked off. His cheeks felt hot, and his eyes smarted with tears. It was to Pollyanna that he owed it all – this great good that had come to him; and he knew it. And it was to Pollyanna that he had just now been saying –

He kicked a small stone fiercely, then another, and another. He thought those hot tears in his eyes were going to spill over and roll down his cheeks in spite of himself. He kicked another stone, then another; then he picked up a third stone and threw it with all his might. A minute later he strolled back to Pollyanna still sitting on the stone wall.

'I bet you I can hit that pine tree down there before you can,' he challenged airily.

'Bet you can't,' cried Pollyanna, scrambling down from her perch.

The race was not run after all, for Pollyanna remembered just in time that running fast was yet one of the forbidden luxuries for her. But so far as Jimmy was concerned, it did not matter. His cheeks were no longer hot, his eyes were not threatening to overflow with tears. Jimmy was himself again.

CHAPTER 3

A Dose of Pollyanna

As the eighth of September approached – the day Pollyanna was to arrive – Mrs Ruth Carew became more and more nervously exasperated with herself. She declared that she had regretted just *once* her promise to take the child – and that was ever since she had given it. Before twenty-four hours had passed she had, indeed, written to her sister demanding that she be released from the agreement; but Della had answered that it was quite too late, as already both she and Dr Ames had written the Chiltons.

Soon after that had come Della's letter saying that Mrs Chilton had given her consent, and would in a few days come to Boston to make arrangements as to school, and the like. So there was nothing to be done, naturally, but to let matters take their course. Mrs Carew realised that, and submitted to the inevitable, but with poor grace. True, she tried to be decently civil when Della and Mrs Chilton made their expected appearance; but she was very glad that limited time made Mrs Chilton's stay of very short duration, and full to the brim of business.

It was well, indeed, perhaps, that Pollyanna's arrival was to be at a date no later than the eighth; for time, instead of reconciling Mrs Carew to the prospective new member of her household, was filling her with angry impatience at what she was pleased to call her 'absurd yielding to Della's crazy scheme'.

Nor was Della herself in the least unaware of her sister's state of mind. If outwardly she maintained a bold front, inwardly she was very fearful as to results; but on Pollyanna she was pinning her faith, and because she did pin her faith on Pollyanna, she determined on the bold stroke of leaving the little girl to begin her fight entirely unaided and alone. She contrived, therefore, that Mrs Carew should meet them at the station upon their arrival; then, as soon as greetings and introductions were over, she hurriedly pleaded a previous engagement and took herself off. Mrs Carew, therefore, had scarcely time to look at her new charge before she found herself alone with the child.

'Oh, but Della, Della, you mustn't – I can't – ' she called agitatedly, after the retreating figure of the nurse.

But Della, if she heard, did not heed; and, plainly annoyed and vexed, Mrs Carew turned back to the child at her side.

'What a shame! She didn't hear, did she?' Pollyanna was saying, her eyes, also, wistfully following the nurse. 'And I didn't *want* her to go now a bit. But then, I've got you, haven't I? I can be glad for that.'

'Oh, yes, you've got me – and I've got you,' returned the lady, not very graciously. 'Come, we go this way,' she directed, with a motion towards the right.

Obediently Pollyanna turned and trotted at Mrs Carew's side, through the huge station; but she looked up once or twice rather anxiously into the lady's unsmiling face.

At last she spoke hesitatingly. 'I expect maybe you thought – I'd be pretty,' she hazarded, in a troubled voice.

'P–pretty?' repeated Mrs Carew.

'Yes – with curls, you know, and all that. And of course you did wonder how I *did* look, just as I did you. Only I *knew* you'd be pretty and nice, on account of your sister. I had her to go by, and you didn't have anybody. And of course I'm not pretty, on account of the freckles, and it *isn't* nice when you've been expecting a *pretty* little girl, to have one come like me; and – '

'Nonsense, child!' interrupted Mrs Carew, a trifle sharply. 'Come, we'll see to your trunk now, then we'll go home. I had hoped that my sister would come with us; but it seems she didn't see fit – even for this one night.'

Pollyanna smiled and nodded.

'I know; but she couldn't, probably. Somebody wanted her, I expect. Somebody was always wanting her at the Sanatorium. It's a bother, of course, when folks do want you all the time, isn't it? – 'cause you can't have yourself when you want yourself, lots of times. Still, you can be kind of glad for that, for it *is* nice to be wanted, isn't it?'

There was no reply – perhaps because for the first time in her life Mrs Carew was wondering if anywhere in the world there was any one who really wanted her – not that she *wished* to be wanted, of course, she told herself angrily, pulling herself up with a jerk, and frowning down at the child by her side.

Pollyanna did not see the frown. Pollyanna's eyes were on the hurrying throngs about them.

'My! what a lot of people,' she was saying happily. 'There's even more of them than there was the other time I was here; but I haven't seen anybody, yet, that I saw then, though I've looked for them everywhere. Of course the lady and the little baby lived in Honolulu, so probably *they wouldn't* be here; but there was a little girl, Susie Smith – she lived right here in Boston. Maybe you know her though. Do you know Susie Smith?'

'No, I don't know Susie Smith,' replied Mrs Carew, dryly.

'Don't you? She's awfully nice, and *she's* pretty – black curls, you know; the kind I'm going to have when I go to heaven. But never mind; maybe I can find her for you so you *will* know her. Oh, my! what a perfectly lovely automobile! And are we going to ride in it?' broke off Pollyanna, as they came to a pause before a handsome limousine, the door of which a liveried chauffeur was holding open.

The chauffeur tried to hide a smile – and failed. Mrs Carew, however, answered with the weariness of one to whom 'rides' are never anything but a means of locomotion from one tiresome place to another probably quite as tiresome.

'Yes, we're going to ride in it.' Then, 'Home, Perkins,' she added to the deferential chauffeur.

'Oh, my, is it yours?' asked Pollyanna, detecting the unmistakable air of ownership in her hostess's manner. 'How perfectly lovely! Then you must be rich – awfully – I mean *exceedingly* rich, more than the kind that just has carpets in every room and ice cream Sundays, like the Whites – one of my Ladies' Aiders, you know. (That is, *she* was a Ladies' Aider.) I used to think *they* were rich, but I know now that being really rich means you've got diamond rings and hired girls and sealskin coats, and dresses made of silk and velvet for every day, and an automobile. Have you got all those?'

'Why, y–yes, I suppose I have,' admitted Mrs Carew, with a faint smile.

'Then you are rich, of course,' nodded Pollyanna, wisely. 'My Aunt Polly has them, too, only her automobile is a horse. My! but don't I just love to ride in these things,' exulted Pollyanna, with a happy little bounce. 'You see I never did before, except the one that ran over me. They put me *in* that one after they'd got me out from under it; but of course I didn't know about it, so I couldn't enjoy it. Since then I haven't been in one at all. Aunt Polly doesn't like them. Uncle Tom does, though, and he wants one. He says he's got to have one, in his business. He's a doctor, you know, and all the other doctors in town have got them now. I don't know how it will come out. Aunt Polly is all stirred up over it. You see, she wants Uncle Tom to have what he wants, only she wants him to want what she wants him to want. See?'

Mrs Carew laughed suddenly.

'Yes, my dear, I think I see,' she answered demurely, though her eyes still carried – for them – a most unusual twinkle.

'All right,' sighed Pollyanna contentedly. 'I thought you would; still, it did sound sort of mixed when I said it. Oh, Aunt Polly says she wouldn't mind having an automobile, so much, if she could have the only one there was in the world, so there wouldn't be anyone else to run into her; but – My! what a lot of houses!' broke off Pollyanna, looking about her with round eyes of wonder. 'Don't they ever stop? Still, there'd have to be a lot of them for all those folks to live in, of course, that I saw at the station, besides all these here on the streets. And of course where there *are* more folks, there are more to know. I love folks. Don't you?'

'*Love folks!*'

'Yes, just folks, I mean. Anybody – everybody.'

'Well, no, Pollyanna, I can't say that I do,' replied Mrs Carew, coldly, her brows contracted.

Mrs Carew's eyes had lost their twinkle. They were turned rather mistrustfully, indeed, on Pollyanna. To herself Mrs Carew was saying: 'Now for preachment number one, I suppose, on my duty to mix with my fellow-men, *à la* Sister Della!'

'Don't you? Oh, I do,' sighed Pollyanna. 'They're all so nice and so different, you know. And down here there must be such a lot of them to be nice and different. Oh, you don't know how glad I am so soon that I came! I knew I would be, anyway, just as soon as I found out you were *you* – that is, Miss Wetherby's sister, I mean. I love Miss Wetherby, so I knew I should you, too; for of course you'd be alike – being sisters – even if you weren't twins like Mrs Jones and Mrs Peck – and they weren't quite alike, anyway, on account of the wart. But I reckon you don't know what I mean, so I'll tell you.'

And thus it happened that Mrs Carew, who had been steeling

herself for a preachment on social ethics, found herself, much to her surprise and a little to her discomfiture, listening to the story of a wart on the nose of one Mrs Peck, Ladies' Aider.

By the time the story was finished the limousine had turned into Commonwealth Avenue, and Pollyanna immediately began to exclaim at the beauty of a street which had such a 'lovely big long yard all the way up and down through the middle of it', and which was all the nicer, she said, 'after all those little narrow streets'.

'Only I should think everyone would want to live on it,' she commented enthusiastically.

'Very likely; but that would hardly be possible,' retorted Mrs Carew, with uplifted eyebrows.

Pollyanna, mistaking the expression on her face for one of dissatisfaction that her own home was not on the beautiful Avenue, hastened to make amends.

'Why, no, of course not,' she agreed. 'And I didn't mean that the narrower streets weren't just as nice,' she hurried on; 'and even better, maybe, because you could be glad you didn't have to go so far when you wanted to run across the way to borrow eggs or soda, and – Oh, but *do* you live here?' she interrupted herself, as the car came to a stop before the imposing Carew doorway. 'Do you live here, Mrs Carew?'

'Why, yes, of course I live here,' returned the lady, with just a touch of irritation.

'Oh, how glad, *glad* you must be to live in such a perfectly lovely place!' exulted the little girl, springing to the sidewalk and looking eagerly about her. 'Aren't you glad?'

Mrs Carew did not reply. With unsmiling lips and frowning brow she was stepping from the limousine.

For the second time in five minutes, Pollyanna hastened to make amends.

'Of course I don't mean the kind of glad that's sinfully proud,' she explained, searching Mrs Carew's face with anxious eyes. 'Maybe you thought I did, same as Aunt Polly used to, sometimes. I don't mean the kind that's glad because you've got something somebody else can't have; but the kind that just – just makes you want to shout and yell and bang doors, you know, even if it isn't proper,' she finished, dancing up and down on her toes.

The chauffeur turned his back precipitately, and busied himself with the car. Mrs Carew, still with unsmiling lips and frowning brow, led the way up the broad stone steps.

'Come, Pollyanna,' was all she said, crisply.

It was five days later that Della Wetherby received the letter from her sister, and very eagerly she tore it open. It was the first that had come since Pollyanna's arrival in Boston.

MY DEAR SISTER – For pity's sake, Della, why didn't you give me some sort of an idea what to expect from this child you have insisted upon my taking? I'm nearly wild – and I simply can't send her away. I've tried to three times, but every time, before I get the words out of my mouth, she stops them by telling me what a perfectly lovely time she is having, and how glad she is to be here, and how good I am to let her live with me while her Aunt Polly has gone to Germany. Now how, pray, in the face of that, can I turn around and say, 'Well, won't you please go home; I don't want you'? And the absurd part of it is, I don't believe it has ever entered her head that I don't *want* her here; and I can't seem to make it enter her head, either.

Of course, if she begins to preach, and to tell me to count my blessings, I *shall* send her away. You know I told you, to begin with, that I wouldn't permit that. And I won't. Two or three times I have thought she was going to (preach, I mean), but so far she has always ended up with some ridiculous story about those Ladies' Aiders of hers; so the sermon gets sidetracked – luckily for her, if she wants to stay.

But, really, Della, she is impossible. Listen. In the first place she is wild with delight over the house. The very first day she got here she begged me to open every room; and she was not satisfied until every shade in the house was up, so that she might 'see all the perfectly lovely things', which, she declared, were even nicer than Mr John Pendleton's – whoever he may be, somebody in

Beldingsville, I believe. Anyhow, he isn't a Ladies' Aider. I've found out that much.

Then, as if it wasn't enough to keep me running from room to room (as if I were the guide on a 'personally conducted'), what did she do but discover a white satin evening gown that I hadn't worn for years, and beseech me to put it on. And I did put it on – why, I can't imagine, only that I found myself utterly helpless in her hands.

But that was only the beginning. She begged then to see everything that I had, and she was so perfectly funny in her stories of the missionary barrels, which she used to 'dress out of', that I had to laugh – though I almost cried, too, to think of the wretched things that poor child had to wear. Of course gowns led to jewels, and she made such a fuss over my two or three rings that I foolishly opened the safe, just to see her eyes pop out. And, Della, I thought that child would go crazy. She put on to me every ring, brooch, bracelet and necklace that I owned, and insisted on fastening both diamond tiaras in my hair (when she found out what they were), until there I sat, hung with pearls and diamonds and emeralds, and feeling like a heathen goddess in a Hindu temple, especially when that preposterous child began to dance round and round me, clapping her hands and chanting, 'Oh, how perfectly lovely, how perfectly lovely! How I would love to hang you on a string in the window – you'd make such a beautiful prism!'

I was just going to ask her what on earth she meant by that when down she dropped in the middle of the floor and began to cry. And what do you suppose she was crying for? Because she was so glad she'd got eyes that could see! Now what do you think of that?

Of course this isn't all. It's only the beginning. Pollyanna has been here four days, and she's filled every one of them full. She already numbers among her friends the ash-man, the policeman on the beat and the paper boy, to say nothing of every servant in my employ. They seem actually bewitched with her, every one of them. But please do not think *I* am, for I'm not. I would send the child back to you at once if I didn't feel obliged to fulfil my promise to keep her this winter. As for her making me forget Jamie and my great sorrow – that is impossible. She only makes me feel my loss all the more keenly – because I have her instead of him. But, as I said, I shall keep her – until she begins to preach. Then back she goes to you. But she hasn't preached yet.

Lovingly but distractedly yours,

RUTH

' "Hasn't preached yet", indeed!' chuckled Della Wetherby to herself, folding up the closely-written sheets of her sister's letter. 'Oh, Ruth, Ruth! and yet you admit that you've opened every room, raised every shade, decked yourself in satin and jewels – and Pollyanna hasn't been there a week yet. But she hasn't preached – oh, no, she hasn't preached!'

CHAPTER 4

The Game and Mrs Carew

Boston, to Pollyanna, was a new experience, and certainly Pollyanna, to Boston – such part of it as was privileged to know her, was very much of a new experience.

Pollyanna said she liked Boston, but that she did wish it was not quite so big.

'You see,' she explained earnestly to Mrs Carew, the day following her arrival, 'I want to see and know it *all*, and I can't. It's just like Aunt Polly's company dinners; there's so much to eat – I mean, to see – that you don't eat – I mean, see – anything, because you're always trying to decide what to eat – I mean, to see.

'Of course you can be glad there *is* such a lot,' resumed Pollyanna, after taking breath, ' 'cause a whole lot of anything is nice – that is, *good* things; not such things as medicine and funerals, of course! – but at the same time I couldn't used to help wishing Aunt Polly's company dinners could be spread out a little over the days when there wasn't any cake and pie; and I feel the same way about Boston. I wish I could take part of it home with me up to Beldingsville so I'd have *something* new next summer. But of course I can't. Cities aren't like frosted cake – and, anyhow, even the cake didn't keep very well. I tried it, and it dried up, specially the frosting. I reckon the time to take frosting and good times is while they are going; so I want to see all I can now while I'm here.'

Pollyanna, unlike the people who think that to see the world one must begin at the most distant point, began her 'seeing Boston' by a thorough exploration of her immediate surroundings – the beautiful Commonwealth Avenue residence which was now her home. This, with her school work, fully occupied her time and attention for some days.

There was so much to see, and so much to learn; and everything was so marvellous and so beautiful, from the tiny buttons in the wall that flooded the rooms with light, to the great silent ballroom hung with mirrors and pictures. There were so many delightful people to know, too, for besides Mrs Carew herself there were Mary, who dusted the drawing-rooms, answered the bell and accompanied Pollyanna to and from school each day; Bridget, who lived in the kitchen and cooked; Jennie, who waited at table, and Perkins, who drove the automobile. And they were all so delightful – yet so different!

Pollyanna had arrived on a Monday, so it was almost a week before the first Sunday. She came downstairs that morning with a beaming countenance.

'I love Sundays,' she sighed happily.

'Do you?' Mrs Carew's voice had the weariness of one who loves no day.

'Yes, on account of church, you know, and Sunday school. Which do you like best, church or Sunday school?'

'Well, really, I – ' began Mrs Carew, who seldom went to church and never went to Sunday school.

' 'Tis hard to tell, isn't it?' interposed Pollyanna, with luminous but serious eyes. 'But you see *I* like church best, on account of father. You know he was a minister, and of course he's really up in heaven with mother and the rest of us, but I try to imagine him down here, lots of times; and it's easiest in church, when the minister is talking. I shut my eyes and imagine it's father up there; and it helps lots. I'm so glad we can imagine things, aren't you?'

'I'm not so sure of that, Pollyanna.'

'Oh, but just think how much nicer our *imagined* things are than our really truly ones – that is, of course, yours aren't, because your *real* ones are so nice.' Mrs Carew angrily started to speak, but Pollyanna was hurrying on. 'And of course *my* real ones are ever so much nicer than they used to be. But all that time I was hurt, when my legs didn't go, I just had to keep imagining all the time, just as hard as I could. And of course now there are lots of times when I do it – like about father, and all that. And so today I'm just going to imagine it's father up there in the pulpit. What time do we go?'

'*Go?*'

'To church, I mean.'

'But, Pollyanna, I don't – that is, I'd rather not – ' Mrs Carew cleared her throat and tried again to say that she was not going to church at all; that she almost never went. But with Pollyanna's confident little face and happy eyes before her, she could not do it.

'Why, I suppose – about quarter past ten – if we walk,' she said then, almost crossly. 'It's only a little way.'

Thus it happened that Mrs Carew on that bright September morning occupied for the first time in months the Carew pew in the very fashionable and elegant church to which she had gone as a girl, and which she still supported liberally – so far as money went.

To Pollyanna that Sunday morning service was a great wonder and joy. The marvellous music of the vested choir, the opalescent rays from the jewelled windows, the impassioned voice of the preacher, and the reverent hush of the worshipping throng filled her with an ecstasy that left her for a time almost speechless.

Not until they were nearly home did she fervently breathe: 'Oh, Mrs Carew, I've just been thinking how glad I am we don't have to live but just one day at a time!'

Mrs Carew frowned and looked down sharply. Mrs Carew was in

no mood for preaching. She had just been obliged to endure it from the pulpit, she told herself angrily, and she would *not* listen to it from this chit of a child. Moreover, this 'living one day at a time' theory was a particularly pet doctrine of Della's. Was not Della always saying: 'But you only have to live one minute at a time, Ruth, and anyone can endure anything for one minute at a time!'

'Well?' said Mrs Carew now, tersely.

'Yes. Only think what I'd do if I had to live yesterday and today and tomorrow all at once,' sighed Pollyanna. 'Such a lot of perfectly lovely things, you know. But I've had yesterday, and now I'm living today, and I've got tomorrow still coming, and next Sunday, too. Honestly, Mrs Carew, if it wasn't Sunday now, and on this nice quiet street, I should just dance and shout and yell. I couldn't help it. But it's being Sunday, so, I shall have to wait till I get home and then take a hymn – the most rejoicingest hymn I can think of. What is the most rejoicingest hymn? Do you know, Mrs Carew?'

'No, I can't say that I do,' answered Mrs Carew, faintly, looking very much as if she were searching for something she had lost. For a woman who expects, because things are so bad, to be told that she need stand only one day at a time, it is disarming, to say the least, to be told that, because things are so good, it is lucky she does not *have* to stand but one day at a time!

On Monday, the next morning, Pollyanna went to school for the first time alone. She knew the way perfectly now, and it was only a short walk. Pollyanna enjoyed her school very much. It was a small private school for girls, and was quite a new experience, in its way; but Pollyanna liked new experiences.

Mrs Carew, however, did not like new experiences, and she was having a good many of them these days. For one who is tired of everything to be in so intimate a companionship with one to whom everything is a fresh and fascinating joy must needs result in annoyance, to say the least. And Mrs Carew was more than annoyed. She was exasperated. Yet to herself she was forced to admit that if anyone asked her why she was exasperated, the only reason she could give would be, 'Because Pollyanna is so glad' – and even Mrs Carew would hardly like to give an answer like that.

To Della, however, Mrs Carew did write that the word 'glad' had got on her nerves, and that sometimes she wished she might never hear it again. She still admitted that Pollyanna had not preached – that she had not even once tried to make her play the game. What the child did do, however, was invariably to take Mrs Carew's 'gladness' as a matter of course, which, to one who *had* no gladness, was most provoking.

It was during the second week of Pollyanna's stay that Mrs Carew's annoyance overflowed into irritable remonstrance. The immediate cause thereof was Pollyanna's glowing conclusion to a story about one of her Ladies' Aiders.

'She was playing the game, Mrs Carew. But maybe you don't know what the game is. I'll tell you. It's a lovely game.'

But Mrs Carew held up her hand. 'Never mind, Pollyanna,' she demurred. 'I know all about the game. My sister told me, and – and I must say that I – I should not care for it.'

'Why, of course not, Mrs Carew!' exclaimed Pollyanna in quick apology. 'I didn't mean the game for you. You couldn't play it, of course.'

'I *couldn't* play it!' ejaculated Mrs Carew, who, though she *would* not play this silly game, was in no mood to be told that she *could* not.

'Why, no, don't you see?' laughed Pollyanna, gleefully. 'The game is to find something in everything to be glad about; and you couldn't even begin to hunt, for there isn't anything about you but what you *could* be glad about. There wouldn't *be* any game to it for you! Don't you see?'

Mrs Carew flushed angrily. In her annoyance she said more than perhaps she meant to say.

'Well, no, Pollyanna, I can't say that I do,' she differed coldly. 'As it happens, you see, I can find nothing whatever to be – glad for.'

For a moment Pollyanna stared blankly. Then she fell back in amazement.

'Why, *Mrs Carew*!' she breathed.

'Well, what is there – for me?' challenged the woman, forgetting all about, for the moment, the resolution that she was never going to allow Pollyanna to 'preach'.

'Why, there's – there's everything,' murmured Pollyanna, still with that dazed unbelief. 'There – there's this beautiful house.'

'It's just a place to eat and sleep – and I don't want to eat and sleep.'

'But there are all these perfectly lovely things,' faltered Pollyanna.

'I'm tired of them.'

'And your automobile that will take you anywhere.'

'I don't want to go anywhere.'

Pollyanna quite gasped aloud.

'But think of the people and things you could see, Mrs Carew.'

'They would not interest me, Pollyanna.'

Once again Pollyanna stared in amazement. The troubled frown on her face deepened.

'But, Mrs Carew, I don't see,' she urged. 'Always, before, there have been *bad* things for folks to play the game on, and the badder they are the more fun 'tis to get them out – find the things to be glad for, I mean. But where there *aren't* any bad things, I shouldn't know how to play the game myself.'

There was no answer for a time. Mrs Carew sat with her eyes out the window. Gradually the angry rebellion on her face changed to a look of hopeless sadness. Very slowly then she turned and said: 'Pollyanna, I had thought I wouldn't tell you this; but I've decided that I will. I'm going to tell you why nothing that I have can make me – glad.' And she began the story of Jamie, the little four-year-old boy who, eight long years before, had stepped as into another world, leaving the door fast shut between.

'And you've never seen him since – anywhere?' faltered Pollyanna, with tear-wet eyes, when the story was done.

'Never.'

'But we'll find him, Mrs Carew – I'm sure we'll find him.'

Mrs Carew shook her head sadly.

'But I can't. I've looked everywhere, even in foreign lands.'

'But he must be somewhere.'

'He may be – dead, Pollyanna.'

Pollyanna gave a quick cry.

'Oh, no, Mrs Carew. Please don't say that! Let's imagine he's alive. We *can* do that, and that'll help; and when we get him *imagined* alive we can just as well imagine we're going to find him. And that'll help a whole lot more.'

'But I'm afraid he's – dead, Pollyanna,' choked Mrs Carew.

'You don't know it for sure, do you?' besought the little girl, anxiously.

'N–no.'

'Well, then, you're just imagining it,' maintained Pollyanna, in triumph. 'And if you can imagine him dead, you can just as well imagine him alive, and it'll be a whole lot nicer while you're doing it. Don't you see? And some day, I'm just sure you'll find him. Why, Mrs Carew, you *can* play the game now! You can play it on Jamie. You can be glad every day, for every day brings you just one day nearer to the time when you're going to find him. See?'

But Mrs Carew did not 'see'. She rose drearily to her feet and said: 'No, no, child! You don't understand – you don't understand. Now run away, please, and read, or do anything you like. My head aches. I'm going to lie down.'

And Pollyanna, with a troubled, sober face, slowly left the room.

CHAPTER 5

Pollyanna Takes a Walk

It was on the second Saturday afternoon that Pollyanna took her memorable walk. Heretofore Pollyanna had not walked out alone, except to go to and from school. That she would ever attempt to explore Boston streets by herself, never occurred to Mrs Carew, hence she naturally had never forbidden it. In Beldingsville, however, Pollyanna had found – especially at the first – her chief diversion in strolling about the rambling old village streets in search of new friends and new adventures.

On this particular Saturday afternoon Mrs Carew had said, as she often did say: 'There, there, child, run away; please do. Go where you like and do what you like, only don't, please, ask me any more questions today!'

Until now, left to herself, Pollyanna had always found plenty to interest her within the four walls of the house; for, if inanimate things failed, there were yet Mary, Jennie, Bridget and Perkins. Today, however, Mary had a headache, Jennie was trimming a new hat, Bridget was making apple pies and Perkins was nowhere to be found. Moreover it was a particularly beautiful September day, and nothing within the house was so alluring as the bright sunlight and balmy air outside. So outside Pollyanna went and dropped herself down on the steps.

For some time she watched in silence the well-dressed men, women and children who walked briskly by the house, or else sauntered more leisurely through the parkway that extended up and down the middle of the Avenue. Then she got to her feet, skipped down the steps, and stood looking, first to the right, then to the left.

Pollyanna had decided that she, too, would take a walk. It was a beautiful day for a walk, and not once, yet, had she taken one at all – not a *real* walk. Just going to and from school did not count. So she would take one today. Mrs Carew would not mind. Had she not told her to do just what she pleased so long as she asked no more questions? And there was the whole long afternoon before her. Only think what a lot one might see in a whole long afternoon! And it really was such a beautiful day. She would go – this way! And with a little whirl and skip of pure joy, Pollyanna turned and walked blithely down the Avenue.

Into the eyes of those she met Pollyanna smiled joyously. She was disappointed – but not surprised – that she received no answering smile in return. She was used to that now – in Boston. She still smiled, however, hopefully: there might be someone, sometime, who would smile back.

Mrs Carew's home was very near the beginning of Commonwealth Avenue, so it was not long before Pollyanna found herself at the edge of a street crossing her way at right angles. Across the street, in all its autumn glory, lay what to Pollyanna was the most beautiful 'yard' she had ever seen – the Boston Public Garden.

For a moment Pollyanna hesitated, her eyes longingly fixed on the wealth of beauty before her. That it was the private grounds of some rich man or woman, she did not for a moment doubt. Once, with Dr Ames at the Sanatorium, she had been taken to call on a lady who lived in a beautiful house surrounded by just such walks and trees and flower-beds as these.

Pollyanna wanted now very much to cross the street and walk in those grounds, but she doubted if she had the right. To be sure, others were there, moving about, she could see; but they might be invited guests, of course. After she had seen two women, one man, and a little girl unhesitatingly enter the gate and walk briskly down the path, however, Pollyanna concluded that she, too, might go. Watching her chance she skipped nimbly across the street and entered the Garden.

It was even more beautiful close at hand than it had been at a distance. Birds twittered over her head, and a squirrel leaped across the path ahead of her. On benches here and there sat men, women and children. Through the trees flashed the sparkle of the sun on water; and from somewhere came the shouts of children and the sound of music.

Once again Pollyanna hesitated; then, a little timidly, she accosted a handsomely-dressed young woman coming towards her.

'Please, is this – a party?' she asked.

The young woman stared.

'A party!' she repeated dazedly.

'Yes'm. I mean, is it all right for me – to be here?'

'For you to be here? Why, of course. It's for – for everybody!' exclaimed the young woman.

'Oh, that's all right, then. I'm glad I came,' beamed Pollyanna.

The young woman said nothing; but she turned back and looked at Pollyanna still dazedly as she hurried away.

Pollyanna, not at all surprised that the owner of this beautiful place should be so generous as to give a party to everybody, continued on her way. At the turn of the path she came upon a small girl and a doll carriage. She stopped with a glad little cry, but she had not said a dozen words before from somewhere came a young woman with hurrying steps and a disapproving voice; a young woman who held out her hand to the small girl, and said sharply: 'Here, Gladys, Gladys, come away with me. Hasn't mama told you not to talk to strange children?'

'But I'm not strange children,' explained Pollyanna in eager defence. 'I live right here in Boston, now, and – ' But the young woman and the little girl dragging the doll carriage were already far down the path; and with a half-stifled sigh Pollyanna fell back. For a moment she stood silent, plainly disappointed; then resolutely she lifted her chin and went forward.

'Well, anyhow, I can be glad for that,' she nodded to herself, 'for now maybe I'll find somebody even nicer – Susie Smith, perhaps, or even Mrs Carew's Jamie. Anyhow, I can *imagine* I'm going to find them; and if I don't find *them*, I can find *somebody*!' she finished, her wistful eyes on the self-absorbed people all about her.

Undeniably Pollyanna was lonesome. Brought up by her father and the Ladies' Aid Society in a small Western town, she had counted every house in the village her home, and every man, woman and child her friend. Coming to her aunt in Vermont at eleven years of age, she had promptly assumed that conditions would differ only in that the homes and the friends would be new, and therefore even more delightful, possibly, for they would be 'different' – and Pollyanna did so love 'different' things and people! Her first and always her supreme delight in Beldingsville, therefore, had been her long rambles about the town and the charming visits with the new friends she had made. Quite naturally, in consequence, Boston, as she first saw it, seemed to Pollyanna even more delightfully promising in its possibilities.

Thus far, however, Pollyanna had to admit that in one respect, at least, it had been disappointing: she had been here nearly two weeks and she did not yet know the people who lived across the street, or even next door. More inexplicable still, Mrs Carew herself did not know many of them, and not any of them well. She seemed, indeed, utterly indifferent to her neighbours, which was most amazing from Pollyanna's point of view; but nothing she could say appeared to change Mrs Carew's attitude in the matter at all.

'They do not interest me, Pollyanna,' was all she would say; and with this, Pollyanna – whom they did interest very much – was forced to be content.

Today, on her walk, however, Pollyanna had started out with high hopes, yet thus far she seemed destined to be disappointed. Here all about her were people who were doubtless most delightful – if she only knew them. But she did not know them. Worse yet, there seemed to be no prospect that she would know them, for they did not, apparently, wish to know her: Pollyanna was still smarting under the nurse's sharp warning concerning 'strange children'.

'Well, I reckon I'll just have to show 'em that I'm not strange children,' she said at last to herself, moving confidently forward again.

Pursuant of this idea Pollyanna smiled sweetly into the eyes of the next person she met, and said blithely: 'It's a nice day, isn't it?'

'Er – what? Oh, y–yes, it is,' murmured the lady addressed, as she hastened on a little faster.

Twice again Pollyanna tried the same experiment, but with like disappointing results. Soon she came upon the little pond that she had seen sparkling in the sunlight through the trees. It was a beautiful pond, and on it were several pretty little boats full of laughing children. As she watched them, Pollyanna felt more and more dissatisfied to remain by herself. It was then that, spying a man sitting alone not far away, she advanced slowly towards him and sat down on the other end of the bench. Once Pollyanna would have danced unhesitatingly to the man's side and suggested acquaintanceship with a cheery confidence that had no doubt of a welcome; but recent rebuffs had filled her with unaccustomed diffidence. Covertly she looked at the man now.

He was not very good to look at. His garments, though new, were dusty, and plainly showed lack of care. They were of the cut and style (though Pollyanna of course did not know this) that the State gives its prisoners as a freedom suit. His face was a pasty white, and was adorned with a week's beard. His hat was pulled far down over his eyes. With his hands in his pockets he sat idly staring at the ground.

For a long minute Pollyanna said nothing; then hopefully she began: 'It *is* a nice day, isn't it?'

The man turned his head with a start.

'Eh? Oh – er – what did you say?' he questioned, with a curiously frightened look around to make sure the remark was addressed to him.

'I said 'twas a nice day,' explained Pollyanna in hurried earnestness; 'but I don't care about that especially. That is, of course I'm glad it's a nice day, but I said it just as a beginning to things, and I'd just as soon talk about something else – anything else. It's only that I wanted you to talk – about something, you see.'

The man gave a low laugh. Even to Pollyanna the laugh sounded a little queer, though she did not know (as did the man) that a laugh to his lips had been a stranger for many months.

'So you want me to talk, do you?' he said a little sadly. 'Well, I don't see but what I shall have to do it, then. Still, I should think a nice little lady like you might find lots nicer people to talk to than an old duffer like me.'

'Oh, but I like old duffers,' exclaimed Pollyanna quickly; 'that is, I like the *old* part, and I don't know what a duffer is, so I can't dislike that. Besides, if you are a duffer, I reckon I like duffers. Anyhow, I like you,' she finished, with a contented little settling of herself in her seat that carried conviction.

'Humph! Well, I'm sure I'm flattered,' smiled the man, ironically. Though his face and words expressed polite doubt, it might have been noticed that he sat a little straighter on the bench. 'And, pray, what shall we talk about?'

'It's – it's infinitesimal to me. That means I don't care, doesn't it?' asked Pollyanna, with a beaming smile. 'Aunt Polly says that, whatever I talk about, anyhow, I always bring up at the Ladies' Aiders. But I reckon that's because they brought me up first, don't you? We might talk about the party. I think it's a perfectly beautiful party – now that I know someone.'

'P–party?'

'Yes – this, you know – all these people here today. It *is* a party, isn't it? The lady said it was for everybody, so I stayed – though I haven't got to where the house is, yet, that's giving the party.'

The man's lips twitched.

'Well, little lady, perhaps it is a party, in a way,' he smiled; 'but the "house" that's giving it is the city of Boston. This is the Public Garden – a public park, you understand, for everybody.'

'Is it? Always? And I may come here any time I want to? Oh, how perfectly lovely! That's even nicer than I thought it could be. I'd worried for fear I couldn't ever come again, after today, you see. I'm glad now, though, that I didn't know it just at the first, for it's all the nicer now. Nice things are nicer when you've been worrying for fear they won't be nice, aren't they?'

'Perhaps they are – if they ever turn out to be nice at all,' conceded the man, a little gloomily.

'Yes, I think so,' nodded Pollyanna, not noticing the gloom. 'But isn't it beautiful – here?' she gloried. 'I wonder if Mrs Carew knows about it – that it's for anybody, so. Why, I should think everybody would want to come here all the time, and just stay and look around.'

The man's face hardened.

'Well, there are a few people in the world who have got a job – who've got something to do besides just to come here and stay and look around; but I don't happen to be one of them.'

'Don't you? Then you can be glad for that, can't you?' sighed Pollyanna, her eyes delightedly following a passing boat.

The man's lips parted indignantly, but no words came. Pollyanna was still talking.

'I wish *I* didn't have anything to do but that. I have to go to school. Oh, I like school; but there's such a whole lot of things I like better. Still I'm glad I *can* go to school. I'm specially glad when I remember how last winter I didn't think I could ever go again. You see, I lost my legs for a while – I mean, they didn't go; and you know you never know how much you use things, till you don't have 'em. And eyes, too. Did you ever think what a lot you do with eyes? I didn't till I went to the Sanatorium. There was a lady there who had just got blind the year before. I tried to get her to play the game – finding something to be glad about, you know – but she said she couldn't; and if I wanted to know why, I might tie up my eyes with my handkerchief for just one hour. And I did. It was awful. Did you ever try it?'

'Why, n–no, I didn't.' A half-vexed, half-baffled expression was coming to the man's face.

'Well, don't. It's awful. You can't do anything – not anything that you want to do. But I kept it on the whole hour. Since then I've been so glad, sometimes – when I see something perfectly lovely like this, you know – I've been so glad I wanted to cry – 'cause I *could* see it, you know. She's playing the game now, though – that blind lady is. Miss Wetherby told me.'

'The – *game?*'

'Yes; the glad game. Didn't I tell you? Finding something in everything to be glad about. Well, she's found it now – about her eyes, you know. Her husband is the kind of a man that goes to help make the laws, and she had him ask for one that would help blind people, specially little babies. And she went herself and talked and told those men how it felt to be blind. And they made it – that law. And they said that she did more than anybody else, even her husband, to help make it, and that they didn't believe there would have been any law at all if it hadn't been for her. So now she says she's glad she lost her eyes, 'cause she's kept so many little babies from growing up to be blind like her. So you see she's playing it – the game. But I reckon you don't know about the game yet, after all; so I'll tell you. It started this way.' And Pollyanna, with her eyes on the shimmering beauty all about her, told of the little pair of crutches of long ago, which should have been a doll.

When the story was finished there was a long silence; then, a little abruptly the man got to his feet.

'Oh, are you going away *now?*' she asked in open disappointment.

'Yes, I'm going now.' He smiled down at her a little queerly.

'But you're coming back sometime?'

He shook his head – but again he smiled.

'I hope not – and I believe not, little girl. You see, I've made a great discovery today. I thought I was down and out. I thought there was no place for me anywhere – now. But I've just discovered that I've got two eyes, two arms and two legs. Now I'm going to use them – and I'm going to *make* somebody understand that I know how to use them!'

The next moment he was gone.

'Why, what a funny man!' mused Pollyanna. 'Still, he was nice – and he was different, too,' she finished, rising to her feet and resuming her walk.

Pollyanna was now once more her usual cheerful self, and she stepped with the confident assurance of one who has no doubt. Had not the man said that this was a public park, and that she had as good a right as anybody to be there? She walked nearer to the pond and crossed the bridge to the starting-place of the little boats. For some time she watched the children happily, keeping a particularly sharp lookout for the possible black curls of Susie Smith. She would have liked to take a ride in the pretty boats, herself, but the sign said 'Five cents' a trip, and she did not have any money with her. She smiled hopefully into the faces of several women, and twice she spoke tentatively. But no one spoke first to her, and those whom she addressed eyed her coldly, and made scant response.

After a time she turned her steps into still another path. Here she found a white-faced boy in a wheelchair. She would have spoken to him, but he was so absorbed in his book that she turned away after a moment's wistful gazing. Soon then she came upon a pretty but sad-looking young girl sitting alone, staring at nothing, very much as the man had sat. With a contented little cry Pollyanna hurried forward.

'Oh, how do you do?' she beamed. 'I'm so glad I found you! I've been hunting ever so long for you,' she asserted, dropping herself down on the unoccupied end of the bench.

The pretty girl turned with a start, an eager look of expectancy in her eyes.

'Oh!' she exclaimed, falling back in plain disappointment. 'I thought – Why, what do you mean?' she demanded aggrievedly. 'I never set eyes on you before in my life.'

'No, I didn't you, either,' smiled Pollyanna; 'but I've been hunting for you, just the same. That is, of course I didn't know you were going to be *you* exactly. It's just that I wanted to find someone that looked lonesome, and that didn't have anybody. Like me, you know. So many here today have got folks. See?'

'Yes, I see,' nodded the girl, falling back into her old listlessness. 'But, poor little kid, it's too bad *you* should find it out – so soon.'

'Find what out?'

'That the lonesomest place in all the world is in a crowd in a big city.'

Pollyanna frowned and pondered.

'Is it? I don't see how it can be. I don't see how you can be lonesome when you've got folks all around you. Still – ' she hesitated, and the frown deepened, 'I *was* lonesome this afternoon, and there *were* folks all around me; only they didn't seem to – to think – or notice.'

The pretty girl smiled bitterly.

'That's just it. They don't ever think – or notice, crowds don't.'

'But some folks do. We can be glad some do,' urged Pollyanna. 'Now when I – '

'Oh, yes, some do,' interrupted the other. As she spoke she shivered and looked fearfully down the path beyond Pollyanna. 'Some notice – too much.'

Pollyanna shrank back in dismay. Repeated rebuffs that afternoon had given her a new sensitiveness.

'Do you mean – me?' she stammered. 'That you wished I hadn't – noticed – you?'

'No, no, kiddie! I meant – someone quite different from you. Someone that hadn't ought to notice. I was glad to have you speak, only – I thought at first it was someone from home.'

'Oh, then you don't live here, either, any more than I do – I mean, for keeps.'

'Oh, yes, I live here now,' sighed the girl; 'that is, if you can call it living – what I do.'

'What do you do?' asked Pollyanna interestedly.

'Do? I'll tell you what I do,' cried the other, with sudden bitterness. 'From morning till night I sell fluffy laces and perky bows to girls that laugh and talk and *know* each other. Then I go home to a little back room up three flights just big enough to hold a lumpy cot-bed, a washstand with a nicked pitcher, one rickety chair, and me. It's like a furnace in the summer and an ice box in the winter; but it's all the place I've got, and I'm supposed to stay in it – when I ain't workin'. But I've come out today. I ain't goin' to stay in that room, and I ain't goin' to go to any old library to read, neither. It's our last half-holiday this year – and an extra one, at that; and I'm going to have a good time – for once. I'm just as young, and I like to laugh and joke just as well as them girls I sell bows to all day. Well, today I'm going to laugh and joke.'

Pollyanna smiled and nodded her approval.

'I'm glad you feel that way. I do, too. It's a lot more fun – to be happy, isn't it? Besides, the Bible tells us to – rejoice and be glad, I mean. It tells us to eight hundred times. Probably you know about 'em, though – the rejoicing texts.'

The pretty girl shook her head. A queer look came to her face.

'Well, no,' she said dryly. 'I can't say I *was* thinkin' – of the Bible.'

'Weren't you? Well, maybe not; but, you see, *my* father was a minister, and he – '

'A *minister*?'

'Yes. Why, was yours, too?' cried Pollyanna, answering something she saw in the other's face.

'Y–yes.' A faint colour crept up to the girl's forehead.

'Oh, and has he gone like mine to be with God and the angels?'

The girl turned away her head.

'No. He's still living – back home,' she answered, half under her breath.

'Oh, how glad you must be,' sighed Pollyanna, enviously. 'Sometimes I get to thinking if only I could just *see* father once – but you do see your father, don't you?'

'Not often. You see, I'm down – here.'

'But you *can* see him – and I can't, mine. He's gone to be with mother and the rest of us up in heaven, and – Have you got a mother, too – an earth mother?'

'Y–yes.' The girl stirred restlessly, and half moved as if to go.

'Oh, then you can see both of them,' breathed Pollyanna, un-utterable longing in her face. 'Oh, how glad you must be! For there just isn't anybody, is there, that really *cares* and notices quite so much as fathers and mothers. You see I know, for I had a father until

I was eleven years old; but, for a mother, I had Ladies' Aiders for ever so long, till Aunt Polly took me. Ladies' Aiders are lovely, but of course they aren't like mothers, or even Aunt Pollys; and – '

On and on Pollyanna talked. Pollyanna was in her element now. Pollyanna loved to talk. That there was anything strange or unwise or even unconventional in this intimate telling of her thoughts and her history to a total stranger on a Boston park bench did not once occur to Pollyanna. To Pollyanna all men, women and children were friends, either known or unknown; and thus far she had found the unknown quite as delightful as the known, for with them there was always the excitement of mystery and adventure – while they were changing from the unknown to the known.

To this young girl at her side, therefore, Pollyanna talked unreservedly of her father, her Aunt Polly, her Western home, and her journey East to Vermont. She told of new friends and old friends, and of course she told of the game. Pollyanna almost always told everybody of the game, either sooner or later. It was, indeed, so much a part of her very self that she could hardly have helped telling of it.

As for the girl – she said little. She was not now sitting in her old listless attitude, however, and to her whole self had come a marked change. The flushed cheeks, frowning brow, troubled eyes and nervously working fingers were plainly the signs of some inward struggle. From time to time she glanced apprehensively down the path beyond Pollyanna, and it was after such a glance that she clutched the little girl's arm.

'See here, kiddie, for just a minute don't you leave me. Do you hear? Stay right where you are? There's a man I know comin'; but no matter what he says, don't you pay no attention, and *don't you go*. I'm goin' to stay with *you*. See?'

Before Pollyanna could more than gasp her wonderment and surprise, she found herself looking up into the face of a very handsome young gentleman, who had stopped before them.

'Oh, here you are,' he smiled pleasantly, lifting his hat to Pollyanna's companion. 'I'm afraid I'll have to begin with an apology – I'm a little late.'

'It don't matter, sir,' said the young girl, speaking hurriedly. 'I – I've decided not to go.'

The young man gave a light laugh.

'Oh, come, my dear, don't be hard on a chap because he's a little late!'

'It isn't that, really,' defended the girl, a swift red flaming into her cheeks. 'I mean – I'm not going.'

'Nonsense!' The man stopped smiling. He spoke sharply. 'You said yesterday you'd go.'

'I know; but I've changed my mind. I told my little friend here – I'd stay with her.'

'Oh, but if you'd rather go with this nice young gentleman,' began Pollyanna, anxiously; but she fell back silenced at the look the girl gave her.

'I tell you I had rather *not* go. I'm not going.'

'And, pray, why this sudden right-about face?' demanded the young man with an expression that made him suddenly look, to Pollyanna, not quite so handsome. 'Yesterday you said – '

'I know I did,' interrupted the girl, feverishly. 'But I knew then that I hadn't ought to. Let's call it – that I know it even better now. That's all.' And she turned away resolutely.

It was not all. The man spoke again, twice. He coaxed, then he sneered with a hateful look in his eyes. At last he said something very low and angry, which Pollyanna did not understand. The next moment he wheeled about and strode away.

The girl watched him tensely till he passed quite out of sight, then, relaxing, she laid a shaking hand on Pollyanna's arm.

'Thanks, kiddie. I reckon I owe you – more than you know. Goodbye.'

'But you aren't going away *now*!' bemoaned Pollyanna.

The girl sighed wearily.

'I got to. He might come back, and next time I might not be able to – ' She clipped the words short and rose to her feet. For a moment she hesitated, then she choked bitterly: 'You see, he's the kind that – notices too much, and that hadn't ought to notice – *me* – at all!' With that she was gone.

'Why, what a funny lady,' murmured Pollyanna, looking wistfully after the vanishing figure. 'She was nice, but she was sort of different, too,' she commented, rising to her feet and moving idly down the path.

CHAPTER 6

Jerry to the Rescue

It was not long before Pollyanna reached the edge of the Garden at a corner where two streets crossed. It was a wonderfully interesting corner, with its hurrying cars, automobiles, carriages and pedestrians. A huge red bottle in a drug-store window caught her eye, and from down the street came the sound of a hurdy-gurdy. Hesitating only a moment Pollyanna darted across the corner and skipped lightly down the street towards the entrancing music.

Pollyanna found much to interest her now. In the store windows were marvellous objects, and around the hurdy-gurdy, when she had reached it, she found a dozen dancing children, most fascinating to watch. So altogether delightful, indeed, did this pastime prove to be that Pollyanna followed the hurdy-gurdy for some distance, just to see those children dance. Presently she found herself at a corner so busy that a very big man in a belted blue coat helped the people across the street. For an absorbed minute she watched him in silence; then, a little timidly, she herself started to cross.

It was a wonderful experience. The big, blue-coated man saw her at once and promptly beckoned to her. He even walked to meet her. Then, through a wide lane with puffing motors and impatient horses on either hand, she walked unscathed to the further kurb. It gave her a delightful sensation, so delightful that, after a minute, she walked back. Twice again, after short intervals, she trod the fascinating way so magically opened at the lifting of the big man's hand. But the last time her conductor left her at the kerb, he gave a puzzled frown.

'See here, little girl, ain't you the same one what crossed a minute ago?' he demanded. 'And again before that?'

'Yes, sir,' beamed Pollyanna. 'I've been across four times!'

'Well!' the officer began to bluster; but Pollyanna was still talking. 'And it's been nicer every time!'

'Oh–h, it has – has it?' mumbled the big man, lamely. Then, with a little more spirit he sputtered: 'What do you think I'm here for – just to tote you back and forth?'

'Oh, no, sir,' dimpled Pollyanna. 'Of course you aren't just for me! There are all these others. I know what you are. You're a policeman. We've got one of you out where I live at Mrs Carew's, only he's the kind that just walks on the sidewalk, you know. I used to think you were soldiers, on account of your gold buttons and blue hats; but I know better now. Only I think you *are* a kind of a soldier, 'cause you're so brave – standing here like this, right in the middle of all these teams and automobiles, helping folks across.'

'Ho – ho! Brrrr!' spluttered the big man, colouring like a school-boy and throwing back his head with a hearty laugh. 'Ho – ho! Just as if – ' He broke off with a quick lifting of his hand. The next moment he was escorting a plainly very much frightened little old lady from kurb to kurb. If his step were a bit more pompous, and his chest a bit more full, it must have been only an unconscious tribute to the watching eyes of the little girl back at the starting-point. A moment later, with a haughtily permissive wave of his hand towards the chafing drivers and chauffeurs, he strolled back to Pollyanna.

'Oh, that was splendid!' she greeted him, with shining eyes. 'I love to see you do it – and it's just like the Children of Israel crossing the Red Sea, isn't it? – with you holding back the waves for the people to cross. And how glad you must be all the time, that you can do it! I used to think being a doctor was the very gladdest business there was, but I reckon, after all, being a policeman is gladder yet – to help frightened people like this, you know. And – ' But with another 'Brrrr!' and an embarrassed laugh, the big blue-coated man was back in the middle of the street, and Pollyanna was all alone on the kerbstone.

For only a minute longer did Pollyanna watch her fascinating 'Red Sea', then, with a regretful backward glance, she turned away.

'I reckon maybe I'd better be going home now,' she meditated. 'It must be 'most dinner time.' And briskly she started to walk back by the way she had come.

Not until she had hesitated at several corners, and unwittingly made two false turns, did Pollyanna grasp the fact that 'going back home' was not to be so easy as she had thought it to be. And not until she came to a building which she knew she had never seen before, did she fully realise that she had lost her way.

She was on a narrow street, dirty and ill-paved. Dingy tenement blocks and a few unattractive stores were on either side. All about were jabbering men and chattering women – though not one word of what they said could Pollyanna understand. Moreover, she could not help seeing that the people looked at her very curiously, as if they knew she did not belong there.

Several times, already, she had asked her way, but in vain. No one seemed to know where Mrs Carew lived; and, the last two times, those addressed had answered with a gesture and a jumble of words which Pollyanna, after some thought, decided must be 'Dutch', the kind the Haggermans – the only foreign family in Beldingsville – used.

On and on, down one street and up another, Pollyanna trudged. She was thoroughly frightened now. She was hungry, too, and very tired. Her feet ached, and her eyes smarted with the tears she was trying so hard to hold back. Worse yet, it was unmistakably beginning to grow dark.

'Well, anyhow,' she choked to herself, 'I'm going to be glad I'm lost, 'cause it'll be so nice when I get found. I *can* be glad for that!'

It was at a noisy corner where two broader streets crossed that Pollyanna finally came to a dismayed stop. This time the tears quite overflowed, so that, lacking a handkerchief, she had to use the backs of both hands to wipe them away.

'Hullo, kid, why the weeps?' queried a cheery voice. 'What's up?'

With a relieved little cry Pollyanna turned to confront a small boy carrying a bundle of newspapers under his arm.

'Oh, I'm so glad to see you!' she exclaimed. 'I've so wanted to see someone who didn't talk Dutch!'

The small boy grinned.

'Dutch nothin'!' he scoffed. 'You mean Dago, I bet ye.'

Pollyanna gave a slight frown.

'Well, anyway, it – it wasn't English,' she said doubtfully; 'and they couldn't answer my questions. But maybe you can. Do you know where Mrs Carew lives?'

'Nix! You can search me.'

'Wha–at?' queried Pollyanna, still more doubtfully.

The boy grinned again.

'I guess I ain't acquainted with the lady.'

'But isn't there anybody anywhere that is?' implored Pollyanna. 'You see, I just went out for a walk and I got lost. I've been ever and ever so far, but I can't find the house at all; and it's supper – I mean dinner time and getting dark. I want to get back. I *must* get back.'

'Gee! Well, I should worry!' sympathised the boy.

'Yes, and I'm afraid Mrs Carew'll worry, too,' sighed Pollyanna.

'Gorry! if you ain't the limit,' chuckled the youth, unexpectedly. 'But, say, listen! Don't ye know the name of the street ye want?'

'No – only that it's some kind of an avenue,' desponded Pollyanna.

'A ave*noo*, is it? Sure, now, some class to that! We're doin' fine. What's the number of the house? Can ye tell me that? Just scratch your head!'

'Scratch – my – head?' Pollyanna frowned questioningly, and raised a tentative hand to her hair.

The boy eyed her with disdain.

'Aw, come off yer perch! Ye ain't so dippy as all that. I say, don't ye know the number of the house ye want?'

'N–no, except there's a seven in it,' returned Pollyanna, with a faintly hopeful air.

'Won't ye listen ter that?' gibed the scornful youth. 'There's a seven in it – an' she expects me ter know it when I see it!'

'Oh, I should know the house, if I could only see it,' declared Pollyanna, eagerly; 'and I think I'd know the street, too, on account of the lovely long yard running right up and down through the middle of it.'

This time it was the boy who gave a puzzled frown.

'*Yard?*' he queried, 'in the middle of a street?'

'Yes – trees and grass, you know, with a walk in the middle of it, and seats, and – ' But the boy interrupted her with a whoop of delight.

'Gee whiz! Commonwealth Avenue, sure as yer livin'! Wouldn't that get yer goat, now?'

'Oh, do you know – do you, really?' besought Pollyanna. 'That sounded like it – only I don't know what you meant about the goat part. There aren't any goats there. I don't think they'd allow – '

'Goats nothin'!' scoffed the boy. 'You bet yer sweet life I know where 'tis! Don't I tote Sir James up there to the Garden 'most ev'ry day? An' I'll take *you*, too. Jest ye hang out here till I get on ter my job again, an' sell out my stock. Then we'll make tracks for that 'ere Avenue 'fore ye can say Jack Robinson.'

'You mean you'll take me – home?' appealed Pollyanna, still plainly not quite understanding.

'Sure! It's a cinch – if you know the house.'

'Oh, yes, I know the house,' replied the literal Pollyanna, anxiously, 'but I don't know whether it's a – a cinch, or not. If it isn't, can't you – '

But the boy only threw her another disdainful glance and darted off into the thick of the crowd. A moment later Pollyanna heard his strident call of, 'Paper, paper! *Herald, Globe* – paper, sir?'

With a sigh of relief Pollyanna stepped back into a doorway and waited. She was tired, but she was happy. In spite of sundry puzzling aspects of the case, she yet trusted the boy, and she had perfect confidence that he could take her home.

'He's nice, and I like him,' she said to herself, following with her eyes the boy's alert, darting figure. 'But he does talk funny. His words *sound* English, but some of them don't seem to make any sense with the rest of what he says. But then, I'm glad he found me, anyway,' she finished with a contented little sigh.

It was not long before the boy returned, his hands empty.

'Come on, kid. All aboard,' he called cheerily. 'Now we'll hit the trail for the Avenue. If I was the real thing, now, I'd tote ye home in style in a buzz-wagon; but seein' as how I hain't got the dough, we'll have ter hoof it.'

It was, for the most part, a silent walk. Pollyanna, for once in her life, was too tired to talk, even of the Ladies' Aiders; and the boy was intent on picking out the shortest way to his goal.

When the Public Garden was reached, Pollyanna did exclaim joyfully: 'Oh, now I'm 'most there! I remember this place. I had a perfectly lovely time here this afternoon. It's only a little bit of a ways home now.'

'That's the stuff! Now we're gettin' there,' crowed the boy. 'What'd I tell ye? We'll just cut through here to the Avenue, an' then it'll be up ter you ter find the house.'

'Oh, I can find the house,' exulted Pollyanna, with all the confidence of one who has reached familiar ground.

It was quite dark when Pollyanna led the way up the broad Carew steps. The boy's ring at the bell was very quickly answered, and Pollyanna found herself confronted by not only Mary, but by Mrs Carew, Bridget and Jennie as well. All four of the women were white-faced and anxious-eyed.

'Child, child, where *have* you been?' demanded Mrs Carew, hurrying forward.

'Why, I – I just went to walk,' began Pollyanna, 'and I got lost, and this boy – '

'Where did you find her?' cut in Mrs Carew, turning imperiously to Pollyanna's escort, who was, at that moment, gazing in frank admiration at the wonders about him in the brilliantly lighted hall.

'Where did you find her, boy?' she repeated sharply.

For a brief moment the boy met her gaze unflinchingly; then something very like a twinkle came into his eyes, though his voice, when he spoke, was gravity itself.

'Well, I found her around Bowdoin Square, but I reckon she'd been doin' the North End, only she couldn't catch on ter the lingo of the Dagos, so I don't think she give 'em the glad hand, ma'am.'

'The North End – that child – alone! Pollyanna!' shuddered Mrs Carew.

'Oh, I wasn't alone, Mrs Carew,' fended Pollyanna. 'There were ever and ever so many people there, weren't there, boy?'

But the boy, with an impish grin, was disappearing through the door. Pollyanna learned many things during the next half-hour. She learned that nice little girls do not take long walks alone in unfamiliar cities, nor sit on park benches and talk to strangers. She learned, also, that it was only by a 'perfectly marvellous miracle' that she had reached home at all that night, and that she had escaped many, many very disagreeable consequences of her foolishness. She learned that Boston was not Beldingsville, and that she must not think it was.

'But, Mrs Carew,' she finally argued despairingly, 'I *am* here, and I didn't get lost for keeps. Seems as if I ought to be glad for that instead of thinking all the time of the sorry things that might have happened.'

'Yes, yes, child, I suppose so, I suppose so,' sighed Mrs Carew; 'but you have given me such a fright, and I want you to be sure, *sure*, *sure* never to do it again. Now come, dear, you must be hungry.'

It was just as she was dropping off to sleep that night that Pollyanna murmured drowsily to herself: 'The thing I'm the very sorriest for of anything is that I didn't ask that boy his name nor where he lived. Now I can't ever say thank you to him!'

CHAPTER 7

A New Acquaintance

Pollyanna's movements were most carefully watched over after her adventurous walk; and, except to go to school, she was not allowed out of the house unless Mary or Mrs Carew herself accompanied her. This, to Pollyanna, however, was no cross, for she loved both Mrs Carew and Mary, and delighted to be with them. They were, too, for a while, very generous with their time. Even Mrs Carew, in her terror of what might have happened, and her relief that it had not happened, exerted herself to entertain the child.

Thus it came about that, with Mrs Carew, Pollyanna attended

concerts and matinees, and visited the Public Library and the Art Museum; and with Mary she took the wonderful 'seeing Boston' trips, and visited the State House and the Old South Church.

Greatly as Pollyanna enjoyed the automobile, she enjoyed the trolley cars more, as Mrs Carew, much to her surprise, found out one day.

'Do we go in the trolley car?' Pollyanna asked eagerly.

'No. Perkins will take us,' answered Mrs Carew. Then, at the unmistakable disappointment in Pollyanna's face, she added in surprise: 'Why, I thought you liked the auto, child!'

'Oh, I do,' acceded Pollyanna, hurriedly; 'and I wouldn't say anything, anyway, because of course I know it's cheaper than the trolley car, and – '

' "Cheaper than the trolley car"!' exclaimed Mrs Carew, amazed into an interruption.

'Why, yes,' explained Pollyanna, with widening eyes; 'the trolley car costs five cents a person, you know, and the auto doesn't cost anything, 'cause it's yours. And of course I *love* the auto, anyway,' she hurried on, before Mrs Carew could speak. 'It's only that there are so many more people in the trolley car, and it's such fun to watch them! Don't you think so?'

'Well, no, Pollyanna, I can't say that I do,' responded Mrs Carew, dryly, as she turned away.

As it chanced, not two days later, Mrs Carew heard something more of Pollyanna and trolley cars – this time from Mary.

'I mean, it's queer, ma'am,' explained Mary earnestly, in answer to a question her mistress had asked, 'it's queer how Miss Polly-anna just gets round *everybody* – and without half trying. It isn't that she *does* anything. She doesn't. She just – just looks glad, I guess, that's all. But I've seen her get into a trolley car that was full of cross-looking men and women, and whimpering children, and in five minutes you wouldn't know the place. The men and women have stopped scowling and the children have forgot what they're cryin' for.

'Sometimes it's just somethin' that Miss Pollyanna has said to me, and they've heard it. Sometimes it's just the "Thank you", she gives when somebody insists on givin' us their seat – and they're always doin' that – givin' us seats, I mean. And sometimes it's the way she smiles at a baby or a dog. All dogs everywhere wag their tails at her, anyway, and all babies, big and little, smile and reach out to her. If we get held up it's a joke, and if we take the wrong car, it's the funniest thing that ever happened. And that's the way 'tis about everythin'. One just can't stay grumpy, with Miss Pollyanna, even if you're only one of a trolley car full of folks that don't know her.'

'Hm–m; very likely,' murmured Mrs Carew, turning away.

October proved to be, that year, a particularly warm, delightful month, and as the golden days came and went, it was soon very evident that to keep up with Pollyanna's eager little feet was a task which would consume altogether too much of somebody's time and patience; and, while Mrs Carew had the one, she had not the other, neither had she the willingness to allow Mary to spend quite so much of *her* time (whatever her patience might be) in dancing attendance to Pollyanna's whims and fancies.

To keep the child indoors all through those glorious October afternoons was, of course, out of the question. Thus it came about that, before long, Pollyanna found herself once more in the 'lovely big yard' – the Boston Public Garden – and alone. Apparently she was as free as before, but in reality she was surrounded by a high stone wall of regulations.

She must not talk to strange men or women; she must not play with strange children; and under no circumstances must she step foot outside the Garden except to come home. Furthermore, Mary, who had taken her to the Garden and left her, made very sure that she knew the way home – that she knew just where Commonwealth Avenue came down to Arlington Street across from the Garden. And always she must go home when the clock in the church tower said it was half-past four.

Pollyanna went often to the Garden after this. Occasionally she went with some of the girls from school. More often she went alone. In spite of the somewhat irksome restrictions she enjoyed herself very much. She could *watch* the people even if she could not talk to them; and she could talk to the squirrels and pigeons and sparrows

that so eagerly came for the nuts and grain which she soon learned
to carry to them every time she went.

Pollyanna often looked for her old friends of that first day – the
man who was so glad he had his eyes and legs and arms, and the
pretty young lady who would not go with the handsome man; but
she never saw them. She did frequently see the boy in the wheel
chair, and she wished she could talk to him. The boy fed the birds
and squirrels, too, and they were so tame that the doves would perch
on his head and shoulders, and the squirrels would burrow in his
pockets for nuts. But Pollyanna, watching from a distance, always
noticed one strange circumstance: in spite of the boy's very evident
delight in serving his banquet, his supply of food always ran short
almost at once; and though he invariably looked fully as disappointed
as did the squirrel after a nutless burrowing, yet he never remedied
the matter by bringing more food the next day – which seemed most
short-sighted to Pollyanna.

When the boy was not playing with the birds and squirrels he was
reading – always reading. In his chair were usually two or three
worn books, and sometimes a magazine or two. He was nearly
always to be found in one especial place, and Pollyanna used to
wonder how he got there. Then, one unforgettable day, she found
out. It was a school holiday, and she had come to the Garden in the
forenoon; and it was soon after she reached the place that she saw
him being wheeled along one of the paths by a snub-nosed, sandy-
haired boy. She gave a keen glance into the sandy-haired boy's face,
then ran towards him with a glad little cry.

'Oh, you – you! I know you – even if I don't know your name. You
found me! Don't you remember? Oh, I'm so glad to see you! I've so
wanted to say thank you!'

'Gee, if it ain't the swell little lost kid of the Ave*noo*!' grinned the
boy. 'Well, what do you know about that! Lost again?'

'Oh, no!' exclaimed Pollyanna, dancing up and down on her toes
in irrepressible joy. 'I can't get lost any more – I have to stay right
here. And I mustn't talk, you know. But I can to you, for I *know you*;
and I can to him – after you introduce me,' she finished, with a
beaming glance at the lame boy, and a hopeful pause.

The sandy-haired youth chuckled softly, and tapped the shoulder of the boy in the chair.

'Listen ter that, will ye? Ain't that the real thing, now? Just you wait while I intro*dooce* ye!' And he struck a pompous attitude. 'Madam, this is me friend, Sir James, Lord of Murphy's Alley, and – ' But the boy in the chair interrupted him.

'Jerry, quit your nonsense!' he cried vexedly. Then to Pollyanna he turned a glowing face. 'I've seen you here lots of times before. I've watched you feed the birds and squirrels – you always have such a lot for them! And I think *you* like Sir Lancelot the best, too. Of course, there's the Lady Rowena – but wasn't she rude to Guinevere yesterday – snatching her dinner right away from her like that?'

Pollyanna blinked and frowned, looking from one to the other of the boys in plain doubt. Jerry chuckled again. Then, with a final push he wheeled the chair into its usual position, and turned to go.

Over his shoulder he called to Pollyanna: 'Say, kid, jest let me put ye wise ter somethin'. This chap ain't drunk nor crazy. See? Them's jest names he's give his young friends here' – with a flourish of his arms towards the furred and feathered creatures that were gathering from all directions. 'An' they ain't even names of *folks*. They're just guys out of books. Are ye on? Yet he'd ruther feed them than feed hisself. Ain't he the limit? Ta–ta, Sir James,' he added, with a grimace, to the boy in the chair.'Buck up, now – nix on the no grub racket for you! See you later.' And he was gone.

Pollyanna was still blinking and frowning when the lame boy turned with a smile.

'You mustn't mind Jerry. That's just his way. He'd cut off his right hand for me – Jerry would; but he loves to tease. Where'd you see him? Does he know you? He didn't tell me your name.'

'I'm Pollyanna Whittier. I was lost and he found me and took me home,' answered Pollyanna, still a little dazedly.

'I see. Just like him,' nodded the boy. 'Don't he tote me up here every day?'

A quick sympathy came to Pollyanna's eyes.

'Can't you walk – at all – er – Sir J–James?'

The boy laughed gleefully.

' "Sir James," indeed! That's only more of Jerry's nonsense. I ain't a "Sir".'

Pollyanna looked clearly disappointed.

'You aren't? Nor a – a lord, like he said?'

'I sure ain't.'

'Oh, I hoped you were – like Little Lord Fauntleroy, you know,' rejoined Pollyanna. 'And – '

But the boy interrupted her with an eager: 'Do *you* know Little Lord Fauntleroy? And do you know about Sir Lancelot, and the Holy Grail, and King Arthur and his Round Table, and the Lady Rowena, and Ivanhoe, and all those? *Do* you?'

Pollyanna gave her head a dubious shake.

'Well, I'm afraid maybe I don't know *all* of 'em,' she admitted. 'Are they all – in books?'

The boy nodded.

'I've got 'em here – some of 'em,' he said. 'I like to read 'em over and over. There's always *something* new in 'em. Besides, I hain't got no others, anyway. These were father's. Here, you little rascal – quit that!' he broke off in laughing reproof as a bushy-tailed squirrel leaped to his lap and began to nose in his pockets. 'Gorry, guess we'd better give them their dinner or they'll be tryin' to eat us,' chuckled the boy. 'That's Sir Lancelot. He's always first, you know.'

From somewhere the boy produced a small pasteboard box which he opened guardedly, mindful of the numberless bright little eyes that were watching every move. All about him now sounded the whir and flutter of wings, the cooing of doves, the saucy twitter of the sparrows. Sir Lancelot, alert and eager, occupied one arm of the wheelchair. Another bushy-tailed little fellow, less venturesome, sat back on his haunches five feet away. A third squirrel chattered noisily on a neighbouring tree-branch.

From the box the boy took a few nuts, a small roll and a doughnut. At the latter he looked longingly, hesitatingly.

'Did you – bring anything?' he asked then.

'Lots – in here,' nodded Pollyanna, tapping the paper bag she carried.

'Oh, then perhaps I *will* eat it today,' sighed the boy, dropping the doughnut back into the box with an air of relief.

Pollyanna, on whom the significance of this action was quite lost, thrust her fingers into her own bag, and the banquet was on.

It was a wonderful hour. To Pollyanna it was, in a way, the most wonderful hour she had ever spent, for she had found someone who could talk faster and longer than she could. This strange youth seemed to have an inexhaustible fund of marvellous stories of brave knights and fair ladies, of tournaments and battles. Moreover, so vividly did he draw his pictures that Pollyanna saw with her own eyes the deeds of valour, the knights in armour, and the fair ladies with their jewelled gowns and tresses, even though she was really looking at a flock of fluttering doves and sparrows and a group of frisking squirrels on a wide sweep of sunlit grass.

The Ladies' Aiders were forgotten. Even the glad game was not thought of. Pollyanna, with flushed cheeks and sparkling eyes was trailing down the golden ages led by a romance-fed boy who – though she did not know it – was trying to crowd into this one short hour of congenial companionship countless dreary days of loneliness and longing.

Not until the noon bells sent Pollyanna hurrying homeward did she remember that she did not even yet know the boy's name.

'I only know it isn't "Sir James",' she sighed to herself, frowning with vexation. 'But never mind. I can ask him tomorrow.'

CHAPTER 8

Jamie

Pollyanna did not see the boy 'tomorrow'. It rained, and she could not go to the Garden at all. It rained the next day, too. Even on the third day she did not see him, for, though the sun came out bright and warm, and though she went very early in the afternoon to the

Garden and waited long, he did not come at all. But on the fourth day he was there in his old place, and Pollyanna hastened forward with a joyous greeting.

'Oh, I'm so glad, *glad* to see you! But where've you been? You weren't here yesterday at all.'

'I couldn't. The pain wouldn't let me come yesterday,' explained the lad, who was looking very white.

'The *pain*! Oh, does it – ache?' stammered Pollyanna, all sympathy at once.

'Oh, yes, always,' nodded the boy, with a cheerfully matter-of-fact air. 'Most generally I can stand it and come here just the same, except when it gets *too* bad, same as 'twas yesterday. Then I can't.'

'But how can you stand it – to have it ache – always?' gasped Pollyanna.

'Why, I have to,' answered the boy, opening his eyes a little wider. 'Things that are so are *so*, and they can't be any other way. So what's the use thinking how they might be? Besides, the harder it aches one day, the nicer 'tis to have it let-up the next.'

'I know! That's like the ga – ' began Pollyanna; but the boy interrupted her.

'Did you bring a lot this time?' he asked anxiously. 'Oh, I hope you did! You see I couldn't bring them any today. Jerry couldn't spare even a penny for peanuts this morning and there wasn't really enough stuff in the box for me this noon.'

Pollyanna looked shocked.

'You mean – that you didn't have enough to eat – yourself? – for *your* luncheon?'

'Sure!' smiled the boy. 'But don't worry. 'Tisn't the first time – and 'twon't be the last. I'm used to it. Hi, there! here comes Sir Lancelot.'

Pollyanna, however, was not thinking of squirrels.

'And wasn't there any more at home?'

'Oh, no, there's *never* any left at home,' laughed the boy. 'You see, mumsey works out – stairs and washings – so she gets some of her feed in them places, and Jerry picks his up where he can, except nights and mornings; he gets it with us then – if we've got any.'

Pollyanna looked still more shocked.

'But what do you do when you don't have anything to eat?'

'Go hungry, of course.'

'But I never *heard* of anybody who didn't have *anything* to eat,' gasped Pollyanna. 'Of course father and I were poor, and we had to eat beans and fish balls when we wanted turkey. But we had *something*. Why don't you tell folks – all these folks everywhere, that live in these houses? '

'What's the use?'

'Why, they'd give you something, of course!'

The boy laughed once more, this time a little queerly.

'Guess again, kid. You've got another one coming. Nobody I know is dishin' out roast beef and frosted cakes for the askin'. Besides, if you didn't go hungry once in a while, you wouldn't know how good 'taters and milk can taste; and you wouldn't have so much to put in your Jolly Book.'

'Your *what*?'

The boy gave an embarrassed laugh and grew suddenly red.

'Forget it! I didn't think, for a minute, but you was mumsey or Jerry.'

'But what *is* your Jolly Book?' pleaded Pollyanna. 'Please tell me. Are there knights and lords and ladies in that?'

The boy shook his head. His eyes lost their laughter and grew dark and fathomless.

'No; I wish't there was,' he sighed wistfully. 'But when you – you can't even *walk*, you can't fight battles and win trophies, and have fair ladies hand you your sword, and bestow upon you the golden guerdon.' A sudden fire came to the boy's eyes. His chin lifted itself as if in response to a bugle call. Then, as suddenly, the fire died, and the boy fell back into his old listlessness.

'You just can't do nothin',' he resumed wearily, after a moment's silence. 'You just have to sit and think; and times like that your *think* gets to be something awful. Mine did, anyhow. I wanted to go to school and learn things – more things than just mumsey can teach me; and I thought of that. I wanted to run and play ball with the other boys; and I thought of that. I wanted to go out and sell papers with Jerry; and I thought of that. I didn't want to be taken care of all my life; and I thought of that.'

'I know, oh, I know,' breathed Pollyanna, with shining eyes. 'Didn't I lose *my* legs for a while?'

'Did you? Then you do know, some. But you've got yours again. I hain't, you know,' sighed the boy, the shadow in his eyes deepening.

'But you haven't told me yet about – the Jolly Book,' prompted Pollyanna, after a minute.

The boy stirred and laughed shamefacedly.

'Well, you see, it ain't much, after all, except to me. *You* wouldn't see much in it. I started it a year ago. I was feelin' specially bad that day. Nothin' was right. For a while I grumped it out, just thinkin'; and then I picked up one of father's books and tried to read. And the first thing I see was this: I learned it afterwards, so I can say it now.

> Pleasures lie thickest where no pleasures seem;
> There's not a leaf that falls upon the ground
> But holds some joy, of silence or of sound.

'Well, I was mad. I wished I could put the guy that wrote that in my place, and see what kind of joy he'd find in my "leaves". I was so mad I made up my mind I'd prove he didn't know what he was talkin' about, so I begun to hunt for 'em – the joys in my "leaves", you know. I took a little old empty notebook that Jerry had given me, and I said to myself that I'd write 'em down. Everythin' that had anythin' about it that I liked I'd put down in the book. Then I'd just show how many "joys" I had.'

'Yes, yes!' cried Pollyanna, absorbedly, as the boy paused for breath.

'Well, I didn't expect to get many, but – do you know? – I got a lot. There was somethin' about 'most everythin' that I liked a *little*, so in it had to go. The very first one was the book itself – that I'd got it, you know, to write in. Then somebody give me a flower in a pot, and Jerry found a dandy book in the subway. After that it was really fun to hunt 'em out – I'd find 'em in such queer places, sometimes. Then one day Jerry got hold of the little notebook, and found out what 'twas. Then he give it its name – the Jolly Book. And – and that's all.'

'All – *all*!' cried Pollyanna, delight and amazement struggling for the mastery on her glowing little face. 'Why, that's the game! You're playing the glad game, and don't know it – only you're playing it ever and ever so much better than I ever could! Why, I – I couldn't play it at all, I'm afraid, if I – I didn't have enough to eat, and couldn't ever walk, or anything,' she choked.

'The game? What game? I don't know anything about any game,' frowned the boy.

Pollyanna clapped her hands.

'I know you don't – I know you don't, and that's why it's so perfectly lovely, and so – so wonderful! But listen. I'll tell you what the game is.'

And she told him. 'Gee!' breathed the boy appreciatively, when she had finished. 'Now what do you think of that!'

'And here you are, playing *my* game better than anybody I ever saw, and I don't even know your name yet, nor anything!' exclaimed Pollyanna, in almost awestruck tones. 'But I want to – I want to know everything.'

'Pooh! there's nothing to know,' rejoined the boy, with a shrug. 'Besides, see, here's poor Sir Lancelot and all the rest, waiting for their dinner,' he finished.

'Dear me, so they are,' sighed Pollyanna, glancing impatiently at the fluttering and chattering creatures all about them. Recklessly she turned her bag upside down and scattered her supplies to the four winds. 'There, now, that's done, and we can talk again,' she rejoiced. 'And there's such a lot I want to know. First, please, what *is* your name? I only know it isn't "Sir James".'

The boy smiled.

'No, it isn't; but that's what Jerry 'most always calls me. Mumsey and the rest call me "Jamie".'

' "*Jamie!*" ' Pollyanna caught her breath and held it suspended. A wild hope had come to her eyes. It was followed almost instantly, however, by fearful doubt.

'Does "mumsey" mean – mother?'

'Sure!'

Pollyanna relaxed visibly. Her face fell. If this Jamie had a mother, he could not, of course, be Mrs Carew's Jamie, whose mother had died long ago. Still, even as he was, he was wonderfully interesting.

'But where do you live?' she catechised eagerly. 'Is there anybody else in your family but your mother and – and Jerry? Do you always come here every day? Where is your Jolly Book? Mayn't I see it? Don't the doctors say you can ever walk again? And where was it you said you got it? – this wheelchair, I mean.'

The boy chuckled.

'Say, how many of them questions do you expect me to answer all at once? I'll begin at the last one, anyhow, and work backwards, maybe, if I don't forget what they are. I got this chair a year ago. Jerry knew one of them fellers what writes for papers, you know, and he put in it about me – how I couldn't ever walk, and all that, and – and the Jolly Book, you see. The first thing I knew, a whole lot of men and women come one day toting this chair, and said 'twas for me. That they'd read all about me, and they wanted me to have it to remember them by.'

'My! how glad you must have been!'

'I was. It took a whole page of my Jolly Book to tell about that chair.'

'But can't you *ever* walk again?' Pollyanna's eyes were blurred with tears.

'It don't look like it. They said I couldn't.'

'Oh, but that's what they said about me, and then they sent me to Dr Ames, and I stayed 'most a year; and *he* made me walk. Maybe he could *you*!'

The boy shook his head.

'He couldn't – you see; I couldn't go to him, anyway. 'Twould cost too much. We'll just have to call it that I can't ever – walk again. But never mind.' The boy threw back his head impatiently. 'I'm trying not to *think* of that. You know what it is when – when your *think* gets to going.'

'Yes, yes, of course – and here I am talking about it!' cried Pollyanna, penitently. 'I *said* you knew how to play the game better than I did, now. But go on. You haven't told me half, yet. Where do you live? And is Jerry all the brothers and sisters you've got?'

A swift change came to the boy's face. His eyes glowed.

'Yes – and he ain't mine, really. He ain't any relation, nor mumsey ain't, neither. And only think how good they've been to me!'

'What's that?' questioned Pollyanna, instantly on the alert. 'Isn't that – that "mumsey" your mother at all?'

'No; and that's what makes – '

'And haven't you got any mother?' interrupted Pollyanna, in growing excitement.

'No; I never remember any mother, and father died six years ago.'

'How old were you?'

'I don't know. I was little. Mumsey says she guesses maybe I was about six. That's when they took me, you see.'

'And your name is Jamie?' Pollyanna was holding her breath.

'Why, yes, I told you that.'

'And what's the other name?' Longingly, but fearfully, Pollyanna asked this question.

'I don't know.'

'*You don't know!*'

'I don't remember. I was too little, I suppose. Even the Murphys don't know. They never knew me as anything but Jamie.'

A great disappointment came to Pollyanna's face, but almost immediately a flash of thought drove the shadow away.

'Well, anyhow, if you don't know what your name is, you can't know it isn't "Kent"!' she exclaimed.

' "Kent"?' puzzled the boy.

'Yes,' began Pollyanna, all excitement. 'You see, there was a little boy named Jamie Kent that – ' She stopped abruptly and bit her lip. It had occurred to Pollyanna that it would be kinder not to let this boy know yet of her hope that he might be the lost Jamie. It would be better that she make sure of it before raising any expectations, otherwise she might be bringing him sorrow rather than joy. She had not forgotten how disappointed Jimmy Bean had been when she had been obliged to tell him that the Ladies' Aid did not want him, and again when at first Mr Pendleton had not wanted him, either. She was determined that she would not make the same mistake a third time; so very promptly now she assumed an air of elaborate indifference on this most dangerous subject, as she said: 'But never mind about Jamie Kent. Tell me about yourself. I'm *so* interested!'

'There isn't anything to tell. I don't know anything nice,' hesitated the boy. 'They said father was – was queer, and never talked. They didn't even know his name. Everybody called him the "Professor".' Mumsey says he and I lived in a little back room on the top floor of the house in Lowell where they used to live. They were poor then, but they wasn't near so poor as they are now. Jerry's father was alive them days, and had a job.'

'Yes, yes, go on,' prompted Pollyanna.

'Well, mumsey says my father was sick a lot, and he got queerer and queerer, so that they had me downstairs with them a good deal. I could walk then, a little, but my legs wasn't right. I played with Jerry, and the little girl that died. Well, when father died there wasn't anybody to take me, and some men were goin' to put me in an orphan asylum; but mumsey says I took on so, and Jerry took on so, that they said they'd keep me. And they did. The little girl had just died, and they said I might take her place. And they've had me ever since. And I fell and got worse, and they're awful poor now, too, what with Jerry's father dyin'. But they've kept me. Now ain't that what you call bein' pretty good to a feller?'

'Yes, oh, yes,' cried Pollyanna. 'But they'll get their reward – I know they'll get their reward!' Pollyanna was quivering with delight now. The last doubt had fled. She had found the lost Jamie. She was sure of it. But not yet must she speak. First Mrs Carew must see him. Then – *then* – ! Even Pollyanna's imagination failed when it came to picturing the bliss in store for Mrs Carew and Jamie at that glad reunion.

She sprang lightly to her feet in utter disregard of Sir Lancelot who had come back and was nosing in her lap for more nuts.

'I've got to go now, but I'll come again tomorrow. Maybe I'll have a lady with me that you'll like to know. You'll be here tomorrow, won't you?' she finished anxiously.

'Sure, if it's pleasant. Jerry totes me up here 'most every mornin'. They fixed it so he could, you know; and I bring my dinner and stay till four o'clock. Jerry's good to me – he is!'

'I know, I know,' nodded Pollyanna. 'And maybe you'll find some-body else to be good to you, too,' she carolled. With which cryptic statement and a beaming smile, she was gone.

CHAPTER 9

Plans and Plottings

On the way home Pollyanna made joyous plans. Tomorrow, in some way or other, Mrs Carew must be persuaded to go with her for a walk in the Public Garden. Just how this was to be brought about Pollyanna did not know; but brought about it must be.

To tell Mrs Carew plainly that she had found Jamie, and wanted her to go to see him, was out of the question. There was, of course, a bare chance that this might not be her Jamie; and if it were not, and if she had thus raised in Mrs Carew false hopes, the result might be disastrous. Pollyanna knew, from what Mary had told her, that twice already Mrs Carew had been made very ill by the great disappointment of following alluring clues that had led to some boy very different from her dead sister's son. So Pollyanna knew that she could not tell Mrs Carew why she wanted her to go to walk tomorrow in the Public Garden. But there would be a way, declared Pollyanna to herself as she happily hurried homeward.

Fate, however, as it happened, once more intervened in the shape of a heavy rainstorm; and Pollyanna did not have to more than look out of doors the next morning to realise that there would be no Public Garden stroll that day. Worse yet, neither the next day nor the next saw the clouds dispelled; and Pollyanna spent all three afternoons wandering from window to window, peering up into the sky, and anxiously demanding of everyone: '*Don't* you think it looks a *little* like clearing up?'

So unusual was this behaviour on the part of the cheery little girl, and so irritating was the constant questioning, that at last Mrs Carew lost her patience.

'For pity's sake, child, what is the trouble?' she cried. 'I never knew you to fret so about the weather. Where's that wonderful glad game of yours today?'

Pollyanna reddened and looked abashed.

'Dear me, I reckon maybe I did forget the game this time,' she admitted. 'And of course there *is* something about it I can be glad for, if I'll only hunt for it. I can be glad that – that it will *have* to stop raining sometime 'cause God said he *wouldn't* send another flood. But you see, I did so want it to be pleasant today.'

'Why, especially?'

'Oh, I – I just wanted to go to walk in the Public Garden.' Pollyanna was trying hard to speak unconcernedly. 'I – I thought maybe you'd like to go with me, too.' Outwardly Pollyanna was nonchalance itself. Inwardly, however, she was aquiver with excitement and suspense.

'*I* go to walk in the Public Garden?' queried Mrs Carew, with brows slightly uplifted. 'Thank you, no, I'm afraid not,' she smiled.

'Oh, but you – you wouldn't *refuse*!' faltered Pollyanna, in quick panic.

'I have refused.'

Pollyanna swallowed convulsively. She had grown really pale.

'But, Mrs Carew, please, *please* don't say you *won't* go, when it gets pleasant,' she begged. 'You see, for a – a special reason I wanted you to go – with me – just this once.'

Mrs Carew frowned. She opened her lips to make the 'no' more decisive; but something in Pollyanna's pleading eyes must have changed the words, for when they came they were a reluctant acquiescence.

'Well, well, child, have your own way. But if I promise to go, *you* must promise not to go near the window for an hour, and not to ask again today if I think it's going to clear up.'

'Yes'm, I will – I mean, I won't,' palpitated Pollyanna. Then, as a pale shaft of light that was almost a sunbeam, came aslant through the window, she cried joyously: 'But you *do* think it *is* going to – Oh!' she broke off in dismay, and ran from the room.

Unmistakably it 'cleared up' the next morning. But, though the sun shone brightly, there was a sharp chill in the air, and by afternoon, when Pollyanna came home from school, there was a brisk wind. In spite of protests, however, she insisted that it was a beautiful day out, and that she should be perfectly miserable if Mrs Carew would not come for a walk in the Public Garden. And Mrs Carew went, though still protesting.

As might have been expected, it was a fruitless journey. Together the impatient woman and the anxious-eyed little girl hurried shiveringly up one path and down another. (Pollyanna, not finding the boy in his accustomed place, was making frantic search in every nook and corner of the Garden. To Pollyanna it seemed that she could not have it so. Here she was in the Garden, and here with her was Mrs Carew; but not anywhere to be found was Jamie – and yet not one word could she say to Mrs Carew.) At last, thoroughly chilled and exasperated, Mrs Carew insisted on going home; and despairingly Pollyanna went.

Sorry days came to Pollyanna then. What to her was perilously near a second deluge – but according to Mrs Carew was merely 'the usual autumn rains' – brought a series of damp, foggy, cold, cheerless days, filled with either a dreary drizzle of rain, or, worse yet, a steady downpour. If perchance occasionally there came a day of sunshine, Pollyanna always flew to the Garden; but in vain. Jamie was never there. It was the middle of November now, and even the Garden itself was full of dreariness. The trees were bare, the benches almost empty, and not one boat was on the little pond. True, the squirrels and pigeons were there, and the sparrows were as pert as ever, but to feed them was almost more of a sorrow than a joy, for every saucy switch of Sir Lancelot's feathery tail but brought bitter memories of the lad who had given him his name – and who was not there.

'And to think I didn't find out where he lived!' mourned Pollyanna to herself over and over again, as the days passed. 'And he was Jamie – I just know he was Jamie. And now I'll have to wait and wait till spring comes, and it's warm enough for him to come here again. And then, maybe, *I* shan't be coming here by that time. Oh dear, Oh dear – and he *was* Jamie, I know he was Jamie!'

Then, one dreary afternoon, the unexpected happened. Polly-anna, passing through the upper hallway heard angry voices in the hall below, one of which she recognised as being Mary's, while the other – the other –

The other voice was saying: 'Not on yer life! It's nix on the beggin' business. Do yer get me? I wants ter see the kid, Pollyanna. I got a message for her from – from Sir James. Now beat it, will ye, and trot out the kid, if ye don't mind.'

With a glad little cry Pollyanna turned and fairly flew down the stairway.

'Oh, I'm here, I'm here, I'm right here!' she panted, stumbling forward. 'What is it? Did Jamie send you?'

In her excitement she had almost flung herself with outstretched arms upon the boy when Mary interposed a shocked, restraining hand.

'Miss Pollyanna, Miss Pollyanna, do you mean to say you know this – this beggar boy?'

The boy flushed angrily; but before he could speak Pollyanna interposed valiant championship.

'He isn't a beggar boy. He belongs to one of my very best friends. Besides, he's the one that found me and brought me home that time I was lost.' Then to the boy she turned with impetuous questioning. 'What is it? Did Jamie send you?'

'Sure he did. He hit the hay a month ago, and he hain't been up since.'

'He hit – what?' puzzled Pollyanna.

'Hit the hay – went ter bed. He's sick, I mean, and he wants ter see ye. Will ye come?'

'Sick? Oh, I'm so sorry!' grieved Pollyanna. 'Of course I'll come. I'll go get my hat and coat right away.'

'Miss Pollyanna!' gasped Mary in stern disapproval. 'As if Mrs Carew would let you go *anywhere* with a strange boy like this!'

'But he isn't a strange boy,' objected Pollyanna. 'I've known him ever so long, and I *must* go. I – '

'What in the world is the meaning of this?' demanded Mrs Carew icily from the drawing-room doorway. 'Pollyanna, who is this boy, and what is he doing here?'

Pollyanna turned with a quick cry.

'Oh, Mrs Carew, you'll let me go, won't you?'

'Go where?'

'To see my brother, ma'am,' cut in the boy hurriedly, and with an obvious effort to be very polite. 'He's sort of off his feed, ye know, and he wouldn't give me no peace till I come up – after her,' with an awkward gesture toward Pollyanna. 'He thinks a sight an' all of her.'

'I may go, mayn't I?' pleaded Pollyanna.

Mrs Carew frowned.

'Go with this boy – *you*? Certainly not, Pollyanna! I wonder you are wild enough to think of it for a moment.'

'Oh, but I want you to come, too,' began Pollyanna.

'I? Absurd, child! That is impossible. You may give this boy here a little money, if you like, but – '

'Thank ye, ma'am, but I didn't come for money,' resented the boy, his eyes flashing. 'I come for – her.'

'Yes, and Mrs Carew, it's Jerry – Jerry Murphy, the boy that found me when I was lost, and brought me home,' appealed Pollyanna. '*Now* won't you let me go?'

Mrs Carew shook her head.

'It is out of the question, Pollyanna.'

'But he says Ja – the other boy is sick, and wants me!'

'I can't help that.'

'And I know him real well, Mrs Carew. I do, truly. He reads books – lovely books, all full of knights and lords and ladies, and he feeds the birds and squirrels and gives 'em names, and everything. And he can't walk, and he doesn't have enough to eat, lots of days,' panted Pollyanna; 'and he's been playing my glad game for a year, and didn't know it. And he plays it ever and ever so much better than I do. And I've hunted and hunted for him, ever and ever so many days. Honest and truly, Mrs Carew, I've just *got* to see him,' almost sobbed Pollyanna. 'I can't lose him again!'

An angry colour flamed into Mrs Carew's cheeks.

'Pollyanna, this is sheer nonsense. I am surprised. I am amazed at you for insisting upon doing something you know I disapprove of. I *cannot* allow you to go with this boy. Now please let me hear no more about it.'

A new expression came to Pollyanna's face. With a look half-terrified, half-exalted, she lifted her chin and squarely faced Mrs Carew. Tremulously, but determinedly, she spoke. 'Then I'll have to tell you. I didn't mean to – till I was sure. I wanted you to see him first. But now I've got to tell. I can't lose him again. I think, Mrs Carew, he's – Jamie.'

'Jamie! Not – my – Jamie!' Mrs Carew's face had grown very white.

'Yes.'

'Impossible!'

'I know; but, please, his name *is* Jamie, and he doesn't know the other one. His father died when he was six years old, and he can't remember his mother. He's twelve years old, he thinks. These folks took him in when his father died, and his father was queer, and didn't tell folks his name, and – '

But Mrs Carew had stopped her with a gesture. Mrs Carew was even whiter than before, but her eyes burned with a sudden fire.

'We'll go at once,' she said. 'Mary, tell Perkins to have the car here as soon as possible. Pollyanna, get your hat and coat. Boy, wait here, please. We'll be ready to go with you immediately.' The next minute she had hurried upstairs.

In the hall the boy drew a long breath.

'Gee whiz!' he muttered softly. 'If we ain't goin' ter go in a buzz-wagon! Some class ter that! Gorry! what'll Sir James say?'

CHAPTER 10

In Murphy's Alley

With the opulent purr that seems to be peculiar to luxurious limousines, Mrs Carew's car rolled down Commonwealth Avenue and out upon Arlington Street to Charles. Inside sat a shining-eyed little girl and a white-faced, tense woman. Outside, to give directions to the plainly disapproving chauffeur, sat Jerry Murphy, inordinately proud and insufferably important.

When the limousine came to a stop before a shabby doorway in a narrow, dirty alley, the boy leaped to the ground, and, with a ridiculous imitation of the liveried pomposities he had so often watched, threw open the door of the car and stood waiting for the ladies to alight.

Pollyanna sprang out at once, her eyes widening with amazement and distress as she looked about her. Behind her came Mrs Carew, visibly shuddering as her gaze swept the filth, the sordidness and the ragged children that swarmed shrieking and chattering out of the dismal tenements and surrounded the car in a second.

Jerry waved his arms angrily.

'Here, you, beat it!' he yelled to the motley throng. 'This ain't no free movies! *Can* that racket and get a move on ye. Lively, now! We gotta get by. Jamie's got comp'ny.'

Mrs Carew shuddered again, and laid a trembling hand on Jerry's shoulder.

'Not – *here*!' she recoiled.

But the boy did not hear. With shoves and pushes from sturdy fists and elbows, he was making a path for his charges; and before Mrs Carew knew quite how it was done, she found herself with the boy and Pollyanna at the foot of a rickety flight of stairs in a dim, evil-smelling hallway.

Once more she put out a shaking hand.

'Wait,' she commanded huskily. 'Remember! Don't either of you say a word about – about his being possibly the boy I'm looking for. I must see for myself first, and – question him.'

'Of course!' agreed Pollyanna.

'Sure! I'm on,' nodded the boy. 'I gotta go right off anyhow, so I won't bother ye none. Now toddle easy up these 'ere stairs. There's always holes, and most generally there's a kid or two asleep somewheres. An' the elevator ain't runnin' terday,' he gibed cheerfully. 'We gotta go ter the top, too!'

Mrs Carew found the 'holes' – broken boards that creaked and bent fearsomely under her shrinking feet; and she found one 'kid' – a two-year-old baby playing with an empty tin can on a string which he was banging up and down the second flight of stairs. On all sides doors were opened, now boldly, now stealthily, but always disclosing women with tousled heads or peering children with dirty faces. Somewhere a baby was wailing piteously. Somewhere else a man was cursing. Everywhere was the smell of bad whiskey, stale cabbage and unwashed humanity.

At the top of the third and last stairway the boy came to a pause before a closed door.

'I'm just a-thinkin' what Sir James'll say when he's wise ter the prize package I'm bringin' him,' he whispered in a throaty voice. 'I know what mumsey'll do – she'll turn on the weeps in no time ter see Jamie so tickled.' The next moment he threw wide the door with a gay: 'Here we be – an' we come in a buzz-wagon! Ain't that goin' some, Sir James?'

It was a tiny room, cold and cheerless and pitifully bare, but scrupulously neat. There were here no tousled heads, no peering children, no odours of whiskey, cabbage and unclean humanity. There were two beds, three broken chairs, a dry-goods-box table, and a stove with a faint glow of light that told of a fire not nearly brisk enough to heat even that tiny room. On one of the beds lay a lad with flushed cheeks and fever-bright eyes. Near him sat a thin, white-faced woman, bent and twisted with rheumatism.

Mrs Carew stepped into the room and, as if to steady herself, paused a minute with her back to the wall. Pollyanna hurried forward with a low cry just as Jerry, with an apologetic 'I gotta go now; goodbye!' dashed through the door.

'Oh, Jamie, I'm so glad I've found you,' cried Pollyanna. 'You don't know how I've looked and looked for you every day. But I'm so sorry you're sick!'

Jamie smiled radiantly and held out a thin white hand.

'I ain't sorry – I'm *glad*,' he emphasised meaningly; ' 'cause it's brought you to see me. Besides, I'm better now, anyway. Mumsey, this is the little girl, you know, that told me the glad game – and mumsey's playing it, too,' he triumphed, turning back to Pollyanna. 'First she cried 'cause her back hurts too bad to let her work; then when I was took worse she was *glad* she couldn't work, 'cause she could be here to take care of me, you know.'

At that moment Mrs Carew hurried forward, her eyes half-fearfully, half-longingly on the face of the lame boy in the bed.

'It's Mrs Carew. I've brought her to see you, Jamie,' introduced Pollyanna, in a tremulous voice.

The little twisted woman by the bed had struggled to her feet by this time, and was nervously offering her chair. Mrs Carew accepted it without so much as a glance. Her eyes were still on the boy in the bed.

'Your name is – Jamie?' she asked, with visible difficulty.

'Yes, ma'am.' The boy's bright eyes looked straight into hers.

'What is your other name?'

'I don't know.'

'He is not your son?' For the first time Mrs Carew turned to the twisted little woman who was still standing by the bed.

'No, madam.'

'And you don't know his name?'

'No, madam. I never knew it.'

With a despairing gesture Mrs Carew turned back to the boy.

'But think, think – don't you remember *anything* of your name but – Jamie?'

The boy shook his head. Into his eyes was coming a puzzled wonder.

'No, nothing.'

'Haven't you anything that belonged to your father, with possibly his name in it?'

'There wasn't anythin' worth savin' but them books,' interposed Mrs Murphy. 'Them's his. Maybe you'd like to look at 'em,' she suggested, pointing to a row of worn volumes on a shelf across the room. Then, in plainly uncontrollable curiosity, she asked: 'Was you thinkin' you knew him, ma'am?'

'I don't know,' murmured Mrs Carew, in a half-stifled voice, as she rose to her feet and crossed the room to the shelf of books.

There were not many – perhaps ten or a dozen. There was a volume of Shakespeare's plays, an *Ivanhoe*, a much-thumbed *Lady of the Lake*, a book of miscellaneous poems, a coverless Tennyson, a dilapidated *Little Lord Fauntleroy* and two or three books of ancient and medieval history. But, though Mrs Carew looked carefully through every one, she found nowhere any written word. With a despairing sigh she turned back to the boy and to the woman, both of whom now were watching her with startled, questioning eyes.

'I wish you'd tell me – both of you – all you know about yourselves,' she said brokenly, dropping herself once more into the chair by the bed.

And they told her. It was much the same story that Jamie had told Pollyanna in the Public Garden. There was little that was new, nothing that was significant, in spite of the probing questions that Mrs Carew asked. At its conclusion Jamie turned eager eyes on Mrs Carew's face.

'Do you think you knew – my father?' he begged.

Mrs Carew closed her eyes and pressed her hand to her head.

'I don't – know,' she answered. 'But I think – not.'

Pollyanna gave a quick cry of keen disappointment, but as quickly she suppressed it in obedience to Mrs Carew's warning glance. With new horror, however, she surveyed the tiny room.

Jamie, turning his wondering eyes from Mrs Carew's face, suddenly awoke to his duties as host.

'Wasn't you good to come!' he said to Pollyanna, gratefully. 'How's Sir Lancelot? Do you ever go to feed him now?' Then, as Pollyanna did not answer at once, he hurried on, his eyes going from her face to the somewhat battered pink in a broken-necked bottle in the window. 'Did you see my posy? Jerry found it. Somebody dropped it and he picked it up. Ain't it pretty? And it *smells* a little.'

But Pollyanna did not seem even to have heard him. She was still gazing, wide-eyed about the room, clasping and unclasping her hands nervously.

'But I don't see how you can ever play the game here at all, Jamie,' she faltered. 'I didn't suppose there could be anywhere such a perfectly awful place to live,' she shuddered.

'Ho!' scoffed Jamie, valiantly. 'You'd oughter see the Pikes' downstairs. Theirs is a whole lot worse'n this. You don't know what a lot of nice things there is about this room. Why, we get the sun in that winder there for 'most two hours every day, when it shines. And if you get real near it you can see a whole lot of sky from it. If we could only *keep* the room! – but you see we've got to leave, we're afraid. And that's what's worrin' us.'

'Leave!'

'Yes. We got behind on the rent – mumsey bein' sick so, and not earnin' anythin'.' In spite of a courageously cheerful smile, Jamie's voice shook. 'Mis' Dolan downstairs – the woman what keeps my wheelchair for me, you know – is helpin' us out this week. But of course she can't do it always, and then we'll have to go – if Jerry don't strike it rich, or somethin'.'

'Oh, but can't we – ' began Pollyanna.

She stopped short. Mrs Carew had risen to her feet abruptly with a hurried: 'Come, Pollyanna, we must go.' Then to the woman she turned wearily. 'You won't have to leave. I'll send you money and food at once, and I'll mention your case to one of the charity organisations in which I am interested, and they will – '

In surprise she ceased speaking. The bent little figure of the woman opposite had drawn itself almost erect. Mrs Murphy's cheeks were flushed. Her eyes showed a smouldering fire.

'Thank you, no, Mrs Carew,' she said tremulously, but proudly. 'We're poor – God knows; but we ain't charity folks.'

'Nonsense!' cried Mrs Carew, sharply. 'You're letting the woman downstairs help you. This boy said so.'

'I know; but that ain't charity,' persisted the woman, still tremulously. 'Mrs Dolan is my *friend*. She knows *I'd* do *her* a good turn just as quick – I have done 'em for her in times past. Help from *friends* ain't charity. They *care*; and that – that makes a difference. We wasn't always as we are now, you see; and that makes it hurt all the more – all this. Thank you; but we couldn't take – your money.'

Mrs Carew frowned angrily. It had been a most disappointing, heart-breaking, exhausting hour for her. Never a patient woman, she was exasperated now, besides being utterly tired out.

'Very well, just as you please,' she said coldly. Then, with vague irritation, she added: 'But why don't you go to your landlord and insist that he make you even decently comfortable while you do stay? Surely you're entitled to something besides broken windows stuffed with rags and papers! And those stairs that I came up are positively dangerous.'

Mrs Murphy sighed in a discouraged way. Her twisted little figure had fallen back into its old hopelessness.

'We have tried to have something done, but it's never amounted to anything. We never see anybody but the agent, of course; and he says the rents are too low for the owner to put out any more money on repairs.'

'Nonsense!' snapped Mrs Carew, with all the sharpness of a nervous, distraught woman who has at last found an outlet for her exasperation. 'It's shameful! What's more, I think it's a clear case of violation of the law – those stairs are, certainly. I shall make it my business to see that he's brought to terms. What is the name of that agent, and who is the owner of this delectable establishment?'

'I don't know the name of the owner, madam; but the agent is Mr Dodge.'

'Dodge!' Mrs Carew turned sharply, an odd look on her face. 'You don't mean – Henry Dodge?'

'Yes, madam. His name is Henry, I think.'

A flood of colour swept into Mrs Carew's face, then receded, leaving it whiter than before.

'Very well, I – I'll attend to it,' she murmured, in a half-stifled voice, turning away. 'Come, Pollyanna, we must go now.'

Over at the bed Pollyanna was bidding Jamie a tearful goodbye.

'But I'll come again. I'll come real soon,' she promised brightly, as she hurried through the door after Mrs Carew.

Not until they had picked their precarious way down the three long flights of stairs and through the jabbering, gesticulating crowd of men, women and children that surrounded the scowling Perkins and the limousine, did Pollyanna speak again. But then she scarcely waited for the irate chauffeur to slam the door upon them before she pleaded: 'Dear Mrs Carew, please, please say that it was Jamie! Oh, it would be so nice for him to be Jamie.'

'But he isn't Jamie!'

'Oh dear! Are you sure?'

There was a moment's pause, then Mrs Carew covered her face with her hands.

'No, I'm not sure – and that's the tragedy of it,' she moaned. 'I don't think he is; I'm almost positive he isn't. But, of course, there *is* a chance – and that's what's killing me.'

'Then can't you just *think* he's Jamie,' begged Pollyanna, 'and play he was? Then you could take him home, and – ' But Mrs Carew turned fiercely.

'Take that boy into my home when he *wasn't* Jamie? Never, Pollyanna! I couldn't.'

'But if you *can't* help Jamie, I should think you'd be so glad there was someone like him you *could* help,' urged Pollyanna, tremulously. 'What if your Jamie was like this Jamie, all poor and sick, wouldn't you want someone to take him in and comfort him, and – '

'Don't – don't, Pollyanna,' moaned Mrs Carew, turning her head from side to side, in a frenzy of grief. 'When I think that maybe, somewhere, our Jamie is like that – ' Only a choking sob finished the sentence.

'That's just what I mean – that's just what I mean!' triumphed Pollyanna, excitedly. 'Don't you see? If this *is* your Jamie, of course you'll want him; and if it isn't, you couldn't be doing any harm to the other Jamie by taking this one, and you'd do a whole lot of good, for you'd make this one so happy – so happy! And then, by and by, if you should find the real Jamie, you wouldn't have lost anything, but you'd have made two little boys happy instead of one; and – '

But again Mrs Carew interrupted her. 'Don't, Pollyanna, don't! I want to think – I want to think.'

Tearfully Pollyanna sat back in her seat. By a very visible effort she kept still for one whole minute. Then, as if the words fairly bubbled forth of themselves, there came this: 'Oh, but what an awful, awful place that was! I just wish the man that owned it had to live in it himself – and then see what he'd have to be glad for!'

Mrs Carew sat suddenly erect. Her face showed a curious change. Almost as if in appeal she flung out her hand towards Pollyanna.

'Don't!' she cried. 'Perhaps – she didn't know, Pollyanna. Perhaps she didn't know. I'm sure she didn't know – she owned a place like that. But it will be fixed now – it will be fixed.'

'*She!* Is it a woman that owns it, and do you know her? And do you know the agent, too?'

'Yes.' Mrs Carew bit her lips. 'I know her, and I know the agent.'

'Oh, I'm so glad,' sighed Pollyanna. 'Then it'll be all right now.'

'Well, it certainly will be – better,' avowed Mrs Carew with emphasis, as the car stopped before her own door.

Mrs Carew spoke as if she knew what she was talking about. And perhaps, indeed, she did – better than she cared to tell Pollyanna. Certainly, before she slept that night, a letter left her hands addressed to one Henry Dodge, summoning him to an immediate conference as to certain changes and repairs to be made at once in tenements she owned. There were, moreover, several scathing sentences concerning 'rag-stuffed windows', and 'rickety stairways', that caused this same Henry Dodge to scowl angrily, and to say a sharp word behind his teeth – though at the same time he paled with something very like fear.

CHAPTER II

A Surprise for Mrs Carew

The matter of repairs and improvements having been properly and efficiently attended to, Mrs Carew told herself that she had done her duty, and that the matter was closed. She would forget it. The boy was not Jamie – he could not be Jamie. That ignorant, sickly, crippled boy her dead sister's son? Impossible! She would cast the whole thing from her thoughts.

It was just here, however, that Mrs Carew found herself against an immovable, impassable barrier: the whole thing refused to be cast from her thoughts. Always before her eyes was the picture of that bare little room and the wistful-faced boy. Always in her ears was that heartbreaking, 'What if it *were* Jamie?' And always, too, there was Pollyanna; for even though Mrs Carew might (as she did) silence the pleadings and questionings of the little girl's tongue, there was no getting away from the prayers and reproaches of the little girl's eyes.

Twice again in desperation Mrs Carew went to see the boy, telling herself each time that only another visit was needed to convince her that the boy was not the one she sought. But, even though while there in the boy's presence, she told herself that she *was* convinced, once away from it, the old, old questioning returned. At last, in still greater desperation, she wrote to her sister, and told her the whole story. After she had stated the bare facts of the case, she went on:

I had not meant to tell you. I thought it a pity to harrow you up, or to raise false hopes. I am so sure it is not he – and yet, even as I write these words, I know I am *not* sure. That is why I want you to come – why you must come. I must have you see him.

I wonder – oh, I wonder what you'll say! Of course we haven't seen our Jamie since he was four years old. He would be twelve now. This boy is twelve, I should judge. (He doesn't know his age.) He has hair and eyes not unlike our Jamie's. He is crippled, but that condition came upon him through a fall, six years ago, and was made worse through another one four years later. Anything like a complete description of his father's appearance seems impossible to obtain; but what I have learned contains nothing conclusive either for or against his being poor Doris's husband. He was called the 'Professor', was very queer and seemed to own nothing save a few books. This might, or might not signify. John Kent was certainly always queer, and a good deal of a bohemian in his tastes. Whether he cared for books or not I don't remember. Do you? And of course the title 'Professor' might easily have been assumed, if he wished, or it might have been merely given him by others. As for this boy – I don't know, I don't know – but I do hope *you* will!

Your distracted sister,

RUTH

Della came at once, and she went immediately to see the boy; but she did not 'know'. Like her sister, she said she did not think it was their Jamie, but at the same time there was that chance – it might be he, after all. Like Pollyanna, however, she had what she thought was a very satisfactory way out of the dilemma.

'But why don't you take him, dear?' she proposed to her sister. 'Why don't you take him and adopt him? It would be lovely for him – poor little fellow – and – ' But Mrs Carew shuddered and would not even let her finish.

'No, no, I can't, I can't!' she moaned. 'I want my Jamie, my own Jamie – or no one.' And with a sigh Della gave it up and went back to her nursing.

If Mrs Carew thought that this closed the matter, however, she was again mistaken; for her days were still restless, and her nights were still either sleepless or filled with dreams of a 'may be' or a 'might be' masquerading as an 'it is so'. She was, moreover, having a difficult time with Pollyanna.

Pollyanna was puzzled. She was filled with questionings and unrest. For the first time in her life Pollyanna had come face to face with real poverty. She knew people who did not have enough to eat, who wore ragged clothing and who lived in dark, dirty and very tiny rooms. Her first impulse, of course, had been 'to help'. With Mrs Carew she made two visits to Jamie, and greatly did she rejoice at the changed conditions she found there after 'that man Dodge' had 'tended to things'. But this, to Pollyanna, was a mere drop in the bucket. There were yet all those other sick-looking men, unhappy-looking women, and ragged children out in the street – Jamie's neighbours. Confidently she looked to Mrs Carew for help for them, also.

'Indeed!' exclaimed Mrs Carew, when she learned what was expected of her, 'so you want the whole street to be supplied with fresh paper, paint, and new stairways, do you? Pray, is there anything else you'd like?'

'Oh, yes, lots of things,' sighed Pollyanna, happily. 'You see, there are so many things they need – all of them! And what fun it will be to get them! How I wish I was rich so I could help, too; but I'm 'most as glad to be with you when you get them.'

Mrs Carew quite gasped aloud in her amazement. She lost no time – though she did lose not a little patience – in explaining that she had no intention of doing anything further in 'Murphy's Alley', and that there was no reason why she should. No one would expect her to. She had cancelled all possible obligations, and had even been really very generous, anyone would say, in what she had done for the tenement where lived Jamie and the Murphys. (That she owned the tenement building she did not think it necessary to state.) At some length she explained to Pollyanna that there were charitable institutions, both numerous and efficient, whose business it was to aid all the worthy poor, and that to these institutions she gave frequently and liberally.

Even then, however, Pollyanna was not convinced.

'But I don't see,' she argued, 'why it's any better, or even so nice, for a whole lot of folks to club together and do what everybody would like to do for themselves. I'm sure I'd much rather give Jamie a – a nice book, now, than to have some old Society do it; and I *know* he'd like better to have me do it, too.'

'Very likely,' returned Mrs Carew, with some weariness and a little exasperation. 'But it is just possible that it would not be so well for Jamie as – as if that book were given by a body of people who knew what sort of one to select.'

This led her to say much, also (none of which Pollyanna in the least understood), about 'pauperising the poor', the 'evils of indiscriminate giving' and the 'pernicious effect of unorganised charity'.

'Besides,' she added, in answer to the still perplexed expression on Pollyanna's worried little face, 'very likely if I offered help to these people they would not take it. You remember Mrs Murphy declined, at the first, to let me send food and clothing – though they accepted it readily enough from their neighbours on the first floor, it seems.'

'Yes, I know,' sighed Pollyanna, turning away. 'There's something there somehow that I don't understand. But it doesn't seem right that *we* should have such a lot of nice things, and that *they* shouldn't have anything, hardly.'

As the days passed, this feeling on the part of Pollyanna increased rather than diminished; and the questions she asked and the comments she made were anything but a relief to the state of mind in which Mrs Carew herself was. Even the test of the glad game, in this case, Pollyanna was finding to be very near a failure; for, as she expressed it: 'I don't see how you can find anything about this poor-people business to be glad for. Of course we can be glad for ourselves that we aren't poor like them; but whenever I'm thinking how glad I am for that, I get so sorry for them that I *can't* be glad any longer. Of course we *could* be glad there were poor folks, because we could help them. But if we *don't* help them, where's the glad part of that coming in?' And to this Pollyanna could find no one who could give her a satisfactory answer.

Especially she asked this question of Mrs Carew; and Mrs Carew, still haunted by the visions of the Jamie that was, and the Jamie that might be, grew only more restless, more wretched and more utterly despairing. Nor was she helped any by the approach of Christmas. Nowhere was there glow of holly or flash of tinsel that did not carry its pang to her; for always to Mrs Carew it but symbolised a child's empty stocking – a stocking that might be – Jamie's.

Finally, a week before Christmas, she fought what she thought was the last battle with herself. Resolutely, but with no real joy in her face, she gave terse orders to Mary, and summoned Pollyanna.

'Pollyanna,' she began, almost harshly, 'I have decided to – to take Jamie. The car will be here at once. I'm going after him now – to bring him home. You may come with me if you like.'

A great light transfigured Pollyanna's face.

'Oh, oh, oh, how glad I am!' she breathed. 'Why, I'm so glad I – I want to cry! Mrs Carew, why is it, when you're the very gladdest of anything, you always want to cry?'

'I don't know, I'm sure, Pollyanna,' rejoined Mrs Carew, abstractedly. On Mrs Carew's face there was still no look of joy.

Once in the Murphys' little one-room tenement, it did not take Mrs Carew long to tell her errand. In a few short sentences she told the story of the lost Jamie, and of her first hopes that this Jamie might be he. She made no secret of her doubts that he was the one; at the same time, she said she had decided to take him home with her and give him every possible advantage. Then, a little wearily, she told what were the plans she had made for him.

At the foot of the bed Mrs Murphy listened, crying softly. Across the room Jerry Murphy, his eyes dilating, emitted an occasional low 'Gee! Can ye beat that, now?' As to Jamie – Jamie, on the bed, had listened at first with the air of one to whom suddenly a door has opened into a longed-for paradise; but gradually, as Mrs Carew talked, a new look came to his eyes. Very slowly he closed them, and turned away his face.

When Mrs Carew ceased speaking there was a long silence before Jamie turned his head and answered. They saw then that his face was very white, and that his eyes were full of tears.

'Thank you, Mrs Carew, but – I can't go,' he said simply.

'You can't – what?' cried Mrs Carew, as if she doubted the evidence of her own ears.

'Jamie!' gasped Pollyanna.

'Oh, come, kid, what's eatin' ye?' scowled Jerry, hurriedly coming forward. 'Don't ye know a good thing when ye see it?'

'Yes; but I can't – go,' said the crippled boy, again.

'But, Jamie, Jamie, think, *think* what it would mean to you!' quavered Mrs Murphy, at the foot of the bed.

'I am a-thinkin',' choked Jamie. 'Don't you suppose I know what I'm doin' – what I'm givin' up?' Then to Mrs Carew he turned tear-wet eyes. 'I can't,' he faltered. 'I can't let you do all that for me. If you – *cared* it would be different. But you don't care – not really. You don't *want* me – not *me*. You want the real Jamie, and I ain't the real Jamie. You don't think I am. I can see it in your face.'

'I know. But – but – ' began Mrs Carew, helplessly.

'And it isn't as if – as if I was like other boys, and could walk, either,' interrupted the cripple, feverishly. 'You'd get tired of me in no time. And I'd see it comin'. I couldn't stand it – to be a burden like that. Of course, if you *cared* – like mumsey here – ' He threw out his hand, choked back a sob, then turned his head away again. 'I'm not the Jamie you want. I – can't – go,' he said. With the words, his thin, boyish hand fell clenched till the knuckles showed white against the tattered old shawl that covered the bed.

There was a moment's breathless hush, then, very quietly, Mrs Carew got to her feet. Her face was colourless; but there was that in it that silenced the sob that rose to Pollyanna's lips.

'Come, Pollyanna,' was all she said.

'Well, if you ain't the fool limit!' babbled Jerry Murphy to the boy on the bed, as the door closed a moment later.

But the boy on the bed was crying very much as if the closing door had been the one that had led to paradise – and that had closed now for ever.

CHAPTER 12

From Behind a Counter

Mrs Carew was very angry. To have brought herself to the point where she was willing to take this lame boy into her home, and then to have the lad calmly refuse to come, was unbearable. Mrs Carew was not in the habit of having her invitations ignored, or her wishes scorned. Furthermore, now that she could not have the boy, she was conscious of an almost frantic terror lest he were, after all, the real Jamie. She knew then that her true reason for wanting him had been – not because she cared for him, not even because she wished to help him and make him happy – but because she hoped, by taking him, that she would ease her own mind, and forever silence that awful eternal questioning on her part: 'What if he *were* her own Jamie?'

It certainly had not helped matters any that the boy had divined her state of mind, and had given as the reason for his refusal that she 'did not care'. To be sure, Mrs Carew now very proudly told herself that she did not indeed 'care', that he was *not* her sister's boy, and that she would 'forget all about it'.

But she did not forget all about it. However insistently she might disclaim responsibility and relationship, just as insistently responsibility and relationship thrust themselves upon her in the shape of panicky doubts; and however resolutely she turned her thoughts to other matters, just so resolutely visions of a wistful-eyed boy in a poverty-stricken room loomed always before her.

Then, too, there was Pollyanna. Clearly Pollyanna was not herself at all. In a most unPollyanna-like spirit she moped about the house, finding apparently no interest anywhere.

'Oh, no, I'm not sick,' she would answer, when remonstrated with, and questioned.

'But what *is* the trouble?'

'Why, nothing. It – it's only that I was thinking of Jamie, you know – how *he* hasn't got all these beautiful things – carpets, and pictures, and curtains.'

It was the same with her food. Pollyanna was actually losing her appetite; but here again she disclaimed sickness.

'Oh, no,' she would sigh mournfully. 'It's just that I don't seem hungry. Some way, just as soon as I begin to eat, I think of Jamie, and how *he* doesn't have only old doughnuts and dry rolls; and then I – I don't want anything.'

Mrs Carew, spurred by a feeling that she herself only dimly understood, and recklessly determined to bring about some change in Pollyanna at all costs, ordered a huge tree, two dozen wreaths, and quantities of holly and Christmas baubles. For the first time in many years the house was aflame and aglitter with scarlet and tinsel. There was even to be a Christmas party, for Mrs Carew had told Pollyanna to invite half a dozen of her schoolgirl friends for the tree on Christmas Eve.

But even here Mrs Carew met with disappointment; for, though Pollyanna was always grateful, and at times interested and even excited, she still carried frequently a sober little face. And in the end the Christmas party was more of a sorrow than a joy; for the first glimpse of the glittering tree sent her into a storm of sobs.

'Why, Pollyanna!' ejaculated Mrs Carew. 'What in the world is the matter now?'

'N–n–nothing,' wept Pollyanna. 'It's only that it's so perfectly, perfectly beautiful that I just had to cry. I was thinking how Jamie would love to see it.'

It was then that Mrs Carew's patience snapped.

' "Jamie, Jamie, Jamie"!' she exclaimed. 'Pollyanna, *can't* you stop talking about that boy? You know perfectly well that it is not my fault that he is not here. I asked him to come here to live. Besides, where is that glad game of yours? I think it would be an excellent idea if you would play it on this.'

'I *am* playing it,' quavered Pollyanna. 'And that's what I don't understand. I never knew it to act so funny. Why, before, when I've been glad about things, I've been happy. But now, about Jamie – I'm so glad I've got carpets and pictures and nice things to eat, and that I can walk and run, and go to school, and all that; but the harder I'm glad for myself, the sorrier I am for him. I never knew the game to act so funny, and I don't know what ails it. Do you?'

But Mrs Carew, with a despairing gesture, merely turned away without a word.

It was the day after Christmas that something so wonderful happened that Pollyanna, for a time, almost forgot Jamie. Mrs Carew had taken her shopping, and it was while Mrs Carew was trying to decide between a duchesse-lace and a point-lace collar, that Pollyanna chanced to spy farther down the counter a face that looked vaguely familiar. For a moment she regarded it frowningly; then, with a little cry, she ran down the aisle.

'Oh, it's you – it *is* you!' she exclaimed joyously to a girl who was putting into the showcase a tray of pink bows. 'I'm so glad to see you!'

The girl behind the counter lifted her head and stared at Pollyanna in amazement. But almost immediately her dark, sombre face lighted with a smile of glad recognition.

'Well, well, if it isn't my little Public Garden kiddie!' she ejaculated.

'Yes. I'm so glad you remembered,' beamed Pollyanna. 'But you never came again. I looked for you lots of times.'

'I couldn't. I had to work. That was our last half-holiday, and – Fifty cents, madam,' she broke off, in answer to a sweet-faced old lady's question as to the price of a black-and-white bow on the counter.

'Fifty cents? Hm-m!' The old lady fingered the bow, hesitated, then laid it down with a sigh. 'Hm, yes; well, it's very pretty, I'm sure, my dear,' she said, as she passed on.

Immediately behind her came two bright-faced girls who, with much giggling and bantering, picked out a jewelled creation of scarlet velvet, and a fairy-like structure of tulle and pink buds. As the girls turned chattering away Pollyanna drew an ecstatic sigh.

'Is this what you do all day? My, how glad you must be you chose this!'

'*Glad!*'

'Yes. It must be such fun – such lots of folks, you know, and all different! And you can talk to 'em. You *have* to talk to 'em – it's your business. I should love that. I think I'll do this when I grow up. It must be such fun to see what they all buy!'

'Fun! Glad!' bristled the girl behind the counter. 'Well, child, I guess if you knew half – That's a dollar, madam,' she interrupted herself hastily, in answer to a young woman's sharp question as to the price of a flaring yellow bow of beaded velvet in the showcase.

'Well, I should think 'twas time you told me,' snapped the young woman. 'I had to ask you twice.'

The girl behind the counter bit her lip.

'I didn't hear you, madam.'

'I can't help that. It is your business *to* hear. You are paid for it, aren't you? How much is that black one?'

'Fifty cents.'

'And that blue one?'

'One dollar.'

'No impudence, miss! You needn't be so short about it, or I shall report you. Let me see that tray of pink ones.'

The salesgirl's lips opened, then closed in a thin, straight line. Obediently she reached into the showcase and took out the tray of pink bows; but her eyes flashed, and her hands shook visibly as she set the tray down on the counter. The young woman whom she was serving picked up five bows, asked the price of four of them, then turned away with a brief: 'I see nothing I care for.'

'Well,' said the girl behind the counter, in a shaking voice, to the wide-eyed Pollyanna, 'what do you think of my business now? Anything to be glad about there?'

Pollyanna giggled a little hysterically.

'My, wasn't she cross? But she was kind of funny, too – don't you think? Anyhow, you can be glad that – that they aren't *all* like *her*, can't you?'

'I suppose so,' said the girl, with a faint smile, 'But I can tell you right now, kiddie, that glad game of yours you was tellin' me about that day in the Garden may be all very well for you; but – ' Once more she stopped with a tired: 'Fifty cents, madam,' in answer to a question from the other side of the counter.

'Are you as lonesome as ever?' asked Pollyanna wistfully, when the salesgirl was at liberty again.

'Well, I can't say I've given more'n five parties, nor been to more'n seven, since I saw you,' replied the girl so bitterly that Pollyanna detected the sarcasm.

'Oh, but you did something nice for Christmas, didn't you?'

'Oh, yes. I stayed in bed all day with my feet done up in rags and read four newspapers and one magazine. Then at night I hobbled out to a restaurant where I had to fork out thirty-five cents for chicken pie instead of a quarter.'

'But what ailed your feet?'

'Blistered. Standin' on 'em – Christmas rush.'

'Oh!' shuddered Pollyanna, sympathetically. 'And you didn't have any tree, or party, or anything?' she cried, distressed and shocked.

'Well, hardly!'

'Oh dear! How I wish you could have seen mine!' sighed the little girl. 'It was just lovely, and – But, oh, say!' she exclaimed joyously. 'You can see it, after all. It isn't gone yet. Now, can't you come out tonight, or tomorrow night, and – '

'Poll*anna*!' interrupted Mrs Carew in her chilliest accents. 'What in the world does this mean? Where have you been? I have looked everywhere for you. I even went way back to the suit department.'

Pollyanna turned with a happy little cry.

'Oh, Mrs Carew, I'm so glad you've come,' she rejoiced. 'This is – well, I don't know her name yet, but I know *her*, so it's all right. I met her in the Public Garden ever so long ago. And she's lonesome, and doesn't know anybody. And her father was a minister like mine, only he's alive. And she didn't have any Christmas tree only blistered feet and chicken pie; and I want her to see mine, you know – the tree, I mean,' plunged on Pollyanna, breathlessly. 'I've asked her to come out tonight, or tomorrow night. And you'll let me have it all lighted up again, won't you?'

'Well, really, Pollyanna,' began Mrs Carew, in cold disapproval. But the girl behind the counter interrupted with a voice quite as cold, and even more disapproving.

'Don't worry, madam. I've no notion of goin'.'

'Oh, but *please*,' begged Pollyanna. 'You don't know how I want you, and – '

'I notice the lady ain't doin' any askin',' interrupted the salesgirl, a little maliciously.

Mrs Carew flushed an angry red, and turned as if to go; but Pollyanna caught her arm and held it, talking meanwhile almost frenziedly to the girl behind the counter, who happened, at the moment, to be free from customers.

'Oh, but she will, she will,' Pollyanna was saying. 'She wants you to come – I know she does. Why, you don't know how good she is, and how much money she gives to – to charitable 'sociations and everything.'

'Poll*yanna!*' remonstrated Mrs Carew, sharply. Once more she would have gone, but this time she was held spellbound by the ringing scorn in the low, tense voice of the salesgirl.

'Oh, yes, I know! There's lots of 'em that'll give to *rescue*work. There's always plenty of helpin' hands stretched out to them that has gone wrong. And that's all right. I ain't findin' no fault with that. Only sometimes I wonder there don't some of 'em think of helpin' the girls *before* they go wrong. Why don't they give *good* girls pretty homes with books and pictures and soft carpets and music, and somebody round 'em to care? Maybe then there wouldn't be so many – Good heavens, what am I sayin'?' she broke off, under her breath. Then, with the old weariness, she turned to a young woman who had stopped before her and picked up a blue bow.

'That's fifty cents, madam,' Mrs Carew heard, as she hurried Pollyanna away.

CHAPTER 13

A Waiting and a Winning

It was a delightful plan. Pollyanna had it entirely formulated in about five minutes; then she told Mrs Carew. Mrs Carew did not think it was a delightful plan, and she said so very distinctly.

'Oh, but I'm sure *they'll* think it is,' argued Pollyanna, in reply to Mrs Carew's objections. 'And just think how easy we can do it! The tree is just as it was – except for the presents, and we can get more of those. It won't be so very long till New Year's Eve; and only think how glad she'll be to come! Wouldn't *you* be, if you hadn't had anything for Christmas only blistered feet and chicken pie?'

'Dear, dear, what an impossible child you are!' frowned Mrs Carew. 'Even yet it doesn't seem to occur to you that we don't know this young person's name.'

'So we don't! And isn't it funny, when I feel that I know *her* so well?' smiled Pollyanna. 'You see, we had such a good talk in the Garden that day, and she told me all about how lonesome she was, and that she thought the lonesomest place in the world was in a crowd in a big city, because folks didn't think nor notice. Oh, there was one that noticed; but he noticed too much, she said, and he hadn't ought to notice her any – which is kind of funny, isn't it, when you come to think of it. But anyhow, he came for her there in the Garden to go somewhere with him, and she wouldn't go, and he was a real handsome gentleman, too – until he began to look so cross, just at the last. Folks aren't so pretty when they're cross, are they? Now there was a lady today looking at bows, and she said – well, lots of things that weren't nice, you know. And *she* didn't look pretty, either, after – after she began to talk. But you will let me have the tree New Year's Eve, won't you, Mrs Carew? – and invite this girl who sells bows, and Jamie? He's better, you know, now, and he *could* come. Of course Jerry would have to wheel him – but then, we'd want Jerry, anyway.'

'Oh, of course, *Jerry*!' exclaimed Mrs Carew in ironic scorn. 'But why stop with Jerry? I'm sure Jerry has hosts of friends who would love to come. And – '

'Oh, Mrs Carew, *may* I?' broke in Pollyanna, in uncontrollable delight. 'Oh, how good, *good*, *good* you are! I've so wanted – '

But Mrs Carew fairly gasped aloud in surprise and dismay. 'No, no, Pollyanna, I – ' she began, protestingly.

But Pollyanna, entirely mistaking the meaning of her interruption, plunged in again in stout championship.

'Indeed you *are* good – just the bestest ever; and I shan't let you say you aren't. Now I reckon I'll have a party all right! There's Tommy Dolan and his sister Jennie, and the two Macdonald children, and three girls whose names I don't know that live under the Murphys, and a whole lot more, if we have room for 'em. And only think how glad they'll be when I tell 'em! Why, Mrs Carew, seems to me as if I never knew anything so perfectly lovely in all my life – and it's all your doing! Now mayn't I begin right away to invite 'em – so they'll *know* what's coming to 'em?'

And Mrs Carew, who would not have believed such a thing possible, heard herself murmuring a faint 'yes', which, she knew, bound her to the giving of a Christmas-tree party on New Year's Eve to a dozen children from Murphy's Alley and a young salesgirl whose name she did not know.

Perhaps in Mrs Carew's memory was still lingering a young girl's 'Sometimes I wonder there don't some of 'em think of helpin' the girls *before* they go wrong.' Perhaps in her ears was still ringing Pollyanna's story of that same girl who had found a crowd in a big city the loneliest place in the world, yet who had refused to go with the handsome man that had 'noticed too much'. Perhaps in Mrs Carew's heart was the undefined hope that somewhere in it all lay the peace she had so longed for. Perhaps it was a little of all three combined with utter helplessness in the face of Pollyanna's amazing twisting of her irritated sarcasm into the wide-sweeping hospitality of a willing hostess. Whatever it was, the thing was done; and at once Mrs Carew found herself caught into a veritable whirl of plans and plottings, the centre of which was always Pollyanna and the party.

To her sister, Mrs Carew wrote distractedly of the whole affair, closing with: 'What I'm going to do I don't know; but I suppose I shall have to keep right on doing as I am doing. There is no other way. Of course, if Pollyanna once begins to preach – but she hasn't yet; so I can't, with a clear conscience, send her back to you.'

Della, reading this letter at the Sanatorium, laughed aloud at the conclusion.

' "Hasn't preached yet", indeed!' she chuckled to herself. 'Bless her dear heart! And yet you, Ruth Carew, own up to giving two Christmas-tree parties within a week, and, as I happen to know, your home, which used to be shrouded in death-like gloom, is aflame with scarlet and green from top to toe. But she hasn't preached yet – oh, no, she hasn't preached yet!'

The party was a great success. Even Mrs Carew admitted that. Jamie, in his wheelchair, Jerry, with his startling but expressive vocabulary, and the girl (whose name proved to be Sadie Dean) vied with each other in amusing the more diffident guests. Sadie Dean, much to the others' surprise – and perhaps to her own – disclosed an intimate knowledge of the most fascinating games; and these games, with Jamie's stories and Jerry's good-natured banter, kept everyone in gales of laughter until supper and the generous distribution of presents from the laden tree sent the happy guests home with tired sighs of content.

If Jamie (who with Jerry was the last to leave) looked about him a bit wistfully, no one apparently noticed it. Yet Mrs Carew, when she bade him good-night, said low in his ear, half impatiently, half embarrassedly: 'Well, Jamie, have you changed your mind – about coming?'

The boy hesitated. A faint colour stole into his cheeks. He turned and looked into her eyes wistfully, searchingly. Then very slowly he shook his head.

'If it could always be – like tonight, I – could,' he sighed. 'But it wouldn't. There'd be tomorrow, and next week, and next month, and next year comin'; and I'd know before next week that I hadn't oughter come.'

If Mrs Carew had thought that the New Year's Eve party was to end the matter of Pollyanna's efforts on behalf of Sadie Dean, she was soon undeceived; for the very next morning Pollyanna began to talk of her.

'And I'm so glad I found her again,' she prattled contentedly. 'Even if I haven't been able to find the real Jamie for you, I've found somebody else for you to love – and of course you'll love to love her, 'cause it's just another way of loving Jamie.'

Mrs Carew drew in her breath and gave a little gasp of exasperation. This unfailing faith in her goodness of heart, and unhesitating belief in her desire to 'help everybody' was most disconcerting, and some-times most annoying. At the same time it was a most difficult thing to disclaim – under the circumstances, especially with Pollyanna's happy, confident eyes full on her face.

'But, Pollyanna,' she objected impotently, at last, feeling very much as if she were struggling against invisible silken cords, 'I – you – this girl really isn't Jamie, at all, you know.'

'I know she isn't,' sympathised Pollyanna quickly. 'And of course I'm just as sorry she *isn't* Jamie as can be. But she's somebody's Jamie – that is, I mean she hasn't got anybody down here to love her and – and notice, you know; and so whenever you remember Jamie I should think you couldn't be glad enough there was *somebody* you could help, just as you'd want folks to help Jamie, wherever *he* is.'

Mrs Carew shivered and gave a little moan.

'But I want *my* Jamie,' she grieved.

Pollyanna nodded with understanding eyes.

'I know – the "child's presence". Mr Pendleton told me about it – only you've *got* the "woman's hand".'

'"Woman's hand"?'

'Yes – to make a home, you know. He said that it took a woman's hand or a child's presence to make a home. That was when he wanted me, and I found him Jimmy, and he adopted him instead.'

'*Jimmy?*' Mrs Carew looked up with the startled something in her eyes that always came into them at the mention of any variant of that name.

'Yes; Jimmy Bean.'

'Oh – *Bean*,' said Mrs Carew, relaxing.

'Yes. He was from an Orphans' Home, and he ran away. I found him. He said he wanted another kind of a home with a mother in it instead of a Matron. I couldn't find him the mother-part, but I found him Mr Pendleton, and he adopted him. His name is Jimmy Pendleton now.'

'But it was – Bean?'

'Yes, it was Bean.'

'Oh!' said Mrs Carew, this time with a long sigh.

Mrs Carew saw a good deal of Sadie Dean during the days that followed the New Year's Eve party. She saw a good deal of Jamie, too. In one way and another Pollyanna contrived to have them frequently at the house; and this, Mrs Carew, much to her surprise and vexation, could not seem to prevent. Her consent and even her delight were taken by Pollyanna as so much a matter of course that she found herself helpless to convince the child that neither approval nor satisfaction entered into the matter at all, as far as she was concerned.

But Mrs Carew, whether she herself realised it or not, was learning many things – things she never could have learned in the old days, shut up in her rooms, with orders to Mary to admit no one. She was learning something of what it means to be a lonely young girl in a big city, with one's living to earn, and with no one to care – except one who cares too much, and too little.

'But what did you mean?' she nervously asked Sadie Dean one evening; 'what did you mean that first day in the store – what you said – about helping the girls?'

Sadie Dean coloured distressfully.

'I'm afraid I was rude,' she apologised.

'Never mind that. Tell me what you meant. I've thought of it so many times since.'

For a moment the girl was silent; then, a little bitterly she said: ' 'Twas because I knew a girl once, and I was thinkin' of her. She came from my town, and she was pretty and good, but she wasn't over strong. For a year we pulled together, sharin' the same room, boiling our eggs over the same gas-jet, and eatin' our hash and fish balls for supper at the same cheap restaurant. There was never anything to do evenin's but to walk in the Common, or go to the movies, if we had the dime to blow in, or just stay in our room. Well, our room wasn't very pleasant. It was hot in summer, and cold in winter, and the gas-jet was so measly and so flickery that we couldn't sew or read, even if we hadn't been too fagged out to do either – which we 'most generally was. Besides, over our heads was a squeaky board that someone was always rockin' on, and under us was a feller that was learnin' to play the cornet. Did you ever hear anyone learn to play the cornet?'

'N–no, I don't think so,' murmured Mrs Carew.

'Well, you've missed a lot,' said the girl, dryly. Then, after a moment, she resumed her story.

'Sometimes, specially at Christmas and holidays, we used to walk up here on the Avenue, and other streets, huntin' for windows where the curtains were up, and we could look in. You see, we were pretty lonesome, them days specially, and we said it did us good to see homes with folks, and lamps on the centre-tables, and children playin' games; but we both of us knew that really it only made us feel worse than ever, because we were so hopelessly out of it all. 'Twas even harder to see the automobiles, and the gay young folks in them, laughing and chatting. You see, we were young, and I suspect we wanted to laugh and chatter. We wanted a good time, too; and, by and by – my chum began to have it – this good time.

'Well, to make a long story short, we broke partnership one day, and she went her way, and I mine. I didn't like the company she was keepin', and I said so. She wouldn't give 'em up, so we quit. I didn't see her again for 'most two years, then I got a note from her, and I went. This was just last month. She was in one of them rescue homes. It was a lovely place: soft rugs, fine pictures, plants, flowers and books, a piano, a beautiful room, and everything possible done for her. Rich women came in their automobiles and carriages to take her driving, and she was taken to concerts and matinées. She was learnin' stenography, and they were going to help her to a position just as soon as she could take it. Everybody was wonderfully good to her, she said, and showed they wanted to help her in every way. But she said something else, too.

'She said: "Sadie, if they'd taken one half the pains to show me they cared and wanted to help long ago when I was an honest, self-respectin', hard-workin' homesick girl – I wouldn't have been here for them to help now." And – well, I never forgot it. That's all. It ain't that I'm objectin' to the rescue work – it's a fine thing, and they ought to do it. Only I'm thinkin' there wouldn't be quite so much of it for them to do – if they'd just show a little of their interest earlier in the game.'

'But I thought there were working-girls' homes, and – and settlement-houses that – that did that sort of thing,' faltered Mrs Carew in a voice that few of her friends would have recognised.

'There are. Did you ever see the inside of one of them?'

'Why, n–no; though I – I have given money to them.' This time Mrs Carew's voice was almost apologetically pleading in tone.

Sadie Dean smiled curiously.

'Yes, I know. There are lots of good women that have given money to them – and have never seen the inside of one of them. Please don't understand that I'm sayin' anythin' against the homes. I'm not. They're good things. They're almost the only thing that's doing anything to help; but they're only a drop in the bucket to what is really needed. I tried one once; but there was an air about it – somehow I felt – But there, what's the use? Probably they aren't all like that one, and maybe the fault was with me. If I should try to tell you, you wouldn't understand. You'd have to live in it – and you haven't even seen the inside of one. But I can't help wonderin' sometimes why so many of those good women never seem to put the real *heart* and *interest* into the preventin' that they do into the rescuin'. But there! I didn't mean to talk such a lot. But – you asked me.'

'Yes, I asked you,' said Mrs Carew in a half-stifled voice, as she turned away.

Not only from Sadie Dean, however, was Mrs Carew learning things never learned before, but from Jamie, also.

Jamie was there a great deal. Pollyanna liked to have him there, and he liked to be there. At first, to be sure, he had hesitated; but very soon he had quieted his doubts and yielded to his longings by telling himself (and Pollyanna) that, after all, visiting was not 'staying for keeps'.

Mrs Carew often found the boy and Pollyanna contentedly settled on the library window-seat, with the empty wheelchair close by. Sometimes they were poring over a book. (She heard Jamie tell Pollyanna one day that he didn't think he'd mind so very much being lame if he had so many books as Mrs Carew, and that he guessed he'd be so happy he'd fly clean away if he had both books and legs.) Sometimes the boy was telling stories, and Pollyanna was listening, wide-eyed and absorbed.

Mrs Carew wondered at Pollyanna's interest – until one day she herself stopped and listened. After that she wondered no longer – but she listened a good deal longer. Crude and incorrect as was much of the boy's language, it was always wonderfully vivid and picturesque, so that Mrs Carew found herself, hand in hand with Pollyanna, trailing down the golden ages at the beck of a glowing-eyed boy.

Dimly Mrs Carew was beginning to realise, too, something of what it must mean, to be in spirit and ambition the centre of brave deeds and wonderful adventures, while in reality one was only a crippled boy in a wheelchair. But what Mrs Carew did not realise was the part this crippled boy was beginning to play in her own life. She did not realise how much a matter of course his presence was becoming, nor how interested she now was in finding something new 'for Jamie to see'. Neither did she realise how day by day he was coming to seem to her more and more the lost Jamie, her dead sister's child.

As February, March and April passed, however, and May came, bringing with it the near approach of the date set for Pollyanna's homegoing, Mrs Carew did suddenly awake to the knowledge of what that homegoing was to mean to her.

She was amazed and appalled. Up to now she had, in belief, looked forward with pleasure to the departure of Pollyanna. She had said that then once again the house would be quiet, with the glaring sun shut out. Once again she would be at peace, and able to hide herself away from the annoying, tiresome world. Once again she would be free to summon to her aching consciousness all those dear memories of the lost little lad who had so long ago stepped into that vast unknown and closed the door behind him. All this she had believed would be the case when Pollyanna should go home.

But now that Pollyanna was really going home, the picture was far different. The 'quiet house with the sun shut out' had become one that promised to be 'gloomy and unbearable'. The longed-for 'peace' would be 'wretched loneliness'; and as for her being able to 'hide herself away from the annoying, tiresome world,' and be 'free to summon to her aching consciousness all those dear memories of that lost little lad' – just as if anything could blot out those other aching memories of the new Jamie (who yet might be the old Jamie) with his pitiful, pleading eyes!

Full well now Mrs Carew knew that without Pollyanna the house would be empty; but that without the lad, Jamie, it would be worse than that. To her pride this knowledge was not pleasing. To her heart it was torture – since the boy had twice said that he would not come. For a time, during those last few days of Pollyanna's stay, the struggle was a bitter one, though pride always kept the ascendancy. Then, on what Mrs Carew knew would be Jamie's last visit, her heart triumphed, and once more she asked Jamie to come and be to her the Jamie that was lost.

What she said she never could remember afterwards; but what the boy said, she never forgot. After all, it was compassed in six short words.

For what seemed a long, long minute his eyes had searched her face; then to his own had come a transfiguring light, as he breathed: 'Oh, yes! Why, you – *care*, now!'

CHAPTER 14

Jimmy and the Green-Eyed Monster

This time Beldingsville did not literally welcome Pollyanna home with brass bands and bunting – perhaps because the hour of her expected arrival was known to but few of the townspeople. But there certainly was no lack of joyful greetings on the part of everybody from the moment she stepped from the railway train with her Aunt Polly and Dr Chilton. Nor did Pollyanna lose any time in starting on a round of fly-away minute calls on all her old friends. Indeed, for the next few days, according to Nancy, 'There wasn't no putting of your finger on her anywheres, for by the time you'd got your finger down she wasn't there.'

And always, everywhere she went, Pollyanna met the question: 'Well, how did you like Boston?' Perhaps to no one did she answer this more fully than she did to Mr Pendleton. As was usually the case when this question was put to her, she began her reply with a troubled frown.

'Oh, I liked it – I just loved it – some of it.'

'But not all of it?' smiled Mr Pendleton.

'No. There's parts of it – Oh, I was glad to be there,' she explained hastily. 'I had a perfectly lovely time, and lots of things were so queer and different, you know – like eating dinner at night instead of noons, when you ought to eat it. But everybody was so good to me, and I saw such a lot of wonderful things – Bunker Hill, and the Public Garden, and the Seeing Boston autos, and miles of pictures and statues and store-windows and streets that didn't have any end. And folks. I never saw such a lot of folks.'

'Well, I'm sure – I thought you liked folks,' commented the man.

'I do.' Pollyanna frowned again and pondered. 'But what's the use of such a lot of them if you don't know 'em? And Mrs Carew wouldn't let me. She didn't know 'em herself. She said folks didn't, down there.'

There was a slight pause, then, with a sigh, Pollyanna resumed.

'I reckon maybe that's the part I don't like the most – that folks don't know each other. It would be such a lot nicer if they did! Why, just think, Mr Pendleton, there are lots of folks that live on dirty, narrow streets, and don't even have beans and fish balls to eat, nor things even as good as missionary barrels to wear. Then there are other folks – Mrs Carew, and a whole lot like her – that live in perfectly beautiful houses, and have more things to eat and wear than they know what to do with. Now if *those* folks only knew the other folks – ' But Mr Pendleton interrupted with a laugh.

'My dear child, did it ever occur to you that these people don't *care* to know each other?' he asked quizzically.

'Oh, but some of them do,' maintained Pollyanna, in eager defence. 'Now there's Sadie Dean – she sells bows, lovely bows in a big store – she *wants* to know people; and I introduced her to Mrs Carew, and we had her up to the house, and we had Jamie and lots of others there, too; and she was *so* glad to know them! And that's what made me think that if only a lot of Mrs Carew's kind could know the other kind – but of course *I* couldn't do the introducing. I didn't know many of them myself, anyway. But if they *could* know each other, so that the rich people could give the poor people part of their money – '

But again Mr Pendleton interrupted with a laugh.

'Oh, Pollyanna, Pollyanna,' he chuckled; 'I'm afraid you're getting into pretty deep water. You'll be a rabid little socialist before you know it.'

'A – what?' questioned the little girl, dubiously. 'I – I don't think I know what a socialist is. But I know what being *sociable* is – and I like folks that are that. If it's anything like that, I don't mind being one, a mite. I'd like to be one.'

'I don't doubt it, Pollyanna,' smiled the man. 'But when it comes to this scheme of yours for the wholesale distribution of wealth – you've got a problem on your hands that you might have difficulty with.'

Pollyanna drew a long sigh. 'I know,' she nodded. 'That's the way Mrs Carew talked. She says I don't understand; that 'twould – er – pauperise her and be indiscriminate and pernicious, and – Well, it was *something* like that, anyway,' bridled the little girl, aggrievedly, as the man began to laugh. 'And, anyway, I *don't* understand why some folks should have such a lot, and other folks shouldn't have anything; and I *don't* like it. And if I ever have a lot I shall just give some of it to folks who don't have any, even if it does make me pauperised and pernicious, and – ' But Mr Pendleton was laughing so hard now that Pollyanna, after a moment's struggle, surrendered and laughed with him.

'Well, anyway,' she reiterated, when she had caught her breath, 'I don't understand it, all the same.'

'No, dear, I'm afraid you don't,' agreed the man, growing suddenly very grave and tender-eyed; 'nor any of the rest of us, for that matter. But, tell me,' he added, after a minute, 'who is this Jamie you've been talking so much about since you came?'

And Pollyanna told him.

In talking of Jamie, Pollyanna lost her worried, baffled look. Pollyanna loved to talk of Jamie. Here was something she understood. Here was no problem that had to deal with big, fearsome-sounding words. Besides, in this particular instance, would not Mr Pendleton be especially interested in Mrs Carew's taking the boy into her home, for who better than himself could understand the need of a child's presence?

For that matter, Pollyanna talked to everybody about Jamie. She assumed that everybody would be as interested as she herself was. On most occasions she was not disappointed in the interest shown; but one day she met with a surprise. It came through Jimmy Pendleton.

'Say, look a-here,' he demanded one afternoon, irritably. 'Wasn't there *anybody* else down to Boston but just that everlasting "Jamie"?'

'Why, Jimmy Bean, what do you mean?' cried Pollyanna.

The boy lifted his chin a little.

'I'm not Jimmy Bean. I'm Jimmy Pendleton. And I mean that I should think, from your talk, that there wasn't *anybody* down to

Boston but just that loony boy who calls them birds and squirrels "Lady Lancelot", and all that tommyrot.'

'Why, Jimmy Be – Pendleton!' gasped Pollyanna. Then, with some spirit: 'Jamie isn't loony! He is a very nice boy. And he knows a lot – books and stories! Why, he can *make* stories right out of his own head! Besides, it isn't "Lady Lancelot" – it's "Sir Lancelot". If you knew half as much as he does you'd know that, too!' she finished, with flashing eyes.

Jimmy Pendleton flushed miserably and looked utterly wretched. Growing more and more jealous moment by moment, still doggedly he held his ground.

'Well, anyhow,' he scoffed, 'I don't think much of his name. 'Jamie'! Humph! – sounds sissy! And I know somebody else that said so, too.'

'Who was it?'

There was no answer.

'*Who was it?*' demanded Pollyanna, more peremptorily.

'Dad.' The boy's voice was sullen.

'Your – dad?' repeated Pollyanna, in amazement. 'Why, how could he know Jamie?'

'He didn't. 'Twasn't about that Jamie. 'Twas about me.' The boy still spoke sullenly, with his eyes turned away. Yet there was a curious softness in his voice that was always noticeable whenever he spoke of his father.

'*You!*'

'Yes. 'Twas just a little while before he died. We stopped 'most a week with a farmer. Dad helped about the hayin' – and I did, too, some. The farmer's wife was awful good to me, and pretty quick she was callin' me "Jamie". I don't know why, but she just did. And one day father heard her. He got awful mad – so mad that I remembered it always – what he said. He said "Jamie" wasn't no sort of a name for a boy, and that no son of his should ever be called it. He said 'twas a sissy name, and he hated it. 'Seems so I never saw him so mad as he was that night. He wouldn't even stay to finish the work, but him and me took to the road again that night. I was kind of sorry, 'cause I liked her – the farmer's wife, I mean. She was good to me.'

Pollyanna nodded, all sympathy and interest. It was not often that

Jimmy said much of that mysterious past life of his, before she had known him.

'And what happened next?' she prompted. Pollyanna had, for the moment, forgotten all about the original subject of the controversy – the name Jamie that was dubbed sissy.

The boy sighed.

'We just went on till we found another place. And 'twas there dad – died. Then they put me in the 'sylum.'

'And then you ran away and I found you that day, down by Mrs Snow's,' exulted Pollyanna, softly. 'And I've known you ever since.'

'Oh, yes – and you've known me ever since,' repeated Jimmy – but in a far different voice: Jimmy had suddenly come back to the present, and to his grievance. 'But, then, I ain't *Jamie*, you know,' he finished with scornful emphasis, as he turned loftily away, leaving a distressed, bewildered Pollyanna behind him.

'Well, anyway, I can be glad he doesn't always act like this,' sighed the little girl, as she mournfully watched the sturdy, boyish figure with its disagreeable, amazing swagger.

CHAPTER 15

Aunt Polly takes Alarm

Pollyanna had been at home about a week when the letter from Della Wetherby came to Mrs Chilton. She wrote:

I wish I could make you see what your little niece has done for my sister, but I'm afraid I can't. You would have to know what she was before. You did see her, to be sure, and perhaps you saw something of the hush and gloom in which she has shrouded herself for so many years. But you can have no conception of her bitterness of heart, her lack of aim and interest, her insistence upon eternal mourning.

Then came Pollyanna. Probably I didn't tell you, but my sister regretted her promise to take the child, almost the minute it was given; and she made the stern stipulation that the moment Pollyanna began to preach, back she should come to me. Well, she hasn't preached – at least, my sister says she hasn't; and my sister ought to know. And yet – well, just let me tell you what I found when I went to see her yesterday. Perhaps nothing else could give you a better idea of what that wonderful little Pollyanna of yours has accomplished.

To begin with, as I approached the house, I saw that nearly all the shades were up: they used to be down – way down to the sill. The minute I stepped into the hall I heard music – *Parsifal*. The drawing-rooms were open, and the air was sweet with roses.

'Mrs Carew and Master Jamie are in the music-room,' said the maid. And there I found them – my sister, and the youth she has taken into her home, listening to one of those modern contrivances that can hold an entire opera company, including the orchestra.

The boy was in a wheelchair. He was pale, but plainly beatifically happy. My sister looked ten years younger. Her usually colourless cheeks showed a faint pink, and her eyes glowed and sparkled. A little later, after I had talked a few minutes with the boy, my sister and I went upstairs to her own rooms; and there she talked to me – of Jamie. Not of the old Jamie, as she used to, with tear-wet eyes and hopeless sighs, but of the new Jamie – and there were no sighs nor tears now. There was, instead, the eagerness of enthusiastic interest.

'Della, he's wonderful,' she began. 'Everything that is best in music, art and literature seems to appeal to him in a perfectly marvellous fashion, only, of course, he needs development and training. That's what I'm going to see that he gets. A tutor is coming tomorrow. Of course his language is something awful; at the same time, he has read so many good books that his vocabulary is quite amazing – and you should hear the stories he can reel off! Of course in general education he is very deficient; but he's eager to learn, so that will soon be remedied. He loves music, and I shall give him what training in that he wishes. I have already put in a stock of carefully selected records. I wish you could have seen his face when he first heard that *Holy Grail* music. He knows all about King Arthur and his Round Table, and he prattles of knights and lords and ladies as you and I do of the members of our own family – only sometimes I don't know whether his Sir Lancelot means the ancient knight or a squirrel in the Public Garden. And, Della, I believe he can be made to walk. I'm going to have Dr Ames see him, anyway, and –'

And so on and on she talked, while I sat amazed and tongue-tied, but, oh, so happy! I tell you all this, dear Mrs Chilton, so you can see for yourself how interested she is, how eagerly she is going to watch this boy's growth and development, and how, in spite of herself, it is all going to change her attitude towards life. She *can't* do what she is doing for this boy, Jamie, and not transform herself at the same time. Never again, I believe, will she be the soured, morose woman she was before. And it's all because of Pollyanna.

Pollyanna! Dear child – and the best part of it is, she is so unconscious of the whole thing. I don't believe even my sister yet quite realises what is taking place within her own heart and life, and certainly Pollyanna doesn't – least of all does she realise the part she played in the change.

And now, dear Mrs Chilton, how can I thank you? I know I can't; so I'm not even going to try. Yet in your heart I believe you know how grateful I am to both you and Pollyanna.

DELLA WETHERBY

'Well, it seems to have worked a cure, all right,' smiled Dr Chilton, when his wife had finished reading the letter to him.

To his surprise she lifted a quick, remonstrative hand.

'Thomas, don't, please!' she begged.

'Why, Polly, what's the matter? Aren't you glad that – that the medicine worked?'

Mrs Chilton dropped despairingly back in her chair.

'There you go again, Thomas,' she sighed. 'Of *course* I'm glad that this misguided woman has forsaken the error of her ways and found that she can be of use to someone. And of course I'm glad that

Pollyanna did it. But I am not glad to have that child continually spoken of as if she were a – a bottle of medicine, or a "cure". Don't you see?'

'Nonsense! After all, where's the harm? I've called Pollyanna a tonic ever since I knew her.'

'Harm! Thomas Chilton, that child is growing older every day. Do you want to spoil her? Thus far she has been utterly unconscious of her extraordinary power. And therein lies the secret of her success. The minute she *consciously* sets herself to reform somebody, you know as well as I do that she will be simply impossible. Consequently, heaven forbid that she ever gets it into her head that she's anything like a cure-all for poor, sick, suffering humanity.'

'Nonsense! I wouldn't worry,' laughed the doctor.

'But I do worry, Thomas.'

'But, Polly, think of what she's done,' argued the doctor. 'Think of Mrs Snow and John Pendleton, and quantities of others – why, they're not the same people at all that they used to be, any more than Mrs Carew is. And Pollyanna did do it – bless her heart!'

'I know she did,' nodded Mrs Polly Chilton, emphatically. 'But I don't want Pollyanna to know she did it! Oh, of course she knows it, in a way. She knows she taught them to play the glad game with her, and that they are lots happier in consequence. And that's all right. It's a game – *her* game, and they're playing it together. To you I will admit that Pollyanna has preached to us one of the most powerful sermons I ever heard; but the minute *she* knows it – well, I don't want her to. That's all. And right now let me tell you that I've decided that I will go to Germany with you this autumn. At first I thought I wouldn't. I didn't want to leave Pollyanna – and I'm not going to leave her now. I'm going to take her with me.'

'Take her with us? Good! Why not?'

'I've got to. That's all. Furthermore, I should be glad to plan to stay a few years, just as you said you'd like to. I want to get Pollyanna away, quite away from Beldingsville for a while. I'd like to keep her sweet and unspoiled, if I can. And she shall not get silly notions into her head if I can help myself. Why, Thomas Chilton, do we want that child made an insufferable little prig?'

'We certainly don't,' laughed the doctor. 'But, for that matter, I don't believe anything or anybody could make her so. However, this Germany idea suits me to a T. You know I didn't want to come away when I did – if it hadn't been for Pollyanna. So the sooner we get back there the better I'm satisfied. And I'd like to stay – to practice a little, as well as study.'

'Then that's settled.' And Aunt Polly gave a satisfied sigh.

CHAPTER 16

When Pollyanna was Expected

All Beldingsville was fairly aquiver with excitement. Not since Pollyanna Whittier came home from the Sanatorium, *walking*, had there been such a chatter of talk over back-yard fences and on every street corner. Today, too, the centre of interest was Pollyanna. Once again Pollyanna was coming home – but so different a Pollyanna, and so different a homecoming!

Pollyanna was twenty now. For six years she had spent her winters in Germany, her summers leisurely travelling with Dr Chilton and his wife. Only once during that time had she been in Beldingsville, and then it was for but a short four weeks the summer she was sixteen. Now she was coming home – to stay, report said; she and her Aunt Polly.

The doctor would not be with them. Six months before, the town had been shocked and saddened by the news that the doctor had died suddenly. Beldingsville had expected then that Mrs Chilton and Pollyanna would return at once to the old home. But they had not come. Instead had come word that the widow and her niece would remain abroad for a time. The report said that, in entirely new surroundings, Mrs Chilton was trying to seek distraction and relief from her great sorrow.

Very soon, however, vague rumours, and rumours not so vague, began to float through the town that, financially, all was not well with Mrs Polly Chilton. Certain railroad stocks, in which it was known that the Harrington estate had been heavily interested, wavered uncertainly, then tumbled into ruin and disaster. Other investments, according to report, were in a most precarious condition. From the doctor's estate, little could be expected. He had not been a rich man, and his expenses had been heavy for the past six years. Beldingsville was not surprised, therefore, when, not quite six months after the doctor's death, word came that Mrs Chilton and Pollyanna were coming home.

Once more the old Harrington homestead, so long closed and silent, showed up-flung windows and wide-open doors. Once more Nancy – now Mrs Timothy Durgin – swept and scrubbed and dusted until the old place shone in spotless order.

'No, I hain't had no instructions ter do it; I hain't, I hain't,' Nancy explained to curious friends and neighbours who halted at the gate, or came more boldly up to the doorways. 'Mother Durgin's had the key, 'course, and has come in regerler to air up and see that things was all right; and Mis' Chilton just wrote and said she and Miss Pollyanna was comin' this week Friday, and ter please see that the rooms and sheets was aired, and ter leave the key under the side-door mat on that day.

'Under the mat, indeed! Just as if I'd leave them two poor things ter come into this house alone, and all forlorn like that – and me only a mile away, a-sittin' in my own parlour like as if I was a fine lady an' hadn't no heart at all, at all! Just as if the poor things hadn't enough ter stand without that – a-comin' into this house an' the doctor gone – bless his kind heart! – an' never comin' back. An' no money, too. Did ye hear about that? An' ain't it a shame, a shame! Think of Miss Polly – I mean, Mis' Chilton – bein' poor! My stars and stockings, I can't sense it – I can't, I can't!'

Perhaps to no one did Nancy speak so interestedly as she did to a tall, good-looking young fellow with peculiarly frank eyes and a particularly winning smile, who cantered up to the side door on a mettlesome thoroughbred at ten o'clock that Thursday morning. At the same time, to no one did she talk with so much evident embarrassment, so far as the manner of address was concerned; for her tongue stumbled and blundered out a 'Master Jimmy – er – Mr Bean – I mean, Mr Pendleton, Master Jimmy!' with a nervous precipitation that sent the young man himself into a merry peal of laughter.

'Never mind, Nancy! Let it go at whatever comes handiest,' he chuckled. 'I've found out what I wanted to know: Mrs Chilton and her niece really are expected tomorrow.'

'Yes, sir, they be, sir,' curtseyed Nancy, ' – more's the pity! Not but that I shall be glad enough ter see 'em, you understand, but it's the *way* they're a-comin'.'

'Yes, I know. I understand,' nodded the youth, gravely, his eyes sweeping the fine old house before him. 'Well, I suppose that part can't be helped. But I'm glad you're doing – just what you are doing. That *will* help a whole lot,' he finished with a bright smile, as he wheeled about and rode rapidly down the driveway.

Back on the steps Nancy wagged her head wisely. 'I ain't surprised, Master Jimmy,' she declared aloud, her admiring eyes following the handsome figures of horse and man. 'I ain't surprised that you ain't lettin' no grass grow under your feet 'bout enquirin' for Miss Pollyanna. I said long ago 'twould come sometime, an' it's bound to – what with your growin' so handsome and tall. An' I hope 'twill; I do, I do. It'll be just like a book, what with her a-findin' you an' gettin' you into that grand home with Mr Pendleton. My, but who'd ever take you now for that little Jimmy Bean that used to be! I never did see such a change in anybody – I didn't, I didn't!' she answered, with one last look at the rapidly disappearing figures far down the road.

Something of the same thought must have been in the mind of John Pendleton some time later that same morning, for, from the veranda of his big grey house on Pendleton Hill, John Pendleton was watching the rapid approach of that same horse and rider; and in his eyes was an expression very like the one that had been in Mrs Nancy Durgin's. On his lips, too, was an admiring, 'Jove! what a handsome pair!' as the two dashed by on the way to the stable.

Five minutes later the youth came around the corner of the house and slowly ascended the veranda steps.

'Well, my boy, is it true? Are they coming?' asked the man, with visible eagerness.

'Yes.'

'When?'

'Tomorrow.' The young fellow dropped himself into a chair.

At the crisp terseness of the answer, John Pendleton frowned. He threw a quick look into the young man's face. For a moment he hesitated; then, a little abruptly, he asked: 'Why, son, what's the matter?'

'Matter? Nothing, sir.'

'Nonsense! I know better. You left here an hour ago so eager to be off that wild horses could not have held you. Now you sit humped up in that chair and look as if wild horses couldn't drag you out of it. If I didn't know better I'd think you weren't glad that our friends are coming.'

He paused, evidently for a reply. But he did not get it.

'Why, Jim, *aren't* you glad they're coming?'

The young fellow laughed and stirred restlessly.

'Why, yes, of course.'

'Humph! You act like it.'

The youth laughed again. A boyish red flamed into his face.

'Well, it's only that I was thinking – of Pollyanna.'

'Pollyanna! Why, man alive, you've done nothing but prattle of Pollyanna ever since you came home from Boston and found she was expected. I thought you were dying to see Pollyanna.'

The other leaned forward with curious intentness.

'That's exactly it! See? You said it a minute ago. It's just as if yesterday wild horses couldn't keep me from seeing Pollyanna; and now, today, when I know she's coming – they couldn't drag me to see her.'

'Why, *Jim!*'

At the shocked incredulity on John Pendleton's face, the younger man fell back in his chair with an embarrassed laugh.

'Yes, I know. It sounds nutty, and I don't expect I can make you understand. But, somehow, I don't think – I ever wanted Pollyanna to grow up. She was such a dear, just as she was. I like to think of her as I saw her last, her earnest, freckled little face, her yellow pigtails, her tearful: "Oh, yes, I'm glad I'm going; but I think I shall be a little gladder when I come back." That's the last time I saw her. You know we were in Egypt that time she was here four years ago.'

'I know. I see exactly what you mean, too. I think I felt the same way – till I saw her last winter in Rome.'

The other turned eagerly.

'Sure enough, you have seen her! Tell me about her.'

A shrewd twinkle came into John Pendleton's eyes.

'Oh, but I thought you didn't want to know Pollyanna – grown up.'

With a grimace the young fellow tossed this aside.

'Is she pretty?'

'Oh, you young men!' shrugged John Pendleton, in mock despair. 'Always the first question – "Is she pretty?"!'

'Well, is she?' insisted the youth.

'I'll let you judge for yourself. If you – On second thoughts, though, I believe I won't. You might be too disappointed. Pollyanna isn't pretty, so far as regular features, curls and dimples go. In fact, to my certain knowledge the great cross in Pollyanna's life thus far is that she is so sure she isn't pretty. Long ago she told me that black curls were one of the things she was going to have when she got to heaven; and last year in Rome she said something else. It wasn't much, perhaps, so far as words went, but I detected the longing beneath. She said she did wish that sometime someone would write a novel with a heroine who had straight hair and a freckle on her nose; but that she supposed she ought to be glad girls in books didn't have to have them.'

'That sounds like the old Pollyanna.'

'Oh, you'll still find her – Pollyanna,' smiled the man, quizzically. 'Besides, *I* think she's pretty. Her eyes are lovely. She is the picture of health. She carries herself with all the joyous springiness of youth, and her whole face lights up so wonderfully when she talks that you quite forget whether her features are regular or not.'

'Does she still – play the game?'

John Pendleton smiled fondly.

'I imagine she plays it, but she doesn't say much about it now, I fancy. Anyhow, she didn't to me, the two or three times I saw her.'

There was a short silence; then, a little slowly, young Pendleton said: 'I think that was one of the things that was worrying me. That game has been so much to so many people. It has meant so much everywhere, all through the town! I couldn't bear to think of her giving it up and *not* playing it. At the same time I couldn't fancy a grown-up Pollyanna perpetually admonishing people to be glad for something. Someway, I – well, as I said, I – I just didn't want Pollyanna to grow up, anyhow.'

'Well, I wouldn't worry,' shrugged the elder man, with a peculiar smile. 'Always, with Pollyanna, you know, it was the "clearing-up shower", both literally and figuratively; and I think you'll find she lives up to the same principle now – though perhaps not quite in the same way. Poor child, I fear she'll need some kind of game to make existence endurable, for a while, at least.'

'Do you mean because Mrs Chilton has lost her money? Are they so very poor, then?'

'I suspect they are. In fact, they are in rather bad shape, so far as money matters go, as I happen to know. Mrs Chilton's own fortune has shrunk unbelievably, and poor Tom's estate is very small, and hopelessly full of bad debts – professional services never paid for, and that never will be paid for. Tom could never say no when his help was needed, and all the dead beats in town knew it and imposed on him accordingly. Expenses have been heavy with him lately. Besides, he expected great things when he should have completed this special work in Germany. Naturally he supposed his wife and Pollyanna were more than amply provided for through the Harrington estate, so he had no worry in that direction.'

'Hm–m; I see, I see. Too bad, too bad!'

'But that isn't all. It was about two months after Tom's death that I saw Mrs Chilton and Pollyanna in Rome, and Mrs Chilton then was in a terrible state. In addition to her sorrow, she had just begun to get an inkling of the trouble with her finances, and she was nearly frantic. She refused to come home. She declared she never wanted to see Beldingsville, or anybody in it, again. You see, she has always been a peculiarly proud woman, and it was all affecting her in a rather curious way. Pollyanna said that her aunt seemed possessed with the idea that Beldingsville had not approved of her marrying Dr Chilton in the first place, at her age; and now that he was dead, she felt that they were utterly out of sympathy in any grief that she might show. She resented keenly, too, the fact that they must now know that she was poor as well as widowed. In short, she had worked herself into an utterly morbid, wretched state, as unreasonable as it was terrible. Poor little Pollyanna! It was a marvel to me how she stood it. All is, if Mrs Chilton kept it up, and continues to keep it up, that child will be a wreck. That's why I said Pollyanna would need some kind of a game if ever anybody did.'

'The pity of it! – to think of that happening to Pollyanna!' exclaimed the young man, in a voice that was not quite steady.

'Yes; and you can see all is not right by the way they are coming today – so quietly, with not a word to anybody. That was Polly Chilton's doings, I'll warrant. She didn't *want* to be met by anybody. I understand she wrote to no one but her Old Tom's wife, Mrs Durgin, who had the keys.'

'Yes, so Nancy told me – good old soul! She'd got the whole house open, and had contrived somehow to make it look as if it wasn't a tomb of dead hopes and lost pleasures. Of course the grounds looked fairly well, for Old Tom has kept them up, after a fashion. But it made my heart ache – the whole thing.'

There was a long silence, then, curtly, John Pendleton suggested: 'They ought to be met.'

'They will be met.'

'Are *you* going to the station?'

'I am.'

'Then you know what train they're coming on.'

'Oh, no. Neither does Nancy.'

'Then how will you manage?'

'I'm going to begin in the morning and go to every train till they come,' laughed the young man, a bit grimly. 'Timothy's going, too, with the family carriage. After all, there aren't many trains, anyway, that they can come on, you know.'

'Hm–m, I know,' said John Pendleton. 'Jim, I admire your nerve, but not your judgement. I'm glad you're going to follow your nerve and not your judgement, however – and I wish you good luck.'

'Thank you, sir,' smiled the young man dolefully. 'I need 'em – your good wishes – all right, all right, as Nancy says.'

CHAPTER 17

When Pollyanna Came

As the train neared Beldingsville, Pollyanna watched her aunt anxiously. All day Mrs Chilton had been growing more and more restless, more and more gloomy; and Pollyanna was fearful of the time when the familiar home station should be reached.

As Pollyanna looked at her aunt, her heart ached. She was thinking that she would not have believed it possible that anyone could have changed and aged so greatly in six short months. Mrs Chilton's eyes were lustreless, her cheeks pallid and shrunken, and her forehead crossed and recrossed by fretful lines. Her mouth drooped at the corners, and her hair was combed tightly back in the unbecoming fashion that had been hers when Pollyanna first had seen her, years before. All the softness and sweetness that seemed to have come to her with her marriage had dropped from her like a cloak, leaving uppermost the old hardness and sourness that had been hers when she was Miss Polly Harrington, unloved and unloving.

'Pollyanna!' Mrs Chilton's voice was incisive.

Pollyanna started guiltily. She had an uncomfortable feeling that her aunt might have read her thoughts.

'Yes, auntie.'

'Where is that black bag – the little one?'

'Right here.'

'Well, I wish you'd get out my black veil. We're nearly there.'

'But it's so hot and thick, auntie!'

'Pollyanna, I asked for that black veil. If you'd please learn to do what I ask without arguing about it, it would be a great deal easier for me. I want that veil. Do you suppose I'm going to give all Beldingsville a chance to see how I "take it"?'

'Oh, auntie, they'd never be there in *that* spirit,' protested Polly-anna, hurriedly rummaging in the black bag for the much-wanted veil. 'Besides, there won't be anybody there, anyway, to meet us. We didn't tell anyone we were coming, you know.'

'Yes, I know. We didn't *tell* anyone to meet us. But we instructed Mrs Durgin to have the rooms aired and the key under the mat for today. Do you suppose Mary Durgin has kept that information to herself? Not much! Half the town knows we're coming today, and a dozen or more will "happen around" the station about train time. I know them! They want to see what Polly Harrington *Poor* looks like. They – '

'Oh, auntie, auntie,' begged Pollyanna, with tears in her eyes.

'If I wasn't so alone. If – the doctor were only here, and – ' She stopped speaking and turned away her head. Her mouth worked convulsively. 'Where is – that veil?' she choked huskily.

'Yes, dear. Here it is – right here,' comforted Pollyanna, whose only aim now, plainly, was to get the veil into her aunt's hands with all haste. 'And here we are now almost there. Oh, auntie, I do wish you'd had Old Tom or Timothy meet us!'

'And ride home in state, as if we could *afford* to keep such horses and carriages? And when we know we shall have to sell them tomorrow? No, I thank you, Pollyanna. I prefer to use the public carriage, under those circumstances.'

'I know, but – ' The train came to a jolting, jarring stop, and only a fluttering sigh finished Pollyanna's sentence.

As the two women stepped to the platform, Mrs Chilton, in her black veil, looked neither to the right nor the left. Pollyanna, how-ever, was nodding and smiling tearfully in half a dozen directions before she had taken twice as many steps. Then, suddenly, she found herself looking into a familiar, yet strangely unfamiliar face.

'Why, it isn't – it *is* – Jimmy!' she beamed, reaching forth a cordial hand. 'That is, I suppose I should say "*Mr Pendleton*",' she corrected herself with a shy smile that said plainly: 'Now that you've grown so tall and fine!'

'I'd like to see you try it,' challenged the youth, with a very Jimmy-like tilt to his chin. He turned then to speak to Mrs Chilton; but that lady, with her head half averted, was hurrying on a little in advance.

He turned back to Pollyanna, his eyes troubled and sympathetic. 'If you'd please come this way – both of you,' he urged hurriedly. 'Timothy is here with the carriage.'

'Oh, how good of him,' cried Pollyanna, but with an anxious glance at the sombre veiled figure ahead. Timidly she touched her aunt's arm. 'Auntie, dear, Timothy's here. He's come with the carriage. He's over this side. And – this is Jimmy Bean, auntie. You remember Jimmy Bean!'

In her nervousness and embarrassment Pollyanna did not notice that she had given the young man the old name of his boyhood. Mrs Chilton, however, evidently did notice it. With palpable reluctance she turned and inclined her head ever so slightly.

'Mr – Pendleton is very kind, I am sure; but – I am sorry that he or Timothy took quite so much trouble,' she said frigidly.

'No trouble – no trouble at all, I assure you,' laughed the young man, trying to hide his embarrassment. 'Now if you'll just let me have your checks, so I can see to your baggage.'

'Thank you,' began Mrs Chilton, 'but I am very sure we can –'

But Pollyanna, with a relieved little 'thank you!' had already passed over the checks; and dignity demanded that Mrs Chilton say no more.

The drive home was a silent one. Timothy, vaguely hurt at the reception he had met with at the hands of his former mistress, sat up in front stiff and straight, with tense lips. Mrs Chilton, after a weary, 'Well, well, child, just as you please; I suppose we shall have to ride home in it now!' had subsided into stern gloom. Pollyanna, however, was neither stern, nor tense, nor gloomy. With eager, though tearful eyes she greeted each loved landmark as they came to it.

Only once did she speak, and that was to say: 'Isn't Jimmy fine? How he has improved! And hasn't he the nicest eyes and smile?'

She waited hopefully, but as there was no reply to this, she contented herself with a cheerful: 'Well, I think he has, anyhow.'

Timothy had been both too aggrieved and too afraid to tell Mrs Chilton what to expect at home; so the wide-flung doors and flower-adorned rooms with Nancy curtseying on the porch were a complete surprise to Mrs Chilton and Pollyanna.

'Why, Nancy, how perfectly lovely!' cried Pollyanna, springing lightly to the ground. 'Auntie, here's Nancy to welcome us. And only see how charming she's made everything look!'

Pollyanna's voice was determinedly cheerful, though it shook audibly. This home-coming without the dear doctor whom she had loved so well was not easy for her; and if hard for her, she knew something of what it must be for her aunt. She knew, too, that the one thing her aunt was dreading was a breakdown before Nancy, than which nothing could be worse in her eyes. Behind the heavy black veil the eyes were brimming and the lips were trembling, Pollyanna knew. She knew, too, that to hide these facts her aunt would probably seize the first opportunity for fault-finding, and make her anger a cloak to hide the fact that her heart was breaking. Pollyanna was not surprised, therefore, to hear her aunt's few cold words of greeting to Nancy followed by a sharp: 'Of course all this was very kind, Nancy; but, really, I would have much preferred that you had not done it.'

All the joy fled from Nancy's face. She looked hurt and frightened.

'Oh, but Miss Polly – I mean, Mis' Chilton,' she entreated; 'it seemed as if I couldn't let you – '

'There, there, never mind, Nancy,' interrupted Mrs Chilton. 'I – I don't want to talk about it.' And, with her head proudly high, she swept out of the room. A minute later they heard the door of her bedroom shut upstairs.

Nancy turned in dismay.

'Oh, Miss Pollyanna, what is it? What have I done? I thought she'd *like* it. I meant it all right!'

'Of course you did,' wept Pollyanna, fumbling in her bag for her handkerchief. 'And 'twas lovely to have you do it, too, – just lovely.'

'But *she* didn't like it.'

'Yes, she did. But she didn't want to show she liked it. She was afraid if she did she'd show – other things, and – Oh, Nancy, Nancy, I'm so glad just to c–cry!' And Pollyanna was sobbing on Nancy's shoulder.

'There, there, dear; so she shall, so she shall,' soothed Nancy, patting the heaving shoulders with one hand, and trying, with the other, to make the corner of her apron serve as a handkerchief to wipe her own tears away.

'You see, I mustn't – cry – before – *her*,' faltered Pollyanna; 'and it *was* hard – coming here – the first time, you know, and all. And I *knew* how she was feeling.'

'Of course, of course, poor lamb,' crooned Nancy. 'And to think the first thing *I* should have done was somethin' ter vex her, and – '

'Oh, but she wasn't vexed at that,' corrected Pollyanna, agitatedly. 'It's just her way, Nancy. You see, she doesn't like to show how badly she feels about – about the doctor. And she's so afraid she *will* show it that she – she just takes anything for an excuse to – to talk about. She does it to me, too, just the same. So I know all about it. See?'

'Oh, yes, I see, I do, I do.' Nancy's lips snapped together a little severely, and her sympathetic pats, for the minute, were even more loving, if possible. 'Poor lamb! I'm glad I come, anyhow, for your sake.'

'Yes, so am I,' breathed Pollyanna, gently drawing herself away and wiping her eyes. 'There, I feel better. And I do thank you ever so much, Nancy, and I appreciate it. Now don't let us keep you when it's time for you to go.'

'Ho! I'm thinkin' I'll stay for a spell,' sniffed Nancy.

'Stay! Why, Nancy, I thought you were married. Aren't you Timothy's wife?'

'Sure! But he won't mind – for you. He'd *want* me to stay – for you.'

'Oh, but, Nancy, we couldn't let you,' demurred Pollyanna. 'We can't have anybody – now, you know. I'm going to do the work. Until we know just how things are, we shall live very economically, Aunt Polly says.'

'Ho! as if I'd take money from – ' began Nancy, in bridling wrath; but at the expression on the other's face she stopped, and let her words dwindle off in a mumbling protest, as she hurried from the room to look after her creamed chicken on the stove.

Not until supper was over, and everything put in order, did Mrs Timothy Durgin consent to drive away with her husband; then she went with evident reluctance, and with many pleadings to be allowed to come 'just ter help out a bit' at any time.

After Nancy had gone, Pollyanna came into the living-room where Mrs Chilton was sitting alone, her hand over her eyes.

'Well, dearie, shall I light up?' suggested Pollyanna, brightly.

'Oh, I suppose so.'

'Wasn't Nancy a dear to fix us all up so nice?'

No answer.

'Where in the world she found all these flowers I can't imagine. She has them in every room down here, and in both bedrooms, too.'

Still no answer.

Pollyanna gave a half-stifled sigh and threw a wistful glance into her aunt's averted face. After a moment she began again hopefully.

'I saw Old Tom in the garden. Poor man, his rheumatism is worse than ever. He was bent nearly double. He enquired very particularly for you, and – '

Mrs Chilton turned with a sharp interruption.

'Pollyanna, what are we going to do?'

'Do? Why, the best we can, of course, dearie.'

Mrs Chilton gave an impatient gesture.

'Come, come, Pollyanna, do be serious for once. You'll find it is serious, fast enough. *What* are we going to *do*? As you know, my income has almost entirely stopped. Of course, some of the things are worth something, I suppose; but Mr Hart says very few of them will pay anything at present. We have something in the bank, and a little coming in, of course. And we have this house. But of what earthly use is the house? We can't eat it, or wear it. It's too big for us, the way we shall have to live; and we couldn't sell it for half what it's really worth, unless we *happened* to find just the person that wanted it.'

'Sell it! Oh, auntie, you wouldn't – this beautiful house full of lovely things!'

'I may have to, Pollyanna. We have to eat – unfortunately.'

'I know it; and I'm always *so* hungry,' mourned Pollyanna, with a rueful laugh. 'Still, I suppose I ought to be glad my appetite is so good.'

'Very likely. You'd find something to be glad about, of course. But what shall we do, child? I do wish you'd be serious for a minute.'

A quick change came to Pollyanna's face.

'I am serious, Aunt Polly. I've been thinking. I – I wish I could earn some money.'

'Oh, child, child, to think of my ever living to hear you say that!' moaned the woman; ' – a daughter of the Harringtons having to earn her bread!'

'Oh, but that isn't the way to look at it,' laughed Pollyanna. 'You ought to be glad if a daughter of the Harringtons is *smart* enough to earn her bread! That isn't any disgrace, Aunt Polly.'

'Perhaps not; but it isn't very pleasant to one's pride, after the position we've always occupied in Beldingsville, Pollyanna.'

Pollyanna did not seem to have heard. Her eyes were musingly fixed on space.

'If only I had some talent! If only I could do something better than anybody else in the world,' she sighed at last. 'I can sing a little, play a little, embroider a little and darn a little; but I can't do any of them well – not well enough to be paid for it.

'I think I'd like best to cook,' she resumed, after a minute's silence, 'and keep house. You know I loved that in Germany winters, when Gretchen used to bother us so much by not coming when we wanted her. But I don't exactly want to go into other people's kitchens to do it.'

'As if I'd let you! Pollyanna!' shuddered Mrs Chilton again.

'And of course, to just work in our own kitchen here doesn't bring in anything,' bemoaned Pollyanna, ' – not any money, I mean. And it's money we need.'

'It most emphatically is,' sighed Aunt Polly.

There was a long silence, broken at last by Pollyanna.

'To think that after all you've done for me, auntie – to think that now, if I only could, I'd have such a splendid chance to help! And yet – I can't do it. Oh, why wasn't I born with something that's worth money?'

'There, there, child, don't, don't! Of course, if the doctor – ' The words choked into silence.

Pollyanna looked up quickly, and sprang to her feet.

'Dear, dear, this will never do!' she exclaimed, with a complete change of manner. 'Don't you fret, auntie. What'll you wager that I don't develop the most marvellous talent going, one of these days? Besides, *I* think it's real exciting – all this. There's so much uncertainty in it. There's a lot of fun in wanting things – and then watching for them to come. Just living along and *knowing* you're going to have everything you want is so – so humdrum, you know,' she finished, with a gay little laugh.

Mrs Chilton, however, did not laugh. She only sighed and said: 'Dear me, Pollyanna, what a child you are!'

CHAPTER 18

A Matter of Adjustment

The first few days at Beldingsville were not easy either for Mrs Chilton or for Pollyanna. They were days of adjustment; and days of adjustment are seldom easy.

From travel and excitement it was not easy to put one's mind to the consideration of the price of butter and the delinquencies of the butcher. From having all one's time for one's own, it was not easy to attend always to the next task clamouring to be done. Friends and neighbours called, too, and although Pollyanna welcomed them with glad cordiality, Mrs Chilton, when possible, excused herself; and always she said bitterly to Pollyanna: 'Curiosity, I suppose, to see how Polly Harrington likes being poor.'

Of the doctor Mrs Chilton seldom spoke, yet Pollyanna knew very well that almost never was he absent from her thoughts; and that more than half her taciturnity was but her usual cloak for a deeper emotion which she did not care to show.

Jimmy Pendleton Pollyanna saw several times during that first month. He came first with John Pendleton for a somewhat stiff and ceremonious call – not that it was either stiff or ceremonious until after Aunt Polly came into the room; then it was both. For some reason Aunt Polly had not excused herself on this occasion. After that Jimmy had come by himself, once with flowers, once with a book for Aunt Polly, twice with no excuse at all. Pollyanna welcomed him with frank pleasure always. Aunt Polly, after that first time, did not see him at all.

To the most of their friends and acquaintances Pollyanna said little about the change in their circumstances. To Jimmy, however, she talked freely, and always her constant cry was: 'If only I could do something to bring in some money!'

'I'm getting to be the most mercenary little creature you ever saw,' she laughed dolefully. 'I've got so I measure everything with a dollar bill, and I actually think in quarters and dimes. You see, Aunt Polly does feel so poor!'

'It's a shame!' stormed Jimmy.

'I know it. But, honestly, I think she feels a little poorer than she needs to – she's brooded over it so. But I do wish I could help!'

Jimmy looked down at the wistful, eager face with its luminous eyes, and his own eyes softened.

'What do you *want* to do – if you could do it?' he asked.

'Oh, I want to cook and keep house,' smiled Pollyanna, with a pensive sigh. 'I just love to beat eggs and sugar, and hear the soda gurgle its little tune in the cup of sour milk. I'm happy if I've got a day's baking before me. But there isn't any money in that – except in somebody else's kitchen, of course. And I – I don't exactly love it well enough for that!'

'I should say not!' ejaculated the young fellow.

Once more he glanced down at the expressive face so near him. This time a queer look came to the corners of his mouth. He pursed his lips, then spoke, a slow red mounting to his forehead.

'Well, of course you might – marry. Have you thought of that – Miss Pollyanna?'

Pollyanna gave a merry laugh. Voice and manner were unmistakably those of a girl quite untouched by even the most far-reaching of Cupid's darts.

'Oh, no, I shall never marry,' she said blithely. 'In the first place I'm not pretty, you know; and in the second place, I'm going to live with Aunt Polly and take care of her.'

'Not pretty, eh?' smiled Pendleton, quizzically. 'Did it ever – er – occur to you that there might be a difference of opinion on that, Pollyanna?'

Pollyanna shook her head.

'There couldn't be. I've got a mirror, you see,' she objected, with a merry glance.

It sounded like coquetry. In any other girl it would have been coquetry, Pendleton decided. But, looking into the face before him now, Pendleton knew that it was not coquetry. He knew, too, suddenly, why Pollyanna had seemed so different from any girl he had ever known. Something of her old literal way of looking at things still clung to her.

'Why aren't you pretty?' he asked.

Even as he uttered the question, and sure as he was of his estimate of Pollyanna's character, Pendleton quite held his breath at his temerity. He could not help thinking of how quickly any other girl he knew would have resented that implied acceptance of her claim to no beauty. But Pollyanna's first words showed him that even this lurking fear of his was quite groundless.

'Why, I just am not,' she laughed, a little ruefully. 'I wasn't made that way. Maybe you don't remember, but long ago, when I was a little girl, it always seemed to me that one of the nicest things heaven was going to give me when I got there was black curls.'

'And is that your chief desire now?'

'N–no, maybe not,' hesitated Pollyanna. 'But I still think I'd like them. Besides, my eyelashes aren't long enough, and my nose isn't Grecian, or Roman, or any of those delightfully desirable ones that belong to a "type". It's just a *nose*. And my face is too long, or too short, I've forgotten which; but I measured it once with one of those "correct-for-beauty" tests, and it wasn't right, anyhow. And they said the width of the face should be equal to five eyes, and the width of the eyes equal to – to something else. I've forgotten that, too – only that mine wasn't.'

'What a lugubrious picture!' laughed Pendleton. Then, with his gaze admiringly regarding the girl's animated face and expressive eyes, he asked: 'Did you ever look in the mirror when you were talking, Pollyanna?'

'Why, no, of course not!'

'Well, you'd better try it sometime.'

'What a funny idea! Imagine my doing it,' laughed the girl. 'What shall I say? Like this? "Now, you, Pollyanna, what if your eyelashes aren't long, and your nose is just a nose, be glad you've got *some* eyelashes and *some* nose!" '

Pendleton joined in her laugh, but an odd expression came to his face.

'Then you still play – the game,' he said, a little diffidently.

Pollyanna turned soft eyes of wonder full upon him.

'Why, of course! Why, Jimmy, I don't believe I could have lived – the last six months – if it hadn't been for that blessed game.' Her voice shook a little.

'I haven't heard you say much about it,' he commented.

She changed colour.

'I know. I think I'm afraid – of saying too much – to outsiders, who don't care, you know. It wouldn't sound quite the same from me now, at twenty, as it did when I was ten. I realise that, of course. Folks don't like to be preached at, you know,' she finished with a whimsical smile.

'I know,' nodded the young fellow gravely. 'But I wonder sometimes, Pollyanna, if you really understand yourself what that game is, and what it has done for those who are playing it.'

'I know – what it has done for myself.' Her voice was low, and her eyes were turned away.

'You see, it really *works*, if you play it,' he mused aloud, after a short silence. 'Somebody said once that it would revolutionise the world if everybody would really play it. And I believe it would.'

'Yes; but some folks don't want to be revolutionised,' smiled Pollyanna. 'I ran across a man in Germany last year. He had lost his money, and was in hard luck generally. Dear, dear, but he was gloomy! Somebody in my presence tried to cheer him up one day by saying, "Come, come, things might be worse, you know!" Dear, dear, but you should have heard that man then!

' "If there is anything on earth that makes me mad clear through," he snarled, "it is to be told that things might be worse, and to be thankful for what I've got left. These people who go around with an everlasting grin on their faces carolling forth that they are thankful that they can breathe, or eat, or walk, or lie down, I have no use for. I don't *want to* breathe, or eat, or walk, or lie down – if things are as they are now with me. And when I'm told that I ought to be thankful for some such tommyrot as that, it makes me just want to go out and shoot somebody!" Imagine what *I'd* have gotten if I'd have introduced the glad game to that man!' laughed Pollyanna.

'I don't care. He needed it,' answered Jimmy.

'Of course he did – but he wouldn't have thanked me for giving it to him.'

'I suppose not. But, listen! As he was, under his present philosophy and scheme of living, he made himself and everybody else wretched, didn't he? Well, just suppose he was playing the game. While he was trying to hunt up something to be glad about in everything that had happened to him, he *couldn't* be at the same time grumbling and growling about how bad things were; so that much would be gained. He'd be a whole lot easier to live with, both for himself and for his friends. Meanwhile, just thinking of the doughnut instead of the hole couldn't make things any worse for him, and it might make things better; for it wouldn't give him such a gone feeling in the pit of his stomach, and his digestion would be better. I tell you, troubles are poor things to hug. They've got too many prickers.'

Pollyanna smiled appreciatively.

'That makes me think of what I told a poor old lady once. She was one of my Ladies' Aiders out West, and was one of the kind of people that really *enjoys* being miserable and telling over her causes for unhappiness. I was perhaps ten years old, and was trying to teach her the game. I reckon I wasn't having very good success, and evidently I at last dimly realised the reason, for I said to her triumphantly: "Well, anyhow, you can be glad you've got such a lot of things to make you miserable, for you love to be miserable so well!" '

'Well, if that wasn't a good one on her,' chuckled Jimmy.

Pollyanna raised her eyebrows.

'I'm afraid she didn't enjoy it any more than the man in Germany would have if I'd told him the same thing.'

'But they ought to be told, and you ought to tell – ' Pendleton stopped short with so queer an expression on his face that Pollyanna looked at him in surprise.

'Why, Jimmy, what is it?'

'Oh, nothing. I was only thinking,' he answered, puckering his lips. 'Here I am urging you to do the very thing I was afraid you *would* do before I saw you, you know. That is, I was afraid before I saw you, that – that – ' He floundered into a helpless pause, looking very red indeed.

'Well, Jimmy Pendleton,' bridled the girl, 'you needn't think you can stop there, sir. Now just what do you mean by all that, please?'

'Oh, er – n–nothing, much.'

'I'm waiting,' murmured Pollyanna. Voice and manner were calm and confident, though the eyes twinkled mischievously.

The young fellow hesitated, glanced at her smiling face, and capitulated.

'Oh, well, have it your own way,' he shrugged. 'It's only that I was worrying – a little – about that game, for fear you *would* talk it just as you used to, you know, and – ' But a merry peal of laughter interrupted him.

'There, what did I tell you? Even you were worried, it seems, lest I should be at twenty just what I was at ten!'

'N–no, I didn't mean – Pollyanna, honestly, I thought – of course I knew – ' But Pollyanna only put her hands to her ears and went off into another peal of laughter.

CHAPTER 19

Two Letters

It was towards the latter part of June that the letter came to Pollyanna from Della Wetherby.

I am writing to ask you a favour. I am hoping you can tell me of some quiet private family in Beldingsville that will be willing to take my sister to board for the summer. There would be three of them, Mrs Carew, her secretary and her adopted son Jamie. (You remember Jamie, don't you?) They do not like to go to an ordinary hotel or boarding house. My sister is very tired, and the doctor has advised her to go into the country for a complete rest and change. He suggested Vermont or New Hampshire. We immediately thought of Beldingsville and you; and we wondered if you couldn't recommend just the right place to us. I told Ruth I would write you. They would like to go right away, early in July, if possible. Would it be asking too much to request you to let us know as soon as you conveniently can if you do know of a place? Please address me here. My sister is with us here at the Sanatorium for a few weeks' treatment.

Hoping for a favourable reply, I am,

Most cordially yours,

DELLA WETHERBY

For the first few minutes after the letter was finished, Pollyanna sat with frowning brow, mentally searching the homes of Beldingsville for a possible boarding house for her old friends. Then a sudden something gave her thoughts a new turn, and with a joyous exclamation she hurried to her aunt in the living-room.

'Auntie, auntie,' she panted; 'I've got just the loveliest idea. I told you something would happen, and that I'd develop that wonderful talent sometime. Well, I have. I have right now. Listen! I've had a letter from Miss Wetherby, Mrs Carew's sister – where I stayed that winter in Boston, you know – and they want to come into the country to board for the summer, and Miss Wetherby's written to see if I didn't know a place for them. They don't want a hotel or an ordinary boarding house, you see. And at first I didn't know of one; but now I do. I do, Aunt Polly! Just guess where 'tis.'

'Dear me, child,' ejaculated Mrs Chilton, 'how you do run on! I should think you were a dozen years old instead of a woman grown. Now what are you talking about?'

'About a boarding place for Mrs Carew and Jamie. I've found it,' babbled Pollyanna.

'Indeed! Well, what of it? Of what possible interest can that be to me, child?' murmured Mrs Chilton, drearily.

'Because it's *here*. I'm going to have them here, auntie.'

'Pollyanna!' Mrs Chilton was sitting erect in horror.

'Now, auntie, please don't say no – please don't,' begged Pollyanna, eagerly. 'Don't you see? This is my chance, the chance I've been waiting for; and it's just dropped right into my hands. We can do it lovely. We have plenty of room, and you know I *can* cook and keep house. And now there'd be money in it, for they'd pay well, I know; and they'd love to come, I'm sure. There'd be three of them – there's a secretary with them.'

'But, Pollyanna, I can't! Turn this house into a boarding house? – the Harrington homestead a common boarding house? Oh, Pollyanna, I can't, I can't!'

'But it wouldn't be a common boarding house, dear. 'Twill be an uncommon one. Besides, they're our friends. It would be like having our friends come to see us; only they'd be *paying* guests, so meanwhile we'd be earning money – money that we *need*, auntie, money that we need,' she emphasised significantly.

A spasm of hurt pride crossed Polly Chilton's face. With a low moan she fell back in her chair.

'But how could you do it?' she asked at last, faintly. 'You couldn't do the work part alone, child!'

'Oh, no, of course not,' chirped Pollyanna. (Pollyanna was on sure ground now. She knew her point was won.) 'But I could do the cooking and the overseeing, and I'm sure I could get one of Nancy's younger sisters to help about the rest. Mrs Durgin would do the laundry part just as she does now.'

'But, Pollyanna, I'm not well at all – you know I'm not. I couldn't do much.'

'Of course not. There's no reason why you should,' scorned Pollyanna, loftily. 'Oh, auntie, won't it be splendid? Why, it seems too good to be true – money just dropped into my hands like that!'

'Dropped into your hands, indeed! You still have some things to learn in this world, Pollyanna, and one is that summer boarders don't drop money into anybody's hands without looking very sharply to it that they get ample return. By the time you fetch and carry and bake and brew until you are ready to sink, and by the time you nearly kill yourself trying to serve everything to order from fresh-laid eggs to the weather, you will believe what I tell you.'

'All right, I'll remember,' laughed Pollyanna. 'But I'm not doing any worrying now; and I'm going to hurry and write Miss Wetherby at once so I can give it to Jimmy Bean to mail when he comes out this afternoon.'

Mrs Chilton stirred restlessly.

'Pollyanna, I do wish you'd call that young man by his proper name. That "Bean" gives me the shivers. His name is "Pendleton" now, as I understand it.'

'So it is,' agreed Pollyanna, 'but I do forget it half the time. I even call him that to his face, sometimes, and of course that's dreadful, when he really is adopted, and all. But you see I'm so excited,' she finished, as she danced from the room.

She had the letter all ready for Jimmy when he called at four o'clock. She was still quivering with excitement, and she lost no time in telling her visitor what it was all about.

'And I'm crazy to see them, besides,' she cried, when she had told him of her plans. 'I've never seen either of them since that winter. You know I told you – didn't I tell you? – about Jamie.'

'Oh, yes, you told me.' There was a touch of constraint in the young man's voice.

'Well, isn't it splendid, if they can come?'

'Why, I don't know as I should call it exactly splendid,' he parried.

'Not splendid that I've got such a chance to help Aunt Polly out, for even this little while? Why, Jimmy, of course it's splendid.'

'Well, it strikes me that it's going to be rather *hard*– for you,' bridled Jimmy, with more than a shade of irritation.

'Yes, of course, in some ways. But I shall be so glad for the money coming in that I'll think of that all the time. You see,' she sighed, 'how mercenary I am, Jimmy.'

For a long minute there was no reply; then, a little abruptly, the young man asked: 'Let's see, how old is this Jamie now?'

Pollyanna glanced up with a merry smile.

'Oh, I remember – you never did like his name, "Jamie",' she twinkled. 'Never mind; he's adopted now, legally, I believe, and has taken the name of Carew. So you can call him that.'

'But that isn't telling me how old he is,' reminded Jimmy, stiffly.

'Nobody knows, exactly, I suppose. You know he couldn't tell; but I imagine he's about your age. I wonder how he is now. I've asked all about it in this letter, anyway.'

'Oh, you have!' Pendleton looked down at the letter in his hand and flipped it a little spitefully. He was thinking that he would like to drop it, to tear it up, to give it to somebody, to throw it away, to do anything with it – but mail it.

Jimmy knew perfectly well that he was jealous, that he always had been jealous of this youth with the name so like and yet so unlike his own. Not that he was in love with Pollyanna, he assured himself wrathfully. He was not that, of course. It was just that he did not care to have this strange youth with the sissy name come to Beldingsville and be always around to spoil all their good times. He almost said as much to Pollyanna, but something stayed the words on his lips; and after a time he took his leave, carrying the letter with him.

That Jimmy did not drop the letter, tear it up, give it to anybody, or throw it away was evidenced a few days later, for Pollyanna received a prompt and delighted reply from Miss Wetherby; and when Jimmy came next time he heard it read – or rather he heard part of it, for Pollyanna prefaced the reading by saying: 'Of course the first part is just where she says how glad they are to come, and all that. I won't read that. But the rest I thought you'd like to hear, because you've heard me talk so much about them. Besides, you'll know them yourself pretty soon, of course. I'm depending a whole lot on you, Jimmy, to help me make it pleasant for them.'

'Oh, are you!'

'Now don't be sarcastic, just because you don't like Jamie's name,' reproved Pollyanna, with mock severity. 'You'll like *him*, I'm sure, when you know him; and you'll *love* Mrs Carew.'

'Will I, indeed?' retorted Jimmy huffily. 'Well, that *is* a serious prospect. Let us hope, if I do, the lady will be so gracious as to reciprocate.'

'Of course,' dimpled Pollyanna. 'Now listen, and I'll read to you about her. This letter is from her sister, Della – Miss Wetherby, you know, at the Sanatorium.'

'All right. Go ahead!' directed Jimmy, with a somewhat too evident attempt at polite interest. And Pollyanna, still smiling mischievously, began to read.

'You ask me to tell you everything about everybody. That is a large commission, but I'll do the best I can. To begin with, I think you'll find my sister quite changed. The new interests that have come into her life during the last six years have done wonders for her. Just now she is a bit thin and tired from overwork, but a good rest will soon remedy that, and you'll see how young and blooming and happy she looks. Please notice I said *happy*. That won't mean so much to you as it does to me, of course, for you were too young to realise quite how unhappy she was when you first knew her that winter in Boston. Life was such a dreary, hopeless thing to her then; and now it is so full of interest and joy.

First she has Jamie, and when you see them together you won't need to be told what he is to her. To be sure, we are no nearer knowing whether he is the *real* Jamie, or not, but my sister loves him like an own son now, and has legally adopted him, as I presume you know.

Then she has her girls. Do you remember Sadie Dean, the

salesgirl? Well, from getting interested in her, and trying to help her to a happier living, my sister has broadened her efforts little by little, until she has scores of girls now who regard her as their own best and particular good angel. She has started a Home for Working Girls along new lines. Half a dozen wealthy and influential men and women are associated with her, of course, but she is head and shoulders of the whole thing, and never hesitates to give *herself* to each and every one of the girls. You can imagine what that means in nerve strain. Her chief support and right-hand man is her secretary, this same Sadie Dean. You'll find *her* changed, too, yet she is the same old Sadie.

As for Jamie – poor Jamie! The great sorrow of his life is that he knows now he can never walk. For a time we all had hopes. He was here at the Sanatorium under Dr Ames for a year, and he improved to such an extent that he can go now with crutches. But the poor boy will always be a cripple – so far as his feet are concerned, but never as regards anything else. Someway, after you know Jamie, you seldom think of him as a cripple, his *soul* is so free. I can't explain it, but you'll know what I mean when you see him; and he has retained, to a marvellous degree, his old boyish enthusiasm and joy of living. There is just one thing – and only one, I believe – that would utterly quench that bright spirit and cast him into utter despair; and that is to find that he is not Jamie Kent, our nephew. So long has he brooded over this, and so ardently has he wished it, that he has come actually to believe that he *is* the real Jamie; but if he isn't, I hope he will never find it out.

'There, that's all she says about them,' announced Pollyanna, folding up the closely-written sheets in her hands. 'But isn't that interesting?'

'Indeed it is!' There was a ring of genuineness in Jimmy's voice now. Jimmy was thinking suddenly of what his own good legs meant to him. He even, for the moment, was willing that this poor crippled youth should have a *part* of Pollyanna's thoughts and attentions, if he were not so presuming as to claim too much of them, of course! 'By George! it is tough for the poor chap, and no mistake.'

'Tough! You don't know anything about it, Jimmy Bean,' choked Pollyanna; 'but *I* do. *I* couldn't walk once. *I know!*'

'Yes, of course, of course,' frowned the youth, moving restively in his seat. Jimmy, looking into Pollyanna's sympathetic face and brimming eyes, was suddenly not so sure, after all, that he *was* willing to have this Jamie come to town – if just to *think* of him made Pollyanna look like that!

CHAPTER 20

The Paying Guests

The few intervening days before the expected arrival of 'those dreadful people', as Aunt Polly termed her niece's paying guests, were busy ones indeed for Pollyanna – but they were happy ones, too, as Pollyanna refused to be weary, or discouraged, or dismayed, no matter how puzzling were the daily problems she had to meet.

Summoning Nancy, and Nancy's younger sister Betty to her aid, Pollyanna systematically went through the house, room by room, and arranged everything for the comfort and convenience of her expected boarders. Mrs Chilton could do but little to assist. In the first place she was not well. In the second place her mental attitude towards the whole idea was not conducive to aid or comfort, for at her side stalked always the Harrington pride of name and race, and on her lips was the constant moan: 'Oh, Pollyanna, Pollyanna, to think of the Harrington homestead ever coming to this!'

'It isn't, dearie,' Pollyanna at last soothed laughingly. 'It's the Carews that are *coming to the Harrington homestead*!'

But Mrs Chilton was not to be so lightly diverted, and responded only with a scornful glance and a deeper sigh, so Pollyanna was forced to leave her to travel alone her road of determined gloom.

Upon the appointed day, Pollyanna with Timothy (who owned the Harrington horses now) went to the station to meet the afternoon train. Up to this hour there had been nothing but confidence and joyous anticipation in Pollyanna's heart. But with the whistle of the engine there came to her a veritable panic of doubt, shyness and dismay. She realised suddenly what she, Pollyanna, almost alone and unaided, was about to do. She remembered Mrs Carew's wealth, position and fastidious tastes. She recollected, too, that this would be a new, tall, young-man Jamie, quite unlike the boy she had known.

For one awful moment she thought only of getting away – somewhere, anywhere.

'Timothy, I – I feel sick. I'm not well. I – tell 'em – er – not to come,' she faltered, poising as if for flight.

'Ma'am!' exclaimed the startled Timothy.

One glance into Timothy's amazed face was enough. Pollyanna laughed and threw back her shoulders alertly.

'Nothing. Never mind! I didn't mean it, of course, Timothy. Quick – see! They're almost here,' she panted. And Pollyanna hurried forward, quite herself once more.

She knew them at once. Even had there been any doubt in her mind, the crutches in the hands of the tall, brown-eyed young man would have piloted her straight to her goal.

There were a brief few minutes of eager hand-clasps and incoherent exclamations, then, somehow, she found herself in the carriage with Mrs Carew at her side, and Jamie and Sadie Dean in front. She had a chance, then, for the first time, really to see her friends, and to note the changes the six years had wrought.

In regard to Mrs Carew, her first feeling was one of surprise. She had forgotten that Mrs Carew was so lovely. She had forgotten that the eyelashes were so long, that the eyes they shaded were so beautiful. She even caught herself thinking enviously of how exactly that perfect face must tally, figure by figure, with that dread beauty-test-table. But more than anything else she rejoiced in the absence of the old fretful lines of gloom and bitterness.

Then she turned to Jamie. Here again she was surprised, and for much the same reason. Jamie, too, had grown handsome. To herself, Pollyanna declared that he was really distinguished looking. His dark eyes, rather pale face and dark, waving hair she thought most attractive. Then she caught a glimpse of the crutches at his side, and a spasm of aching sympathy contracted her throat.

From Jamie, Pollyanna turned to Sadie Dean.

Sadie, so far as features went, looked much as she had when Pollyanna first saw her in the Public Garden; but Pollyanna did not need a second glance to know that Sadie, so far as hair, dress, temper, speech and disposition were concerned, was a very different Sadie indeed.

Then Jamie spoke.

'How good you were to let us come,' he said to Pollyanna. 'Do you know what I thought of when you wrote that we could come?'

'Why, n–no, of course not,' stammered Pollyanna. Pollyanna was still seeing the crutches at Jamie's side, and her throat was still tightened from that aching sympathy.

'Well, I thought of the little maid in the Public Garden with her bag of peanuts for Sir Lancelot and Lady Guinevere, and I knew that you were just putting us in their places, for if you had a bag of peanuts, and we had none, you wouldn't be happy till you'd shared it with us.'

'A bag of peanuts, indeed!' laughed Pollyanna.

'Oh, of course in this case your bag of peanuts happened to be airy country rooms, and cow's milk, and real eggs from a real hen's nest,' returned Jamie whimsically; 'but it amounts to the same thing. And maybe I'd better warn you – you remember how greedy Sir Lancelot was? – well – ' He paused meaningly.

'All right, I'll take the risk,' dimpled Pollyanna, thinking how glad she was that Aunt Polly was not present to hear her worst predictions so nearly fulfilled thus early. 'Poor Sir Lancelot! I wonder if anybody feeds him now, or if he's there at all.'

'Well, if he's there, he's fed,' interposed Mrs Carew, merrily. 'This ridiculous boy still goes down there at least once a week with his pockets bulging with peanuts and I don't know what all. He can be traced any time by the trail of small grains he leaves behind him; and, half the time, when I order my cereal for breakfast it isn't forthcoming because, forsooth, "Master Jamie has fed it to the pigeons, ma'am!" '

'Yes, but let me tell you – ' plunged in Jamie, enthusiastically. And the next minute Pollyanna found herself listening with all the old fascination to a story of a couple of squirrels in a sunlit garden. Later she saw what Della Wetherby had meant in her letter, for when the house was reached, it came as a distinct shock to her to see Jamie pick up his crutches and swing himself out of the carriage with their aid. She knew then that already in ten short minutes he had made her forget that he was lame.

To Pollyanna's great relief that first dreaded meeting between Aunt Polly and the Carew party passed off much better than she had feared. The newcomers were so frankly delighted with the old house and everything in it that it was an utter impossibility for the mistress and owner of it all to continue her stiff attitude of disapproving resignation to their presence. Besides, as was plainly evident before an hour had passed, the personal charm and magnetism of Jamie had pierced even Aunt Polly's armour of distrust; and Pollyanna knew that at least one of her own most dreaded problems was a problem no longer, for already Aunt Polly was beginning to play the stately, yet gracious hostess to these, her guests.

Notwithstanding her relief at Aunt Polly's change of attitude, however, Pollyanna did not find that all was smooth sailing, by any means. There was work, and plenty of it, that must be done. Nancy's sister, Betty, was pleasant and willing, but she was not Nancy, as Pollyanna soon found. She needed training, and training took time. Pollyanna worried, too, for fear everything should not be quite right. To Pollyanna, those days, a dusty chair was a crime and a fallen cake a tragedy.

Gradually, however, after incessant arguments and pleadings on the part of Mrs Carew and Jamie, Pollyanna came to take her tasks more easily, and to realise that the real crime and tragedy in her friends' eyes was not the dusty chair nor the fallen cake but the frown of worry and anxiety on her own face.

'Just as if it wasn't enough for you to *let* us come,' Jamie declared, 'without just killing yourself with work to get us something to eat.'

'Besides, we ought not to eat so much, anyway,' Mrs Carew laughed, 'or else we shall get "digestion", as one of my girls calls it when her food disagrees with her.'

It was wonderful, after all, how easily the three new members of the family fitted into the daily life. Before twenty-four hours had passed, Mrs Carew had Mrs Chilton asking really interested questions about the new Home for Working Girls, and Sadie Dean and Jamie were quarrelling over the chance to help with the pea-shelling or the flower-picking.

The Carews had been at the Harrington homestead nearly a week when one evening John Pendleton and Jimmy called. Pollyanna had been hoping they would come soon. She had, indeed, urged it very strongly before the Carews came. She made the introductions now with visible pride.

'You are such good friends of mine, I want you to know each other, and be good friends together,' she explained.

That Jimmy and Mr Pendleton should be clearly impressed with the charm and beauty of Mrs Carew did not surprise Pollyanna in the least; but the look that came into Mrs Carew's face at sight of Jimmy did surprise her very much. It was almost a look of recognition.

'Why, Mr Pendleton, haven't I met you before?' Mrs Carew cried.

Jimmy's frank eyes met Mrs Carew's gaze squarely, admiringly.

'I think not,' he smiled back at her. 'I'm sure I never have met you. I should have remembered it – if *I* had met *you*,' he bowed.

So unmistakable was his significant emphasis that everybody laughed, and John Pendleton chuckled: 'Well done, son – for a youth of your tender years. I couldn't have done half so well myself.'

Mrs Carew flushed slightly and joined in the laugh.

'No, but really,' she urged; 'joking aside, there certainly is a strangely familiar something in your face. I think I must have *seen* you somewhere, if I haven't actually met you.'

'And maybe you have,' cried Pollyanna, 'in Boston. Jimmy goes to the technical college there in the winters, you know. Jimmy's going to build bridges and dams, you see – when he grows up, I mean,' she finished with a merry glance at the big six-foot fellow still standing before Mrs Carew.

Everybody laughed again – that is, everybody but Jamie; and only Sadie Dean noticed that Jamie, instead of laughing, closed his eyes as if at the sight of something that hurt. And only Sadie Dean knew how – and why – the subject was so quickly changed, for it was Sadie herself who changed it. It was Sadie, too, who, when the opportunity came, saw to it that books and flowers and beasts and birds – things that Jamie knew and understood – were talked about as well as dams and bridges, which (as Sadie knew) Jamie could never build. That Sadie did all this, however, was not realised by anybody, least of all by Jamie, the one who most of all was concerned.

When the call was over and the Pendletons had gone, Mrs Carew referred again to the curiously haunting feeling that somewhere she had seen young Pendleton before.

'I have, I know I have – somewhere,' she declared musingly. 'Of course it may have been in Boston; but – ' She let the sentence remain unfinished; then, after a minute she added: 'He's a fine young fellow, anyway. I like him.'

'I'm so glad! I do, too,' nodded Pollyanna. 'I've always liked Jimmy.'

'You've known him some time, then?' queried Jamie, a little wistfully.

'Oh, yes. I knew him years ago when I was a little girl, you know. He was Jimmy Bean then.'

'Jimmy *Bean*! Why, isn't he Mr Pendleton's son?' asked Mrs Carew, in surprise.

'No, only by adoption.'

'Adoption!' exclaimed Jamie. 'Then *he* isn't a real son any more than I am.' There was a curious note of almost joy in the lad's voice.

'No. Mr Pendleton hasn't any children. He never married. He – he was going to, once, but he – he didn't.' Pollyanna blushed and spoke with sudden diffidence. Pollyanna had never forgotten that it was her mother who, in the long ago, had said no to this same John Pendleton, and who had thus been responsible for the man's long, lonely years of bachelorhood.

Mrs Carew and Jamie, however, being unaware of this, and seeing now only the blush on Pollyanna's cheek and the diffidence in her manner, drew suddenly the same conclusion.

'Is it possible,' they asked themselves, 'that this man, John Pendleton, ever had a love affair with Pollyanna, child that she is?'

Naturally they did not say this aloud; so, naturally, there was no answer possible. Naturally, too, perhaps, the thought, though un-spoken, was still not forgotten, but was tucked away in a corner of their minds for future reference – if need arose.

CHAPTER 21

Summer Days

Before the Carews came, Pollyanna had told Jimmy that she was depending on him to help her entertain them. Jimmy had not expressed himself then as being overwhelmingly desirous to serve her in this way; but before the Carews had been in town a fortnight, he had shown himself as not only willing but anxious – judging by the frequency and length of his calls, and the lavishness of his offers of the Pendleton horses and motor cars.

Between him and Mrs Carew there sprang up at once a warm friendship based on what seemed to be a peculiarly strong attraction for each other. They walked and talked together, and even made sundry plans for the Home for Working Girls, to be carried out the following winter when Jimmy should be in Boston. Jamie, too, came in for a good measure of attention, nor was Sadie Dean forgotten. Sadie, as Mrs Carew plainly showed, was to be regarded as if she were quite one of the family; and Mrs Carew was careful to see that she had a full share in any plans for merrymaking.

Nor did Jimmy always come alone with his offers for entertain-ment. More and more frequently John Pendleton appeared with him. Rides and drives and picnics were planned and carried out, and long delightful afternoons were spent over books and fancy-work on the Harrington veranda.

Pollyanna was delighted. Not only were her paying guests being kept from any possibilities of ennui and homesickness, but her good friends, the Carews, were becoming delightfully acquainted with her other good friends, the Pendletons. So, like a mother hen with a brood of chickens, she hovered over the veranda meetings, and did everything in her power to keep the group together and happy.

Neither the Carews nor the Pendletons, however, were at all satisfied to have Pollyanna merely an onlooker in their pastimes, and very strenuously they urged her to join them. They would not take no for an answer, indeed, and Pollyanna very frequently found the way opened for her.

'Just as if we were going to have you poked up in this hot kitchen frosting cake!' Jamie scolded one day, after he had penetrated the fastnesses of her domain. 'It is a perfectly glorious morning, and we're all going over to the Gorge and take our luncheon. And *you* are going with us.'

'But, Jamie, I can't – indeed I can't,' refused Pollyanna.

'Why not? You won't have dinner to get for us, for we shan't be here to eat it.'

'But there's the – the luncheon.'

'Wrong again. We'll have the luncheon with us, so you *can't* stay home to get that. Now what's to hinder your going along *with* the luncheon, eh?'

'Why, Jamie, I – I can't. There's the cake to frost – '

'Don't want it frosted.'

'And the dusting – '

'Don't want it dusted.'

'And the ordering to do for tomorrow.'

'Give us crackers and milk. We'd lots rather have you and crackers and milk than a turkey dinner and not you.'

'But I can't begin to tell you the things I've got to do today.'

'Don't want you to begin to tell me,' retorted Jamie, cheerfully. 'I want you to stop telling me. Come, put on your bonnet. I saw Betty in the dining room, and she says she'll put our luncheon up. Now hurry.'

'Why, Jamie, you ridiculous boy, I can't go,' laughed Pollyanna, holding feebly back, as he tugged at her dress-sleeve. 'I can't go on that picnic with you!'

But she went. She went not only then, but again and again. She could not help going, indeed, for she found arrayed against her not

only Jamie, but Jimmy and Mr Pendleton, to say nothing of Mrs
Carew and Sadie Dean, and even Aunt Polly herself.

'And of course I *am* glad to go,' she would sigh happily, when
some dreary bit of work was taken out of her hands in spite of all
protesting. 'But, surely, never before were there any boarders like
mine – teasing for crackers and milk and cold things; and never
before was there a boarding mistress like me – running around the
country after this fashion!'

The climax came when one day John Pendleton (and Aunt Polly
never ceased to exclaim because it *was* John Pendleton) – suggested
that they all go on a two weeks' camping trip to a little lake up
among the mountains forty miles from Beldingsville.

The idea was received with enthusiastic approbation by everybody
except Aunt Polly. Aunt Polly said, privately, to Pollyanna, that it
was all very good and well and desirable that John Pendleton should
have gotten out of the sour, morose aloofness that had been his
state for so many years, but that it did not necessarily follow that it
was equally desirable that he should be trying to turn himself into a
twenty-year-old boy again; and that was what, in her opinion, he
seemed to be doing now! Publicly she contented herself with saying
coldly that *she* certainly should not go on any insane camping trip
to sleep on damp ground and eat bugs and spiders, under the guise
of 'fun', nor did she think it a sensible thing for anybody over forty
to do.

If John Pendleton felt any wound from this shaft, he made no
sign. Certainly there was no diminution of apparent interest and
enthusiasm on his part, and the plans for the camping expedition
came on apace, for it was unanimously decided that even if Aunt
Polly would not go that was no reason why the rest should not.

'And Mrs Carew will be all the chaperon we need, anyhow,' Jimmy
had declared airily.

For a week, therefore, little was talked of but tents, food supplies,
cameras and fishing tackle, and little was done that was not a
preparation in some way for the trip.

'And let's make it the real thing,' proposed Jimmy, eagerly, ' – yes,
even to Mrs Chilton's bugs and spiders,' he added, with a merry

smile straight into that lady's severely disapproving eyes. 'None of your log-cabin-central-dining-room idea for us! We want real campfires with potatoes baked in the ashes, and we want to sit around and tell stories and roast corn on a stick.'

'And we want to swim and row and fish,' chimed in Pollyanna. 'And – ' She stopped suddenly, her eyes on Jamie's face. 'That is, of course,' she corrected quickly, 'we wouldn't want to – to do those things all the time. There'd be a lot of *quiet* things we'd want to do, too – read and talk, you know.'

Jamie's eyes darkened. His face grew a little white. His lips parted, but before any words came, Sadie Dean was speaking.

'Oh, but on camping trips and picnics, you know, we *expect* to do outdoor stunts,' she interposed feverishly; 'and I'm sure we *want* to. Last summer we were down in Maine, and you should have seen the fish Mr Carew caught. It was – You tell it,' she begged, turning to Jamie.

Jamie laughed and shook his head.

'They'd never believe it,' he objected; ' – a fish story like that!'

'Try us,' challenged Pollyanna.

Jamie still shook his head – but the colour had come back to his face, and his eyes were no longer sombre as if with pain. Pollyanna, glancing at Sadie Dean, vaguely wondered why she suddenly settled back in her seat with so very evident an air of relief.

At last the appointed day came, and the start was made in John Pendleton's big new touring car with Jimmy at the wheel. A whir, a throbbing rumble, a chorus of goodbyes, and they were off, with one long shriek of the siren under Jimmy's mischievous fingers.

In after days Pollyanna often went back in her thoughts to that first night in camp. The experience was so new and so wonderful in so many ways.

It was four o'clock when their forty-mile automobile journey came to an end. Since half-past three their big car had been ponderously picking its way over an old logging-road not designed for six-cylinder automobiles. For the car itself, and for the hand at the wheel, this part of the trip was a most wearing one; but for the merry passengers, who had no responsibility concerning hidden holes and muddy curves, it was nothing but a delight growing more poignant with every new vista through the green arches, and with every echoing laugh that dodged the low-hanging branches.

The site for the camp was one known to John Pendleton years before, and he greeted it now with a satisfied delight that was not unmingled with relief.

'Oh, how perfectly lovely!' chorused the others.

'Glad you like it! I thought it would be about right,' nodded John Pendleton. 'Still, I was a little anxious, after all, for these places do change, you know, most remarkably sometimes. And of course this has grown up to bushes a little – but not so much that we can't easily clear it.'

Everybody fell to work then, clearing the ground, putting up the two little tents, unloading the automobile, building the campfire, and arranging the 'kitchen and pantry'.

It was then that Pollyanna began especially to notice Jamie, and to fear for him. She realised suddenly that the hummocks and hollows and pine-littered knolls were not like a carpeted floor for a pair of crutches, and she saw that Jamie was realising it, too. She saw, also, that in spite of his infirmity, he was trying to take his share in the work; and the sight troubled her. Twice she hurried forward and intercepted him, taking from his arms the box he was trying to carry.

'Here, let me take that,' she begged. 'You've done enough.' And the second time she added: 'Do go and sit down somewhere to rest, Jamie. You look so tired!'

If she had been watching closely she would have seen the quick colour sweep to his forehead. But she was not watching, so she did not see it. She did see, however, to her intense surprise, Sadie Dean hurry forward a moment later, her arms full of boxes, and heard her cry: 'Oh, Mr Carew, please, if you *would* give me a lift with these!'

The next moment, Jamie, once more struggling with the problem of managing a bundle of boxes and two crutches, was hastening towards the tents.

With a quick word of protest on her tongue, Pollyanna turned to Sadie Dean. But the protest died unspoken, for Sadie, her finger to her lips, was hurrying straight towards her.

'I know you didn't think,' she stammered in a low voice, as she reached Pollyanna's side. 'But, don't you see? – it *hurts* him to have you think he can't do things like other folks. There, look! See how happy he is now.'

Pollyanna looked, and she saw. She saw Jamie, his whole self alert, deftly balance his weight on one crutch and swing his burden to the ground. She saw the happy light on his face, and she heard him say nonchalantly: 'Here's another contribution from Miss Dean. She asked me to bring this over.'

'Why, yes, I see,' breathed Pollyanna, turning to Sadie Dean. But Sadie Dean had gone.

Pollyanna watched Jamie a good deal after that, though she was careful not to let him, or anyone else, see that she was watching him. And as she watched, her heart ached. Twice she saw him essay a task and fail: once with a box too heavy for him to lift; once with a folding-table too unwieldy for him to carry with his crutches. And each time she saw his quick glance about him to see if others noticed. She saw, too, that unmistakably he was getting very tired, and that his face, in spite of its gay smile, was looking white and drawn, as if he were in pain.

'I should think we might have known more,' stormed Pollyanna hotly to herself, her eyes blinded with tears. 'I should think we might have known more than to have let him come to a place like this. Camping, indeed! – and with a pair of crutches! Why couldn't we have remembered before we started?'

An hour later, around the campfire after supper, Pollyanna had her answer to this question; for, with the glowing fire before her, and the soft, fragrant dark all about her, she once more fell under the spell of the witchery that fell from Jamie's lips; and she once more forgot Jamie's crutches.

CHAPTER 22

Comrades

They were a merry party – the six of them – and a congenial one. There seemed to be no end to the new delights that came with every new day, not the least of which was the new charm of companionship that seemed to be a part of this new life they were living.

As Jamie said one night, when they were all sitting about the fire: 'You see, we seem to know each other so much better up here in the woods – better in a week than we would in a year in town.'

'I know it. I wonder why,' murmured Mrs Carew, her eyes dreamily following the leaping blaze.

'I think it's something in the air,' sighed Pollyanna, happily. 'There's something about the sky and the woods and the lake so – so – well, there just is; that's all.'

'I think you mean, because the world is shut out,' cried Sadie Dean, with a curious little break in her voice. (Sadie had not joined in the laugh that followed Pollyanna's limping conclusion.) 'Up here everything is so real and true that we, too, can be our real true selves – not what the world *says* we are because we are rich, or poor, or great, or humble; but what we really are, *ourselves*.'

'Ho!' scoffed Jimmy, airily. 'All that sounds very fine; but the real common-sense reason is because we don't have any Mrs Tom and Dick and Harry sitting on their side porches and commenting on every time we stir, and wondering among themselves where we are going, why we are going there, and how long we're intending to stay!'

'Oh, Jimmy, how you do take the poetry out of things,' reproached Pollyanna, laughingly.

'But that's my business,' flashed Jimmy. 'How do you suppose I'm going to build dams and bridges if I don't see something besides poetry in the waterfall?'

'You can't, Pendleton! And it's the bridge – that counts – every time,' declared Jamie in a voice that brought a sudden hush to the group about the fire. It was for only a moment, however, for almost at once Sadie Dean broke the silence with a gay: 'Pooh! I'd rather have the waterfall every time, without *any* bridge around – to spoil the view!'

Everybody laughed – and it was as if a tension somewhere snapped. Then Mrs Carew rose to her feet.

'Come, come, children, your stern chaperon says it's bedtime!' And with a merry chorus of good-nights the party broke up.

And so the days passed. To Pollyanna they were wonderful days, and still the most wonderful part was the charm of close companionship – a companionship that, while differing as to details with each one, was yet delightful with all.

With Sadie Dean she talked of the new Home, and of what marvellous work Mrs Carew was doing. They talked, too, of the old days when Sadie was selling bows behind the counter, and of what Mrs Carew had done for her. Pollyanna heard, also, something of the old father and mother 'back home', and of the joy that Sadie, in her new position, had been able to bring into their lives.

'And after all it's really *you* that began it, you know,' she said one day to Pollyanna. But Pollyanna only shook her head at this with an emphatic: 'Nonsense! It was all Mrs Carew.'

With Mrs Carew herself Pollyanna talked also of the Home, and of her plans for the girls. And once, in the hush of a twilight walk, Mrs Carew spoke of herself and of her changed outlook on life. And she, like Sadie Dean, said brokenly: 'After all, it's really you that began it, Pollyanna.' But Pollyanna, as in Sadie Dean's case, would have none of this; and she began to talk of Jamie, and of what *he* had done.

'Jamie's a dear,' Mrs Carew answered affectionately. 'And I love him like an own son. He couldn't be dearer to me if he were really my sister's boy.'

'Then you don't think he is?'

'I don't know. We've never learned anything conclusive. Sometimes I'm sure he is. Then again I doubt it. I think *he* really believes he is – bless his heart! At all events, one thing is sure: he has good blood in him from somewhere. Jamie's no ordinary waif of the streets, you know, with his talents; and the wonderful way he has responded to teaching and training proves it.'

'Of course,' nodded Pollyanna. 'And as long as you love him so well, it doesn't really matter, anyway, does it, whether he's the real Jamie or not?'

Mrs Carew hesitated. Into her eyes crept the old somberness of heartache.

'Not so far as he is concerned,' she sighed, at last. 'It's only that sometimes I get to thinking: if he isn't our Jamie, where is – Jamie Kent? Is he well? Is he happy? Has he anyone to love him? When I get to thinking like that, Pollyanna, I'm nearly wild. I'd give – everything I have in the world, it seems to me, to really *know* that this boy is Jamie Kent.'

Pollyanna used to think of this conversation sometimes, in her after talks with Jamie. Jamie was so sure of himself.

'It's just somehow that I *feel* it's so,' he said once to Pollyanna. 'I believe I am Jamie Kent. I've believed it quite a while. I'm afraid I've believed it so long now that – that I just couldn't bear it, to find out I wasn't he. Mrs Carew has done so much for me; just think if, after all, I were only a stranger!'

'But she – loves you, Jamie.'

'I know she does – and that would only hurt all the more – don't you see? – because it would be hurting her. *She* wants me to be the real Jamie. I know she does. Now if I could only *do* something for her – make her proud of me in some way! If I could only do something to support myself, even, like a man! But what can I do, with – these?' He spoke bitterly, and laid his hand on the crutches at his side.

Pollyanna was shocked and distressed. It was the first time she had heard Jamie speak of his infirmity since the old boyhood days. Frantically she cast about in her mind for just the right thing to say, but before she had thought of anything, Jamie's face had undergone a complete change.

'But, there, forget it! I didn't mean to say it,' he cried gaily. 'And 'twas rank heresy to the game, wasn't it? I'm sure I'm *glad* I've got the crutches. They're a whole lot nicer than the wheelchair!'

'And the Jolly Book – do you keep it now?' asked Pollyanna, in a voice that trembled a little.

'Sure! I've got a whole library of jolly books now,' he retorted. 'They're all in leather, dark red, except the first one. That is the same little old notebook that Jerry gave me.'

'Jerry! And I've been meaning all the time to ask for him,' cried Pollyanna. 'Where is he?'

'In Boston; and his vocabulary is just as picturesque as ever, only he has to tone it down at times. Jerry's still in the newspaper business – but he's *getting* the news, not selling it. Reporting, you know. I *have* been able to help him and mumsey. And don't you suppose I was glad? Mumsey's in a sanatorium for her rheumatism.'

'And is she better?'

'Very much. She's coming out pretty soon, and going to housekeeping with Jerry. Jerry's been making up some of his lost schooling during these past few years. He's let me help him – but only as a loan. He's been very particular to stipulate that.'

'Of course,' nodded Pollyanna, in approval. 'He'd want it that way, I'm sure. I should. It isn't nice to be under obligations that you can't pay. I know how it is. That's why I so wish I could help Aunt Polly out – after all she's done for me!'

'But you are helping her this summer.'

Pollyanna lifted her eyebrows.

'Yes, I'm keeping summer boarders. I look it, don't I?' she challenged, with a flourish of her hands towards her surroundings. 'Surely, never was a boarding-house mistress's task quite like mine! And you should have heard Aunt Polly's dire predictions of what summer boarders would be,' she chuckled irrepressibly.

'What was that?'

Pollyanna shook her head decidedly.

'Couldn't possibly tell you. That's a dead secret. But – ' She stopped and sighed, her face growing wistful again. 'This isn't going to last, you know. It can't. Summer boarders don't. I've got to do something in the winters. I've been thinking. I believe – I'll write stories.'

Jamie turned with a start.

'You'll – what?' he demanded.

'Write stories – to sell, you know. You needn't look so surprised! Lots of folks do that. I knew two girls in Germany who did.'

'Did you ever try it?' Jamie still spoke a little queerly.

'N–no; not yet,' admitted Pollyanna. Then, defensively, in answer to the expression on his face, she bridled: 'I *told* you I was keeping summer boarders now. I can't do both at once.'

'Of course not!'

She threw him a reproachful glance.

'You don't think I can ever do it?'

'I didn't say so.'

'No; but you look it. I don't see why I can't. It isn't like singing. You don't have to have a voice for it. And it isn't like an instrument that you have to learn how to play.'

'I think it is – a little – like that.' Jamie's voice was low. His eyes were turned away.

'How? What do you mean? Why, Jamie, just a pencil and paper, so – that isn't like learning to play the piano or violin!'

There was a moment's silence. Then came the answer, still in that low, diffident voice; still with the eyes turned away.

'The instrument that you play on, Pollyanna, will be the great heart of the world; and to me that seems the most wonderful instrument of all – to learn. Under your touch, if you are skilful, it will respond with smiles or tears, as you will.'

Pollyanna drew a tremulous sigh. Her eyes grew wet.

'Oh, Jamie, how beautifully you do put things – always! I never thought of it that way. But it's so, isn't it? How I would love to do it! Maybe I couldn't do – all that. But I've read stories in the magazines, lots of them. Seems as if I could write some like those, anyway. I *love* to tell stories. I'm always repeating those you tell, and I always laugh and cry, too, just as I do when *you* tell them.'

Jamie turned quickly.

'*Do* they make you laugh and cry, Pollyanna – really?' There was a curious eagerness in his voice.

'Of course they do, and you know it, Jamie. And they used to long ago, too, in the Public Garden. Nobody can tell stories like you, Jamie. *You* ought to be the one writing stories; not I. And, say, Jamie, why don't you? You could do it lovely, I know!'

There was no answer. Jamie, apparently, did not hear; perhaps because he called, at that instant, to a chipmunk that was scurrying through the bushes near by.

It was not always with Jamie, nor yet with Mrs Carew and Sadie Dean that Pollyanna had delightful walks and talks, however; very often it was with Jimmy, or John Pendleton.

Pollyanna was sure now that she had never before known John Pendleton. The old taciturn moroseness seemed entirely gone since they came to camp. He rowed and swam and fished and tramped with fully as much enthusiasm as did Jimmy himself, and with almost as much vigour. Around the campfire at night he quite rivalled Jamie with his story-telling of adventures, both laughable and thrilling, that had befallen him in his foreign travels.

'In the "Desert of Sarah", Nancy used to call it,' laughed Pollyanna one night, as she joined the rest in begging for a story.

Better than all this, however, in Pollyanna's opinion, were the times when John Pendleton, with her alone, talked of her mother as he used to know her and love her, in the days long gone. That he did so talk with her was a joy to Pollyanna, but a great surprise, too; for never in the past had John Pendleton talked so freely of the girl whom he had so loved – hopelessly. Perhaps John Pendleton himself felt some of the surprise, for once he said to Pollyanna, musingly: 'I wonder why I'm talking to you like this.'

'Oh, but I love to have you,' breathed Pollyanna.

'Yes, I know – but I wouldn't think I would do it. It must be, though, that it's because you are so like her, as I knew her. You are very like your mother, my dear.'

'Why, I thought my mother was *beautiful*!' cried Pollyanna, in unconcealed amazement.

John Pendleton smiled quizzically.

'She was, my dear.'

Pollyanna looked still more amazed.

'Then I don't see how I *can be* like her!'

The man laughed outright.

'Pollyanna, if some girls had said that, I – well, never mind what I'd say. You little witch! – you poor, homely little Pollyanna!'

Pollyanna flashed a genuinely distressed reproof straight into the man's merry eyes.

'Please, Mr Pendleton, don't look like that, and don't tease me – about *that*. I'd so *love* to be beautiful – though of course it sounds silly to say it. And I *have* a mirror, you know.'

'Then I advise you to look in it – when you're talking sometime,' observed the man sententiously.

Pollyanna's eyes flew wide open.

'Why, that's just what Jimmy said,' she cried.

'Did he, indeed – the young rascal!' retorted John Pendleton, dryly. Then, with one of the curiously abrupt changes of manner peculiar to him, he said, very low: 'You have your mother's eyes and smile, Pollyanna; and to me you are – beautiful.'

And Pollyanna, her eyes blinded with sudden hot tears, was silenced.

Dear as were these talks, however, they still were not quite like the talks with Jimmy, to Pollyanna. For that matter, she and Jimmy did not need to *talk* to be happy. Jimmy was always so comfortable, and comforting; whether they talked or not did not matter. Jimmy always understood. There was no pulling on her heart-strings for sympathy, with Jimmy – Jimmy was delightfully big, and strong, and happy. Jimmy was not sorrowing for a long-lost nephew, nor pining for the loss of a boyhood sweetheart. Jimmy did not have to swing himself painfully about on a pair of crutches – all of which was so hard to see, and know, and think of. With Jimmy one could be just glad, and happy, and free. Jimmy was such a dear! He always rested one so – did Jimmy!

CHAPTER 23

'Tied to Two Sticks'

It was on the last day at camp that it happened. To Pollyanna it seemed such a pity that it should have happened at all, for it was the first cloud to bring a shadow of regret and unhappiness to her heart during the whole trip, and she found herself futilely sighing: 'I wish we'd gone home the day before yesterday; then it wouldn't have happened.'

But they had not gone home 'the day before yesterday', and it had happened; and this was the manner of it.

Early in the morning of that last day they had all started on a two-mile tramp to 'the Basin'.

'We'll have one more bang-up fish dinner before we go,' Jimmy had said. And the rest had joyfully agreed.

With luncheon and fishing tackle, therefore, they had made an early start. Laughing and calling gaily to each other they followed the narrow path through the woods, led by Jimmy, who best knew the way.

At first, close behind Jimmy had walked Pollyanna; but gradually she had fallen back with Jamie, who was last in the line: Pollyanna had thought she detected on Jamie's face the expression which she had come to know was there only when he was attempting something that taxed almost to the breaking-point his skill and powers of endurance. She knew that nothing would so offend him as to have her openly notice this state of affairs. At the same time, she also knew that from her, more willingly than from anyone else, would he accept an occasional steadying hand over a troublesome log or stone. Therefore, at the first opportunity to make the change without apparent design, she had dropped back step by step until she had reached her goal, Jamie. She had been rewarded instantly in the way

Jamie's face brightened, and in the easy assurance with which he met and conquered a fallen tree-trunk across their path, under the pleasant fiction (carefully fostered by Pollyanna) of 'helping her across'.

Once out of the woods, their way led along an old stone wall for a time, with wide reaches of sunny, sloping pastures on each side, and a more distant picturesque farmhouse. It was in the adjoining pasture that Pollyanna saw the golden-rod which she immediately coveted.

'Jamie, wait! I'm going to get it,' she exclaimed eagerly. 'It'll make such a beautiful bouquet for our picnic table!' And nimbly she scrambled over the high stone wall and dropped herself down on the other side.

It was strange how tantalising was that golden-rod. Always just ahead she saw another bunch, and yet another, each a little finer than the one within her reach. With joyous exclamations and gay little calls back to the waiting Jamie, Pollyanna – looking particularly attractive in her scarlet sweater – skipped from bunch to bunch, adding to her store. She had both hands full when there came the hideous bellow of an angry bull, the agonised shout from Jamie and the sound of hoofs thundering down the hillside.

What happened next was never clear to her. She knew she dropped her golden-rod and ran – ran as she never ran before, ran as she thought she never could run – back towards the wall and Jamie. She knew that behind her the hoof-beats were gaining, gaining, always gaining. Dimly, hopelessly far ahead of her, she saw Jamie's agonised face, and heard his hoarse cries. Then, from somewhere, came a new voice – Jimmy's – shouting a cheery call of courage.

Still on and on she ran blindly, hearing nearer and nearer the thud of those pounding hoofs. Once she stumbled and almost fell. Then, dizzily she righted herself and plunged forward. She felt her strength quite gone when suddenly, close to her, she heard Jimmy's cheery call again. The next minute she felt herself snatched off her feet and held close to a great throbbing something that dimly she realised was Jimmy's heart. It was all a horrid blur then of cries, hot, panting breaths, and pounding hoofs thundering nearer, ever nearer. Then, just as she knew those hoofs to be almost upon her, she felt herself flung, still in Jimmy's arms, sharply to one side, and yet not so far but that she still could feel the hot breath of the maddened animal as he dashed by. Almost at once then she found herself on the other side of the wall, with Jimmy bending over her, imploring her to tell him she was not dead.

With an hysterical laugh that was yet half a sob, she struggled out of his arms and stood upon her feet.

'Dead? No, indeed – thanks to you, Jimmy. I'm all right. I'm all right. Oh, how glad, glad, glad I was to hear your voice! Oh, that was splendid! How did you do it?' she panted.

'Pooh! That was nothing. I just – ' An inarticulate choking cry brought his words to a sudden halt. He turned to find Jamie face down on the ground, a little distance away. Pollyanna was already hurrying towards him.

'Jamie, Jamie, what is the matter?' she cried. 'Did you fall? Are you hurt?'

There was no answer.

'What is it, old fellow? *Are* you hurt?' demanded Jimmy.

Still there was no answer. Then, suddenly, Jamie pulled himself half upright and turned. They saw his face then, and fell back, shocked and amazed.

'Hurt? Am I hurt?' he choked huskily, flinging out both his hands. 'Don't you suppose it hurts to see a thing like that and not be able to do anything? To be tied, helpless, to a pair of sticks? I tell you there's no hurt in all the world to equal it!'

'But – but – Jamie,' faltered Pollyanna.

'Don't!' interrupted the cripple, almost harshly. He had struggled to his feet now. 'Don't say – anything. I didn't mean to make a scene – like this,' he finished brokenly, as he turned and swung back along the narrow path that led to the camp.

For a minute, as if transfixed, the two behind him watched him go.

'Well, by – Jove!' breathed Jimmy, then, in a voice that shook a little, 'That was – tough on him!'

'And I didn't think, and *praised* you, right before him,' half-sobbed Pollyanna. 'And his hands – did you see them? They were – *bleeding* where the nails had cut right into the flesh,' she finished, as she turned and stumbled blindly up the path.

'But, Pollyanna, w–where are you going?' cried Jimmy.

'I'm going to Jamie, of course! Do you think I'd leave him like that? Come, we must get him to come back.'

And Jimmy, with a sigh that was not all for Jamie, went.

CHAPTER 24

Jimmy Wakes Up

Outwardly the camping trip was pronounced a great success; but inwardly –

Pollyanna wondered sometimes if it were all herself, or if there really were a peculiar, indefinable constraint in everybody with everybody else. Certainly she felt it, and she thought she saw evidences that the others felt it, too. As for the cause of it all – unhesitatingly she attributed it to that last day at camp with its unfortunate trip to the Basin.

To be sure, she and Jimmy had easily caught up with Jamie, and had, after considerable coaxing, persuaded him to turn about and go on to the Basin with them. But, in spite of everybody's very evident efforts to act as if nothing out of the ordinary had happened, nobody really succeeded in doing so. Pollyanna, Jamie and Jimmy overdid their gaiety a bit, perhaps; and the others, while not knowing exactly what had happened, very evidently felt that something was not quite right, though they plainly tried to hide the fact that they did feel so. Naturally, in this state of affairs, restful happiness was out of the question. Even the anticipated fish dinner was flavourless; and early in the afternoon the start was made back to the camp.

Once home again, Pollyanna had hoped that the unhappy episode of the angry bull would be forgotten. But she could not forget it, so in all fairness she could not blame the others if they could not.

Always she thought of it now when she looked at Jamie. She saw again the agony on his face, the crimson stain on the palms of his hands. Her heart ached for him, and because it did so ache, his mere presence had come to be a pain to her. Remorsefully she confessed to herself that she did not like to be with Jamie now, nor to talk with him – but that did not mean that she was not often with him. She was with him, indeed, much oftener than before, for so remorseful was she, and so fearful was she that he would detect her unhappy frame of mind, that she lost no opportunity of responding to his overtures of comradeship; and sometimes she deliberately sought him out. This last she did not often have to do, however, for more and more frequently these days Jamie seemed to be turning to her for companionship.

The reason for this, Pollyanna believed, was to be found in this same incident of the bull and the rescue. Not that Jamie ever referred to it directly. He never did that. He was, too, even gayer than usual; but Pollyanna thought she detected sometimes a bitterness underneath it all that was never there before. Certainly she could not help seeing that at times he seemed almost to want to avoid the others, and that he actually sighed, as if with relief, when he found himself alone with her. She thought she knew why this was so, after he said to her, as he did say one day, while they were watching the others play tennis: 'You see, after all, Pollyanna, there isn't anyone who can quite understand as you can.'

' "Understand"?' Pollyanna had not known what he meant at first. They had been watching the players for five minutes without a word between them.

'Yes; for you, once – couldn't walk – yourself.'

'Oh–h, yes, I know,' faltered Pollyanna; and she knew that her great distress must have shown in her face, for so quickly and so blithely did he change the subject, after a laughing: 'Come, come, Pollyanna, why don't you tell me to play the game? I would if I were in your place. Forget it, please. I was a brute to make you look like that!'

And Pollyanna smiled, and said: 'No, no – no, indeed!' But she did not 'forget it'. She could not. And it all made her only the more anxious to be with Jamie and help him all she could.

'As if *now* I'd ever let him see that I was ever anything but glad when he was with me!' she thought fervently, as she hurried forward a minute later to take her turn in the game.

Pollyanna, however, was not the only one in the party who felt a new awkwardness and constraint. Jimmy Pendleton felt it, though he, too, tried not to show it.

Jimmy was not happy these days. From a carefree youth whose visions were of wonderful spans across hitherto unbridgeable chasms, he had come to be an anxious-eyed young man whose visions were of a feared rival bearing away the girl he loved.

Jimmy knew very well now that he was in love with Pollyanna. He suspected that he had been in love with her for some time. He stood aghast, indeed, to find himself so shaken and powerless before this thing that had come to him. He knew that even his beloved bridges were as nothing when weighed against the smile in a girl's eyes and the word on a girl's lips. He realised that the most wonderful span in the world to him would be the thing that could help him to cross the chasm of fear and doubt that he felt lay between him and Pollyanna – doubt because of Pollyanna; fear because of Jamie.

Not until he had seen Pollyanna in jeopardy that day in the pasture had he realised how empty would be the world – his world – without her. Not until his wild dash for safety with Pollyanna in his arms had he realised how precious she was to him. For a moment, indeed, with his arms about her, and hers clinging about his neck, he had felt that she was indeed his; and even in that supreme moment of danger he knew the thrill of supreme bliss. Then, a little later, he had seen Jamie's face, and Jamie's hands. To him they could mean but one thing: Jamie, too, loved Pollyanna, and Jamie had to stand by, helpless – 'tied to two sticks'. That was what he had said. Jimmy believed that, had he himself been obliged to stand by helpless, 'tied to two sticks', while another rescued the girl that he loved, he would have looked like that.

Jimmy had gone back to camp that day with his thoughts in a turmoil of fear and rebellion. He wondered if Pollyanna cared for Jamie; that was where the fear came in. But even if she did care, a little, must he stand aside, weakly, and let Jamie, without a struggle, make her learn to care more? That was where the rebellion came in. Indeed, no, he would not do it, decided Jimmy. It should be a fair fight between them.

Then, all by himself as he was, Jimmy flushed hot to the roots of his hair. Would it be a 'fair' fight? Could any fight between him and Jamie be a 'fair' fight? Jimmy felt suddenly as he had felt years before when, as a lad, he had challenged a new boy to a fight for an apple they both claimed, then, at the first blow, had discovered that the new boy had a crippled arm. He had purposely lost then, of course, and had let the crippled boy win. But he told himself fiercely now that this case was different. It was no apple that was at stake. It was his life's happiness. It might even be Pollyanna's life's happiness, too. Perhaps she did not care for Jamie at all, but would care for her old friend, Jimmy, if he but once showed her he wanted her to care. And he would show her. He would –

Once again Jimmy blushed hotly. But he frowned, too, angrily: if only he *could* forget how Jamie had looked when he had uttered that moaning 'tied to two sticks!' If only – But what was the use? It was *not* a fair fight, and he knew it. He knew, too, right there and then, that his decision would be just what it afterwards proved to be: he would watch and wait. He would give Jamie his chance; and if Pollyanna showed that she cared, he would take himself off and away quite out of their lives; and they should never know, either of them, how bitterly he was suffering. He would go back to his bridges – as if any bridge, though it led to the moon itself, could compare for a moment with Pollyanna! But he would do it. He must do it.

It was all very fine and heroic, and Jimmy felt so exalted he was atingle with something that was almost happiness when he finally dropped off to sleep that night. But martyrdom in theory and practice differs woefully, as would-be martyrs have found out from time immemorial. It was all very well to decide alone and in the dark that he would give Jamie his chance; but it was quite another matter really to do it when it involved nothing less than the leaving of Pollyanna and Jamie together almost every time he saw them. Then, too, he was very much worried at Pollyanna's apparent attitude towards the lame youth. It looked very much to Jimmy as if she did indeed care for him, so watchful was she of his comfort, so apparently eager to be with him. Then, as if to settle any possible doubt in Jimmy's mind, there came the day when Sadie Dean had something to say on the subject.

They were all out at the tennis court. Sadie was sitting alone when Jimmy strolled up to her.

'You next with Pollyanna, isn't it?' he queried.

She shook her head.

'Pollyanna isn't playing any more this morning.'

'Isn't playing!' frowned Jimmy, who had been counting on his own game with Pollyanna. 'Why not?'

For a brief minute Sadie Dean did not answer; then with very evident difficulty she said: 'Pollyanna told me last night that she thought we were playing tennis too much; that it wasn't kind to – Mr Carew, as long as he can't play.'

'I know; but – ' Jimmy stopped helplessly, the frown ploughing a deeper furrow into his forehead. The next instant he fairly started with surprise at the tense something in Sadie Dean's voice, as she said: 'But he doesn't want her to stop. He doesn't want any one of us to make any difference – for him. It's that that hurts him so. She doesn't understand. She doesn't understand! But I do. She thinks she does, though!'

Something in words or manner sent a sudden pang to Jimmy's heart. He threw a sharp look into her face. A question flew to his lips. For a moment he held it back; then, trying to hide his earnestness with a bantering smile, he let it come.

'Why, Miss Dean, you don't mean to convey the idea that – that there's any *special* interest in each other – between those two, do you?'

She gave him a scornful glance.

'Where have your eyes been? She worships him! I mean – they worship each other,' she corrected hastily.

Jimmy, with an inarticulate ejaculation, turned and walked away abruptly. He could not trust himself to remain longer. He did not wish to talk any more, just then, to Sadie Dean. So abruptly, indeed, did he turn, that he did not notice that Sadie Dean, too, turned hurriedly, and busied herself looking in the grass at her feet, as if she had lost something. Very evidently, Sadie Dean, also, did not wish to talk any more just then.

Jimmy Pendleton told himself that it was not true at all; that it was all folderol, what Sadie Dean had said. Yet nevertheless, true or not true, he could not forget it. It coloured all his thoughts thereafter, and loomed before his eyes like a shadow whenever he saw Pollyanna and Jamie together. He watched their faces covertly. He listened to the tones of their voices. He came then, in time, to think it was, after all, true: that they did worship each other; and his heart, in consequence, grew like lead within him. True to his promise to himself, however, he turned resolutely away. The die was cast, he told himself. Pollyanna was not to be for him.

Restless days for Jimmy followed. To stay away from the Harrington homestead entirely he did not dare, lest his secret be suspected. To be with Pollyanna at all now was torture. Even to be with Sadie Dean was unpleasant, for he could not forget that it was Sadie Dean who had finally opened his eyes. Jamie, certainly, was no haven of refuge, under the circumstances; and that left only Mrs Carew. Mrs Carew, however, was a host in herself, and Jimmy found his only comfort these days in her society. Gay or grave, she always seemed to know how to fit his mood exactly; and it was wonderful how much she knew about bridges – the kind of bridges he was going to build. She was so wise, too, and so sympathetic, knowing always just the right word to say. He even one day almost told her about The Packet; but John Pendleton interrupted them at just the wrong moment, so the story was not told. John Pendleton was always interrupting them at just the wrong moment, Jimmy thought vexedly, sometimes. Then, when he remembered what John Pendleton had done for him, he was ashamed.

'The Packet' was a thing that dated back to Jimmy's boyhood, and had never been mentioned to anyone save to John Pendleton, and that only once, at the time of his adoption. The Packet was nothing but rather a large white envelope, worn with time, and plump with mystery behind a huge red seal. It had been given him by his father, and it bore the following instructions in his father's hand: 'To my boy, Jimmy. Not to be opened until his thirtieth birthday, except in case of his death, when it shall be opened at once.'

There were times when Jimmy speculated a good deal as to the contents of that envelope. There were other times when he forgot its existence. In the old days, at the Orphans' Home, his chief terror had been that it should be discovered and taken away from him. In those days he wore it always hidden in the lining of his coat. Of late years, at John Pendleton's suggestion, it had been tucked away in the Pendleton safe.

'For there's no knowing how valuable it may be,' John Pendleton had said, with a smile. 'And, anyway, your father evidently wanted you to have it, and we wouldn't want to run the risk of losing it.'

'No, I wouldn't want to lose it, of course,' Jimmy had smiled back, a little soberly. 'But I'm not counting on its being real valuable, sir. Poor dad didn't have anything that was very valuable about him, as I remember.'

It was this packet that Jimmy came so near mentioning to Mrs Carew one day – if only John Pendleton had not interrupted them.

'Still, maybe it's just as well I didn't tell her about it,' Jimmy reflected afterwards, on his way home. 'She might have thought dad had something in his life that wasn't quite – right. And I wouldn't have wanted her to think that – of dad.'

CHAPTER 25

The Game and Pollyanna

Before the middle of September the Carews and Sadie Dean said goodbye and went back to Boston. Much as she knew she would miss them, Pollyanna drew an actual sigh of relief as the train bearing them away rolled out of the Beldingsville station. Pollyanna would not have admitted having this feeling of relief to anyone else, and even to herself she apologised in her thoughts.

'It isn't that I don't love them dearly, every one of them,' she sighed, watching the train disappear around the curve far down the track. 'It's only that – that I'm so sorry for poor Jamie all the time; and – and – I am tired. I shall be glad, for a while, just to go back to the old quiet days with Jimmy.'

Pollyanna, however, did not go back to the old quiet days with Jimmy. The days that immediately followed the going of the Carews were quiet, certainly, but they were not passed 'with Jimmy'. Jimmy rarely came near the house now, and when he did call, he was not the old Jimmy that she used to know. He was moody, restless and silent, or else very gay and talkative in a nervous fashion that was most puzzling and annoying. Before long, too, he himself went to Boston; and then of course she did not see him at all.

Pollyanna was surprised then to see how much she missed him. Even to know that he was in town, and that there was a chance that he might come over, was better than the dreary emptiness of certain absence; and even his puzzling moods of alternating gloominess and gaiety were preferable to this utter silence of nothingness. Then, one day, suddenly she pulled herself up with hot cheeks and shamed eyes.

'Well, Pollyanna Whittier,' she upbraided herself sharply, 'one would think you were in *love* with Jimmy Bean Pendleton! Can't you think of *anything* but him?'

Whereupon, forthwith, she bestirred herself to be very gay and lively indeed, and to put this Jimmy Bean Pendleton out of her thoughts. As it happened, Aunt Polly, though unwittingly, helped her to this.

With the going of the Carews had gone also their chief source of immediate income, and Aunt Polly was beginning to worry again, audibly, about the state of their finances.

'I don't know, really, Pollyanna, what *is* going to become of us,' she would moan frequently. 'Of course we are a little ahead now from this summer's work, and we have a small sum from the estate right along; but I never know how soon that's going to stop, like all the rest. If only we could do something to bring in some ready cash!'

It was after one of these moaning lamentations one day that

Pollyanna's eyes chanced to fall on a prize-story contest offer. It was a most alluring one. The prizes were large and numerous. The conditions were set forth in glowing terms. To read it, one would think that to win out were the easiest thing in the world. It contained even a special appeal that might have been framed for Pollyanna herself:

This is for you – you who read this. What if you never have written a story before! That is no sign you cannot write one. Try it. That's all. Wouldn't *you* like three thousand dollars? Two thousand? One thousand? Five hundred, or even one hundred? Then why not go after it?

'The very thing!' cried Pollyanna, clapping her hands. 'I'm so glad I saw it! And it says I can do it, too. I thought I could, if I'd just try. I'll go tell auntie, so she needn't worry any more.'

Pollyanna was on her feet and halfway to the door when a second thought brought her steps to a pause.

'Come to think of it, I reckon I won't, after all. It'll be all the nicer to surprise her; and if I *should* get the first one – !'

Pollyanna went to sleep that night planning what she *could* do with that three thousand dollars.

Pollyanna began her story the next day. That is, she, with a very important air, got out a quantity of paper, sharpened up half a dozen pencils and established herself at the big old-fashioned Harrington desk in the living-room. After biting restlessly at the ends of two of her pencils, she wrote down three words on the fair white page before her. Then she drew a long sigh, threw aside the second ruined pencil, and picked up a slender green one with a beautiful point. This point she eyed with a meditative frown.

'Oh dear! I wonder *where* they get their titles,' she despaired. 'Maybe, though, I ought to decide on the story first, and then make a title to fit. Anyhow, *I'm* going to do it.' And forthwith she drew a black line through the three words and poised the pencil for a fresh start.

The start was not made at once, however. Even when it was made, it must have been a false one, for at the end of half an hour the whole page was nothing but a jumble of scratched-out lines, with only a few words here and there left to tell the tale.

At this juncture Aunt Polly came into the room. She turned tired eyes upon her niece.

'Well, Pollyanna, what *are* you up to now?' she demanded.

Pollyanna laughed and coloured guiltily.

'Nothing much, auntie. Anyhow, it doesn't look as if it were much – yet,' she admitted, with a rueful smile. 'Besides, it's a secret, and I'm not going to tell it yet.'

'Very well; suit yourself,' sighed Aunt Polly. 'But I can tell you right now that if you're trying to make anything different out of those mortgage papers Mr Hart left, it's useless. I've been all over them myself twice.'

'No, dear, it isn't the papers. It's a whole heap nicer than any papers ever could be,' crowed Pollyanna triumphantly, turning back to her work. In Pollyanna's eyes suddenly had risen a glowing vision of what it might be, with that three thousand dollars once hers.

For still another half-hour Pollyanna wrote and scratched, and chewed her pencils; then, with her courage dulled, but not destroyed, she gathered up her papers and pencils and left the room.

'I reckon maybe I'll do better by myself upstairs,' she was thinking as she hurried through the hall. 'I *thought* I ought to do it at a desk – being literary work, so – but anyhow, the desk didn't help me this morning. I'll try the window seat in my room.'

The window seat, however, proved to be no more inspiring, judging by the scratched and re-scratched pages that fell from Pollyanna's hands; and at the end of another half-hour Pollyanna discovered suddenly that it was time to get dinner.

'Well, I'm glad 'tis, anyhow,' she sighed to herself. 'I'd a lot rather get dinner than do this. Not but that I *want* to do this, of course; only I'd no idea 'twas such an awful job – just a story, so!'

During the following month Pollyanna worked faithfully, doggedly, but she soon found that 'just a story, so' was indeed no small matter to accomplish. Pollyanna, however, was not one to set her hand to the plough and look back. Besides, there was that three-thousand-dollar prize, or even any of the others, if she should not happen to win the first one! Of course even one hundred dollars was something! So day after day she wrote and erased, and rewrote, until finally the story, such as it was, lay completed before her. Then, with some misgivings, it must be confessed, she took the manuscript to Milly Snow to be typewritten.

'It reads all right – that is, it makes sense,' mused Pollyanna doubtfully, as she hurried along towards the Snow cottage; 'and it's a really nice story about a perfectly lovely girl. But there's something somewhere that isn't quite right about it, I'm afraid. Anyhow, I don't believe I'd better count too much on the first prize; then I won't be too much disappointed when I get one of the littler ones.'

Pollyanna always thought of Jimmy when she went to the Snows', for it was at the side of the road near their cottage that she had first seen him as a forlorn little runaway lad from the Orphans' Home years before. She thought of him again today, with a little catch of her breath. Then, with the proud lifting of her head that always came now with the second thought of Jimmy, she hurried up the Snows' doorsteps and rang the bell.

As was usually the case, the Snows had nothing but the warmest of welcomes for Pollyanna; and also as usual it was not long before they were talking of the game: in no home in Beldingsville was the glad game more ardently played than in the Snows'.

'Well, and how are you getting along?' asked Pollyanna, when she had finished the business part of her call.

'Splendidly!' beamed Milly Snow. 'This is the third job I've got this week. Oh, Miss Pollyanna, I'm so glad you had me take up typewriting, for you see I *can* do that at home! And it's all owing to you.'

'Nonsense!' disclaimed Pollyanna, merrily.

'But it is. In the first place, I couldn't have done it anyway if it hadn't been for the game – making mother so much better, you know, that I had some time to myself. And then, at the very first, you suggested typewriting, and helped me to buy a machine. I should like to know if that doesn't come pretty near owing it all to you!'

But once again Pollyanna objected. This time she was interrupted by Mrs Snow from her wheelchair by the window. And so earnestly and gravely did Mrs Snow speak that Pollyanna, in spite of herself, could but hear what she had to say.

'Listen, child, I don't think you know quite what you've done. But I wish you could! There's a little look in your eyes, my dear, today, that I don't like to see there. You are plagued and worried over something, I know. I can see it. And I don't wonder: your uncle's death, your aunt's condition, everything – I won't say more about that. But there's something I do want to say, my dear, and you must let me say it, for I can't bear to see that shadow in your eyes without trying to drive it away by telling you what you've done for me, for this whole town, and for countless other people everywhere.'

'*Mrs Snow!*' protested Pollyanna, in genuine distress.

'Oh, I mean it, and I know what I'm talking about,' nodded the invalid, triumphantly. 'To begin with, look at me. Didn't you find me a fretful, whining creature who never by any chance wanted what she had until she found what she didn't have? And didn't you open my eyes by bringing me three kinds of things so I'd *have* to have what I wanted, for once?'

'Oh, Mrs Snow, was I really ever quite so – impertinent as that?' murmured Pollyanna, with a painful blush.

'It wasn't impertinent,' objected Mrs Snow, stoutly. 'You didn't *mean* it as impertinence – and that made all the difference in the world. You didn't preach, either, my dear. If you had, you'd never have got me to playing the game, nor anybody else, I fancy. But you did get me to playing it – and see what it's done for me, and for Milly! Here I am so much better that I can sit in a wheelchair and go anywhere on this floor in it. That means a whole lot when it comes to waiting on yourself, and giving those around you a chance to breathe – meaning Milly, in this case. And the doctor says it's all owing to the game. Then there's others, quantities of others, right in this town, that I'm hearing of all the time. Nellie Mahoney broke her wrist and was so glad it wasn't her leg that she didn't mind the wrist at all. Old Mrs Tibbits has lost her hearing, but she's so glad 'tisn't her eyesight that she's actually happy. Do you remember cross-eyed Joe that they used to call Cross Joe, because of his temper? Nothing went to suit him either, any more than it did me. Well, somebody's taught him the game, they say, and made a different man of him. And listen, dear. It's not only this town, but other places. I had a letter yesterday from my cousin in Massachusetts, and she told me all about Mrs Tom Payson that used to live here. Do you remember them? They lived on the way up Pendleton Hill.'

'Yes, oh, yes, I remember them,' cried Pollyanna.

'Well, they left here that winter you were in the Sanatorium and went to Massachusetts where my sister lives. She knows them well. She says Mrs Payson told her all about you, and how your glad game actually saved them from a divorce. And now not only do they play it themselves, but they've got quite a lot of others playing it down there, and *they're* getting still others. So you see, dear, there's no telling where that glad game of yours is going to stop. I wanted you to know. I thought it might help even you to play the game sometimes; for don't think I don't understand, dearie, that it *is* hard for you to play your own game – sometimes.'

Pollyanna rose to her feet. She smiled, but her eyes glistened with tears, as she held out her hand in goodbye.

'Thank you, Mrs Snow,' she said unsteadily. 'It *is* hard – sometimes; and maybe I *did* need a little help about my own game. But, anyhow, now – ' her eyes flashed with their old merriment – 'if any time I think I can't play the game myself I can remember that I can still always be *glad* there are some folks playing it!'

Pollyanna walked home a little soberly that afternoon. Touched as she was by what Mrs Snow had said, there was yet an undercurrent of sadness in it all. She was thinking of Aunt Polly – Aunt Polly who played the game now so seldom; and she was wondering if she herself always played it, when she might.

'Maybe I haven't been careful, always, to hunt up the glad side of the things Aunt Polly says,' she thought with undefined guiltiness; 'and maybe if I played the game better myself, Aunt Polly would play it – a little. Anyhow I'm going to try. If I don't look out, all these other people will be playing my own game better than I am myself!'

CHAPTER 26

John Pendleton

It was just a week before Christmas that Pollyanna sent her story (now neatly typewritten) in for the contest. The prize-winners would not be announced until April, the magazine notice said, so Pollyanna settled herself for the long wait with characteristic, philosophical patience.

'I don't know, anyhow, but I'm glad 'tis so long,' she told herself, 'for all winter I can have the fun of thinking it may be the first one instead of one of the others that I'll get. I might just as well think I'm going to get it, then if I do get it, I won't have been unhappy any. While if I don't get it – I won't have had all these weeks of unhappiness beforehand, anyway; and I can be glad for one of the smaller ones, then.' That she might not get any prize was not in Pollyanna's calculations at all. The story, so beautifully typed by Milly Snow, looked almost as good as printed already – to Pollyanna.

Christmas was not a happy time at the Harrington homestead that year, in spite of Pollyanna's strenuous efforts to make it so. Aunt Polly refused absolutely to allow any sort of celebration of the day, and made her attitude so unmistakably plain that Pollyanna could not give even the simplest of presents.

Christmas evening John Pendleton called. Mrs Chilton excused herself, but Pollyanna, utterly worn out from a long day with her aunt, welcomed him joyously. But even here she found a fly in the amber of her content, for John Pendleton had brought with him a letter from Jimmy, and the letter was full of nothing but the plans he and Mrs Carew were making for a wonderful Christmas celebration at the Home for Working Girls; and Pollyanna, ashamed though she was to own it to herself, was not in a mood to hear about Christmas celebrations just then – least of all, Jimmy's.

John Pendleton, however, was not ready to let the subject drop, even when the letter had been read.

'Great doings – those!' he exclaimed, as he folded the letter.

'Yes, indeed; fine!' murmured Pollyanna, trying to speak with due enthusiasm.

'And it's tonight, too, isn't it? I'd like to drop in on them about now.'

'Yes,' murmured Pollyanna again, with still more careful enthusiasm.

'Mrs Carew knew what she was about when she got Jimmy to help her, I fancy,' chuckled the man. 'But I'm wondering how Jimmy likes it – playing Santa Claus to half a hundred young women at once!'

'Why, he finds it delightful, of course!' Pollyanna lifted her chin ever so slightly.

'Maybe. Still, it's a little different from learning to build bridges, you must confess.'

'Oh, yes.'

'But I'll risk Jimmy, and I'll risk wagering that those girls never had a better time than he'll give them tonight, too.'

'Y–yes, of course,' stammered Pollyanna, trying to keep the hated tremulousness out of her voice, and trying very hard *not* to compare her own dreary evening in Beldingsville, with nobody but John Pendleton, to that of those fifty girls in Boston – with Jimmy.

There was a brief pause, during which John Pendleton gazed dreamily at the dancing fire on the hearth.

'She's a wonderful woman – Mrs Carew is,' he said at last.

'She is, indeed!' This time the enthusiasm in Pollyanna's voice was all pure gold.

'Jimmy's written me before something of what she's done for those girls,' went on the man, still gazing into the fire. 'In just the last letter before this he wrote a lot about it, and about her. He said he always admired her, but never so much as now, when he can see what she really is.'

'She's a dear – that's what Mrs Carew is,' declared Pollyanna, warmly. 'She's a dear in every way, and I love her.'

John Pendleton stirred suddenly. He turned to Pollyanna with an oddly whimsical look in his eyes.

'I know you do, my dear. For that matter, there may be others, too – that love her.'

Pollyanna's heart skipped a beat. A sudden thought came to her with stunning, blinding force. *Jimmy!* Could John Pendleton be meaning that Jimmy cared *that way* – for Mrs Carew?

'You mean – ?' she faltered. She could not finish.

With a nervous twitch peculiar to him, John Pendleton got to his feet.

'I mean – the girls, of course,' he answered lightly, still with that whimsical smile. 'Don't you suppose those fifty girls – love her 'most to death?'

Pollyanna said, 'Yes, of course,' and murmured something else appropriate, in answer to John Pendleton's next remark. But her thoughts were in a tumult, and she let the man do most of the talking for the rest of the evening.

Nor did John Pendleton seem averse to this. Restlessly he took a turn or two about the room, then sat down in his old place. And when he spoke, it was on his old subject, Mrs Carew.

'Queer – about that Jamie of hers, isn't it? I wonder if he *is* her nephew.'

As Pollyanna did not answer, the man went on, after a moment's silence.

'He's a fine fellow, anyway. I like him. There's something fine and genuine about him. She's bound up in him. That's plain to be seen, whether he's really her kin or not.'

There was another pause, then, in a slightly altered voice, John Pendleton said: 'Still it's queer, too, when you come to think of it, that she never – married again. She is certainly now – a very beautiful woman. Don't you think so?'

'Yes – yes, indeed she is,' plunged in Pollyanna, with precipitate haste; 'a – a very beautiful woman.'

There was a little break at the last in Pollyanna's voice. Pollyanna, just then, had caught sight of her own face in the mirror opposite – and Pollyanna to herself was never 'a very beautiful woman'.

On and on rambled John Pendleton, musingly, contentedly, his eyes on the fire. Whether he was answered or not seemed not to disturb him. Whether he was even listened to or not, he seemed hardly to know. He wanted, apparently, only to talk; but at last he got to his feet reluctantly and said good-night.

For a weary half-hour Pollyanna had been longing for him to go that she might be alone; but after he had gone she wished he were back. She had found suddenly that she did not want to be alone – with her thoughts.

It was wonderfully clear to Pollyanna now. There was no doubt of it. Jimmy cared for Mrs Carew. That was why he was so moody and restless after she left. That was why he had come so seldom to see her, Pollyanna, his old friend. That was why –

Countless little circumstances of the past summer flocked to Pollyanna's memory now, mute witnesses that would not be denied.

And why should he not care for her? Mrs Carew was certainly beautiful and charming. True, she was older than Jimmy; but young men had married women far older than she, many times. And if they loved each other –

Pollyanna cried herself to sleep that night.

In the morning, bravely she tried to face the thing. She even tried, with a tearful smile, to put it to the test of the glad game. She was reminded then of something Nancy had said to her years before: 'If there *is* a set o' folks in the world that wouldn't have no use for that 'ere glad game o' your'n, it'd be a pair o' quarrellin' lovers!'

'Not that we're "quarrelling", or even "lovers",' thought Pollyanna blushingly; 'but just the same I can be glad *he's* glad, and glad *she's* glad, too, only – ' Even to herself Pollyanna could not finish this sentence.

Being so sure now that Jimmy and Mrs Carew cared for each other, Pollyanna became peculiarly sensitive to everything that tended to strengthen that belief. And being ever on the watch for it, she found it, as was to be expected. First in Mrs Carew's letters.

'I am seeing a lot of your friend, young Pendleton,' Mrs Carew wrote one day; 'and I'm liking him more and more. I do wish, however – just for curiosity's sake – that I could trace to its source that elusive feeling that I've seen him before somewhere.'

Frequently, after this, she mentioned him casually; and, to Polly-anna, in the very casualness of these references lay their sharpest sting; for it showed so unmistakably that Jimmy and Jimmy's presence were now to Mrs Carew a matter of course. From other sources, too, Pollyanna found fuel for the fire of her suspicions. More and more frequently John Pendleton 'dropped in' with his stories of Jimmy, and of what Jimmy was doing; and always here there was mention of Mrs Carew. Poor Pollyanna wondered, indeed, sometimes, if John Pendleton could not talk of anything – but Mrs Carew and Jimmy, so constantly was one or the other of those names on his lips.

There were Sadie Dean's letters, too, and they told of Jimmy, and of what he was doing to help Mrs Carew. Even Jamie, who wrote occasionally, had his mite to add, for he wrote one evening: 'It's ten o'clock. I'm sitting here alone waiting for Mrs Carew to come home. She and Pendleton have been to one of their usual socials down at the Home.'

From Jimmy himself Pollyanna heard very rarely; and for that she told herself mournfully that she *could* be *glad.* 'For if he can't write about *anything* but Mrs Carew and those girls, I'm glad he doesn't write very often!' she sighed.

CHAPTER 27

The Day Pollyanna Did Not Play

And so one by one the winter days passed. January and February slipped away in snow and sleet, and March came in with a gale that whistled and moaned around the old house, and set loose blinds to swinging and loose gates to creaking in a way that was most trying to nerves already stretched to the breaking point.

Pollyanna was not finding it very easy these days to play the game, but she was playing it faithfully, valiantly. Aunt Polly was not playing it at all – which certainly did not make it any the easier for Pollyanna to play it. Aunt Polly was blue and discouraged. She was not well, too, and she had plainly abandoned herself to utter gloom.

Pollyanna still was counting on the prize contest. She had dropped from the first prize to one of the smaller ones, however: Pollyanna had been writing more stories, and the regularity with which they came back from their pilgrimages to magazine editors was beginning to shake her faith in her success as an author.

'Oh, well, I can be glad that Aunt Polly doesn't know anything about it, anyway,' declared Pollyanna to herself bravely, as she twisted in her fingers the 'declined-with-thanks' slip that had just towed in one more shipwrecked story. 'She *can't* worry about this – she doesn't know about it!'

All of Pollyanna's life these days revolved around Aunt Polly, and it is doubtful if even Aunt Polly herself realised how exacting she had become, and how entirely her niece was giving up her life to her.

It was on a particularly gloomy day in March that matters came, in a way, to a climax. Pollyanna, upon arising, had looked at the sky with a sigh – Aunt Polly was always more difficult on cloudy days. With a gay little song, however, that still sounded a bit forced – Pollyanna descended to the kitchen and began to prepare breakfast.

'I reckon I'll make corn muffins,' she told the stove confidentially, 'then maybe Aunt Polly won't mind – other things so much.'

Half an hour later she tapped at her aunt's door.

'Up so soon? Oh, that's fine! And you've done your hair yourself!'

'I couldn't sleep. I had to get up,' sighed Aunt Polly, wearily. 'I had to do my hair, too. *You* weren't here.'

'But I didn't suppose you were ready for me, auntie,' explained Pollyanna, hurriedly. 'Never mind, though. You'll be glad I wasn't when you find what I've been doing.'

'Well, I shan't – not this morning,' frowned Aunt Polly, perversely. 'Nobody could be glad this morning. Look at it rain! That makes the third rainy day this week.'

'That's so – but you know the sun never seems quite so perfectly lovely as it does after a lot of rain like this,' smiled Pollyanna, deftly arranging a bit of lace and ribbon at her aunt's throat. 'Now come. Breakfast's all ready. Just you wait till you see what I've got for you.'

Aunt Polly, however, was not to be diverted, even by corn muffins, this morning. Nothing was right, nothing was even endurable, as she felt; and Pollyanna's patience was sorely taxed before the meal was over. To make matters worse, the roof over the east attic window was found to be leaking, and an unpleasant letter came in the mail. Pollyanna, true to her creed, laughingly declared that, for her part, she was glad they had a roof – to leak; and that, as for the letter, she'd been expecting it for a week, anyway, and she was actually glad she wouldn't have to worry any more for fear it would come. It *couldn't* come now, because it *had* come; and 'twas over with.

All this, together with sundry other hindrances and annoyances, delayed the usual morning work until far into the afternoon – something that was always particularly displeasing to methodical Aunt Polly, who ordered her own life, preferably, by the tick of the clock.

'But it's half-past three, Pollyanna, already! Did you know it?' she fretted at last. 'And you haven't made the beds yet.'

'No, dearie, but I will. Don't worry.'

'But, did you hear what I said? Look at the clock, child. It's after three o'clock!'

'So 'tis, but never mind, Aunt Polly. We can be glad 'tisn't after four.'

Aunt Polly sniffed her disdain.

'I suppose *you* can,' she observed tartly.

Pollyanna laughed.

'Well, you see, auntie, clocks *are* accommodating things, when you stop to think about it. I found that out long ago at the Sanatorium. When I was doing something that I liked, and I didn't *want* the time to go fast, I'd just look at the hour hand, and I'd feel as if I had lots of time – it went so slow. Then, other days, when I had to keep something that hurt on for an hour, maybe, I'd watch the little second hand; and you see then I felt as if Old Time was just humping himself to help me out by going as fast as ever he could. Now I'm watching the hour hand today, 'cause I don't want Time to go fast. See?' she twinkled mischievously, as she hurried from the room before Aunt Polly had time to answer.

It was certainly a hard day, and by night Pollyanna looked pale and worn out. This, too, was a source of worriment to Aunt Polly.

'Dear me, child, you look tired to death!' she fumed. '*What* we're going to do I don't know. I suppose *you'll* be sick next!'

'Nonsense, auntie! I'm not sick a bit,' declared Pollyanna, dropping herself with a sigh on to the couch. 'But I *am* tired. My! how good this couch feels! I'm glad I'm tired, after all – it's so nice to rest.'

Aunt Polly turned with an impatient gesture.

'Glad – glad – glad! Of course you're glad, Pollyanna. You're always glad for everything. I never saw such a girl. Oh, yes, I know it's the game,' she went on, in answer to the look that came to Pollyanna's face. 'And it's a very good game, too; but I think you carry it altogether too far. This eternal doctrine of "it might be worse" has got on my nerves, Pollyanna. Honestly, it would be a real relief if you *wouldn't* be glad for something, sometime!'

'Why, auntie!' Pollyanna pulled herself half erect.

'Well, it would. You just try it sometime, and see.'

'But, auntie, I – ' Pollyanna stopped and eyed her aunt reflectively. An odd look came to her eyes; a slow smile curved her lips. Mrs Chilton, who had turned back to her work, paid no heed; and, after a minute, Pollyanna lay back on the couch without finishing her sentence, the curious smile still on her lips.

It was raining again when Pollyanna got up the next morning, and a north-east wind was still whistling down the chimney. Pollyanna at the window drew an involuntary sigh; but almost at once her face changed.

'Oh, well, I'm glad – ' She clapped her hands to her lips. 'Dear me,' she chuckled softly, her eyes dancing, 'I shall forget – I know I shall; and that'll spoil it all! I must just remember not to be glad for anything – not *anything* today.'

Pollyanna did not make corn muffins that morning. She started the breakfast, then went to her aunt's room.

Mrs Chilton was still in bed.

'I see it rains, as usual,' she observed, by way of greeting.

'Yes, it's horrid – perfectly horrid,' scolded Pollyanna. 'It's rained 'most every day this week, too. I hate such weather.'

Aunt Polly turned with a faint surprise in her eyes; but Pollyanna was looking the other way.

'Are you going to get up now?' she asked a little wearily.

'Why, y–yes,' murmured Aunt Polly, still with that faint surprise in her eyes. 'What's the matter, Pollyanna? Are you especially tired?'

'Yes, I am tired this morning. I didn't sleep well, either. I hate not to sleep. Things always plague so in the night, when you wake up.'

'I guess I know that,' fretted Aunt Polly. 'I didn't sleep a wink after two o'clock myself. And there's that roof! How are we going to have it fixed, pray, if it never stops raining? Have you been up to empty the pans?'

'Oh, yes – and took up some more. There's a new leak now, farther over.'

'A new one! Why, it'll all be leaking yet!'

Pollyanna opened her lips. She had almost said, 'Well, we can be glad to have it fixed all at once, then,' when she suddenly remembered, and substituted, in a tired voice: 'Very likely it will, auntie. It looks like it now, fast enough. Anyway, it's made fuss enough for a whole roof already, and I'm sick of it!' With which statement, Pollyanna, her face carefully averted, turned and trailed listlessly out of the room.

'It's so funny and so – so hard, I'm afraid I'm making a mess of it,' she whispered to herself anxiously, as she hurried downstairs to the kitchen.

Behind her, Aunt Polly, in the bedroom, gazed after her with eyes that were again faintly puzzled.

Aunt Polly had occasion a good many times before six o'clock that night to gaze at Pollyanna with surprised and questioning eyes. Nothing was right with Pollyanna. The fire would not burn, the wind blew one particular blind loose three times, and still a third leak was discovered in the roof. The mail brought to Pollyanna a letter that made her cry (though no amount of questioning on Aunt Polly's part would persuade her to tell why). Even the dinner went wrong, and innumerable things happened in the afternoon to call out fretful, discouraged remarks.

Not until the day was more than half gone did a look of shrewd suspicion suddenly fight for supremacy with the puzzled questioning in Aunt Polly's eyes. If Pollyanna saw this she made no sign. Certainly there was no abatement in her fretfulness and discontent. Long before six o'clock, however, the suspicion in Aunt Polly's eyes became conviction, and drove to ignominious defeat the puzzled questioning. But, curiously enough then, a new look came to take its place, a look that was actually a twinkle of amusement.

At last, after a particularly doleful complaint on Pollyanna's part, Aunt Polly threw up her hands with a gesture of half-laughing despair.

'That'll do, that'll do, child! I'll give up. I'll confess myself beaten at my own game. You can be – *glad* for that, if you like,' she finished with a grim smile.

'I know, auntie, but you said – ' began Pollyanna demurely.

'Yes, yes, but I never will again,' interrupted Aunt Polly, with emphasis. 'Mercy, what a day this has been! I never want to live through another like it.' She hesitated, flushed a little, then went on with evident difficulty: 'Furthermore, I – I want you to know that – that I understand I haven't played the game myself – very well, lately; but, after this, I'm going to – to try – *where's* my handkerchief?' she finished sharply, fumbling in the folds of her dress.

Pollyanna sprang to her feet and crossed instantly to her aunt's side.

'Oh, but Aunt Polly, I didn't mean – It was just a – a joke,' she quavered in quick distress. 'I never thought of your taking it *that* way.'

'Of course you didn't,' snapped Aunt Polly, with all the asperity of a stern, repressed woman who abhors scenes and sentiment, and who is mortally afraid she will show that her heart has been touched. 'Don't you suppose I know you didn't mean it that way? Do you think, if I thought you *had* been trying to teach me a lesson that I'd – I'd – ' But Pollyanna's strong young arms had her in a close embrace, and she could not finish the sentence.

CHAPTER 28

Jimmy and Jamie

Pollyanna was not the only one that was finding that winter a hard one. In Boston Jimmy Pendleton, in spite of his strenuous efforts to occupy his time and thoughts, was discovering that nothing quite erased from his vision a certain pair of laughing blue eyes, and nothing quite obliterated from his memory a certain well-loved, merry voice.

Jimmy told himself that if it were not for Mrs Carew, and the fact that he could be of some use to her, life would not be worth the living. Even at Mrs Carew's it was not all joy, for always there was Jamie; and Jamie brought thoughts of Pollyanna – unhappy thoughts.

Being thoroughly convinced that Jamie and Pollyanna cared for each other, and also being equally convinced that he himself was in honour bound to step to one side and give the handicapped Jamie full right of way, it never occurred to him to question further. Of Pollyanna he did not like to talk or to hear. He knew that both Jamie and Mrs Carew heard from her; and when they spoke of her, he forced himself to listen, in spite of his heartache. But he always changed the subject as soon as possible, and he limited his own letters to her to the briefest and most infrequent epistles possible. For, to Jimmy, a Pollyanna that was not his was nothing but a source of pain and wretchedness; and he had been so glad when the time came for him to leave Beldingsville and take up his studies again in Boston: to be so near Pollyanna, and yet so far from her, he had found to be nothing but torture.

In Boston, with all the feverishness of a restless mind that seeks distraction from itself, he had thrown himself into the carrying out of Mrs Carew's plans for her beloved working girls, and such time as could be spared from his own duties he had devoted to this work, much to Mrs Carew's delight and gratitude.

And so for Jimmy the winter had passed and spring had come – a joyous, blossoming spring full of soft breezes, gentle showers, and tender green buds expanding into riotous bloom and fragrance. To Jimmy, however, it was anything but a joyous spring, for in his heart was still nothing but a gloomy winter of discontent.

'If only they'd settle things and announce the engagement, once for all,' murmured Jimmy to himself, more and more frequently these days. 'If only I could know *something* for sure, I think I could stand it better!'

Then one day late in April, he had his wish – a part of it: he learned 'something for sure'.

It was ten o'clock on a Saturday morning, and Mary, at Mrs Carew's, had ushered him into the music-room with a well-trained: 'I'll tell Mrs Carew you're here, sir. She's expecting you, I think.'

In the music-room Jimmy had found himself brought to a dismayed halt by the sight of Jamie at the piano, his arms outflung upon the rack, and his head bowed upon them. Pendleton had half turned to beat a soft retreat when the man at the piano lifted his head, bringing into view two flushed cheeks and a pair of fever-bright eyes.

'Why, Carew,' stammered Pendleton, aghast, 'has anything – er – happened?'

'Happened! Happened!' ejaculated the lame youth, flinging out both his hands, in each of which, as Pendleton now saw, was an open letter. 'Everything has happened! Wouldn't you think it had if all your life you'd been in prison, and suddenly you saw the gates flung wide open? Wouldn't you think it had if all in a minute you could ask the girl you loved to be your wife? Wouldn't you think it had if – But, listen! You think I'm crazy, but I'm not. Though maybe I am, after all, crazy with joy. I'd like to tell you. May I? I've got to tell somebody!'

Pendleton lifted his head. It was as if, unconsciously, he was bracing himself for a blow. He had grown a little white; but his voice was quite steady when he answered.

'Sure you may, old fellow. I'd be – glad to hear it.'

Carew, however, had scarcely waited for assent. He was rushing on, still a bit incoherently.

'It's not much to you, of course. You have two feet and your freedom. You have your ambitions and your bridges. But I – to me it's everything. It's a chance to live a man's life and do a man's work, perhaps – even if it isn't dams and bridges. It's something! – and it's something I've proved now I *can do*! Listen. In that letter there is the announcement that a little story of mine has won the first prize – three thousand dollars – in a contest. In that other letter there, a big publishing house accepts with flattering enthusiasm my first book manuscript for publication. And they both came today – this morning. Do you wonder I am crazy glad?'

'No! No, indeed! I congratulate you, Carew, with all my heart,' cried Jimmy, warmly.

'Thank you – and you may congratulate me. Think what it means to me. Think what it means if, by and by, I can be independent, like a man. Think what it means if I can, some day, make Mrs Carew proud and glad that she gave the crippled lad a place in her home and heart. Think what it means for me to be able to tell the girl I love that I *do* love her.'

'Yes – yes, indeed, old boy!' Jimmy spoke firmly, though he had grown very white now.

'Of course, maybe I ought not to do that last, even now,' resumed Jamie, a swift cloud shadowing the shining brightness of his countenance. 'I'm still tied to – these.' He tapped the crutches by his side. 'I can't forget, of course, that day in the woods last summer, when I saw Pollyanna – I realise that always I'll have to run the chance of seeing the girl I love in danger and not being able to rescue her.'

'Oh, but Carew – ' began the other huskily.

Carew lifted a peremptory hand. 'I know what you'd say. But don't say it. You can't understand. *You* aren't tied to two sticks. You did the rescuing, not I. It came to me then how it would be, always, with me and – Sadie. I'd have to stand aside and see others – '

'*Sadie!*' cut in Jimmy, sharply.

'Yes; Sadie Dean. You act surprised. Didn't you know? Haven't you suspected – how I felt towards Sadie?' cried Jamie. 'Have I kept it so well to myself, then? I tried to, but – ' He finished with a faint smile and a half-despairing gesture.

'Well, you certainly kept it all right, old fellow – from me, any-how,' cried Jimmy, gayly. The colour had come back to Jimmy's face in a rich flood, and his eyes had grown suddenly very bright indeed. 'So it's Sadie Dean. Good! I congratulate you again, I do, I do, as Nancy says.' Jimmy was quite babbling with joy and excitement now, so great and wonderful had been the reaction within him at the discovery that it was Sadie, not Pollyanna, whom Jamie loved. Jamie flushed and shook his head a bit sadly.

'No congratulations – yet. You see, I haven't spoken to – her. But I think she must know. I supposed everybody knew. Pray, whom did you think it was, if not – Sadie?'

Jimmy hesitated. Then, a little precipitately, he let it out.

'Why, I'd thought of – Pollyanna.'

Jamie smiled and pursed his lips.

'Pollyanna's a charming girl, and I love her – but not that way, any more than she does me. Besides, I fancy somebody else would have something to say about that, eh?'

Jimmy coloured like a happy, conscious boy.

'Do you?' he challenged, trying to make his voice properly impersonal.

'Of course! John Pendleton.'

'*John Pendleton!*' Jimmy wheeled sharply.

'What about John Pendleton?' queried a new voice; and Mrs Carew came forward with a smile.

Jimmy, around whose ears for the second time within five minutes the world had crashed into fragments, barely collected himself enough for a low word of greeting. But Jamie, unabashed, turned with a triumphant air of assurance.

'Nothing; only I just said that I believed John Pendleton would have something to say about Pollyanna's loving anybody – but him.'

'*Pollyanna! John Pendleton!*' Mrs Carew sat down suddenly in the chair nearest her. If the two men before her had not been so deeply absorbed in their own affairs they might have noticed that the smile had vanished from Mrs Carew's lips, and that an odd look as of almost fear had come to her eyes.

'Certainly,' maintained Jamie. 'Were you both blind last summer? Wasn't he with her a lot?'

'Why, I thought he was with – all of us,' murmured Mrs Carew, a little faintly.

'Not as he was with Pollyanna,' insisted Jamie. 'Besides, have you forgotten that day when we were talking about John Pendleton's marrying, and Pollyanna blushed and stammered and said finally that he *had* thought of marrying – once. Well, I wondered then if there wasn't *something* between them. Don't you remember?'

'Y–yes, I think I do – now that you speak of it,' murmured Mrs Carew again. 'But I had – forgotten it.'

'Oh, but I can explain that,' cut in Jimmy, wetting his dry lips. 'John Pendleton *did* have a love affair once, but it was with Pollyanna's mother.'

'Pollyanna's mother!' exclaimed two voices in surprise.

'Yes. He loved her years ago, but she did not care for him at all, I understand. She had another lover – a minister, and she married him instead – Pollyanna's father.'

'Oh–h!' breathed Mrs Carew, leaning forward suddenly in her chair. 'And is that why he's – never married?'

'Yes,' avouched Jimmy. 'So you see there's really nothing to that idea at all – that he cares for Pollyanna. It was her mother.'

'On the contrary I think it adds a whole lot to that idea,' declared Jamie, wagging his head wisely. 'I think it makes my case all the stronger. Listen. He once loved the mother. He couldn't have her. What more absolutely natural than that he should love the daughter now – and win her?'

'Oh, Jamie, you incorrigible spinner of tales!' reproached Mrs Carew, with a nervous laugh. 'This is no tenpenny novel. It's real life. She's too young for him. He ought to marry a woman, not a girl – that is, if he marries anyone, I mean,' she stammeringly corrected, a sudden flood of colour in her face.

'Perhaps; but what if it happens to be a *girl* that he loves?' argued Jamie, stubbornly. 'And, really, just stop to think. Have we had a single letter from her that hasn't told of his being there? And you *know* how *he's* always talking of Pollyanna in his letters.'

Mrs Carew got suddenly to her feet.

'Yes, I know,' she murmured, with an odd little gesture, as if throwing something distasteful aside. 'But – ' She did not finish her sentence, and a moment later she had left the room.

When she came back in five minutes she found, much to her surprise, that Jimmy had gone.

'Why, I thought he was going with us on the girls' picnic!' she exclaimed.

'So did I,' frowned Jamie. 'But the first thing I knew he was explaining or apologising or something about unexpectedly having to leave town, and he'd come to tell you he couldn't go with us. Anyhow, the next thing I knew he'd gone. You see' – Jamie's eyes were glowing again – 'I don't think I knew quite what he did say, anyway. I had something else to think of.' And he jubilantly spread before her the two letters which all the time he had still kept in his hands.

'Oh, Jamie!' breathed Mrs Carew, when she had read the letters through. 'How proud I am of you!' Then suddenly her eyes filled with tears at the look of ineffable joy that illumined Jamie's face.

CHAPTER 29

Jimmy and John

It was a very determined, square-jawed young man that alighted at the Beldingsville station late that Saturday night. And it was an even more determined, square-jawed young man that, before ten o'clock the next morning, stalked through the Sunday-quiet village streets and climbed the hill to the Harrington homestead. Catching sight of a loved and familiar flaxen coil of hair on a well-poised little head just disappearing into the summerhouse, the young man ignored the conventional front steps and doorbell, crossed the lawn, and strode through the garden paths until he came face to face with the owner of the flaxen coil of hair.

'Jimmy!' gasped Pollyanna, falling back with startled eyes. 'Why, where did you – come from?'

'Boston. Last night. I had to see you, Pollyanna.'

'To – see – m–me?' Pollyanna was plainly fencing for time to regain her composure. Jimmy looked so big and strong and *dear* there in the door of the summerhouse that she feared her eyes had been surprised into a telltale admiration, if not more.

'Yes, Pollyanna; I wanted – that is, I thought – I mean, I feared – Oh, hang it all, Pollyanna, I can't beat about the bush like this. I'll have to come straight to the point. It's just this. I stood aside before, but I won't now. It isn't a case any longer of fairness. He isn't crippled like Jamie. He's got feet and hands and a head like mine, and if he wins he'll have to win in a fair fight. *I've* got some rights!'

Pollyanna stared frankly.

'Jimmy Bean Pendleton, whatever in the world are you talking about?' she demanded.

The young man laughed shamefacedly.

'No wonder you don't know. It wasn't very lucid, was it? But I don't think I've been really lucid myself since yesterday – when I found out from Jamie himself.'

'Found out – from Jamie!'

'Yes. It was the prize that started it. You see, he'd just got one, and – '

'Oh, I know about that,' interrupted Pollyanna, eagerly. 'And wasn't it splendid? Just think – the first one – three thousand dollars! I wrote him a letter last night. Why, when I saw his name, and realised it was Jamie – *our Jamie* – I was so excited I forgot all about looking for *my* name, and even when I couldn't find mine at all, and knew that I hadn't got any – I mean, I was so excited and pleased for Jamie that I – I forgot – er – everything else,' corrected Pollyanna, throwing a dismayed glance into Jimmy's face, and feverishly trying to cover up the partial admission she had made.

Jimmy, however, was too intent on his own problem to notice hers.

'Yes, yes, 'twas fine, of course. I'm glad he got it. But Pollyanna, it was what he said *afterwards* that I mean. You see, until then I'd thought that – that he cared – that you cared – for each other, I mean; and – '

'You thought that Jamie and I cared for each other!' exclaimed Pollyanna, into whose face now was stealing a soft, shy colour. 'Why, Jimmy, it's Sadie Dean. 'Twas always Sadie Dean. He used to talk of her to me by the hour. I think she likes him, too.'

'Good! I hope she does; but, you see, I didn't know. I thought 'twas Jamie – and you. And I thought that because he was – was a cripple, you know, that it wouldn't be fair if I – if I stayed around and tried to win you myself.'

Pollyanna stooped suddenly, and picked up a leaf at her feet. When she rose, her face was turned quite away.

'A fellow can't – can't feel square, you know, running a race with a chap that – that's handicapped from the start. So I – I just stayed away and gave him his chance; though it 'most broke my heart to do it, little girl. It just did! Then yesterday morning I found out. But I found out something else, too. Jamie says there is – is somebody else in the case. But I can't stand aside for him, Pollyanna. I can't – even in spite of all he's done for me. John Pendleton is a man, and he's got two whole feet for the race. He's got to take his chances. If you care for him – if you really care for him – '

But Pollyanna had turned, wild-eyed.

'*John Pendleton!* Jimmy, what do you mean? What are you saying – about John Pendleton?'

A great joy transfigured Jimmy's face. He held out both his hands. 'Then you don't – you don't! I can see it in your eyes that you don't – care!'

Pollyanna shrank back. She was white and trembling.

'Jimmy, what do you mean? What do you mean?' she begged piteously.

'I mean – you don't care for Uncle John, that way. Don't you understand? Jamie thinks you do care, and that anyway he cares for you. And then I began to see it – that maybe he did. He's always talking about you; and, of course, there was your mother – '

Pollyanna gave a low moan and covered her face with her hands.

Jimmy came close and laid a caressing arm about her shoulders; but again Pollyanna shrank from him.

'Pollyanna, little girl, don't! You'll break my heart,' he begged. 'Don't you care for me – *any*? Is it that, and you don't want to tell me?'

She dropped her hands and faced him. Her eyes had the hunted look of some wild thing at bay.

'Jimmy, do *you* think – he cares for me – that way?' she entreated, just above a whisper.

Jimmy gave his head an impatient shake.

'Never mind that, Pollyanna – now. I don't know, of course. How should I? But, dearest, that isn't the question. It's you. If *you* don't care for him, and if you'll only give me a chance – half a chance to let me make you care for me – ' He caught her hand, and tried to draw her to him.

'No, no, Jimmy, I mustn't! I can't!' With both her little palms she pushed him from her.

'Pollyanna, you don't mean you *do* care for him?' Jimmy's face whitened.

'No; no, indeed – not that way,' faltered Pollyanna. 'But – don't you see? – if he cares for me, I'll have to – to learn to, someway.'

'*Pollyanna!*'

'Don't! Don't look at me like that, Jimmy!'

'You mean you'd *marry* him, Pollyanna?'

'Oh, no! – I mean – why – er – y–yes, I suppose so,' she admitted faintly.

'Pollyanna, you wouldn't! You couldn't! Pollyanna, you – you're breaking my heart.'

Pollyanna gave a low sob. Her face was in her hands again. For a moment she sobbed on, chokingly; then, with a tragic gesture, she lifted her head and looked straight into Jimmy's anguished, reproachful eyes.

'I know it, I know it,' she chattered frenziedly. 'I'm breaking mine, too. But I'll have to do it. I'd break your heart, I'd break mine – but I'd never break his!'

Jimmy raised his head. His eyes flashed a sudden fire. His whole appearance underwent a swift and marvellous change. With a tender, triumphant cry he swept Pollyanna into his arms and held her close.

'Now I *know* you care for me!' he breathed low in her ear. 'You said it was breaking *your* heart, too. Do you think I'll give you up now to any man on earth? Ah, dear, you little understand a love like mine if you think I'd give you up now. Pollyanna, say you love me – say it with your own dear lips!'

For one long minute Pollyanna lay unresisting in the fiercely tender embrace that encircled her; then with a sigh that was half content, half renunciation, she began to draw herself away.

'Yes, Jimmy, I do love you.' Jimmy's arms tightened, and would have drawn her back to him; but something in the girl's face forbade. 'I love you dearly. But I couldn't ever be happy with you and feel that – Jimmy, don't you see, dear? I'll have to know – that I'm free, first.'

'Nonsense, Pollyanna! Of course you're free!' Jimmy's eyes were mutinous again.

Pollyanna shook her head.

'Not with this hanging over me, Jimmy. Don't you see? It was mother, long ago, that broke his heart – *my mother*. And all these years he's lived a lonely, unloved life in consequence. If now he should come to me and ask me to make that up to him, I'd *have* to do it, Jimmy. I'd *have* to. I couldn't *refuse*! Don't you see?'

But Jimmy did not see; he could not see. He would not see, though Pollyanna pleaded and argued long and tearfully. But Pollyanna, too, was obdurate, though so sweetly and heartbrokenly obdurate that Jimmy, in spite of his pain and anger, felt almost like turning comforter.

'Jimmy, dear,' said Pollyanna, at last, 'we'll have to wait. That's all I can say now. I hope he doesn't care; and I – I don't believe he does care. But I've got to *know*. I've got to be sure. We'll just have to wait, a little, till we find out, Jimmy – till we find out!'

And to this plan Jimmy had to submit, though it was with a most rebellious heart.

'All right, little girl, it'll have to be as you say, of course,' he despaired. 'But, surely, never before was a man kept waiting for his answer till the girl he loved, *and who loved him*, found out if the other man wanted her!'

'I know; but, you see, dear, never before had the other man *wanted* her mother,' sighed Pollyanna, her face puckered into an anxious frown.

'Very well, I'll go back to Boston, of course,' acceded Jimmy reluctantly. 'But you needn't think I've given up – because I haven't. Nor shall I give up, just so long as I know you really care for me, my little sweetheart,' he finished, with a look that sent her palpitatingly into retreat, just out of reach of his arms.

CHAPTER 30

John Pendleton Turns the Key

Jimmy went back to Boston that night in a state that was a most tantalising commingling of happiness, hope, exasperation and rebellion. Behind him he left a girl who was in a scarcely less enviable frame of mind; for Pollyanna, tremulously happy in the wondrous thought of Jimmy's love for her, was yet so despairingly terrified at the thought of the possible love of John Pendleton that there was not a thrill of joy that did not carry its pang of fear.

Fortunately for all concerned, however, this state of affairs was not of long duration; for, as it chanced, John Pendleton, in whose unwitting hands lay the key to the situation, in less than a week after Jimmy's hurried visit turned that key in the lock, and opened the door of doubt.

It was late Thursday afternoon that John Pendleton called to see Pollyanna. As it happened he, like Jimmy, saw Pollyanna in the garden and came straight towards her.

Pollyanna, looking into his face, felt a sudden sinking of the heart.

'It's come – it's come!' she shivered; and involuntarily she turned as if to flee.

'Oh, Pollyanna, wait a minute, please,' called the man hastening his steps. 'You're just the one I wanted to see. Come, can't we go in here?' he suggested, turning towards the summerhouse. 'I want to speak to you about – something.'

'Why, y–yes, of course,' stammered Pollyanna, with forced gaiety. Pollyanna knew that she was blushing, and she particularly wished not to blush just then. It did not help matters, either, that he should have elected to go into the summerhouse for his talk. The summerhouse now, to Pollyanna, was sacred to certain dear memories of Jimmy. 'And to think it should be here – *here!*' she was shuddering frantically. But aloud she said, still gayly, 'It's a lovely evening, isn't it?'

There was no answer. John Pendleton strode into the summerhouse and dropped himself into a rustic chair without even waiting for Pollyanna to seat herself – a most unusual proceeding on the part of John Pendleton. Pollyanna, stealing a nervous glance at his face, found it so startlingly like the old stern, sour visage of her childhood's remembrance that she uttered an involuntary exclamation.

Still John Pendleton paid no heed. Still moodily he sat wrapped in thought. At last, however, he lifted his head and gazed somberly into Pollyanna's startled eyes. 'Pollyanna.'

'Yes, Mr Pendleton.'

'Do you remember the sort of man I was when you first knew me, years ago?'

'Why, y–yes, I think so.'

'Delightfully agreeable specimen of humanity, wasn't I?'

In spite of her perturbation Pollyanna smiled faintly.

'I – *I* liked you, sir.' Not until the words were uttered did Pollyanna realise just how they would sound. She strove then, frantically, to recall or modify them and had almost added a 'that is, I mean, I liked you *then!*' when she stopped just in time: certainly *that* would not have helped matters any! She listened then, fearfully, for John Pendleton's next words. They came almost at once.

'I know you did – bless your little heart! And it was that that was the saving of me. I wonder, Pollyanna, if I could ever make you realise just what your childish trust and liking did for me.'

Pollyanna stammered a confused protest; but he brushed it smilingly aside.

'Oh, yes, it was! It was you, and no one else. I wonder if you remember another thing, too,' resumed the man, after a moment's silence, during which Pollyanna looked furtively but longingly towards the door. 'I wonder if you remember my telling you once that nothing but a woman's hand and heart or a child's presence could make a home.'

Pollyanna felt the blood rush to her face.

'Y—yes, n–no – I mean, yes, I remember it,' she stuttered; 'but I – I don't think it's always so now. I mean – that is, I'm sure your home now is – is lovely just as 'tis, and – '

'But it's my home I'm talking about, child,' interrupted the man, impatiently. 'Pollyanna, you know the kind of home I once hoped to have, and how those hopes were dashed to the ground. Don't think, dear, I'm blaming your mother. I'm not. She but obeyed her heart, which was right; and she made the wiser choice, anyway, as was proved by the dreary waste I've made of life because of that disappointment. After all, Pollyanna, isn't it strange,' added John Pendleton, his voice growing tender, 'that it should be the little hand of her own daughter that led me into the path of happiness, at last?'

Pollyanna moistened her lips convulsively.

'Oh, but Mr Pendleton, I – I – '

Once again the man brushed aside her protests with a smiling gesture.

'Yes, it was, Pollyanna, your little hand in the long ago – you, and your glad game.'

'Oh–h!' Pollyanna relaxed visibly in her seat. The terror in her eyes began slowly to recede.

'And so all these years I've been gradually growing into a different man, Pollyanna. But there's one thing I haven't changed in, my dear.' He paused, looked away, then turned gravely tender eyes back to her face. 'I still think it takes a woman's hand and heart or a child's presence to make a home.'

'Yes; b–but you've g–got the child's presence,' plunged in Pollyanna, the terror coming back to her eyes. 'There's Jimmy, you know.'

The man gave an amused laugh.

'I know; but – I don't think even you would say that Jimmy is – is exactly a *child's* presence any longer,' he remarked.

'N–no, of course not.'

'Besides – Pollyanna, I've made up my mind. I've got to have the woman's hand and heart.' His voice dropped, and trembled a little.

'Oh–h, have you?' Pollyanna's fingers met and clutched each other in a spasmodic clasp. John Pendleton, however, seemed neither to hear nor see. He had leaped to his feet, and was nervously pacing up and down the little house.

'Pollyanna,' he stopped and faced her; 'if – if you were I, and were going to ask the woman you loved to come and make your old grey pile of stone a home, how would you go to work to do it?'

Pollyanna half started from her chair. Her eyes sought the door, this time openly, longingly.

'Oh, but, Mr Pendleton, I wouldn't do it at all, at all,' she stammered, a little wildly. 'I'm sure you'd be – much happier as – as you are.'

The man stared in puzzled surprise, then laughed grimly.

'Upon my word, Pollyanna, is it – quite so bad as that?' he asked.

'B–bad?' Pollyanna had the appearance of being poised for flight.

'Yes. Is that just your way of trying to soften the blow of saying that you don't think she'd have me, anyway?'

'Oh, n–no – no, indeed. She'd say yes – she'd *have* to say yes, you know,' explained Pollyanna, with terrified earnestness. 'But I've been thinking – I mean, I was thinking that if – if the girl didn't love you, you really would be happier without her; and – ' At the look that came into John Pendleton's face, Pollyanna stopped short.

'I shouldn't want her, if she didn't love me, Pollyanna.'

'No, I thought not, too.' Pollyanna began to look a little less distracted.

'Besides, she doesn't happen to be a girl,' went on John Pendleton. 'She's a mature woman who, presumedly, would know her own mind.' The man's voice was grave and slightly reproachful.

'Oh–h–h! Oh!' exclaimed Pollyanna, the dawning happiness in her eyes leaping forth in a flash of ineffable joy and relief. 'Then you love somebody – ' By an almost superhuman effort Pollyanna choked off the 'else' before it left her delighted lips.

'Love somebody! Haven't I just been telling you I did?' laughed John Pendleton, half vexedly. 'What I want to know is – can she be made to love me? That's where I was sort of – of counting on your help, Pollyanna. You see, she's a dear friend of yours.'

'Is she?' gurgled Pollyanna. 'Then she'll just have to love you. We'll make her! Maybe she does, anyway, already. Who is she?'

There was a long pause before the answer came.

'I believe, after all, Pollyanna, I won't – yes, I will, too. It's – can't you guess? – Mrs Carew.'

'Oh!' breathed Pollyanna, with a face of unclouded joy. 'How perfectly lovely! I'm so glad, *glad, glad*!'

A long hour later Pollyanna sent Jimmy a letter. It was confused and incoherent – a series of half-completed, illogical, but shyly joyous sentences, out of which Jimmy gathered much: a little from what was written; more from what was left unwritten. After all, did he really need more than this?

'Oh, Jimmy, he doesn't love me a bit. It's someone else. I mustn't tell you who it is – but her name isn't Pollyanna.'

Jimmy had just time to catch the seven o'clock train for Beldingsville – and he caught it.

CHAPTER 31

After Long Years

Pollyanna was so happy that night after she had sent her letter to Jimmy that she could not quite keep it to herself. Always before going to bed she stepped into her aunt's room to see if anything were needed. Tonight, after the usual questions, she had turned to put out the light when a sudden impulse sent her back to her aunt's bedside. A little breathlessly she dropped on her knees.

'Aunt Polly, I'm so happy I just had to tell someone. I *want* to tell you. May I?'

'Tell me? Tell me what, child? Of course you may tell me. You mean, it's good news – for *me*?'

'Why, yes, dear; I hope so,' blushed Pollyanna. 'I hope it will make you – *glad*, a little, for me, you know. Of course Jimmy will tell you himself all properly some day. But *I* wanted to tell you first.'

'Jimmy!' Mrs Chilton's face changed perceptibly.

'Yes, when – when he – he asks you for me,' stammered Pollyanna, with a radiant flood of colour. 'Oh, I – I'm so happy, I *had* to tell you!'

'Asks me for you! Pollyanna!' Mrs Chilton pulled herself up in bed. 'You don't mean to say there's anything *serious* between you and – Jimmy Bean!'

Pollyanna fell back in dismay.

'Why, auntie, I thought you *liked* Jimmy!'

'So I do – in his place. But that place isn't the husband of my niece.'

'*Aunt Polly!*'

'Come, come, child, don't look so shocked. This is all sheer nonsense, and I'm glad I've been able to stop it before it's gone any further.'

'But, Aunt Polly, it *has* gone further,' quavered Pollyanna. 'Why, I – I already have learned to lo – c–care for him – dearly.'

'Then you'll have to unlearn it, Pollyanna, for never, never will I give my consent to your marrying Jimmy Bean.'

'But – w–why, auntie?'

'First and foremost because we know nothing about him.'

'Why, Aunt Polly, we've always known him, ever since I was a little girl!'

'Yes, and what was he? A rough little runaway urchin from an Orphans' Home! We know nothing whatever about his people, and his pedigree.'

'But I'm not marrying his p–people and his p–pedigree!'

With an impatient groan Aunt Polly fell back on her pillow.

'Pollyanna, you're making me positively ill. My heart is going like a trip hammer. I shan't sleep a wink tonight. *Can't* you let this thing rest till morning?'

Pollyanna was on her feet instantly, her face all contrition.

'Why, yes – yes, indeed; of course, Aunt Polly! And tomorrow you'll feel different, I'm sure. I'm sure you will,' reiterated the girl, her voice quivering with hope again, as she turned to extinguish the light.

But Aunt Polly did not 'feel different' in the morning. If anything, her opposition to the marriage was even more determined. In vain Pollyanna pleaded and argued. In vain she showed how deeply her happiness was concerned. Aunt Polly was obdurate. She would have none of the idea. She sternly admonished Pollyanna as to the possible evils of heredity, and warned her of the dangers of marrying into she knew not what sort of family. She even appealed at last to her sense of duty and gratitude towards herself, and reminded Pollyanna of the long years of loving care that had been hers in the home of her aunt, and she begged her piteously not to break her heart by this marriage as had her mother years before by *her* marriage.

When Jimmy himself, radiant-faced and glowing-eyed, came at ten o'clock, he was met by a frightened, sob-shaken little Pollyanna that tried ineffectually to hold him back with two trembling hands. With whitening cheeks, but with defiantly tender arms that held her close, he demanded an explanation.

'Pollyanna, dearest, what in the world is the meaning of this?'

'Oh, Jimmy, Jimmy, why did you come, why did you come? I was going to write and tell you straight away,' moaned Pollyanna.

'But you did write me, dear. I got it yesterday afternoon, just in time to catch my train.'

'No, no – *again*, I mean. I didn't know then that I – I couldn't.'

'Couldn't! Pollyanna' – his eyes flamed into stern wrath – 'you don't mean to tell me there's anybody *else's* love you think you've got to keep me waiting for?' he demanded, holding her at arm's length.

'No, no, Jimmy! Don't look at me like that. I can't bear it!'

'Then what is it? What is it you can't do?'

'I can't – marry you.'

'Pollyanna, do you love me?'

'Yes. Oh, y—yes.'

'Then you shall marry me,' triumphed Jimmy, his arms enfolding her again.

'No, no, Jimmy, you don't understand. It's – Aunt Polly,' struggled Pollyanna.

'*Aunt Polly!*'

'Yes. She – won't let me.'

'Ho!' Jimmy tossed his head with a light laugh. 'We'll fix Aunt Polly. She thinks she's going to lose you, but we'll just remind her that she – she's going to gain a – a new nephew!' he finished in mock importance.

But Pollyanna did not smile. She turned her head hopelessly from side to side.

'No, no, Jimmy, you don't understand! She – she – oh, how can I tell you? – she objects to – to *you* – for – *me*.'

Jimmy's arms relaxed a little. His eyes sobered.

'Oh, well, I suppose I can't blame her for that. I'm no wonder, of course,' he admitted constrainedly. 'Still' – he turned loving eyes upon her – 'I'd try to make you – happy, dear.'

'Indeed you would! I know you would,' protested Pollyanna, tearfully.

'Then why not give me a chance to try, Pollyanna, even if she doesn't quite approve, at first. Maybe in time, after we were married, we could win her over.'

'Oh, but I couldn't – I couldn't do that,' moaned Pollyanna, 'after what she's said. I couldn't – without her consent. You see, she's done so much for me, and she's so dependent on me. She isn't well a bit, now, Jimmy. And, really, lately she's been so – so loving, and she's been trying so hard to – to play the game, you know, in spite of all her troubles. And she – she cried, Jimmy, and begged me not to break her heart as – as mother did long ago. And – and, Jimmy, I – I just couldn't, after all she's done for me.'

There was a moment's pause; then, with a vivid red mounting to her forehead, Pollyanna spoke again, brokenly.

'Jimmy, if you – if you could only tell Aunt Polly something about – about your father, and your people, and – '

Jimmy's arms dropped suddenly. He stepped back a little. The colour drained from his face.

'Is – that – it?' he asked.

'Yes.' Pollyanna came nearer, and touched his arm timidly. 'Don't think – It isn't for me, Jimmy. I don't care. Besides, I *know* that your father and your people were all – all fine and noble, because *you* are so fine and noble. But she – Jimmy, don't look at me like that!'

But Jimmy, with a low moan, had turned quite away from her. A minute later, with only a few choking words, which she could not understand, he had left the house.

From the Harrington homestead Jimmy went straight home and sought out John Pendleton. He found him in the great crimson-hung library where, some years before, Pollyanna had looked fearfully about for the 'skeleton in John Pendleton's closet'.

'Uncle John, do you remember that packet father gave me?' demanded Jimmy.

'Why, yes. What's the matter, son?' John Pendleton had given a start of surprise at sight of Jimmy's face.

'That packet has got to be opened, sir.'

'But – the conditions!'

'I can't help it. It's got to be. That's all. Will you do it?'

'Why, y–yes, my boy, of course, if you insist; but – ' he paused helplessly.

'Uncle John, as perhaps you have guessed, I love Pollyanna. I asked her to be my wife, and she consented.' The elder man made a delighted exclamation, but the other did not pause, or change his sternly intent expression. 'She says now she can't – marry me. Mrs Chilton objects. She objects to *me*.'

'*Objects to you!*' John Pendleton's eyes flashed angrily.

'Yes. I found out why when – when Pollyanna begged if I couldn't tell her aunt something about – about my father and my people.'

'Shucks! I thought Polly Chilton had more sense – still, it's just like her, after all. The Harringtons have always been inordinately proud of race and family,' snapped John Pendleton. 'Well, could you?'

'*Could I!* It was on the end of my tongue to tell Pollyanna that there couldn't have been a better father than mine was; then, suddenly, I remembered – the packet, and what it said. And I was afraid. I didn't dare say a word till I knew what was inside that packet. There's something dad didn't want me to know till I was thirty years old – when I would be a man grown, and could stand anything. See? There's a secret somewhere in our lives. I've got to know that secret, and I've got to know it now.'

'But, Jimmy, lad, don't look so tragic. It may be a good secret. Perhaps it'll be something you'll *like* to know.'

'Perhaps. But if it had been, would he have been apt to keep it from me till I was thirty years old? No! Uncle John, it was something he was trying to save me from till I was old enough to stand it and not flinch. Understand, I'm not blaming dad. Whatever it was, it was something he couldn't help, I'll warrant. But *what* it was I've got to know. Will you get it, please? It's in your safe, you know.'

John Pendleton rose at once.

'I'll get it,' he said. Three minutes later it lay in Jimmy's hand; but Jimmy held it out at once.

'I would rather you read it, sir, please. Then tell me.'

'But, Jimmy, I – very well.' With a decisive gesture John Pendleton picked up a paper-cutter, opened the envelope and pulled out the contents. There was a package of several papers tied together, and one folded sheet alone, apparently a letter. This John Pendleton opened and read first. And as he read, Jimmy, tense and breathless, watched his face. He saw, therefore, the look of amazement, joy and something else he could not name that leaped into John Pendleton's countenance.

'Uncle John, what is it? What is it?' he demanded.

'Read it – for yourself,' answered the man, thrusting the letter into Jimmy's outstretched hand. And Jimmy read this:

The enclosed papers are the legal proof that my boy Jimmy is really James Kent, son of John Kent, who married Doris Wetherby, daughter of William Wetherby of Boston. There is also a letter in which I explain to my boy why I have kept him from his mother's family all these years. If this packet is opened by him at thirty years of age, he will read this letter, and I hope will forgive a father who feared to lose his boy entirely, so took this drastic course to keep him to himself. If it is opened by strangers, because of his death, I request that his mother's people in Boston be notified at once, and the enclosed package of papers be given, intact, into their hands.

'*John Kent*.'

Jimmy was pale and shaken when he looked up to meet John Pendleton's eyes.

'Am I – the lost – Jamie?' he faltered.

'That letter says you have documents there to prove it,' nodded the other.

'Mrs Carew's nephew?'

'Of course.'

'But, why – what – I can't realise it!' There was a moment's pause before into Jimmy's face flashed a new joy. 'Then, surely now I know who I am! I can tell – Mrs Chilton *something* of my people.'

'I should say you could,' retorted John Pendleton, dryly. 'The Boston Wetherbys can trace straight back to the Crusades, and I don't know but to the year one. That ought to satisfy her. As for your father – he came of good stock, too, Mrs Carew told me, though he was rather eccentric, and not pleasing to the family, as you know, of course.'

'Yes. Poor dad! And what a life he must have lived with me all those years – always dreading pursuit. I can understand – lots of things, now, that used to puzzle me. A woman called me "Jamie" once. Jove! how angry he was! I know now why he hurried me away that night without even waiting for supper. Poor dad! It was right after that he was taken sick. He couldn't use his hands or his feet, and very soon he couldn't talk straight. Something ailed his speech. I remember when he died he was trying to tell me something about this packet. I believe now he was telling me to open it, and go to my mother's people; but I thought then he was just telling me to keep it safe. So that's what I promised him. But it didn't comfort him any. It only seemed to worry him more. You see, I didn't understand. Poor dad!'

'Suppose we take a look at these papers,' suggested John Pendleton. 'Besides, there's a letter from your father to you, I understand. Don't you want to read it?'

'Yes, of course. And then – ' the young fellow laughed shame-facedly and glanced at the clock – 'I was wondering just how soon I could go back – to Pollyanna.'

A thoughtful frown came to John Pendleton's face. He glanced at Jimmy, hesitated, then spoke. 'I know you want to see Pollyanna, lad, and I don't blame you; but it strikes me that, under the circumstances, you should go first to – Mrs Carew, and take these.' He tapped the papers before him.

Jimmy drew his brows together and pondered.

'All right, sir, I will.' he agreed resignedly.

'And if you don't mind, I'd like to go with you,' further suggested John Pendleton, a little diffidently. 'I – I have a little matter of my own that I'd like to see your aunt about. Suppose we go down today on the three o'clock?'

'Good! We will, sir. Gorry! And so I'm Jamie! I can't grasp it yet!' exclaimed the young man, springing to his feet, and restlessly moving about the room. 'I wonder, now,' he stopped, and coloured boyishly, 'do you think – Aunt Ruth – will mind – very much?'

John Pendleton shook his head. A hint of the old sombreness came into his eyes.

'Hardly, my boy. But – I'm thinking of myself. How about it? When you're her boy, where am I coming in?'

'You! Do you think *anything* could put you to one side?' scoffed Jimmy, fervently. 'You needn't worry about that. And *she* won't mind. She has Jamie, you know, and – ' He stopped short, a dawning dismay in his eyes. 'By George! Uncle John, I forgot – Jamie. This is going to be tough on – Jamie!'

'Yes, I'd thought of that. Still, he's legally adopted, isn't he?'

'Oh, yes; it isn't that. It's the fact that he isn't the real Jamie himself – and he with his two poor useless legs! Why, Uncle John, it'll just about kill him. I've heard him talk. I know. Besides, Polly-anna and Mrs Carew both have told me how he feels, how *sure* he is, and how happy he is. Great Scott! I can't take away from him this – But what *can* I do?'

'I don't know, my boy. I don't see as there's anything you can do but what you are doing.'

There was a long silence. Jimmy had resumed his nervous pacing up and down the room. Suddenly he wheeled, his face alight. 'There *is* a way, and I'll do it. I *know* Mrs Carew will agree. *We won't tell!* We won't tell anybody but Mrs Carew herself, and – and Pollyanna and her aunt. I'll *have* to tell them,' he added defensively.

'You certainly will, my boy. As for the rest – ' John Pendleton paused doubtfully.

'It's nobody's business.'

'But, remember, you are making quite a sacrifice – in several ways. I want you to weigh it well.'

'Weigh it? I have weighed it, and there's nothing in it – with Jamie on the other side of the scales, sir. I just couldn't do it. That's all.'

'I don't blame you, and I think you're right,' declared John Pendleton heartily. 'Furthermore, I believe Mrs Carew will agree with you, particularly as she'll *know* now that the real Jamie is found at last.'

'You know she's always said she'd seen me somewhere,' chuckled Jimmy. 'Now how soon does that train go? I'm ready.'

'Well, I'm not,' laughed John Pendleton. 'Luckily for me it doesn't go for some hours yet, anyhow,' he finished, as he got to his feet and left the room.

CHAPTER 32

A New Aladdin

Whatever were John Pendleton's preparations for departure – and they were both varied and hurried – they were done in the open, with two exceptions. The exceptions were two letters, one addressed to Pollyanna and one to Mrs Polly Chilton. These letters, together with careful and minute instructions, were given into the hands of Susan, his housekeeper, to be delivered after they should be gone. But of all this Jimmy knew nothing.

The travellers were nearing Boston when John Pendleton said to Jimmy: 'My boy, I've got one favour to ask – or rather, two. The first is that we say nothing to Mrs Carew until tomorrow afternoon; the other is that you allow me to go first and be your – er – ambassador, you yourself not appearing on the scene until perhaps, say – four o'clock. Are you willing?'

'Indeed I am,' replied Jimmy, promptly; 'not only willing, but delighted. I'd been wondering how I was going to break the ice, and I'm glad to have somebody else do it.'

'Good! Then I'll try to get – *your aunt* on the telephone tomorrow morning and make my appointment.'

True to his promise, Jimmy did not appear at the Carew mansion until four o'clock the next afternoon. Even then he felt suddenly so embarrassed that he walked twice by the house before he summoned sufficient courage to go up the steps and ring the bell. Once in Mrs Carew's presence, however, he was soon his natural self, so quickly did she set him at his ease, and so tactfully did she handle the situation. To be sure, at the very first, there were a few tears, and a few incoherent exclamations. Even John Pendleton had to reach a hasty hand for his handkerchief. But before very long a semblance of normal tranquillity was restored, and only the tender glow in Mrs Carew's eyes, and the ecstatic happiness in Jimmy's and John Pendleton's was left to mark the occasion as something out of the ordinary.

'And I think it's so fine of you – about Jamie!' exclaimed Mrs Carew, after a little. 'Indeed, Jimmy – (I shall still call you Jimmy, for obvious reasons; besides, I like it better, for you) – indeed I think you're just right, if you're willing to do it. And I'm making some sacrifice myself, too,' she went on tearfully, 'for I should be so proud to introduce you to the world as my nephew.'

'And, indeed, Aunt Ruth, I – ' At a half-stifled exclamation from John Pendleton, Jimmy stopped short. He saw then that Jamie and Sadie Dean stood just inside the door. Jamie's face was very white.

'*Aunt Ruth!*' he exclaimed, looking from one to the other with startled eyes. '*Aunt Ruth!* You don't mean – ?'

All the blood receded from Mrs Carew's face, and from Jimmy's, too. John Pendleton, however, advanced jauntily.

'Yes, Jamie; why not? I was going to tell you soon, anyway, so I'll tell you now.' (Jimmy gasped and stepped hastily forward, but John Pendleton silenced him with a look.) 'Just a little while ago Mrs Carew made me the happiest of men by saying yes to a certain question I asked. Now, as Jimmy calls me "Uncle John", why shouldn't he begin right away to call Mrs Carew "Aunt Ruth"?'

'Oh! Oh–h!' exclaimed Jamie, in plain delight, while Jimmy, under John Pendleton's steady gaze, just managed to save the situation by not blurting out *his* surprise and pleasure. Naturally, too, just then, blushing Mrs Carew became the centre of everyone's interest, and the danger point was passed. Only Jimmy heard John Pendleton say low in his ear, a bit later: 'So you see, you young rascal, I'm not going to lose you, after all. We shall *both* have you now.'

Exclamations and congratulations were still at their height, when Jamie, a new light in his eyes, turned without warning to Sadie Dean. 'Sadie, I'm going to tell them now,' he declared triumphantly.

Then, with the bright colour in Sadie's face telling the tender story even before Jamie's eager lips could frame the words, more congratulations and exclamations were in order, and everybody was laughing and shaking hands with everybody else.

Jimmy, however, very soon began to eye them all aggrievedly, longingly.

'This is all very well for *you*,' he complained then. 'You each have each other. But where do I come in? I can just tell you, though, that if only a certain young lady I know were here, *I* should have something to tell *you*, perhaps.'

'Just a minute, Jimmy,' interposed John Pendleton. 'Let's play I was Aladdin, and let me rub the lamp. Mrs Carew, have I your permission to ring for Mary?'

'Why, y–yes, certainly,' murmured that lady, in a puzzled surprise that found its duplicate on the faces of the others.

A few moments later Mary stood in the doorway.

'Did I hear Miss Pollyanna come in a short time ago?' asked John Pendleton.

'Yes, sir. She is here.'

'Won't you ask her to come down, please.'

'Pollyanna here!' exclaimed an amazed chorus, as Mary disappeared. Jimmy turned very white, then very red.

'Yes. I sent a note to her yesterday by my housekeeper. I took the liberty of asking her down for a few days to see you, Mrs Carew. I thought the little girl needed a rest and a holiday; and my housekeeper has instructions to remain and care for Mrs Chilton. I also wrote a note to Mrs Chilton herself,' he added, turning suddenly to Jimmy, with unmistakable meaning in his eyes. 'And I thought after she read what I said that she'd let Pollyanna come. It seems she did, for – here she is.'

And there she was in the doorway, blushing, starry-eyed, yet withal just a bit shy and questioning.

'Pollyanna, dearest!' It was Jimmy who sprang forward to meet her, and who, without one minute's hesitation, took her in his arms and kissed her.

'Oh, Jimmy, before all these people!' breathed Pollyanna in embarrassed protest.

'Pooh! I should have kissed you then, Pollyanna, if you'd been straight in the middle of – of Washington Street itself,' vowed Jimmy. 'For that matter, look at "all these people" and see for yourself if you need to worry about them.'

And Pollyanna looked and she saw, over by one window, backs carefully turned, Jamie and Sadie Dean; and, over by another window, backs also carefully turned, Mrs Carew and John Pendleton.

Pollyanna smiled – so adorably that Jimmy kissed her again.

'Oh, Jimmy, isn't it all beautiful and wonderful?' she murmured softly. 'And Aunt Polly – she knows everything now; and it's all right. I think it would have been all right, anyway. She was beginning to feel so bad – for me. Now she's so glad. And I am, too. Why, Jimmy, I'm glad, *glad*, *GLAD* for – everything, now!'

Jimmy caught his breath with a joy that hurt.

'God grant, little girl, that always it may be so – with you,' he choked unsteadily, his arms holding her close.

'I'm sure it will,' sighed Pollyanna, with shining eyes of confidence.